The Summer Snow

Also by the author

Death of a Nationalist
Law of Return
The Watcher in the Pine

The Summer Snow

Rebecca Pawel

Published by
Soho Press, Inc.
853 Broadway
New York, NY 10003

Library of Congress Cataloging-in-Publication Data

Pawel, Rebecca, 1977–
The summer snow / Rebecca Pawel
p. cm.
ISBN–13: 978-1-56947-443-3
1. Tejada Alonso y Lâón, Carlos (Fictitious character)—Fiction. 2. Older
women—Crimes against—Fiction. 3. Granada (Spain: Province)—Fiction. 4.
Aunts—Crimes against—Fiction. 5. Police—Spain—Fiction. I. Title.

PS3616.A957S86 2006
813'.6–dc22   2005051584

10   9   8   7   6   5   4   3   2   1

For all the people who told me they loved Tejada
and wanted me to reform him,
and all the people who hated Tejada
and begged me to kill him off in the last book.

Chapter 1

It was one of those golden October afternoons when the temperature was warm but no longer oppressive, and the air held just a hint of the winter's moisture. A faint breeze stirred the scent of the ornamental orange trees. In the center of the courtyard, a fountain splashed over a bronze base into a channel lined with brightly colored tiles, whose geometric patterns matched the tiles of the walls. The rustle of the leaves, and the sound of the water were loud enough to mask the swish of Doña Rosalia's skirt over the terrazzo, but they could not quite drown out her angry muttering. "Fools, ingrates! Who do they think they are?"

Doña Rosalia crossed the patio quickly, ignoring its beauty as the familiar background of the last sixty-odd years. "Would never have stood for such a thing in my day . . . won't be allowed to get away with it," she muttered. She reached a massive wooden door at the far end, pulled back the heavy bolt, and unlocked it with a set of keys hanging from a chain around her waist. The keys would not have looked out of place on a medieval chatelaine. Doña Rosalia's dress, though no more than forty years out of style, also somehow managed to convey a sense of dignified antiquity. Something in the ample black skirt mocked the flightiness of twentieth-century innovation. ". . . show them all, if I do have to tell the Guardia. . . ."

The door swung shut behind Doña Rosalia and the old

woman began climbing the stairs quickly, considering her age. She was breathing hard when she reached the end of the second flight, and she leaned against the wall for a moment to catch her breath. Then she headed down the hallway, keeping one hand on the wall for support, unlocked another door, and stumbled forward, catching at a bell pull. An observer might almost have thought that she had grabbed the bell pull for balance, but her repeated vicious jerks on the tattered silk would have belied such an impression immediately.

When María José opened the door a few minutes later, Doña Rosalia was sitting at an open writing desk, apparently absorbed in a letter. "Well? What took you so long, girl?" she demanded, as the maid bobbed a curtsy.

"I'm sorry, Señora."

The old woman brushed aside the apology. "Tell Alberto to summon the Guardia."

"Would you like to telephone them yourself, Señora?" María José asked hopefully.

"Don't you dare telephone them!" Doña Rosalia snapped. "I told you to send Alberto to get them! You never know who's listening on the telephone. I don't want to announce to the entire city that I'm sending for them."

María José kept her expression blank. "Should Alberto give them any special message, Señora?"

"Special message! Huh! Wouldn't you like to know? Prying into the affairs of your betters, peeping and spying on me!"

"I only meant that the Guardia are always busy, Señora, and I don't think they'll come if—"

"Criminals!" Doña Rosalia hit the arm of her chair with one hand. "You don't want the Guardia to come because you're all afraid of them. Thieves and black marketeers, and you think your precious secrets are worth more than my life."

"No, Señora."

"Ingrates!" Doña Rosalia's face was becoming flushed. "I take you into my home, give you work in these times, and this is how you repay me! With larceny and disobedience! I will be obeyed in my own house, girl!"

"Yes, Señora. Alberto will get the Guardia, Señora." María José spoke soothingly, as to a child.

Abruptly, the fight seemed to go out of Doña Rosalia. She slumped in her chair. "What's the point?" She choked slightly. "They'll get me, sooner or later. You're all in league against me. You all want me dead."

"Oh, no, Señora," María José protested. Then, since the white lie bothered her conscience, she added, "I'm sure no one is trying to kill you."

"So it's all in my head, is it? So I'm a crazy old woman who can't see what's in front of her nose? That's what you think of me? That's what everyone thinks of me! That I'm too foolish to see what's going on!"

"No, Señora." María José spoke hastily. "Please, remember what the doctor said about getting excited the last time he checked your heart."

"He's an idiot. He thinks I'm a helpless fool, just like the rest of you."

"I'll go tell Alberto, Señora." María José curtsied again and made a quick escape.

Doña Rosalia made a disgusted noise as the door closed and then returned to her writing. She scribbled furiously for the better part of an hour, until someone knocked at the door. "Go away," she shouted. "I left orders not to be disturbed."

The door swung open. "It's Sergeant Rivas, Señora," María José told her.

"It took you long enough!"

Sergeant Rivas saluted. "Good afternoon, Doña Rosalia. I understand you are in need of some assistance?"

"It's a plot, Sergeant! I've told you before. They're trying to kill me!"

Sergeant Rivas liked to think that the Guardia Civil were the best and brightest in Spain. He comforted himself with the thought that the best and brightest showed no emotion even under the most trying of circumstances. "Who would this be exactly, Doña Rosalia?" he asked politely.

"The Reds, of course! They want to kill me because of what I know, but it's worse this time."

"Of course we're very interested in any criminal activity, Doña. . . ."

"No, you're not!" she snapped. "You're annoyed with me for bothering you. In the old days we had justice. But now the Guardia only care about their own comfort."

Had anyone else made the comment, the sergeant would have pricked up his ears and quietly reported it to the officer in charge of the political section. In the case of Rosalia de Ordoñez, he tried to be selectively deaf. "We'll keep a sharp eye out," he promised, hoping that she would be easily pacified this time.

"Quite a promise from a man who's as good as blind! It's no wonder that the Reds are thriving now, when the Guardia are such idiots. But they're clever, too. They're very clever. . . ."

She had lost two of her sons in the Civil War, torn to death by mobs of enraged peasants, the sergeant reminded himself. Three grandsons had been killed in the attack on Mallorca, and another—a fighter pilot—had died fighting the Russians, in '41. It was only to be expected that an elderly lady would feel unsafe. He just wished that she was less irritating.

"They suborn people, Sergeant," she was saying earnestly now. "Even my nearest and dearest, people I've always thought I could trust. They're in on it, too!"

"I can't believe—"

"You might look at your own post, Sergeant!" she interrupted. "Or you would, if the Guardia were any better than lazy fools."

"Yes, Doña Rosalia." One of Rosalia de Ordoñez's few virtues, from Sergeant Rivas's point of view, was that she kept an excellent cook. Based on previous experience, he and his colleagues had worked out a rough scale of unofficial compensation for visits to her house. Fifteen minutes merited a glass of wine. Half an hour merited a glass of wine and a pastry or a loaf of fresh bread, if it was available. An hour was a meat dish. Anything over an hour was a full meal, or (since Doña Rosalia always seemed to work herself into a state of agitation over the siesta, and send for the Guardia in the early evening) a set of mixed *tapas* and drinks. Doña Rosalia's staff had never argued the point, although the sudden diminution of foodstuffs frequently laid them open to furious tirades about the ingratitude of the Moors and Gypsies she had taken into her home out of the goodness of her heart. Whether they simply feared the Guardia Civil more than their lady or whether they had some sympathy for the harassed guardias who, after encountering Doña Rosalia in a rage, showed up in the kitchen calling for a drink, was not something Sergeant Rivas had ever bothered to consider. Doña Rosalia was exceptionally agitated this evening, and Sergeant Rivas, who had had other work to do, gradually relaxed, as he realized that he would be having dinner at the Casa Ordoñez. He let her ramble on without listening too closely, wondering if there would be any of the stuffed olives that he liked this evening.

The sergeant visited the Casa Ordoñez more frequently than most of his colleagues. His mother's parents and brothers worked on the estates of Don Antonio Ordoñez Guzmán; his mother's family had farmed the Ordoñez lands for longer than anyone could remember. Perhaps because of this, Doña Rosalia seemed to like the sergeant. To put it more accurately, since she could hardly be said to *like* him, she seemed inclined to trust him. When Doña Rosalia had first started to call the Guardia, claiming that people were conspiring to kill her, Sergeant Rivas

had responded quickly and personally because he was worried
that the threat might be real. Señora de Ordoñez had been
recently widowed and was a woman of wealth. Her background
was aristocratic, her politics were impeccable, and her death
from anything other than natural causes would have been highly embarrassing. Rivas had quickly come to the conclusion that
the mysterious threats were delusions and had attempted to del-
egate the problem the next time it arose. Doña Rosalia had
exploded into his office at the post a few hours later, weeping
and furious, and berated him for the better part of an hour. She
had then nearly blighted the careers of the two young guardias
he had sent to deal with her by denouncing them as Reds. A
cautious appeal to her son had cleared the guardias' records,
but Sergeant Rivas's tentative suggestion that Doña Rosalia
might feel less threatened if she were living with family instead
of alone had been met with a firm command to mind his own
business. Over the last three years, Sergeant Rivas had dealt with
the conspiracy against Doña Rosalia de Ordoñez alone or with
the help of subordinates he thought were overeager and needed to be taken down a peg or two.

He finally escaped a little after seven that evening by promising to report the matter to his lieutenant and to put a guard
around the house. Stuffed olives and fresh bread were waiting
for him in the kitchen. He appreciated the attention, although
he would have liked the chance to chat with Luisa, the cook's
pretty assistant. She showed up a few minutes later. "Do you
need anything else, Sergeant?"

"Are there anchovies?" he asked hopefully.

"I'm sorry, Sergeant. We didn't know you were coming until too
late. But there's shrimp in vinegar or cured ham, if you'd like."

Rivas considered. "Ham," he said finally. "If it's from your
own farm."

"Not ours, Sergeant." Luisa was apologetic. "But Señor
Tejada's."

"Good enough."

Luisa turned toward the pantry without saying anything more, and Sergeant Rivas, who wanted to make conversation, looked for a change of subject. "She's in a foul mood today, isn't she?" he remarked.

"Yes, sir." Even muffled by the pantry door, Luisa's agreement was heartfelt. "Ever since Señor Tejada left this morning."

"I'd think a visit from her nephew would cheer her up."

"She doesn't get along with his wife, Doña Consuela," Luisa explained. "Never has, they say."

Sergeant Rivas nodded, wondering absently if Doña Rosalia got along equally badly with her daughter-in-law, and her own daughter. He'd heard that her bachelor son, Felipe, had absolutely refused to live with his mother. "A shame she doesn't have any family she's close to," he said.

"She's never had much use for them, I think. Always quarreling with this one or that one, even before Señor Ordoñez passed away and she became so—" The girl stopped abruptly and flushed as she realized that she had been betrayed into an indiscreet comment. The rest of the sentence was unnecessary anyway. Sergeant Rivas knew perfectly well what she was trying to say. "She was in an even worse mood after Señorito Felipe left on Friday," Luisa finished, embarrassed. The bell in the kitchen suddenly rang violently, and the girl started. "That's her. I have to go."

Sergeant Rivas had finished his meal and departed by the time Luisa took a tray up to Doña Rosalia's room. The old woman greeted her with a mixture of irritation and relief. "What took you so long? I was beginning to think they'd cut the bell cord, so that I couldn't call for help!"

"I'm sorry, Señora." Luisa, who was only responsible for bringing Doña Rosalia her meals, wondered as she always did how poor María José managed to deal with the señora all day long.

"Taste it," Doña Rosalia commanded as Luisa set the tray down.

Luisa sighed. "It's just come up from the kitchen, Señora. I helped make it myself. And I didn't meet anyone on the way up. No one could have tampered with it."

"Taste it!"

Luisa shrugged and took a bite of everything on the plate, taking perhaps a larger mouthful of the ham Sergeant Rivas had already enjoyed than was strictly necessary. It really was very good, and the taste of meat was still rare enough. Doña Rosalia watched her carefully to be sure that she swallowed everything and then nodded her satisfaction. "All right. Tell María José I don't want to be disturbed this evening."

"Yes, Señora." Luisa left, thankful that nothing worse had happened, and went to find María José.

"She'll feel better after she eats probably," Doña Rosalia's maid said optimistically, when she heard Luisa's message. "I'll go up and put her to bed later, and maybe in the morning she'll be more calm."

"God willing!" said Luisa emphatically. "I don't know how you stand it."

"I've been with her a long time." María José's voice was tolerant. "You don't remember what she was like before Señorito Ramón died. And in spite of that—in spite of everything—she was good to us during the war. We've never gone hungry."

Luisa, whose private opinion was that it would have been a good thing if the war had rid the country of Doña Rosalia and all her like, nodded obediently, mumbled something like an assent, and said good night.

María José waited until a little after eleven and then went upstairs to Doña Rosalia's room. She knocked and waited a few moments in silence. No one screeched at her to go away. She pushed open the door, relieved that she had not come too early, and braced herself for Doña Rosalia's angry cry, "What took you so long?" The silence was unbroken.

Doña Rosalia was sitting at her writing desk, her head tilted away from the door, her arms slack. The dinner tray had been pushed to one side, most of its contents eaten. María José, who knew that her lady hated being caught asleep by anyone, stepped forward loudly, clearing her throat, so that the old woman would have time to wake up and pretend that she had not been sleeping. Then María saw that a wineglass was lying on the writing desk, with a few drops of red liquid still caught in the bulb. Afraid that they might spill, she advanced more quickly and then gasped.

The wineglass had clearly been at least half full. Wine had soaked Doña Rosalia's papers and made a dark stain on the wood before dripping into her lap to make a wet spot on her dress. Doña Rosalia's mouth and eyes were open. A little fearfully, María José reached out to touch the old woman's shoulder. Then she crossed the room, picked up a mirror, and held it against the open mouth.

There was a telephone in the living room. But María José had been Doña Rosalia's maid for many years, and habit—or respect for her wishes—died hard. She ran out of the room and down the hallway, crying breathlessly, "Alberto! Alberto, get the Guardia!" Only after she had shooed a reluctant Alberto off to find Sergeant Rivas again did she go to the telephone to call the doctor. It seemed a secondary concern. Rosalia de Ordoñez was clearly past his help.

Chapter 2

" ' Who knows, someday you may be able to eat breakfast in Barcelona and lunch in Madrid. After all, who could have imagined that Barcelona and Madrid would be little more than a day's journey apart a hundred years ago?' The end." Carlos Tejada closed the book.

"Again," his son demanded.

"I don't think we have time tonight, Toño."

"A-gain," Toño repeated, with a little rhythmic bounce to emphasize his request.

"It will be past your bedtime by the time we finish," his father protested.

"Only by five minutes."

"But you *know* the book already. Maybe we could read something else."

"Read this one again." Toño craned his neck backward to stare soulfully up into his father's face. "Please? Only one more time? *Please.*"

"Maybe Mama could read it," his father began cravenly.

"Mama read *Trains, Planes, and Automobiles* eight times this morning." Toño's mother spoke from the rocking chair in the corner of the room, with a slight edge to her voice.

Carlos Tejada sighed again, relaxed onto the pillows piled at the head of his son's bed, and then opened *A Child's History of the Spanish Railway* for the third time that evening. "After this you'll go *right* to bed," he said.

"Promise," Toño agreed.

"*Trains are a common sight today.*" Tejada's voice was quiet and even. "*And you're probably used to seeing them and riding them. It's hard to believe that there were no trains at all in Spain less than a century ago. . . .*"

A few paragraphs later a knock on the apartment door broke the peace of the moment. Unconsciously, Toño cast an appealing glance at his mother, which (though he did not know it) was made more effective by being identical in timing and expression to his father's more conscious look. She pushed herself to her feet. "I'll get it. You finish reading."

"Thanks, Elena." The elder of the readers felt it necessary to express his gratitude. The younger simply assumed that this was what mothers were for. "Where were we?"

They had read only a few sentences when the bedroom door opened again. "I'm sorry, Carlos." His wife stood in the doorway. "There's a long distance call for you."

Toño felt his father's body tense. "I'm sorry, Toño. Mama will finish reading the story." Tejada left the little room reluctantly.

He could still hear his wife's voice, muffled by the door, in the foyer where his jacket was hanging. Extensive experience with the book made him fairly sure of what she was reading as he shrugged his coat on. "*The first Spanish rail line opened in 1849.*" He glanced at his tricorn, the hat that proclaimed his profession, then left it on its hook. *Spain's special narrow-gauge track was built to prevent easy access in case of a French invasion,* he repeated silently as he headed down the stairs, hoping devoutly that this phone call would not be like the last long distance call he had received.

That one had come nearly six months earlier, on a balmy May evening. He had gone outside at sunset to kick a ball around with Toño, who was just learning to dribble. He was crouched in front of an imaginary goal as the little boy prepared for a penalty kick when a voice from across the square in front of the Guardia Civil post startled him. "Lieutenant!"

He looked up and allowed Toño to score a goal. Guardia Torres advanced and saluted. "I beg your pardon for interrupting, sir, but Colonel Suárez is on the phone. He says it's urgent."

Tejada sighed. "All right. You'd better get home, Toño."

"Talk fast," Toño urged. "So you'll be done before it gets dark."

The boy sighed and picked up his ball with such a woebegone expression that Guardia Torres was moved to add, "I can stay with you for a little while, Toño, if your father doesn't object."

Tejada briefly thanked his subordinate and moved toward the post. The last thing he heard as the door closed behind him was Guardia Torres saying good-naturedly, "Can't have you out of training for the Oviedo selection, kid."

The lieutenant picked up the phone, smiling. "Guardia Civil, Tejada."

The clipped voice of his commanding officer banished his good mood. "We're pulling twenty men, Lieutenant. Transports should arrive in a few hours." There were only twenty-four men under his command and all were fully occupied.

"But, sir," he exclaimed. "With all due respect—"

"If you're going to tell me that there's guerrilla activity in the mountains around Potes, I already know," Suárez snapped. "It's the only reason you're not going, along with *all* your men." The connection was static-riddled as always, but it sounded as if the colonel in Santander was raising his voice against slammed doors and shouted commands.

"Yes, sir," Tejada said, recognizing that it would be futile to argue. Yet he was stunned enough to add, "But *why?*"

Stress was starting to tell on the colonel. He broke protocol and gave his subordinate unnecessary information. "All available men are needed at the border," he explained. "The army and the Policía Armada are being sent up as well, as fast as possible, just in case."

"In case what?"

The colonel's voice was ragged with strain. "Invasion. The Germans are finished. The Reds are in Berlin. And if the Allies decide to push south . . . we'll need to be on high alert."

"I'll make sure the men are ready for the transports," Tejada said, shaken. A good deal more than "high alert" would be needed if the awesome wealth and manpower of the Allied war machine turned toward Spain next.

The transports arrived late that evening. That night, after Toño went to bed, Elena turned on the radio. She had listened to the BBC with increasing defiance and frequency as the war progressed, and for the first time Tejada sat beside her and listened to the hysterical joy in London as intently as she.

Then had come tense months of waiting and wondering. The Allies had turned toward Asia. Guerrillas poured south over the French border, but they were still only the once-defeated remnants of the Spanish Communists, weakened now by years of resistance fighting in France. They were not joined by the French, or the English, or Americans. Some of the men under Tejada's command were returned to Potes, and the lieutenant had allowed himself to relax a little and to hope that the Japanese would provide the Allies with a lengthy distraction.

And then, one breathlessly hot August afternoon, word had come: Japan had surrendered, completely and unconditionally. The world was at peace, and the world's rulers had declared their hostility to the Spanish government. Tejada braced himself for the worst. He had bet too much of his life on General Franco's government to retreat from his country or his ideals. But he swallowed his pride and wrote secretly to his brother-in-law in Mexico, asking if Elena and Toño would be welcome there if war broke out. "Come and trade places with me, if you like," his brother-in-law had written back maliciously. "At any rate, you'll eat well here. But I think Elena will be happier in Spain once we get things properly settled there." Tejada received the letter a few days after the proclamation of a limited pardon for political prisoners of the Civil War that had ended six years earlier. The knowledge that his brother-in-law was now absolutely free to return to Spain did not provide him with much comfort. Still no invasion came.

The BBC was reassuringly anti-Communist. Tejada took his family on vacation to Santander for a week at the end of August, where they met Elena's parents. The newspapers in Santander were encouraging, and he became calmer as he watched Toño alternate between the beach and the train station like a blissful little metronome. And still there was no invasion. The leaves turned and the nights grew cool, and no more urgent phone calls came from Colonel Suárez. *Until now*, the lieutenant thought, as he reached his office.

"Sorry to disturb you, sir," said the guardia on duty. "But one of the posts in Granada just put through an emergency call, and the maniac at the other end refuses to speak to anyone but you."

Tejada relaxed. A call from Granada meant some kind of family business: messy and unpleasant, certainly but no threat to the established order of things. He picked up the phone, hoping that he would be able to end the call quickly enough to get back before Toño went to sleep.

Toño was drowsy enough at the end of the third reading to agree to turn out the lights without further protest. He made a determined effort to stay awake, but it had been a long and productive day. He was warm and bathed and fed and the familiar noises of the Guardia Civil post next door were as soothing as a lullaby. He was fast asleep when his bedroom door finally creaked open and a triangle of yellow light fell across the carpet. He did not stir as a tall figure stepped silently through the room, bent to give him a hug, and withdrew without a sound.

His mother was also in bed, but considerably more alert. "You were a long time. What was the phone call?"

Tejada hesitated. His wife recognized the quality of the pause. He only weighed his words like this when what she had asked about was Guardia business and he was considering how much to tell her, if anything. So she was surprised when he said slowly, "It was from Granada. My great-aunt Rosalia's dead."

"Oh." It was Elena's turn to be silent. She had met Rosalia de Ordoñez only once, shortly after her marriage. Tejada had felt it necessary to introduce Elena to his family and had taken her south to spend two weeks at his parents' estate outside Granada on what served as an abbreviated honeymoon. The Tejadas had treated Elena with a painful and condescending politeness. During a rather stilted dinner party, Doña Rosalia had broken the ice with a vengeance, by stating (loudly enough to drown out any other halfhearted attempts at conversation) that it was no wonder Carlos had disgraced the family and married a Red given the way his parents were fool enough to treat him. The memory was not one of Elena's happier ones, and she felt that the conventional condolences on the death of a loved one would ring false. On the other hand, "Thank God, it's about time," was hardly the proper response.

"Shortly before her death, she claimed someone was trying to kill her."

Elena raised her eyebrows. "She *claimed?* You don't believe her."

"Apparently she'd claimed intermittently that people were trying to kill her ever since her husband died." The lieutenant's voice was dry. "And I'll wager that my parents had thought about it years before that. But it's still a little embarrassing."

"And what does your family want you to do about it?" Elena asked.

Tejada sighed and shook his head. "It's not my family. The

call was from the post in Granada where she lodged the complaint. From one Guardia Medina."

"The Guardia in Granada called *you*? Why didn't they call her family?" Elena knew that of course Carlos *was* family, but he understood what she meant. Why the long distance call?

"Guardia Medina called me," Tejada explained. "His superiors knew that it might be Guardia business, and that it was sure to involve my family, and Medina suggested that I be brought in on the investigation. We've known each other for quite a while. Since childhood, actually. His sergant thought it was an inspiration."

Elena raised her eyebrows. Her husband had kept in contact with few companions of his childhood; the majority of them would never have dreamed of entering the Guardia Civil. She was somewhat surprised she had not heard of Medina before. "A school friend?" she asked.

Tejada's mouth twisted. "Hardly. His family are tenants of ours." He frowned, remembering the overloud, nearly hysterical voice that had said as he picked up the phone, "I need to speak to Lieutenant Carlos Tejada Alonso y León. Urgent Guardia business." And then, in response to his curt identification, the barely controlled relief in Medina's voice as he said, "*Señorito Carlos? Is that you? Oh, thank God.*"

Elena did her best not to let her reaction show. She had (more than once) expressed the opinion that her husband's family was disgustingly feudal, but she knew that he was thoroughly caught up in their web of privilege and obligation, however much he deplored it. "Someone you were close to?" she asked neutrally, reframing the question.

He shook his head. "Not by choice. Medina's always been an obnoxious little bully. The sort who hangs around the sidelines giving advice during the game and then takes a lot of credit at the victory celebrations."

"Or explains how if his advice had been followed his team would have won?" suggested Elena.

The lieutenant snorted. "Usually he manages to end up on the winning side."

Elena winced. "Sometimes by denouncing old comrades?"

Tejada shrugged. "I hate people who call me *señorito*."

His wife correctly read this non sequitur as an acknowledgment that Medina probably *had* been responsible for some of the denunciations that had cost thousands of lives in Granada at the outbreak of the Civil War. She knew that her husband would be unwilling to condemn a fellow Falangist outright, even if he found the individual personally distasteful. She shuddered, remembering the executions that had shaken Salamanca and Madrid. Tejada, who had sunk onto the bed to pull off his shoes, gave her a quick affectionate glance. "What does he want you to do about your aunt?" she asked, dropping the subject of the unpleasant Medina with relief.

"Make sure he doesn't get into trouble over it," Tejada said, beginning to undress. "Unfortunately, the way he thinks he's least likely to get into trouble is if the Guardia conduct a full investigation to show their diligence, and if I'm involved in it, to show their respect for my family."

"He doesn't seriously think the Guardia will transfer you at your own request to investigate your aunt's death?" Elena protested.

"No, but his sergeant asked me if I'd be willing to put in for a leave."

"Are you willing?"

Tejada leaned back and wriggled his shoulders into the pillow in a gesture so reminiscent of Toño's that his wife smiled involuntarily. "I don't think Colonel Suárez would approve a request anyway," he said. "That's what I told this Sergeant Rivas."

Elena nodded, grateful for once for the state of perpetual crisis that existed here in the Picos de Europa. "If he thought you wouldn't enjoy it, he'd be happy to," she predicted.

The lieutenant laughed. "Obviously, I'll have to feign great enthusiasm for seeing my family again."

Elena smiled also, but her voice was cautious as she said, "Seriously. Will you ask for leave?"

Tejada stared at the pattern of lamplight on the ceiling. "I don't know. Maybe. Probably. Why don't we sleep on it?"

"It's probably all a mare's nest anyway," Elena comforted, as she reached over to turn out the light.

"I know," the lieutenant agreed. He sighed in the darkness. "I might have known Aunt Rosalia would still be making trouble even after she was dead!"

Chapter 3

"I'm sorry, Señor Tejada." Pablo Almeida had shared a carefree childhood and a wild youth with Andrés Tejada León and had remained a close friend in the intervening fifty years, but Almeida was naturally a formal man, and he had found that a little formality never hurt when breaking bad news. "But Señora de Ordoñez's will appears to be missing."

Andrés Tejada saw no similar need to stand on ceremony. He made an annoyed noise that was at odds with his sixty-five years and dignified appearance. "I might have known the old cat would die intestate! I suppose now we'll have the entire family squabbling over what they can get." He leaned back in his desk chair and closed his eyes with a shudder.

The lawyer coughed apologetically. "Not exactly intestate." Almeida risked a smile at his friend. "That is to say, I know that there *is* a will. I'm just not exactly sure where it is."

Andrés Tejada sat up. "If that's a joke, Pablo, it's in poor taste."

"When do I ever make tasteless jokes about money, Andrés?" Now that the worst was over, Almeida allowed himself to relax slightly. "You know Doña Rosalia changed her will every three months after her husband died. And she came to my office trying to change it an average of every six weeks. She was always very particular about there being an extra copy. One always had to stay in my office, and one went with her, to be put in her safe at home. At least that was where I assume she put it. She always just said that she wanted it in 'a safe place.' You know she never felt secure after what happened to poor Javier and Ramón."

Señor Tejada winced. The deaths of his cousins at the hands of enraged mobs of their own cane cutters, at the outbreak of the Civil War in 1936, still triggered unpleasant memories of fear and fury, even after nearly ten years. The Tejadas, like the Ordoñez family, had been surprised at the outbreak of the war, not in orderly Granada, but at their country house, in territory that had quickly aligned itself with the Communists. He remembered standing guard over the manor house with his oldest son, the two of them armed only with hunting rifles, his wife on her knees before the Virgin in the bedroom upstairs. He remembered his uncle's frantic telephone call, and then the drive through the summer night to Granada, his foot glued to the accelerator in spite of the darkness and the treacherous curves of the mountain passes, determined not to stop, no matter what got in his way. He remembered the long wait for news in Granada and Doña Rosalia's hysterical screams when the Guardia had finally brought her official notice of the deaths of two of her sons. It was the one time his wife had forgotten her dislike of his aunt, and the two women had prayed together, at least until his wife had been insulted by the old lady's monopoly on grief and had tried to argue that her maternal feelings for her younger son (whose whereabouts were still unknown) were as acute as Doña Rosalia's anguish.

"I suppose you can't blame her for that," Señor Tejada said shortly.

"Of course not," Almeida agreed. "That was why I put up with all the nonsense about doing everything in duplicate. The thing is, the last time she changed her will was just a few days before she died. She was very urgent about it, peremptory even. It was a Saturday morning, and since she hadn't formally made an appointment we were rather busy. We typed out a fair copy, but—"

Almeida shifted uncomfortably.—"well, I'd promised Asunción I'd be home in time to meet our guests, and my secretary had specifically asked for the afternoon off as he's getting married in a few weeks, and since I didn't know Doña Rosalia was coming I'd promised him and—well, the long and the short of it is that after we'd done one copy I told Doña Rosalia that we didn't have time to prepare the duplicate original and that she could come back on Monday morning and we'd have it finished."

Doña Rosalia's nephew whistled. "You told her that? You're a brave man."

Almeida looked miserable. "She didn't take it very well," he admitted. "She was a bit abusive. I wish to heaven now that I'd stayed late and made the extra copy as usual but I didn't *know*." He looked pleadingly at his friend, and then sighed and finished his story. "She said if I couldn't be bothered to make a copy I couldn't be trusted to hold onto the one I had made. And then she insisted on having the copy that had been typed properly signed and witnessed—and by the time *that* was done with I was late for lunch. I thought she'd be in again to change its provisions in a few weeks anyway, so she took the only copy home with her. The problem *now* is that it's nowhere to be found."

Señor Tejada sighed. "You must have notes on what the changes were," he suggested. "It can't be that different from all the previous drafts."

Almeida shook his head. "I don't need notes to remember the changes. There were only two important ones. You're still the executor, there are still a few minor bequests to the church and a few charities, and the jewels still go to Daniela, of course."

"And the bulk of the estate?" Andrés Tejada asked with exaggerated casualness.

The lawyer swallowed nervously. "Well, the land has legally belonged to Fernando as the older son ever since his father died. Doña Rosalia was just the beneficiary of a trust that left her its use and income. So it's just her liquid assets and her own property that she could dispose of. She kept dividing it up between you and Daniela and Felipe differently, depending on how she felt at the moment."

"I suppose she finally cut one of us out completely?" Señor Tejada spoke with a heartiness that he did not entirely feel.

Almeida avoided his friend's eyes. "Daniela got nothing but the jewels; Felipe was completely disinherited," he said quietly, "'as a token of their undutiful behavior to their mother and their betrayal of the ideals of their father.' You and Fernando are the sole heirs."

Andrés Tejada made a sound like a balloon being rapidly deflated. Pablo Almeida waited to see if he would make any comment and then said anxiously, "Fernando gets the sugar refinery as well as the farm free and clear now. But you stand to inherit just shy of four hundred thousand pesetas, less taxes. The thing is, the will wasn't in her safe, and I have no idea where it might be. And since it's disappeared, and you're the executor . . ."

"Daniela and Felipe will flay me alive," Tejada whispered. "They'll never believe that she changed her will and that the new will has disappeared." He turned on the lawyer with something like ferocity. "Why didn't you stop her?"

"I advised against it," Almeida pleaded. "But I thought it was just some temporary quarrel and that she'd change her mind soon enough. I told you, she changed her bequests every three months!"

"Great! That means they'll insist she was of unsound mind and that I unfairly influenced her!" Tejada was gaining a second wind. "Unfair influence! God, when I think of the hours I spent dealing with her tantrums because her own children were too sick of her to come running when she called! I *deserve* that bequest! But not a headache like this. Why didn't you *tell* me?"

"I didn't think anyone would have to know. I was sure she'd order a new will in a few weeks. She really just came to my office as a social diversion, you know. And she always seemed healthy as a horse."

Tejada put his head in his hands at the lawyer's last words. "She didn't just go to *your* office," he said grimly. "She's bothered the Guardia at least once every six weeks since my uncle died. She kept claiming there was a conspiracy to kill her. They brushed it off, of course, after Fernando told that idiot sergeant what she was like, but they can't help investigating now. Especially since she always *did* seem as healthy as a horse."

Almeida stared at his friend. "Surely you don't think she was murdered?"

"Of course not," Tejada said. "And neither do they. But if they don't do a proper investigation into the death of a woman who was in perfect health and claimed someone was trying to kill her, and the *reason* they don't do the investigation is because they dismiss the whole thing as the ravings of a senile old bat, we won't have a leg to stand on when we go into court and Daniela and Felipe argue she was of unsound mind so any will of hers would be invalid."

Almeida noted not entirely happily that Tejada had said "when *we* go into court." He liked Andrés and always had. But Daniela and Felipe Ordoñez were old acquaintances and wealthy clients as well. He was uncomfortable with the idea of antagonizing them. "But if the Guardia *do* conduct an investigation and they find out about this will, it gives you a motive for murder," he pointed out unhappily.

"Not if the will's disappeared," Tejada retorted. "If we can't find the will, then she'll either be ruled to have died intestate, or her previous one will stand, and her children stand to benefit most from that one, don't they? But suppose someone murdered her and *stole* her last will to prevent it from going into effect?"

Almeida gulped. "You don't think Daniela or Felipe—," he began.

"I told you, I think she died of perfectly natural causes," Tejada snapped. "But we have to make it clear to the Guardia that we *want* a full investigation. It will give us time to look for the will she took away with her. And if we can't find it, maybe they will."

"The best thing would be for us to locate the will," Almeida agreed, glad to be once more on solid ground. "But it wouldn't be bad to enlist some help. I can't think where else to look. And after all, it's not as if the Guardia go around making wild accusations."

"Of course," Tejada agreed. None of his many relatives had ever been treated by the Guardia Civil with anything except deference. None of Almeida's had either, for that matter. He smiled suddenly. "Aunt Rosalia kept changing her will, and complaining of a conspiracy to murder her to the Guardia, since her husband died. So *any* will she made in the last three years could be held to be made by someone of unsound mind unless the Guardia seriously investigate the alleged conspiracy. I'm sure all her children will understand *that.*"

"Very true." Almeida was relieved at the prospect of the Tejada and Ordoñez clans acting in accord, albeit temporarily. "So the only question is how to make our position clear to the Guardia."

"I've already spoken to Sergeant Rivas," Tejada said confidently. "He seems very anxious to please."

"As long as you're sure that won't make him try to sweep the whole thing under the carpet," Almeida cautioned.

Tejada looked amused. "Pablo, the Guardia's job is to nose into things. They're only too happy to be given a free rein. They're all mad for conspiracy theories themselves, so let them root around. It will make them happy. And if they find anything to support my aunt's delusion, it will make us happy."

The lawyer nodded and held out an envelope. "These are the keys to Doña Rosalia's town house and to the villa. I'll have to give Fernando copies, of course, but if I were you I'd get in there and tear the place apart until you come up with the will."

Tejada deposited the envelope in his desk drawer, with brief thanks, and locked the drawer. Then he ushered the lawyer out and went back into his study. He had always gotten along well with his cousins (except when Daniela and his wife were quarreling) and he felt a certain sympathy for them. But Tejada did not delude himself that his cordial relations with the Ordoñez siblings would survive a legal battle over Doña Rosalia's assets. He wondered if Fernando Ordoñez would support him. Fernando's position as oldest son and head of the family would be unaffected by the outcome of any lawsuit, and his inheritance remained secure no matter who eventually gained control of his mother's other assets. Fernando would want to take charge of his inheritance as quickly as possible, with a minimum of fuss and scandal. *It would be far simpler*, Tejada thought, to search Doña Rosalia's house and country estate with the knowledge and consent of their legal owner, and Fernando might consent if he was convinced that someone would inevitably find his mother's last will and testament anyway. On the other hand, given the circumstances, he might doubt that the will even existed. Or he might resent Doña Rosalia's leaving her wealth to her own side of the family, instead of dividing it amongst her children. Regretfully, Tejada decided that he could not take his oldest cousin into his confidence, at least not for the moment.

Tejada did not share his Aunt Rosalia's prejudice against the telephone. He settled himself into his desk chair and dialed the number of the Guardia Civil. Perhaps because the local guardias still cherished vivid memories of Doña Rosalia, he was transferred to Sergeant Rivas without having to ask for him. "I wondered if you'd made any progress investigating my aunt's murder," Tejada said, after he had identified himself.

There was a faint cough and then Sergeant Rivas said tactfully, "Please don't distress yourself, Señor Tejada. It's likely that your aunt's passing was perfectly natural. After all, she was an elderly lady, in frail health. It's tragic, of course, but there's no reason to think—"

"Have you issued a death certificate?" Tejada interrupted.

"Not yet, Señor, but we should have one within a few days, by the end of the week at the latest. I'll make every effort to see that it's done quickly so that you're not inconvenienced."

"I don't want you to rush to judgment so quickly that if my aunt *was* murdered, her killer gets away scot-free," Tejada said sharply. "She claimed Reds were trying to kill her before she died, didn't she?"

"Well, yes, but . . ." Sergeant Rivas, caught off guard, did not complete his sentence. The pause could easily have been covered by a gesture or smile in face-to-face conversation, but created a revealing silence over the telephone.

"I want an autopsy performed," Tejada insisted. "My aunt seemed to be in perfect health. I can't believe that she'd go so quickly."

"Of course, Señor Tejada, if you and the late woman's children feel—"

"We do," Tejada lied recklessly. "My poor cousins won't rest until they're positive that their mother's untimely death was natural. You do understand, don't you?"

"Yes, sir." Even over the telephone, Rivas's tone made it clear that he did not understand at all. "You realize, sir, that an autopsy and an investigation will result in a delay in issuing a death certificate and therefore a delay in . . . in making other arrangements for the lady?"

"The claims of justice are paramount." Tejada's voice was pious. "I have every confidence in the Guardia Civil."

"Thank you, sir." Rivas sounded miserable. Then, with an attempt at subtlety, he asked, "I imagine your entire family will gather for the poor lady's funeral?"

"I suppose so." Tejada was puzzled by the question. *Maybe they're thinking of interviewing family members about the will,* he thought. *That could get a little ugly, but at least they'll be investigating.*

"Perhaps your son would be willing to—er—offer some informal advice, as he'll be here anyway," hinted Rivas.

It was on the tip of Tejada's tongue to say that his son Juan Andrés had more than enough to do managing his own affairs when the phrase "he'll be here anyway" became clear to him, and he understood that Rivas meant his *younger* son. "If Carlos comes as a member of the family I don't see how he'll be able to interfere in an official investigation," he said, and then added thoughtfully, "unless you were thinking that the Guardia might transfer him to Granada because of his special knowledge in this case."

Rivas suppressed the instinct to say that the Guardia's policy was for officers to serve in regions far from their homes, so that they would not be subject to the pressures of local interests. He was sure that Señor Tejada already knew this, and also fairly sure that what applied to guardias in general might not apply to the Tejadas. He considered how best to admit that he had already contacted Señor Tejada's son. He decided on flattery. "I'm afraid the Guardia in Cantabria prize Lieutenant Tejada too much to let him go. They won't transfer him," he said. "But I had a subordinate speak to the lieutenant a few days ago and ask if he would be willing to put in for personal leave. We would be most grateful for his advice. And, naturally, it would be less distressing for you to have a member of the family in charge of the investigation."

Tejada had always felt that Sergeant Rivas handled his aunt Rosalia's tantrums with great skill. His opinion of the sergeant increased at this speech. Sending for Carlos was a good idea. Even the Ordoñez siblings could hardly object to a few interviews with their own cousin, in the name of insuring justice for their mother. "Well done, Rivas," he said, to the sergeant's relief. "I'd be far happier with Carlos conducting the investigation. Speak to the Guardia in the north and explain that he's needed here."

"Yes, Señor Tejada."

"Oh, and Rivas, if you could hold off any serious investigation until my son arrives? A few days won't make any difference, surely."

Sergeant Rivas said, "Under the circumstances, considering who the victim is, I suppose we could wait."

"Thanks, Rivas." Tejada ended the phone call with a feeling of satisfaction. Doña Rosalia had already been transformed from "the lady" to "the victim" and the sergeant's happy thought of calling for Carlos had bought him extra time for practically nothing. With any luck, Tejada thought, he would be able to find the will even before Carlos arrived.

Chapter 4

The day after his father's conversation with Sergeant Rivas, Carlos Tejada broached the subject of going south at lunch with his wife. "I got another call from Granada this morning," he said. "It seems they're very anxious that there be an investigation of Aunt Rosalia's death."

Elena handed him a bowl of soup. "You've decided to put in for leave, then?"

"I'm not sure. I wouldn't mind putting in for leave if I thought Suárez would grant it, but it sounds like what they really want is for me to be transferred to Granada."

"Why would they want you to transfer?"

"Sergeant Rivas wasn't totally clear. I got the impression that my father was breathing down his neck, but I couldn't tell if it was because he wanted an investigation—with me in charge—or because he didn't want any investigation at all."

Elena considered. She had never fully grasped the subtleties of her husband's relationship with his parents, and she weighed her next words carefully, making sure that her tone was neutral. "Surely your father would send you word if he really needed your help?"

Tejada absentmindedly began to shred a roll into his soup. "He usually avoids doing anything if there's a servant to do it for him." He caught sight of his son's wide eyes and smiled crookedly. "I didn't mean that. My father is a natural leader, and he's very good at delegating things."

Elena laughed. Toño could not understand why, but he had the feeling that his father had deliberately made a joke. He tried to understand what was funny. "What's 'delegating' mean?"

"Getting somebody to do things for you, but in a good way. Never speak ill of your father when he's old and helpless, Toño."

"I won't," Toño agreed readily, although he was comfortably certain that his father would never be old and helpless.

"Do you think the colonel will agree to transfer you?" Elena asked, returning to the subject.

Tejada shook his head. "The Guardia in Granada called Santander and asked him. He doesn't want to put a new man in the mountains with winter coming on. So then they called me, to ask if I'd put in for leave."

"Isn't that a bit discourteous to the colonel?"

Tejada sighed. "Yes. It's bad manners to poach another man's officer, and they know it. That's why I think my father's leaning on them."

"Will you do it?"

The lieutenant shrugged. "I would want Toño to do the same for me."

"How long would you be gone?" asked Elena.

"I don't know. I think Suárez would give me ten days, if I explained it was family business. Maybe two weeks."

"Isn't that a short time to conduct a serious investigation?"

Her husband laughed. "That would barely give us time to finish the paperwork. This is just a formality. Besides I don't want to be away from work for longer than that, and I didn't think you'd want to be away for any length of time either so soon after Santander."

"You weren't planning on all of us going?" exclaimed Elena.

"I wasn't planning to go alone!" her husband retorted.

Elena had little desire to travel all the way to Granada and less to see her husband's parents again, but she was gratified that he did not want to return to his family without her. It was good to know that he was not ashamed of her. She sought something positive to say. "Actually, I might know someone in Granada. There was a girl I knew at university, Cristina Encinas, whose family was from there. Her father was the director of some kind of school for orphans, I think."

Although Tejada was generally unenthusiastic about his wife's college friends, whom he grouped under the heading "rabble-rousing Commie malcontents," he smiled encouragingly. "Maybe you could look her up," he said. "Do you suppose she's still teaching, or has she married?"

"Cristina was studying medicine," Elena corrected. "She was just friendly with teachers because of her father."

Tejada choked on his soup. *A lady doctor,* he thought. *Oh, God, why can't she have normal friends?* He wondered if perhaps it would be better to go to Granada on his own, sparing his wife his parents company, and vice versa. "Of course it would be a lot of traveling in a short time," he said.

Toño had been following a private train of thought. Now he spoke up. "Granada is a long way away?"

Elena nodded. "At least a day of travel."

"And *if* we went to Granada we would probably have to go on the train?" Toño's face was a picture of innocent inquiry.

His parents exchanged glances. "Undoubtedly," his mother agreed gravely.

Carlos Antonio gulped, unable to think of words to frame his request. His quivering body spoke more eloquently than words anyway. The lieutenant smiled. "I guess I'll give the colonel a call this afternoon," he said. "Maybe he won't mind my taking some time off."

Toño was so pleased at the prospect of an actual train trip that he did not notice his parents were both rather nervous in the week before their trip south. He had gathered that they were going to stay with his car-owning uncle, who lived with his wife and children with his father's parents in Granada. The little boy was curious about meeting his father's parents. He had enjoyed his stays with his mother's parents the preceding Christmas, and again in August when they came from Salamanca to the seashore in Santander. Toño had liked them immensely and was happy to discover that he had more grandparents. He noticed, however, that his parents appeared determined to make sure that he was not disappointed by his new relatives. "I don't know them very well. But I'm sure they'll like you. After all, you're their own flesh and blood," his mother said. His father cautioned, "You have to remember that you're the Fernándezes' *only* grandchild. You have three older cousins, and these grandparents know them better. But I'm sure they'll be very fond of you once they meet you."

Toño attributed part of his mother's irritability to unusual activity before their departure. She was suddenly intent on finishing a new dress for herself and a new suit for him. Toño thought she looked pretty in the dress and did not begrudge it to her, although he wished that she did not see a need to make new clothes for him as well. She was also in charge of most of their packing, and the preparations for closing their apartment during their absence. Toño remembered her being short-tempered before they had gone to Santander as well. He was fairly sure that she would become happy once they were well on their way. In fact, he could not understand how anyone going to ride in a sleeping compartment the length of Spain could *not* enjoy the trip.

He was up at sunrise on the day they began their journey. His father had somehow managed to have Don Eduardo, the mayor, drive them to the station in Torrelavega. Toño, sandwiched in the backseat between his mother and the trunks, sat very still during the long ride out of the valley of Liébana through the narrow gorge that led to the coast. He was glad now of his new suit and his freshly cut hair, and was even able to share his mother's regret that he could not wear new shoes to set off on the longest journey of his life. New clothes and grave behavior were an appropriate compliment to the grandeur of the means of transportation.

They reached the station in good time for the 9:28 train to Madrid. Toño was fascinated by the hustle and bustle of boarding the train and enchanted by the compartment his father had reserved. His contentment was complete when his mother agreed that they could pull down the top bunk so that he could have it all to himself. At her suggestion, he climbed into his domain, took the pencils and drawing paper that she passed up to him, and began to draw a picture of the station.

Below him, his parents sank into the seats with sighs of relief. His mother leaned her throbbing temple against the cool glass and stared at the landscape without seeing it. Tejada watched the telephone poles click by, too tired to wonder if it would be possible to take a picture out the window that would be more than a meaningless blur. He took off his tricorn and tossed it onto his folded cloak. The cloak was far too heavy for this weather. Down here, away from the cool of the mountain patrol, switching to winter uniforms at the end of October was ridiculous. *It may be hotter in Granada,* he thought. *Although I suppose I won't have to wear the uniform. I'm visiting family, officially. And conducting an investigation for the Guardia. Unofficially? Or will it be officially? Will I have to wear a uniform? It's only for two weeks. And Toño's happy, bless him. They'll like him. Who couldn't notice what a good boy he is? Not like those brats of Juan's. They ought to be proud of such a grandson. Even if he is Elena's, too.*

He looked at his wife. Her face was drawn with strain, and he knew that she dreaded the meeting with his family. He was not sure what they resented most about Elena: that she was from Salamanca, that her family was impoverished, or that she was a leftist. ("A penniless foreign Red!" his brother had exclaimed on learning of his plans to marry Elena. "My God, Carlos, when you set out to annoy Mama and Papa, you don't do it halfway!") He spared a moment to hope that if she did follow through on her plans to look up her old classmate, his mother would never discover that she was visiting a woman doctor.

He sighed. The visit to Granada was going to be difficult for her. But leaving her behind in Potes had been unthinkable. Tejada doubted that Potes's guerillas would declare open war by attacking an officer's family. Not when the Guardia had easy access to their own parents, siblings, friends, and lovers. Five years earlier he would have feared for Elena's well-being alone in Potes, but now he knew that she would be equally secure, and probably considerably happier there. He had insisted on bringing her and Toño because he did not want to face his family on his own. He wanted to return home as a man in his own right, with the responsibility of a family, not as a prodigal younger son slinking back home at his father's command.

Their train came into the Northern Station in Madrid, and the train to Granada left from Atocha, practically at the other end of the city. They had less than two hours scheduled to make their connection, and their train arrived nearly an hour late. Tejada was left with the nightmare of finding a porter and a taxi and making sure that all of their baggage made the transition from one train station to another along with them. The traffic was terrible, and Tejada, crammed into a corner of the cab with one arm locked around his son, was torn between the nerve-racking conviction that they were going to miss the train and the terror that their driver's recklessness was going to kill them all. Toño was saucer eyed at his first glimpse of the capital and would happily have missed the train to spend the rest of the afternoon wandering around the city naming the make and model of every automobile they passed. Elena, who had spent some of the happiest years of her life in Madrid before the war, was nearly as bad as her son. When they finally reached the Atocha station the two of them ambled through the crowds while Elena wistfully recounted anecdotes of her life in the city. "If we had a little more time, we could go see the Metro," she told Toño regretfully. "That's a train that runs in tunnels under the city."

Tejada turned away from the longing in her face. Her life in Madrid had belonged to a time before the war, and before him. He disliked thinking about the years she had spent as a teacher, a Socialist, and what the Reds had called a "liberated woman," under any circumstances. He especially disliked thinking about them when he was late to catch a train to meet his family. He finally took Toño's hand and all of the Tejadas ran for the train.

Toño thoroughly enjoyed the chance to run down the platform at full speed. Although his glimpse of Madrid had been fascinating, he was not unhappy to be once more ensconced in the upper bunk of a sleeping compartment, and was even resigned to his mother's suggestion that he take a nap. *Someday*, he thought drowsily, staring at the roof of the railroad car as it rolled south across La Mancha, *I'm going to live in Madrid and ride the train every day.*

Thank God we got through Madrid, Tejada thought. *Now we should be all right, provided Juan got the letter about what time to meet us with the car. Elena would have liked more time in Madrid, but she wouldn't want to hear all my mother would have to say about stopping in the capital. God, let them both be decent to Elena. It will be better this time than when we were just married. There's Toño, and lots of things are different.*

Perhaps if Carlos finishes this investigation quickly, we can spend a few days in Madrid on the way back, Elena thought, leaning against his shoulder. *He must have seen how much Toño enjoyed seeing the city. It looks better than it did in '39 at any rate. I wonder if it's changed much? I hope Toño likes Granada. I wonder how Carlos's parents will treat him. I don't care what they say to me, but please, God, don't let them hurt Toño.*

Their thoughts were not comfortable but the car was warm and the hardest part of the journey was over with, and they had been up since before dawn. Toño had been sound asleep for half an hour when Tejada dozed off with his head resting against his wife's. He dreamed that he and his brother were playing tag as they had played when they were children, but that the game wound through the bomb-cratered streets of Madrid after the Civil War. Elena and Toño were hidden somewhere in the rubble and he had to win the game to find them. Finally, some while after her husband and son, Elena slid into an exhausted, dreamless sleep.

Toño woke her a few minutes after nine o'clock because he was hungry. His parents took him to the dining car, which he compared minutely to descriptions in the books he'd had read to him. The Tejadas' dinner was enlivened when Toño struck up a friendship with a group of soldiers heading south to Algeciras. To the little boy's joy, one of them turned out to be the brake-man's cousin, and volunteered to take him to go see the loco-motive. His parents allowed him to go, on the condition that Private Ramos returned him by bedtime. Toño departed, ecstat-ic. When his parents were back in their compartment Tejada began to laugh. "I didn't expect him to run away to join the army until he was eighteen!"

"I didn't expect it at all," Elena said.

"This is what comes of his having your republican instincts to fraternize."

"And your lack of distrust for men with guns!" Elena retorted.

"He won't come to any harm with them," Tejada said sooth-ingly.

"I know," Elena sighed. "He's getting very grown up, isn't he?"

"His first big trip away from home."

"Not really *away*. Just to visit his grandparents," Elena said heroically.

Tejada nodded, and a little silence fell. After a minute or two the lieutenant said slowly, "I think it will be all right. My parents, I mean."

Elena knew he was speaking to reassure himself as much as her. "They'll like Toño."

Tejada silently agreed. Then, looking out the window at the empty landscape he said slowly, "I think they'll be all right about you—about us, I mean. After all, five years is a long time."

Elena remembered a similar anxious conversation at the beginning of their honeymoon. She reached over and took his hand. "It doesn't seem that long," she said with a smile.

He smiled back, remembering their last trip south as well. They had taken a night train then also and had enjoyed proving that although the bunks in the sleeping cars were narrow they definitely could accommodate two people. He had a sudden memory, almost physical in its intensity, of how amazing it had been to travel with a woman on his arm and to refer to "my wife" when he spoke to porters or conductors. How odd it would seem *not* to travel with her now! "A lot has happened," he said, savoring the aftertaste of the memory even as it receded.

She looked skeptical. "I don't know how much will have changed from your parents' point of view."

"A lot's happened in the world," Tejada pointed out. "People felt more strongly about the Reds in 1940."

Elena raised her eyebrows. "I haven't noticed any great resurgence of the Communists."

"Your father was never actually a Communist," Tejada protested, scrupulously censoring the knowledge that Elena herself had been a Socialist during and before the war. It was not a piece of information he planned to share with any of his family. "He supported the Republic, but so did lots of people."

"And the important thing now is to be anti-Communist?" Elena said dryly.

Tejada winced. It had always been important to be anti-

Communist. And in Potes, perhaps, little had changed in the last five years. The peasants of the town were—he did not delude himself—mostly Reds and always had been. They would continue exactly as before regardless of the world outside the valley of Liébana. The Guardia would continue to maintain order, suppressing the peasants' guerrilla activities as necessary. But he suspected that in his family's world—the world of businessmen and landholders—the black and white that had defined the two sides in the Civil War were beginning to blur into shades of gray. In the summer of 1940 the Axis had looked invincible, and the Old Blue Shirts of Spain's own Fascist Party had been an important part of the government. Now things were changing. He did not know how much. He was almost afraid to think how much. But they might change just enough to make his parents courteous to the daughter of an old-fashioned liberal. He edged away from the thought, ashamed that he was capable of believing his own parents would be guilty of trimming their political beliefs to the prevailing winds and ashamed of hoping that their hypocrisy would make them kinder to Elena. "Well, I'm afraid nothing can clear you of being from Salamanca," he said aloud, trying to speak lightly.

Elena shook her head in mock disapproval. "And you could have married a hot-blooded Andalusian," she teased.

Tejada laughed, and put one arm around her. "I think I remember having this discussion five years ago," he said.

Elena kissed him. "Some things haven't changed," she said smugly, and the conversation turned to other things.

Toño was returned promptly at ten, with thanks from his hosts. He was tired and well fed enough to fall asleep shortly afterward. Tejada and his wife put out the lights in the compartment and watched the dusk deepen to royal blue and then to the star-pierced black of night in rural Andalusia. A little before four in the morning the night was banished by the lights of a city. Elena roused a sleepy Toño, who was inclined to be cranky, and made him put his shoes on just as the train creaked to a stop and the cry "Granada! Station stop, Granada!" echoed through the train.

Toño was too sleepy to have a clear impression of the train station. He had a confused memory of trying to lie down on one of the trunks and of his parents conferring rapidly above him, and then his mother picked him up and he was carried out of the station past a line of horse-drawn taxis to a large car that gleamed black under the streetlights. A man with a mustache who looked like his father said, "So this is Carlos Antonio!" and then he was curled in his mother's lap, too tired to keep his eyes open even though he was moving again. He was tired of being always in motion. Finally, his mother stood up and carried him what seemed like a long distance, and he started to cry a little because he wanted to stay where he was and he didn't *want* to be carried anymore, but then she put him down and kissed him good night in what was unmistakably a real bed that wasn't moving. His true memories of Granada started the next morning.

Chapter 5

Sergeant Rivas had gratefully put the awkward case of Rosalia de Ordoñez to one side to focus on other work. Now that Doña Rosalia was not interrupting him so frequently he could accomplish more, and he was almost ashamed that his primary feeling about the old lady's death was relief that she was no longer wasting his time. Doña Rosalia's nephew, Andrés Tejada, had been annoyingly insistent about the need to "pursue an investigation" but after his initial point had been gained he had allowed the Guardia to proceed at their own pace, without further interference or demands for speed. Sergeant Rivas, himself a devout man, thought that putting off an old lady's funeral for an unnecessary autopsy was scandalously irreverent, if not actually sinful, but he was paid to maintain the labyrinthine bureaucracy of the Spanish state, and if the great ones of the land chose to twine themselves in its coils when they could go free, it was no business of his.

The sergeant was somewhat annoyed when Captain Vega, the commander of the post, summoned him as he was about to go on patrol. When he entered the captain's office he saw that Vega was accompanied by a tall man in a lieutenant's uniform, with the dark aquiline features of the Tejada family. Señor Tejada León's attitude toward his aunt's death had won him no respect from Sergeant Rivas, and the sergeant had low expectations of his son, despite—or perhaps because of—Guardia

Medina's recommendation of him. But when the captain presented Lieutenant Tejada and added meaningfully that the Guardia were *very grateful for his help*, Rivas did the only thing possible under the circumstances. "Sir," he said, saluting, "thank you for coming."

"It's nothing." The lieutenant inspected Rivas narrowly and then added, "Forgive me for not making an appointment, Sergeant. I only have two weeks, and I don't want to waste time. But if you show me the file you've assembled so far, I can go over it, and you can finish your patrol."

Rivas blinked, uncertain whether to be relieved or unnerved by the lieutenant's perspicacity. "At your orders, Lieutenant." He hesitated. "How did you know I was going on patrol?"

Tejada smiled. "It's nine o'clock on a Tuesday morning. Your partner is standing in the hallway looking impatient, and the guardia who let me in is obviously on desk duty for the day. Hurry up, Sergeant. I don't want to throw off your patrol schedules."

"Yes, sir. Thank you, sir." Rivas took the lieutenant back to his office. "Here's everything on your lady aunt, sir. If you have questions, or need to interview anyone, don't hesitate to call on my men."

"Has one been assigned to me?" Tejada demanded.

Rivas looked embarrassed. "I made up the duty roster last week, Lieutenant. And I only heard that you were coming yesterday."

"Then I won't need anyone today," Tejada said. The sergeant began to express his gratitude, but the lieutenant cut him off, a little sharply. "Don't look so dumbfounded, Rivas. I was sergeant at a metropolitan post. I know what the job's like. I'm here to smooth things over, not to make waves. Get going."

The sergeant left, relieved and cautiously optimistic about Señor Tejada León's younger son. Rivas was a second-generation member of the Guardia, as proud of his professionalism as he was of having escaped the drudgery of the Ordoñez cane fields that had claimed his mother's family. He could not imag-

ine why a member of the great landowning families would join
the Guardia, and had mentally dismissed the lieutenant as "a
señorito who's probably as dotty as his aunt." Rivas had assumed
that Lieutenant Tejada had joined the Guardia as an officer,
perhaps coming from the amateur militias formed during the
war or after some hushed-up scandal had ended an army career.
But if the lieutenant had served as a sergeant, and understood
clearly what the job entailed, perhaps he would be easy to work
with. On the other hand, a señorito who was so unexpectedly
competent could prove disturbing.

The first thing Lieutenant Tejada did was settle himself in
Sergeant Rivas's chair and read everything in the file about the
late Rosalia Tejada de Ordoñez. He skipped hastily over her family connections and focused on her contacts with the Guardia.
According to Sergeant Rivas's records, she had first approached
the Guardia in the spring of 1943, a few months after her husband's death. The report's tone was carefully neutral:

> According to Señora de Ordoñez, agents of the Russian gov-
> ernment have bugged her telephone and are keeping her
> house under constant surveillance. She has suggested that
> they plan to revenge themselves on her for the part her late
> grandson played in the Blue Division in Russia in 1941. She
> says that her servants are either in league with the Reds or ter-
> rified by them and afford her no protection. Her fear and
> concern are unquestionably genuine.

Tejada smiled. Sergeant Rivas had managed to suggest that
Doña Rosalia's fears were as groundless as they were genuine
with exceptional eloquence and restraint. Anyone reading the
report would have correctly wondered why Russian agents
would have concerned themselves with the elderly grandmother of one of the many young men who had volunteered to fight
Communism and had already given his life doing so.

The next report, dated six months later, was substantially the same, although Doña Rosalia had claimed that the Reds trying to kill her had not only bugged her telephone but planted spies in the house who were watching her every move and reporting to unnamed superiors. "*No new servants have been hired at the Casa Ordoñez,*" the report noted dryly. "*Censors' reports (see attached) show no evidence of unusual correspondence.*" Four months after the second report, the roof of the Casa Ordoñez had suffered damage in a windstorm, and Doña Rosalia had gone to the Guardia demanding the instant arrest of the repairman, who, she insisted, was building a secret compartment in the attic to hide revolutionaries. No secret compartment had been found. The following summer, when new wallpaper was hung in the bedroom, Doña Rosalia had called not only the Guardia but an eminent physician to test the paste and paper, which she was convinced were soaked in a slow-acting poison that would seep into the air and smother her in her sleep. "According to Dr. Navarro, the paste used would only be poisonous if ingested in large quantities," read Sergeant Rivas's report. "I was able to reassure Doña Rosalia that reasonable precautions about what she eats would protect her from being poisoned by the wallpaper." Three months after the wallpaper incident, a chance visit by begging Gypsies had convinced Doña Rosalia that her house had been the subject of a reconnaissance party and was slated to be taken over as a command center by the invading Red army, which was poised to cross the straits from Morocco. There were more reports. Doña Rosalia had possessed a morbid streak of creativity, and none of the plots were exactly the same.

By the time Tejada finished reading, he was torn between amusement at his great-aunt's eccentricities and disgust that she had wasted so much of his colleagues' time. He also had a high opinion of Sergeant Rivas's narrative skills. Anyone who had known Rosalia de Ordoñez would be able to recognize her from the pages of Rivas's reports, in all her querulous and self-absorbed glory. *At least,* the lieutenant thought, *her terror of death had gained her a sort of earthly immortality. She would live on in the Guardia's archives, if anyone ever cared to read them after the case was closed.*

Sergeant Rivas found the lieutenant still occupying his office when he returned from patrol that afternoon. "Well, sir?" he asked. "Did you find anything interesting?"

Tejada stood up, with the trace of a smile. "Your records are very complete, Sergeant. A shame that an elderly lady felt so vulnerable."

Rivas gulped. "We did everything we could—" he began.

"You can't fight phantoms," Tejada interrupted him. "I don't see any credible evidence for a murder plot here. We should get the results of the autopsy by the end of the week, and then we can bury her and be done with it."

"Yes, sir," Rivas said, with relief.

"You dealt with all those complaints personally?" Tejada asked, curious.

"Yes, sir."

The lieutenant whistled. "Congratulations. I don't know if it'll be any good for promotion, but you ought to get years remitted from purgatory for it."

Rivas smiled, a little uncertainly. "I try to do my job."

"So I gather." Tejada frowned. "Off the record, Rivas, why did you open this dossier in the first place? You don't think she was murdered, do you?"

The sergeant made a quick decision. Against all expectations, Lieutenant Tejada struck him as trustworthy. "No, sir. But your father was very anxious . . . to see justice done."

"I thought that was it." Tejada smiled briefly. "I'll get out of your way for now, Sergeant. I'll stop by Thursday or Friday to check on the autopsy report, and then we can both get back to real work."

"Yes, sir." To his own astonishment, Rivas found himself

adding, "But you're certainly welcome at any time, sir. If there's anything we can do for you . . ."

"No, thanks." The lieutenant was definite. He did not add that he had already decided to spend the afternoon showing his son the playground by the Río Genil.

Tejada had deliberately avoided saying how long he intended to spend at the post, so his family had not waited to eat with him. He arrived at his parents' home as the family was finishing lunch. His parents and his brother were still lingering over coffee in the dining room. His sister-in-law and her children had adjourned to the alcove beyond the dining room, where his nephews were absorbed in comic books and his niece was finishing her homework. His brother, Juan Andrés, greeted him first. "Hello, Carlos. Have you eaten?"

"No, not yet." Carlos Tejada's eyes were roaming around the table, counting place mats. "Where's Elena?"

"She went upstairs to put Toño down for his nap," Juan Andrés volunteered.

Señora de Tejada clicked her tongue as her older son spoke. "Honestly, Carlos, you might have the consideration to tell your family when you're coming home so you can eat decently. It's very inconvenient, now that everything's been cleared."

Her younger son shrugged. "I don't want to trouble you, Mama. I can get something from the kitchen."

"Get something from the kitchen!" his mother echoed. "You'll want to go to the side door next! For goodness' sake, you're a member of this family. You might try to act like it, instead of behaving like a"—she made a little moue of distaste—"like a servant."

Tejada gritted his teeth. "I didn't want to inconvenience anyone, Mama. I'm used to eating in a hurry."

Señora de Tejada sniffed. "It's a shame that a married man isn't used to proper meals. In my day, women had more pride."

The lieutenant's nostrils flared, but he bowed his head and

said nothing. He was already turning to leave when his father said peaceably, "Don't peck at the boy. His job has difficult hours. Sit down and relax, Carlos."

"I really should get something to eat."

"It's no trouble to get something for you," His father pulled a bell cord as he spoke. "And I'd like to hear what you've found out about your aunt.

"Bring a plate of soup and some bread for the señorito, Isaura," he added as the door opened and a maid appeared.

The lieutenant felt his teeth grind together as he sat. Fifteen years in the Guardia, a hard-won rank, a painfully acquired habit of independence, and a reasonably happy family life—his parents had managed to deny him all of this in under five minutes. His lunch arrived as he reported on his morning activities to his father, trying to divulge as little information as possible, and feeling like a sulky child all the while.

"It's a shame Aunt Rosalia felt threatened so frequently," Andrés Tejada said, when he'd finished. "I suppose in among Rivas's reports there's no suggestion of any real threats?"

"None at all," his son pointed out.

"Still, she was in perfect health. And her death was so sudden."

"She was eighty-five."

"Eighty-four," Señor Tejada corrected primly. "Her birthday was in December."

"Surely a woman that age—"

"Carlos," his father interrupted, with a hint of asperity, "everyone who knew her thoroughly expected Aunt Rosalia to live another ten years. *You* might have received the impression she was frail, but since you do *not* live here, you did *not* have the same opportunities for observation."

"I'm sorry." The lieutenant accepted his father's implied reproof. After all, Doña Rosalia *had* been irritating and joining the Guardia had provided him an escape from dealing with her. "I'm sure she was in good health. But even so, I've known people who looked indestructible but who were carrying around time bombs in their chests. One minute they're climbing mountains and the next—boom, there isn't even time for a priest to get to them. Why do you suspect she was murdered?"

Andrés Tejada was annoyed. "I thought the guardia were supposed to be zealous about crime! I didn't expect to have to talk you into believing that one had been committed! I thought you became a guardia because you *enjoyed* doing this sort of thing."

The lieutenant flushed and opened his mouth to say that he had chosen his career because he believed that what he did was vitally important to the security of the country he loved, not because he wanted to play detective and look for an imaginary murderer like a little boy playing at being the Masked Warrior. He swallowed the retort, telling himself that he did not want to fight with his parents on his first day at home, although the knowledge that fury would have made him inarticulate probably also had something to do with his decision to keep quiet. "I do what I have to do," he said briefly. "And I was asking that question officially: Do you know of any reason why anyone would want to kill your aunt, Rosalia Tejada de Ordoñez?"

His father laughed. "Come off your high horse, Carlos. I don't have any idea. That's why I asked *you* to look into it."

"In that case, what makes you think she was murdered?"

The lieutenant met his father's eyes. For the first time in the conversation, Andrés Tejada looked uncomfortable. "I don't know. Just a feeling, I suppose. She was an irritating woman— may she rest in peace. And I guess with all that talk of plots . . . no smoke without fire, don't you think?"

"And on the basis of a 'feeling' you pressure Rivas into taking me away from a serious campaign in the mountains?" Tejada exclaimed. "We've only just secured the Valle d'Aran, and there's some real danger of guerrilla activity in the Asturias."

"I'm sorry, Carlos." His father was once more indulgent. "But I wanted a family member in charge of the investigation. I wanted to be sure that if there *was* any evidence of murder someone would discover it."

Carlos finished his soup and stood up. "Well, there will be an autopsy," he said, picking up his plate. "We should get the results by Friday at the latest. Then we'll see if you're right."

"Where are you going?" his father demanded.

"I'm finished." The lieutenant heard himself sounding like a defiant adolescent. Trying to soften his tone he added, "It was very good."

"I'm glad you liked it. But why are you walking off with the dishes?" Andrés Tejada was genuinely bewildered.

Carlos Tejada looked down at the delicate porcelain in his hand and saw a battered tin plate, lone and abandoned on a long trestle table, fifteen years earlier. The voice of his first sergeant echoed in his ears. "What the hell do you think this place is, Guardia? A restaurant? Clean that up!" He turned and set the bowl and plate down on the table. "I don't know," he said, staring at the tablecloth. "I guess I just wasn't thinking."

"You're still tired from the journey," his father said kindly. "Go and get some rest, and everything will be much clearer."

"Yes, Father," Tejada mumbled, and beat a retreat.

He negotiated the halls and stairs of the family mansion automatically and found himself in front of Toño's bedroom. Elena was just emerging from it. She smiled at him and put one finger to her lips in caution. "I just got him to sleep," she murmured, as the latch clicked softly behind her.

Tejada started. He had assumed that Toño was already asleep, and he had intended to search for Elena in their own bedroom. But his body had steered itself to the room he had occupied as a child, not to the guest room where he and Elena were staying. He gave Elena a quick hug, reassured by her presence and his own pleasure in it. "How was your morning?"

Elena shrugged. "All right. Yours?"

"I'm on a wild-goose chase."

"You knew that was probably true before you started," Elena reminded him.

She started toward their room, and Tejada fell into step beside her with relief. In the privacy of their bedroom, he said, "I knew it was probably a waste of time, but I didn't think that the whole thing was set up by my father like—like some sort of game to keep me amused."

"What do you mean?"

The lieutenant sat down, avoiding her eyes. "I talked to Sergeant Rivas this morning. He's got good records, and he runs a decent post. There's no evidence whatsoever of murder. He opened the case because my father told him to. And my *father* amuses himself by cross-examining me on what I found in the records, and then tells me that he has a 'feeling' that Rosalia was murdered, and that I'm supposed to enjoy this sort of thing because I'm a guardia! As if I were about ten years old and didn't have a *real* job!"

"I'm sure he didn't mean that," Elena said soothingly.

"It wouldn't bother me if he'd just say that he disapproved of my being in the Guardia and be done with it." Tejada did not answer her directly. "It's that he treats it as some kind of *joke.* Oh, let's give Carlos a crime to investigate! If he just ordered me to come home, and threatened to disown me otherwise—"

"You wouldn't obey him," Elena pointed out with a smile. "And I thought he *did* say that he disapproved of your being in the Guardia."

"Well, once," Tejada admitted. "Fifteen years ago. But he's never said a word about it since then."

"Some people would call that forbearance."

"If you could have *heard* him just now! Telling my mother when she started in about my being late that the job has long hours and that I should relax."

Elena grimaced. "Did she mention how much weight you've lost?" she demanded bitterly. "She thinks that in the mountains we should eat well, especially with a guardia's ration coupons. Of course, if a woman *wastes* her family's coupons on frivolous items . . ."

The rancor in her voice recalled Tejada from his own self-pity. He squeezed her hand. "Oh, God, love, I'm sorry," he said. "She didn't go on at you like that all morning, did she?"

"No, not exactly. She likes Toño."

"That's good."

"She sent for a seamstress because she says he needs proper clothes."

Tejada winced. "Fourteen more days," he said. "And maybe if I can convince my father I'm not interested in playing games, we can close the case and get away early."

"It will be nice to see some of the sights," Elena offered. "The Alhambra, perhaps?"

"I thought we could take Toño to the park along the Genil this afternoon."

"That will be nice." Elena glanced at the clock on the night table. It was just before four-thirty. "He should be up in an hour or so."

The lieutenant sighed and pulled off his shoes. "I'm going to relax a little until then."

Elena, still tired from the journey, elected to take a siesta as well. Tejada propped his pillow against the bedstead, lit a cigarette, and felt his nerves grow calmer as he listened to his wife's peaceful breathing. When he finished smoking, he lay down and stared at the patterns of afternoon sunlight on the ceiling.

He was not aware of falling asleep until he heard his wife say gently, "Carlos," and he woke up.

"Mmm?"

"I was thinking about your father."

Tejada groaned slightly. "Why did you have to bring him up?"

"He was very decent to me, really."

"I'm glad."

"I was thinking." Elena was hesitant. "I mean, about him being decent. I suppose if he's decent to *me*, it's because he wants to be decent to *you*."

"Maybe." The rings of sunlight on the ceiling were no longer soothing.

"I mean"—Elena paused, and then plunged on—"maybe he isn't wasting your time. Maybe he actually has a reason for thinking your aunt was killed, but he doesn't want to say so."

"He's gone to a lot of trouble to get me here to then not say so," Tejada retorted. "Especially since he's never been diffident."

"What if he thinks it's someone in the family?" Elena said in a small voice. "If he knows one of your family has a motive and doesn't want to be disloyal?"

The lieutenant sighed. "You could be right," he admitted. "But I can't see how I could say to him: 'Excuse me, Father, but did you call me here because you think one of our relatives secretly murdered an old lady and you want me to arrest the culprit, raise a stinking scandal, and start a family feud?'"

"You could think about which of your family members might have wanted to kill her, without asking him," Elena pointed out.

"Everyone who knew her probably *thought* about killing her at some point." Tejada's voice was half amused and half annoyed. "But I can't think of any real motives."

"Honor, love, or money?" Elena summarized, sitting up.

"I think we can rule out the first two," Tejada laughed. "But she was a very rich woman."

"Who does her money go to, then?" Elena was leaning over to put on her shoes, so her voice was muffled.

"Good question." Tejada sat up also. "Tomorrow I'll find out what her will provides."

Chapter 6

Tejada considered stopping by Sergeant Rivas's office the following morning but decided against it. He doubted that the Guardia would be of any help with respect to Doña Rosalia's will. It was not their province of expertise. Besides, he had not confronted his father and he was unwilling to cast suspicion on his own family members without more definite proof. At breakfast he asked his brother if the toy store off the Plaza de la Trinidad was still there. The store had moved after the war, but it still existed. Tejada made sure that Toño was clean and combed and then set out with him and Elena, ostensibly for the toy store.

"Do you mind if I leave you and Toño to go shopping?" he asked when they were well away and walking down the Calle Mesones.

Elena shook her head. "No. We'll be fine. Why?"

"I wanted to find out about Rosalia's will. Her lawyer's offices should be around here."

"How do you know that?"

Tejada's mouth twisted briefly. "Don Pablo's my godfather. He's the one who thought I should go to law school."

Elena would have replied, but a sudden weight on her hand made her look down. Toño was still clinging to her hand, but he was inclined at a forty-five-degree angle to the sidewalk, like a sailor leaning into a high wind. His head was turned away from his mother and his mouth was slightly open. Elena followed his gaze and saw the toy store. "I think that's where we're going," she said and compassionately lengthened her stride so that Toño could get to his destination more quickly.

The little boy let go of her hand when he was a few steps from the store window, and hurried to press his nose against the glass. The store was not very big or very grand, but Toño had never seen a toy store before. He knew that the carpenter, Quico in the village next to Potes, made fine wooden toys, and he had dimly imagined a toy store was a place like a carpenter's workshop, only with more toys and fewer chairs and tables. He had never imagined a picture window with a carefully modeled landscape, populated by tin soldiers. Behind the soldiers sat a row of little metal trucks and—Toño's breath caught in his throat—a locomotive sitting on a tiny, perfectly scaled track. A model airplane hung suspended from wire above the landscape. His parents were still talking above him, but he did not listen, and barely noticed when his father patted him on the head and said that he would see them soon. His attention was focused on the tiny figures, and he was delighted to recognize the uniform of the Guardia Civil.

"Papa, look, there are little guardias!" He looked around, and saw that his father was missing. "Where'd Papa go?"

"He's going to meet us for ice cream in a little while," Mama explained. "Would you like to go in now?"

"In *there*?" Toño asked, to make sure he had not misunderstood.

"Why not? It's only two months until Christmas." Elena smiled, glad that her husband had thought to ask if she needed extra cash.

Tejada, turning the corner toward the Plaza Bib-Rambla, caught a last glimpse of a small figure marching determinedly into the door of the toy store, with a slender, dark-haired woman trailing in his wake. The lieutenant smiled also and then quickened his steps. He did not think that Toño would become bored with the toy store anytime soon, but he wanted to conduct his business in enough time to share at least ice cream with his son.

It took him a few minutes to find Pablo Almeida's offices. He had not wanted to ask his father for the address, and it had been many years since he had visited the lawyer. He was about to give up when a doorway next to the *churrería* at one end of the square struck him as vaguely familiar. As he went over to investigate it he saw that the colored floor tiles and the gleaming bar of the *churrería* were the same as ones he remembered from his childhood. It was the establishment that had always stood next to Almeida's office, where the lawyer took his breakfast on weekdays. He had not recognized it because the canopy and the tables outside had changed in the intervening years.

Encouraged, he went up to the familiar archway and scanned the names next to the bell. Almeida and Berrios, Attorneys, were listed on the first floor. He pressed the doorbell. Nothing happened for some time, and he was about to press the bell again when a shadow appeared in the darkness leading to the interior courtyard. The shadow approached haltingly, until the lieutenant made out a white-haired man on a crutch. "Sorry to keep you waiting, sir."

Tejada blinked as the old man came face to face with him and began to fumble with the lock of the outer door. The crutch clamped under the left elbow, the wispy white hair, and the sharply swallowed consonants of Andalusian dialect all belonged to a past he had thought long dead and buried. He squinted at the doorkeeper again. "Nilo?"

The man looked up at him, startled. "Yes, sir?"

Tejada felt suddenly awkward. "I'm Carlos Tejada. I suppose you don't remember me. I used to come here as a kid sometimes to visit Don Pablo. You . . . you were very kind to me."

"Señorito Carlos!" The old man beamed and pulled back the gate with enthusiasm. "Of course I remember you! Always wanting to hear stories about the bandits and how I got stuck with this blessed stick." He thumped his crutch and took Tejada's elbow with his free hand. "Come in, come in. You'll be wanting to see Don Pablo, I suppose, like old times?"

"Yes." Tejada nodded, staring at the crutch as if mesmerized, with the old feeling that his stare was rude.

"So, I imagine you're a lawyer yourself now, Señorito?" Nilo was saying cheerfully as he hopped toward the stairs. "I heard you were going away to Salamanca to study."

"No." Tejada shook his head. "No, I'm visiting family, on vacation at the moment, but actually I'm . . . a guardia civil."

Nilo swung around, his face split by a broad smile. "No!"

Tejada nodded and grinned, pleased at the doorkeeper's expression. "I joined the corps in '32. Made lieutenant nearly six years ago. I'm stationed in Cantabria. My own command."

"Sir!" Nilo saluted, his entire face alive with gratification. "Congratulations. But by now you must have some stories about bandits yourself!"

Tejada bowed his head, half pleased and half embarrassed. "One or two. Nothing as dramatic as yours."

"Ahh, I probably lied to impress you kids." The ex-guardia laughed. "How'd you end up in the Guardia, anyway? Don Pablo told me you'd gone to study law."

Tejada shrugged. It was a question he seldom asked himself anymore, but when it did come up, the lack of a simple answer always made him uncomfortable. He turned aside the question with a compliment. "I guess I admired all the old guardias I knew."

"What, an old cripple?" Nilo scoffed, but his eyes were still slits of pleasure in a weather-beaten face. "There must have been more to it than that."

"A little more," Tejada admitted. They had reached the staircase that led to the first floor and he put one hand on the banister, unwilling to offend the old man by turning away, but feeling guilty about postponing his meeting with Almeida. "But it's a long story."

"You come and have a drink with me this evening and tell me all about it," the porter invited. "I get off at eight. Can your parents spare you for a few hours?"

Tejada hesitated. "Yes. But . . . ."

Nilo's eyes twinkled. "You have a family of your own?"

The lieutenant nodded.

"Kids?"

"One. He'll be five in April." Tejada's voice was warm with pride.

"Make it a café then, and bring them along," the doorman offered. "I'd love to meet them. That is," he added, "if you don't mind spending time with a nosy old man."

"Of course not," the lieutenant replied.

Nilo named a café on the other side of the square, and suggested a time. Tejada agreed with genuine pleasure and asked if Don Pablo was free. "He'll likely be free to see *you*," the doorman said, patting the lieutenant on the back paternally. "We've all missed you, you know, while you've been off doing great things in the north."

"Then I'll see you at eight-thirty, God willing." Tejada once more turned toward the stairs.

"God willing."

Tejada managed to get up the stairs with only one more pat on the back and a handshake. He was smiling as he knocked on Almeida's door. A secretary his own age let him in. "Can I help you, Señor?"

Tejada identified himself as a family friend and asked to speak to Don Pablo. The secretary, recognizing his surname, hurried into the lawyer's office and returned a moment later, followed by Pablo Almeida himself. "Carlos!" Almeida held out his hand, smiling. "How long has it been?"

"Too long." He submitted to a quick embrace with a better

humor than he might have without Nilo's greeting downstairs. "It's good to see you, Don Pablo."

"Likewise." the lawyer ushered Tejada into his office, speaking in a continuous flow of commonplaces.

Tejada answered Almeida's questions with the slight awkwardness that comes of trying to summarize a decade of living in a few polite phrases. After three minutes that covered the lieutenant's war record, his promotions, his job prospects, his marriage, his son, and whether he would like a cup of coffee, Almeida seemed at a loss. "Well," he repeated. "Well. Doesn't time fly. And your parents, are they well?"

It occurred to the lieutenant that since his parents saw Don Pablo far more frequently than he did, this was a slightly ridiculous question. "They're fine," he replied. "Although of course we're in mourning now, you know."

Don Pablo adjusted his expression. "A great loss. May she rest in peace."

"May she rest in peace," Tejada agreed, with only the faintest hint of irony in his tone. "You knew Doña Rosalia, too, of course."

"Of course. I remember her scolding me as a boy." Don Pablo attempted to make his voice hearty, but he winced slightly as he spoke, as if he remembered more recent scoldings from Doña Rosalia.

"You were her lawyer?"

"Yes." Don Pablo shifted uncomfortably. "Speaking of that, what is the situation of the legal profession like in Cantabria? There used to be some very fine attorneys in Santander."

"I really wouldn't know," the lieutenant said. "We're up in the Picos de Europa."

"A shame." Don Pablo shook his head. "You had talent, you know." He recollected himself and added, "But I'm sure you're doing very valuable work in the Guardia."

Tejada reminded himself that many men would be glad merely

to be patronized in the line of duty instead of shot at. But his smile was a little stiff as he said, "Thank you. I suppose you've heard that the Guardia here are investigating my aunt's death."

"Well, naturally, they have to," the lawyer agreed. "Although, in all honesty, Carlos, I think her time had come."

"You don't think anyone would have any reason to kill her?" Tejada asked, reflecting that his father's opinion appeared to be a minority of one.

"Oh, no." Almeida was emphatic.

"She left a will, I suppose?"

"Yes."

Tejada waited. Doña Rosalia's lawyer coughed, shifted in his chair, and said nothing more. The faintest flicker of suspicion, no stronger than a butterfly's kiss, wafted over the lieutenant. "Her children inherit everything, I suppose?"

"Fernando gets all the real estate, of course," Don Pablo confirmed.

Tejada raised his eyebrows. "You mean it was hers to give? I thought he would have inherited it from his father?"

"He inherited the land in the Vega and the sugar refinery from your great-uncle in trust, with the stipulation that the profits would go to his mother's support while she lived," Don Pablo admitted. "But Doña Rosalia also purchased some lands in the Alpujarras that pass to Fernando as well. She felt very strongly about keeping the estate together, too."

Something nibbled at the edge of Tejada's consciousness. "Was the land a good investment?" he asked.

The lawyer shrugged. "As good as anything, in these times."

"She must have had liquid assets, too, if she was investing?"

"Yes. She was comfortably provided for."

"I imagine she divided those between her two other children?" Tejada said, waiting for the lawyer to lay his suspicion to rest.

"Now, Carlos, you know I can't speak about an unpublished will to a third party." Don Pablo smiled, to show that he was being conciliatory. "It's a violation of confidentiality. But since you're family, I'll tell you that your father's her executor. Why don't you ask him about it?"

Tejada smiled back, ready to repay Don Pablo for being patronizing. "I was only asking because I *am* family," he answered softly. "But the Guardia can seize your records, of course."

"Carlos!" Almeida was shaken. "You can't be serious."

"Who were her heirs?"

"It's a bit complicated."

"I understand." The lieutenant stood and held out his hand. "It was nice to see you, Don Pablo."

"Likewise." The lawyer stood as well, looking relieved.

"I'll speak to Sergeant Rivas this afternoon," Tejada continued as he shook the lawyer's hand. "He'll send someone over to go through your offices tomorrow."

"Carlito, for the love of—!" Don Pablo refused to let go of the lieutenant's hand, tightening his clasp into an almost frantic grip. "Listen to me. Talk to your father tonight. Ask him about the will. Tell him what you've told me, and if he *doesn't* answer all your questions you can come and speak to me again tomorrow. But for goodness' sake, don't drag the Guardia into a private matter. You don't want to upset your cousins and your parents. *Please*, Carlos. How much difference can one day make?"

"I'll talk to my father," Tejada agreed finally, prying his hand out of his godfather's. "But . . ." He hesitated, weighing his words. Don Pablo's reaction had convinced him that something was drastically wrong. "But, Don Pablo, I'm not exactly an outsider. Why can't you just tell me? There's nothing startling about the will, is there? Nothing that would make someone think Doña Rosalia was murdered?"

"Of course not!" Oddly, the lieutenant's suggestion about murder seemed to make Don Pablo more calm. "No one killed her, Carlos. It's just that, well, you know what she was like. It was inevitable that she'd quarrel a bit with her children, and some of the bequests are a bit . . . inequitable. I'm just afraid that Daniela and Felipe will feel that their portions are unjust. I don't want you to get caught up in a family squabble."

"Her children inherited her gift for quarreling?" Tejada suggested dryly.

"Don't speak ill of your elders." The lawyer's response was mechanical, but his voice was friendly. "Trust me, Carlito. I've been in this business since before you were born, and I've seen how even close families can become enemies over estates. You don't want to stir up a hornet's nest."

Tejada nodded. *He doesn't see the Guardia when he talks to me,* he thought. *Just Carlito, who can't be trusted not to start a family squabble. I should have worn a uniform. And Nilo would have liked it.* "All right," he said aloud. "I'll try to avoid upsetting anyone. But if my aunt was killed—"

Don Pablo laughed. His godson would have sworn that the laughter was genuine. "She wasn't. Believe me. Ask your father about the bequests tonight, and likely he'll explain the whole thing to you."

Tejada made his farewells, wondering why Don Pablo was so certain that his father did not believe Doña Rosalia had been murdered. *Maybe Elena was wrong,* he thought, as he left the office. *Maybe no one actually thinks Rosalia was murdered. But then, why all the trouble to get me here to investigate? And why pester Rivas? But if Father and Don Pablo are saying two different things, maybe they don't trust each other. Why?* With a sinking feeling Tejada realized he had committed himself to cross-examining his father, exactly the course of action he had hoped to avoid by interviewing Don Pablo. When he reached the ground floor, Nilo emerged from under the stairs to wish him well and remind him of their evening engagement. Tejada answered affectionately, if a little absently, and regained some of his good humor.

The day was cool and windy, and he enjoyed the brief walk

back to the toy store. Elena and Toño were not there, but when he asked the proprietor about the whereabouts of a little boy who liked trains, the man nodded immediately. "With the lady in the gray suit, Señor? You just missed them. They said they were going to get ice creams at the Suizo."

Tejada thanked the man and sought out his family at the place they had arranged to meet. He found them at a table by the window, with three seats arranged around it. Elena and Toño occupied two of the seats. The third, the lieutenant saw when he attempted to sit down, was taken by a stuffed lion half the size of Toño.

"That's Rodrigo's seat," the little boy informed him. "But you can share with him. He doesn't mind."

Tejada raised his eyebrows at his wife. "Rodrigo?" he asked as he sat down, obediently placing the stuffed animal in his lap.

"First I was going to get trains," Toño explained. "But then Mama said we didn't have room to take home enough to be fun."

"He wanted the deluxe set with enough track to reproduce the entire RENFE network," Elena murmured. "We would have had to ship it separately, or get another trunk."

"And *then* I was going to get toy soldiers," Toño continued, oblivious of the interruption. "But they were expensive and heavy and I thought that maybe Quico could make wooden ones for me when I got home, so I got Rodrigo instead." He indicated the big cat fondly. "But the man said I could go back tomorrow to play with the trains again."

"I see." Tejada scratched Rodrigo's ears. He caught his wife's eye and murmured, "*Combien coute?*"

"*Quarante-cinq pessetes.*"

"*Pour un amant si chere!*"

"Talk Spanish!" Toño commanded.

Tejada smiled at his son. "Sorry. Rodrigo's name reminded me of a silly play in French. How did he come to be named that, by the way?"

"The man in the store said I should call him after El Cid," Toño explained. "You know about El Cid?" His father nodded, and he continued cheerfully. "Well, the man said that El Cid was so brave that lions kneeled before him, so I should call my lion Rodrigo like El Cid, since I was brave to play with him."

"Makes sense to me."

Elena shrugged. "By that logic you should call the lion Carmencita. Look at all those newsreels of Carmencita Franco playing with a lion cub."

"It's a *boy* lion." Toño looked reproachful. He could not understand why Papa was laughing so hard. He was distracted by the arrival of the waiter, bearing Elena's coffee and a large, intriguing-looking ice-cream creation. Ignoring his mother's warnings about not spoiling his appetite for lunch, Toño settled down to enjoy himself. His parents seized the opportunity to talk while he ate.

"Did you see your godfather?" Elena asked.

"Yes. You were right. There's something funny going on with the will."

"Funny?"

"He wouldn't tell me what." Tejada summarized his conversation with the lawyer. "So it looks like I'll have to talk to my father this afternoon," he finished with a sigh.

"So you'll stay home after lunch?" The depth of pleasure and gratitude in Elena's voice startled her husband. So did her suddenly sharp tone as she said, "Toño! Chocolate on your good shirt! Be careful!"

"It's just a shirt," Tejada defended his son as Elena scrubbed the boy's face with a napkin.

Elena turned on the lieutenant. "We missed Toño's fitting with your mother's seamstress this morning," she informed him, "because *you* wanted to go shopping. But your mother says Toño doesn't have decent clothes as it is, and if he gets stains on this one . . ."

Tejada winced. "Sorry. I'll try not to abandon you this afternoon."

"You have to speak with your father," she reminded him acidly.

"I'm not exactly looking forward to it," he retorted.

Elena suppressed another sharp comment and said instead, "Maybe we can go out for a walk this evening then."

He nodded, relieved. "As a matter of fact, we have a date this evening for eight-thirty."

"Oh, who with?" Elena felt another flash of irritation at Carlos's high-handed way of arranging their schedule without consulting her.

"An old—" Tejada hesitated, searching for the right word. "Friend" was too strong and "mentor" implied a formal relationship that had never existed. "Colleague," he finished, and stumblingly explained about Nilo.

Elena's annoyance died away as the lieutenant fumbled for words to explain why he had accepted the doorman's invitation. He had obviously been fond of the old man, for whatever reason, and even if he had not been, decency demanded that he sacrifice a few hours to someone who had been kind to him as a child. But it was not merely Tejada's awkward assurances that she would like Nilo, that reconciled his wife. It was the drawn look on his face and an odd echo in his voice. *He's been seeing ghosts ever since we got here*, Elena thought. *At least I don't have to worry about* that. *Poor Carlos.*

She held her husband's hand on the way home, since Toño's desire to hold Rodrigo left him with only one hand free, making it impossible for him to walk between them as was his custom. Elena was glad that Toño had chosen to cling to his father's other hand so that he was thoroughly surrounded by his present and shielded from his past. *We won't let ghosts get him*, Elena thought protectively, unaware that she was about to meet a ghost of her own.

Chapter 7

Consuela Alonso de Tejada had grown up both rich and beautiful. This combination of traits had naturally led to an indulged taste for fine clothing, which had survived Consuela's youth and middle age. As a girl, Doña Consuela had hated submitting to the judgment of her mother or her *modista*, when she was positive that she could have designed far finer dresses. By the time Consuela became a matriarch, no mere seamstress dared to cross her judgment. The spiteful whispered that Señora de Tejada hired humbler sewing women because she was too stingy to pay the fees of Granada's fashionable *modistas*, but the fact was that Doña Consuela preferred to design her own clothing without reference to professional opinion, and therefore saw no need to pay for advice she had no intention of taking. (She had, in fact, a talent for drawing that she had developed copying and altering sketches from fashion magazines.) One of her secret griefs was that she had not raised a daughter with whom she could have shared her interest in fashion.

Doña Consuela's dormant talents had been recently revived by the pleasant task of dressing her grandchildren, but her daughter-in-law Rosa was a regrettably strong-minded woman, who had—in Doña Consuela's opinion—an unreasonable aversion to "interference" with her children. Since Rosa slavishly followed the fashions of *Blanco y Negro*, and Rosa's husband (to his mother's disgust) slavishly followed Rosa, Doña Consuela's skills had been unfortunately superfluous. So Doña Consuela was delighted when Toño arrived. The fact that he was dressed like an impoverished peasant brat and had a tendency to grubbiness did not distress her at all. She enjoyed a challenge.

Toño's paternal grandmother had quickly discovered that he was a good-natured, biddable child, and she had been annoyed when Carlos had snatched him away immediately after breakfast, muttering something about a family outing. Carlos, his mother thought, would not understand the meaning of the word *family* if he stumbled across it in the dictionary, and as for that wife of his . . . ! She's *done him no good*, Doña Consuela thought grimly. *Of course, poor Carlos was used to living in a barracks before he married, so he probably hardly notices her housekeeping, but he might see that she's practically keeping the child in sackcloth! What can she find to* do *with her time up in the mountains? Probably no better than she should be.*

Doña Consuela had pondered the mystery of her younger son's marriage for some while that morning and had finally decided that this daughter-in-law would have to be endured for Toño's sake, at least during the visit. She comforted herself by thinking that perhaps she would just drop a word of advice in Carlos's ear before he left, about keeping a close eye on his wife. Of course, Carlos was always ridiculously sensitive about such things, but he could hardly object to a friendly caution from his own mother.

Doña Consuela was waiting with a seamstress when Toño and his parents returned from their toy shopping. She dismissed her son with the assurance that he would only be in the way and pounced on Toño. The boy was perfectly willing to spend time with the person he thought of as his *new* grandmother, although he was a little disappointed that she was not more interested in meeting Rodrigo. He submitted amiably enough to being measured, but was at first puzzled, and then annoyed, at being expected to stand still while his grandmother paced around him holding up fabrics. His mother always let him go play after she measured him. He explained this to his grandmother, and she laughed and patted him on the head. Then she made him keep standing still. She did not seem interested when he tried to tell her about the toy store and the ice-cream parlor. He tried telling her about the train ride, and how Private Ramos had taken him to see the locomotive. (He had learned many interesting facts about the locomotive and would have been happy to share them.) She ignored him and talked over his head to the seamstress. Toño began to fidget. She kissed him and told him to stand still.

"He should have something for church," his grandmother commented. "The black wool would do for that, maybe with a matching hat."

"Father Bernardo says it's very important for boys to get exercise," Toño hinted, inspired by the mention of church.

"And a sailor suit, for other occasions," Doña Consuela continued, as if her grandson had not spoken. She smiled and spoke with conscious sweetness. "Wouldn't you like a sailor suit, Carlos Antonio? You could play you were a sea captain."

"No," Toño said with disgust. "I don't want to be a sea captain. I want overalls like a railroad engineer."

For a moment Doña Consuela looked as if she had bitten a lemon. "No, you don't, dear," she said, with a venomous glance in Elena's direction. "Only Reds wear overalls. You'll have a lovely little sailor suit, and then you'll see."

Toño's clothes were a matter of total indifference to him, but he was tired of standing still and tired of being ignored. "I want overalls," he insisted.

His grandmother turned away from him and began sketching something for the seamstress. "Like this," she said. "You can tack the bow *here* and *here*, with a matching belt."

"I don't *want* a sailor suit!"

"Very good, Señora."

"I *want* overalls!"

"And when will it be ready?"

"*Overalls!*"

Elena, who had been sitting like a statue in one corner of the room, intervened sharply. "Toño! That's enough. Thank your grandmother!"

"But I want *overalls*." Toño's voice had deteriorated into a whine. He stamped his foot and eluded his mother as she walked over to pick him up.

"Toño! Behave yourself," his mother hissed.

"I *am* behaving." The words were barely short of a sob.

Doña Consuela concluded her negotiations with the seamstress and saw the woman out. Then she turned to her grandson, whose protests had steadily increased in volume. "Carlos Antonio! The first thing a *well-brought-up* child learns is to be polite to his elders. Your *father* would be very ashamed of you."

Toño's face crumpled. "Papa's not 'shamed of me!" he howled.

Elena hugged her son ferociously and glared at her mother-in-law. "He's overtired." The words were an apology but the tone was a threat.

"Obviously." Doña Consuela once more spoke with artificial sweetness. "It was probably a mistake to take him out this morning. It's not his fault. But, still, I never accepted rudeness from *my* sons. It's important to set a tone." She smiled into her daughter-in-law's frozen face. "You don't mind my saying this, do you? As an experienced mother?"

"Of course not." Elena's voice was as expressionless as her face, but Toño, who was sniffling quietly in her arms, felt her grip tighten convulsively. "If you'll excuse me, I'll take him up to bed for his nap."

Doña Consuela glanced at the clock on the end table. "It's nearly lunchtime."

"He ate a lot earlier in the day."

"It's very important to establish mealtimes. Children will spoil their appetites otherwise."

Elena's throat tightened. "The majority of Spanish children eat when they can because they're always hungry," she said quietly. "I'd think you would thank God your grandchildren are in the lucky minority."

Red, thought Doña Consuela, as Elena walked out, still carrying Toño. Doña Consuela left to check preparations for lunch, well satisfied with the morning. Planning her grandson's wardrobe had been amusing, and his minor misbehavior was no more than could be expected of his age. And she was certain that he would look adorable in his new outfits when they arrived.

Up in his bedroom, Toño was sobbing with confusion and fury and disappointment. Elena did her best to comfort him. She retrieved the forgotten Rodrigo, and patiently reassured the little boy over and over that he could have a pair of overalls when he got home if he wanted, and that his father was *not* ashamed of him. She did not go downstairs to lunch until he had finally fallen asleep.

The afternoon meal was a tense one. The expression on her husband's face told Elena that he had not fared well in his conference with his father. Carlos's brother, Juan Andrés, was preoccupied to the point of rudeness, and his wife, Rosa, irritated by his attitude, sniped at him, with little regard for the rest of the family. All in all, Elena was glad that Toño was spared the ordeal and cheerfully resolved to give up her siesta to play with him if he woke early from his nap.

When she escaped from the table to check on Toño, he was still sleeping soundly. She went to her own room, where she found her husband sitting with his head in his hands. "Your mother—" Elena began.

"Don't start," he warned without looking up. His voice was harsher than she had heard it in many years.

She sat beside him, concerned, and almost frightened by his tone. "What's the matter?"

"I spoke to my father when we got back." Tejada's voice was

cold and steady. "He knows of no reason why Aunt Rosalia should have been murdered. It's not his business to speculate. The Guardia wanted to open an investigation and he had nothing to do with it."

Elena put a hesitant hand on his arm. "I thought Rivas said—"

"I know what Rivas said," Tejada interrupted, still in the same chill monotone. "I'm telling you what my father said. When I asked about Doña Rosalia's will, he said that she'd died intestate."

Elena frowned. "I thought your godfather told you there definitely was a will."

"He also said my father was the executor," Tejada confirmed.

Elena's hand tightened on his arm. "Maybe there's some sort of misunderstanding."

"Don Pablo told me the provisions of her will were inequitable, and asked me to come see him tomorrow if my father didn't tell me all the provisions of the will. Now I'm told there isn't a will. It's as if . . ." Tejada swallowed a few times. "As if one of them was lying to me," he finished softly.

Elena's capacity for comforting had been nearly exhausted by her son earlier, but her husband's hurt perplexity prevented her from saying that *obviously* one or both of the men he had interviewed was lying. She tried for a moment to imagine her own father or her father's friends deceiving her. *Well, they might after I married Carlos,* she thought. *No one trusts the Guardia.* "Did you tell your father you'd spoken to Don Pablo?" she asked gently.

"Of course not!" Elena was relieved to hear the anger in his voice. Anything was better than his grim expressionlessness. "It would have looked like I thought he was lying!"

"Or that you thought Don Pablo was," Elena offered.

He shook his head. "I can't believe Rosalia died without a will. If nothing else, her husband would have urged her to make one, when he was alive. But surely my father would *know* that."

Elena put an arm around him. He turned toward her, and buried his face in her shoulder. "Your father wouldn't have

wanted an investigation of her death if he . . . had anything to
lose by it," she murmured. Tejada nodded, relieved. Elena
stroked his hair. "We'll go home soon."

He laughed faintly. "It'll be a relief to get back to the guerrillas!"

"I've always said they were good people," Elena said.

"At least you know where you are with them," the lieutenant
admitted with a sigh.

"Why don't you write to Guardia Mojica," Elena suggested.
"You never did settle that thing about the repair bills for the
roof, did you?"

"I'll probably be back before a letter gets there!" Nevertheless,
Tejada stood and moved toward the desk in one corner of the
room. The idea of returning to Potes before a letter could make
its way back cheered him immensely.

Elena took out a few sheets of stationery also and curled herself on the bed to write to her parents. The Tejadas wrote in
companionable silence for a while, and the bruises of the morning began to fade.

Elena finished her letter first, and glanced at the clock. Her
husband was still intent on his work, a date book spread open
on the desk beside him. She stood up. "I'm going to check on
Toño. He must be awake by now."

"Fine," Tejada agreed without raising his head. "I'll be done
in a couple of minutes. If he's awake we can go for a walk before
we meet up with Nilo."

As Elena reached Toño's room she heard his voice speaking
animatedly and then a high childish voice raised in reply. The
voice was vaguely familiar, but Elena could not immediately place
it. Perhaps he had made friends with one of his cousins. ". . .
always holding him up as a hero in school," the child's voice was
saying as Elena came near enough to make out the words. She
pushed open the door, and found a girl of about thirteen sitting
in the room's only chair. Toño was sitting comfortably in the girl's

lap, looking at a thick school textbook that she was holding open. He was tracing an illustration with one finger, a sure sign that he was interested. He looked up and smiled at his mother as the door opened, and the girl looked up and smiled also. She gently put Toño to one side, stood up, and bobbed a little curtsy. "Hello, Señorita Fernández," she said. "Do you remember me?"

Toño had awakened from his nap hungry. He'd swung his legs over the side of the bed. It was a funny old-fashioned one with curtains like the sleeping compartment on the train, and the mattress was so high that he had to make a little leap to get down to the floor. He had been charmed by the bed when he first arrived. Now he felt a terrible longing for his own cozy little bed made just for him at home in Potes. Keeping one arm around the patient Rodrigo's neck, he padded to the door in his bare feet, intent on finding Mama and something to eat.

The door handle was made of intricately wrought iron, roughly at his eye level. He dropped Rodrigo and tugged at it with both hands. It moved, but not enough to engage the mechanism, and he found himself trapped. After a minute or so of vain attempts to open the door, he jiggled it with a little cry of frustration. To his amazement, the handle turned smoothly and slowly under his hands, and he had to leap backward to avoid being hit on the nose as the door opened.

A girl was standing on the other side of it. She peered around the door to make sure that he was in no danger of being hit, and then pushed it open all the way. Toño inspected her and classified her as "not quite grown up but almost." She wore braids and a matching vest and skirt, which Toño, who had never before seen a school outfit, nevertheless recognized as a type of unfamiliar uniform. She was thin, and even the little boy could guess that she was not tall for her age. The corners of her mouth turned downward in repose, giving her face a grave but not unpleasant expression. "Sorry about that, Señorito." Her voice was musical, although the accent was slightly unfamiliar to Toño. "There's a trick to the door. I hope I didn't hit you."

The child shook his head. He remembered what his grandmother had said about being polite, and saw an opportunity to atone for his behavior. He smiled widely and put on his best party manners, with an aplomb quite unaffected by his bare feet and pajamas. "My name is Carlos Antonio."

The girl's mouth twitched in an answering smile. "I know. You're Lieutenant Tejada's son, aren't you?"

Toño nodded, unphased by her good information. Everyone in Potes knew he was the lieutenant's son. "What's your name?"

"Alejandra."

Toño gravely held out his right hand. "Nice to meet you, Alejandra."

Alejandra's smile grew a little wider as she shook his hand. "Likewise. Where were you going in such a hurry, Señorito?"

"I wanted to find my mama."

"You should probably get dressed first," Alejandra advised. She paused. "Do you need any help?"

Toño decided that he liked Alejandra. He was pleased that she had thought to ask him if he wanted help dressing, instead of insisting on treating him as if he were a baby or a doll. His answer was courtly. "No. You can wait outside. Except," he added honestly, "sometimes I don't line up my shirt buttons right."

"I'll check on them," the girl promised gravely and withdrew.

In the end, Alejandra only needed to tie his shoelaces. "There." She patted his foot. "All done."

She rose and turned to go. "Wait!" Toño hopped up. "Where are you going now?"

"I have to finish cleaning the other bedrooms," Alejandra explained.

"Can I come with you?" Toño asked. She hesitated and he added, "I can help you. My mama says I'm a good helper."

"I thought you wanted to find your mama." She smiled a little.

"She's probably busy now."

"All right, then." Alejandra held out her hand, and Toño put his into it.

There was a basket with a duster, several rags, and a pile of clean linens sitting outside in the hall. Alejandra picked up the basket with her free hand, and started along the corridor. Toño trotted along beside her, wondering a little if she was a relation. He hoped she was, but he had not met her earlier, so perhaps she was not. "Are you my cousin?" he asked.

"No. My mother is a servant here."

"Oh." Toño thought about the word "servant." He had heard the word before, but was not quite sure what it meant. A housekeeper kept house, and a laundrywoman did laundry. He had gathered that being a servant was something like this. But servants also appeared in Father Bernardo's biblical stories, and Toño had the vague feeling that ancient Israelites probably had not worried about houses and laundry. "Are *you* a servant?" he asked, tactfully fishing for information.

"Yes."

Toño suddenly remembered that one of his playmates in Santander the preceding summer had been cared for by a woman who was not his mother. "Is a nanny a servant?" he asked.

"A kind of servant, yes." They reached the next room, and Alejandra pushed the door open.

"So you could be a servant and help Mama take care of me?"

"Yes, I suppose."

Toño squeezed her hand. "Good," he said, and then added with a confiding smile, "You're nicer than my cousins."

The corners of Alejandra's mouth had been turning ever more firmly downward as Toño questioned her, but now she laughed, and squeezed his hand back. "Thanks," she said, stooping to deposit the basket, and then handing him a rag. "Here. Run this along the baseboards."

Toño obediently squatted by the wall and began to dust with

more goodwill than efficiency. To his delight, Alejandra seemed very interested in hearing about Rodrigo and about the train set. By the time they had finished cleaning two more bedrooms (and Toño had told her all about the train ride from Potes and the taxi in Madrid and how he was learning to ride a pony and the big salmon he had caught that summer), they were fast friends. Toño explained to Alejandra the origin of his new lion's name, and added some slightly confused information about El Cid. Alejandra, sensing that Toño would be grateful for a more complete history, volunteered to go and get one of her school textbooks and read the entire story of El Cid to him.

They were deep into the history of the conquest of Valencia when Elena interrupted them. Toño was happy for the opportunity to introduce his new friend to his mother, and only a little disappointed that Alejandra seemed to know his mother already. Then he got a good look at his mother's face and wondered if she was still mad at him. She did not look angry exactly, only puzzled for a moment and then a little white and sick. "Aleja?" she whispered. "Why . . . yes. Yes, of course I remember you. You . . . you've grown."

Alejandra looked embarrassed at this supremely inane comment. Toño went over to his mother. "You know Alejandra already?" he said. "How come?"

Elena knelt to be at eye level with her son. From this position she had to look up at Alejandra. "Aleja was my student," she said quietly. "In Madrid, before I met Papa."

Chapter 8

"Carlos!"

The lieutenant was just addressing his letter when Elena opened the door, calling his name. He dropped the envelope and stood rapidly, alarmed by her tone and expression. "What happened? What's the matter?"

"Aleja." Elena held out her hands to him unconsciously. "Alejandra Palomino. She's here. She's in Toño's room."

Tejada closed his eyes briefly and for a moment his clothing sat too lightly on him and he missed the familiar weight of a pistol at his waist. Once, long ago, he had used the pistol too quickly and killed someone who had been merely in the wrong place at the wrong time. The murder had introduced him to Elena, so he could not thoroughly regret it. But it had also made him responsible for Alejandra, then a child of seven. His conscience had forced him to make sure that Alejandra's mother was employed and had made him pay for Alejandra's schooling. But he had been content to provide for the girl at a distance. Seeing her brought back too many uncomfortable memories. *Damn*, he thought, as he took his wife's hands between his own and squeezed them. *She's already unhappy here. And now this reminder.* "I suppose Alejandra helps her mother after school," he said aloud, trying to keep his voice steady. "I hope she's being good to Toño."

"Of course she is!" Elena defended her student. "She was reading to him. She—she reads aloud very nicely."

"She had a good teacher," the lieutenant murmured gently, as he embraced his wife. "She must have been glad to see you?"

"I don't know. I—oh, God, Carlos, I was so ashamed."

"Ashamed? Don't be silly. Why?"

"She knew I was Toño's mother." The stresses of the day were starting to tell on Elena. There was a catch in her voice. "So she knew that I'm your wife. I felt like such a hypocrite. Everything I taught her when she was little—. She must hate me."

"Nonsense." Tejada stroked his wife's hair, wondering exactly what she had said about the Guardia to her students during the war. "Fascists" he could accept. It didn't really insult him, any more than she would have been insulted by being called a Socialist. Rebels, perhaps? He disliked the term because it implied that the Movement that had installed General Franco as dictator and saved Spain from the Republic had been nothing more than a band of disobedient malcontents, but that wouldn't have been a *malicious* falsehood, just a half-truth. He gave up trying to imagine how the Reds might have brainwashed their young, and focused on the problem at hand. "Why should she hate someone who's always been good to her?"

Elena heaved a long sigh without raising her head from Tejada's shoulder. Five years of marriage had taught her that trying to explain a classless society—much less its benefits—to her husband was like trying to describe a snowball fight in the tropics: the basic materials were outside both his experience and his imagination. There was no way to explain to him that less than a decade ago she had tried to teach Alejandra that the very wealth he had tried to use for the girl's benefit was evil when kept in private hands. "It's not about being good to her or not," she managed. "It's that she thought I was on her side then, and now . . . I'm one of the winners."

"You have a mania for dividing people into winners and losers."

Tejada tried to speak lightly, censoring the memory of barely overheard rumors that inevitably circled with respect to Elena among the men under his command. *They say the lieutenant's wife is one of the losers. He married the daughter of a loser. Her father was one of the Reds.* "I'm sure Alejandra is too sensible for that."

"No doubt your family make her feel so welcome." Tejada was grateful for the humor, however acid. Elena was recovering.

"Well, she's not one of the family, so they probably mind her less," he said honestly.

Elena sighed. "I guess I overreacted. It's just it was such a shock, seeing her sitting there with Toño."

"It would have caught me off guard, too," Tejada admitted. He glanced at the clock. It was a few minutes before seven. "Why don't we go for a walk? We're supposed to be in the Plaza Bib-Rambla at eight-thirty, but we might walk around the cathedral a bit, if Toño's awake already."

Elena agreed with alacrity. Tejada considered suggesting that since Toño had provided himself with a babysitter, they could enjoy the afternoon alone together, but he thought better of it. He volunteered to go and collect his son, and a little while later the three of them set out along the Gran Vía toward the cathedral. Toño was only politely interested in the tombs of Fernando and Isabel despite his father's attempt to dramatize the story of Granada's conquerors. But he liked the broad, shallow flight of steps in the Plaza de las Pasiegas. There were alley cats slinking through the afternoon shadows, and, at the far end, near the shuttered marketplace, a group of children hopped through boxes chalked on the flagstones. Toño, who had never played hopscotch, was intrigued. He took a few steps toward the children and felt his father's restraining hand on his shoulder. He looked up. "I want to go play."

"Why don't you play on the steps," Tejada suggested, glancing at his watch. "We have time."

"But I want to see what they're doing." Toño shook himself

loose. He noticed that many of the children seemed to have their mothers with them and was struck by a good idea. "I could play with them for a little while and you could go back and look at the paintings like Mama wanted."

Elena smiled, amused and touched by Toño's consideration. She opened her mouth to say that perhaps they should go and introduce themselves before asking someone else's mama to look after a strange little boy. Her husband forestalled her. "No, Toño, you can't play with them. They're Gypsies."

Elena frowned, disapproving. "Carlos—"

He shook his head at her. "No. It's too dangerous." He turned back to his son. "I'll bet you can't hop down all the steps to the first landing on one foot."

"Yes, I can!"

"*And* back up?" Tejada feigned skepticism.

Toño smiled, knowing he was being teased. "I'll race you."

"You're on."

Elena stood in the shadow of the cathedral and watched her family hop, at a safe distance from the Gypsy children. From a distance, the Gypsies did not look so terrible. No poorer or dirtier than some of the village kids in Potes. A better woman, Elena decided, would have walked down the steps to meet them. But Gypsies had not been part of her childhood, and a lurking fear for Toño held her still. All the old stories about Gypsies kidnapping children were ridiculous, of course. And if they turned to begging or theft it was because they were desperately poor, the last hired and the first fired even in good times, persecuted and despised beyond all reason. But Carlos had grown up here, and she was a stranger, and he had been very positive. She wondered if he would have let Alejandra play with Gypsy children. Then, thinking of Alejandra, Elena wondered if she would have gone over to speak to them ten years earlier, before she had known her husband. She shivered as the shadows grew longer and wished that she was at home.

When the church bells tolled eight o'clock, Tejada gently suggested an end to his game with Toño. They kept Toño firmly between them as they passed the Gypsies. They reached the Plaza Bib-Rambla early, but Nilo was waiting for them, enjoying the curiosity he had aroused. The waiters in the plaza all knew Nilo Fuentes. The porter at Number Five frequently spent an hour or so in the square after work before limping home, and he bought a drink or something to eat whenever he could. Some of the younger waiters were impatient with his endless stories of the past, but, after all, Old Nilo didn't seem to have any family, and a man needed to talk to someone. So Manolo, the waiter at the Café-Bar Durandal, had nodded kindly at the porter when he hobbled into the café that evening and took a seat at a table by the window. "Evening, Nilo."

"Evening, son." Nilo propped his cane against the table.

"How are you?" Manolo asked with real concern. "Is your leg bothering you?"

"No, no, can't complain." Nilo was hugging a pleasant secret to himself. He smiled. "Bring a bottle of *costa*, will you. And some bread."

"Here? To the table?" Manolo was hesitant. Table service was an extra three pesetas, and Nilo didn't normally have that kind of money to waste. Sometimes, if his leg was bothering him and business was slow, the manager gave him a seat at a table by the kitchen, instead of making him stand at the bar, and quietly forgot to charge him extra, but a window table was reserved for paying clients.

"I'm dining with friends," Nilo explained grandly. He was clearly receiving three pesetas' worth of pleasure from the explanation. Manolo shrugged and went to get the old man his wine, wondering who on earth would be dining with the porter.

The waiter's curiosity was piqued further when the Tejadas arrived, a few minutes later. Nilo beamed at the group as they entered the café and levered himself out of his chair to greet them. "Hello, Señorito! And this must be your lady." He shook Tejada's hand and then kissed Elena's.

"My wife, Elena Fernández," the lieutenant confirmed. "And this is our son, Carlos Antonio. Toño, this is Guardia Fuentes."

"Pleased to meet you." Nilo bent to greet Toño and then straightened again. "Sit, sit! I've ordered wine, but I didn't know what else you'd want. The cheese is good here usually."

"You know the place," Tejada replied, deferring to his host. He looked around for a waiter, and Manolo, who had been hovering nearby trying to figure out who Old Nilo's guests were, appeared quickly.

The business of ordering took some time, but once their drinks arrived and were tasted, a little silence fell. Nilo broke it by turning to the lieutenant and saying, "And now, tell me what you're doing in Cantabria."

Tejada answered briefly, and then went on at more length under Nilo's prompting. The old guardia listened and asked questions with both interest and intelligence, and by the time the first of their *tapas* arrived, he had somehow shifted to telling a funny story about a rural patrol in the Sierra Nevada thirty years earlier, when his partner had mistaken a bear's den for an outlaw's hideout. The story reminded Tejada of someone he had known at the academy who had nearly ruined a set of exercises by firing on his own side because he was too stubborn to admit he was color-blind. And then Elena couldn't resist describing the time her students had been tested for color blindness and one of them had switched the color codes on the answer cards as a prank. That led, naturally, to Nilo asking about Elena's career as a teacher, and although she knew it was a dangerous subject, she ended up talking about it more than she usually did with strangers. Thankfully, the old man was not shocked by the revelation of her life in Madrid during the Civil War. "It was a bad thing, happening in the summer like that, when so many were away from home," he said, when Elena explained that the war had cut her off from her parents. "Too many people got caught in the wrong zone."

"People who went to Mallorca for two weeks and ended up staying for three years," Tejada agreed, still smiling but serious.

"At least they got home." The old guardia spoke gravely. "Too many didn't."

Tejada was chastened by the old man's tone. "They say the reprisals in Cataluña were terrible."

Nilo nodded. "And not just in Cataluña. Folk guilty of nothing more than belonging to the wrong party." He trailed off, staring into his wine, and then shook himself, as if remembering where he was. "A bad thing, all around. But we're all here, and safe. That's something to be grateful for."

Tejada raised his glass. "To the future."

The others raised their glasses as well, but Toño, tired of a conversation that he could not understand, where no one was laughing, began to swing his legs. Elena noticed his restlessness, and was about to offer to take him out to the plaza when Nilo turned to him and said cheerfully, "And what's in your future, son? Are you going to join the Guardia?"

"Maybe." Toño spoke consideringly. "But I'd really like to be a railroad engineer. Or an architect." Because Guardia Fuentes had been polite to him, he thought it was only reasonable to add, "I wouldn't *mind* being a guardia. But I like trains."

"You could be part of the railroad patrols," Nilo suggested, amused.

"But they're just in stations, and I like being *on* trains," Toño explained.

"Everyone I've known in that division says it's boring work," Nilo admitted.

"Did you ever work in a station?" Toño asked, hoping for a train-related story.

"No, I always did rural patrols. I guess the corps figured a mountain-bred boy was best off in the mountains."

"Were you ever in *our* mountains?" Toño said, interested.

"Sure. I spent a dozen years in Órgiva."

Toño frowned over the unfamiliar name. "Is that in the Asturias?"

"The Asturias!" Nilo repeated. "No, sir! Right here, in our own Alpujarra. A few hours' drive. Longer on a horse, of course." He shot a sidewise glance at the lieutenant. "Never thought I'd meet a Tejada who thought of the Asturias as home!"

"We've lived in Cantabria since before he was born," Tejada excused his son.

Elena sensed her husband's discomfort and quickly said, "So you spent your whole career in the Alpujarra?"

Nilo shook his head. "No, I did four years in Cuba, first. And that was a hellhole, begging your pardon, Señora. Guerrillas everywhere you turned, and damp that gets into your bones and camps out there. Then, after 1898, I came home and they put me in the Sierra Nevada. And I was there and in the Alpujarra for sixteen years. And loved it."

"You're from around here originally?" Elena asked, more for politeness than for information. The man's accent was unmistakable.

"Yes, Señora. I grew up in the Sierra Nevada. A little town called Acequias. I was lucky to be posted to Órgiva. It's only a few hours away, so I was able to get home on leave."

In spite of his travels abroad in his youth, the old man's attitude was similar to that of many of the residents of Potes, Elena thought. There really wasn't much worth seeing outside their own mountains. Except, of course, that both the Granadino and the Cantabrians would have denied that they had anything in common. Wondering what had brought him from his mountains to the metropolis on the plain, she asked, "How did you end up in Granada then?"

Nilo's face darkened. "I had a bit of a run-in with some bandits. It was winter, and I should have known better than to chase them over that road. But I knew it like the back of my hand, and, well, pride goeth before a fall. In my case, pride went before a patch of ice. My horse came down on me."

Elena's breath hissed through her teeth and she closed her eyes momentarily, reminding herself that Carlos was a good horseman and that the roads were better than they had been, and that anyway the Guardia used jeeps whenever they could nowadays. Tejada, who had heard and gloried in the story of the moonlight chase many times in his childhood, now found himself interested in a new facet of Nilo's history. "Did the Guardia sent you to Granada for medical treatment?"

Nilo shook his head. "Oh, no. They picked me up and brought me back to the post, and then the sergeant got the doctor to come take a look at me, but there wasn't much he could do. The problem was when I healed up I had this limp. I couldn't ride, and there was no way I was fit for service. So I went home to Acequias and was just set to go crazy with worry when Don Jesús offered to help."

"Don Jesús?" Elena asked, just as her husband said, "That would be Jesús del Rioseco?"

"That's right," Nilo agreed. "He found me a little house in the city and offered me a place here as a porter. And I've been here ever since." Turning to Elena, he added, "The Riosecos own a lot of land up in the Alpujarra. Don Jesús was the head of the family in those days. My family were tenants of his, and he took care of his people. A fine gentleman, Don Jesús."

"He owned the building where you work?" Elena guessed.

"Yes, and some other properties around the city. His son, Don Ramiro, sold off this one a few years ago, but he told me to come to him if the new owners made any changes. He was like his father."

There was silence for a moment, as Nilo paid tribute to his patron. Toño began to swing his legs again restlessly. Elena, embarrassed by Nilo's feudalism, noticed her son's fidgeting and seized the excuse it offered. "You've been very quiet. Would you like to go look at the fountain?" she asked, stroking the boy's forehead.

Toño agreed enthusiastically and slid out of his seat with a speed that suggested his mother's offer had come none too soon. They excused themselves and headed off to explore the plaza. Nilo watched them go, smiling. "Bright kid."

Tejada bowed his head, pleased. "Thanks. He can't sit still, though."

"Mine couldn't either at that age. But he's a good boy. Like his father." Nilo continued, "You've done well for yourself."

"All right, I suppose."

"No, I mean it." Nilo looked out the window, to watch Toño clambering up the sides of the fountain, while Elena offered him a helping hand. "Becoming a lieutenant. Marrying a pretty, well-educated girl like that. A healthy son. You're a lucky man."

It occurred to Tejada that he had never heard Nilo mention his family. Perhaps the former guardia was a widower. *How did he support his children after he was wounded?* Tejada wondered. *The pension wouldn't have been enough.* He thrust away the unpleasant thought. His parents might dislike Elena, but they would see to it that no grandchild of theirs ever starved. "I didn't know you had children," he said aloud.

"Four girls. All married now, up in the Sierra. And my little Paquito."

"Your son?"

"He would have been about ten years older than you are. He died when he was six. Fever."

"I'm sorry." Tejada cast an involuntary glance toward the window and was reassured by the sight of Toño scampering among the flower sellers, hearty and healthy.

Nilo followed his gaze. "God's will. Probably wouldn't happen nowadays, with all these new medicines."

Tejada nodded absently, still watching Toño. "I'm more blessed than I deserve," he said.

"You are." Nilo looked the lieutenant squarely in the face. "So what are you doing here?"

Tejada blinked, caught off balance, and did not immediately reply. "It's none of my business, of course," Nilo went on. "But it must be more than fifteen years since you last came to visit Don Pablo. What's happening? You're not in any kind of trouble, are you?"

"Trouble? No, of course not." Tejada was not sure if his voice sounded as decided as he hoped. "I'm just here visiting family."

Nilo nodded. "That's good, then. Your parents must be glad you're home. And I'll bet they're proud of their grandson."

"Oh, yes."

"Why didn't you bring him to visit Don Pablo? I'm sure he'd be tickled pink to meet the boy."

"I might, if I get a chance. But I wanted to see Don Pablo on business," Tejada replied absently before he remembered that he had just claimed the purpose of his trip was to visit family.

Nilo raised his eyebrows, but he said nothing. There was silence. Tejada recognized a professional's technique for eliciting a confession. He was an expert at it himself. But it did not seem worth the effort to resist Nilo's curiosity. "My father's aunt Rosalia died a couple of weeks ago," he said. "That's actually why I'm here."

The old man nodded. "I wondered if that was it."

"What?"

"There's not going to be any need to drag the family into court over the will, is there?" Nilo spoke with concern.

"What—?" Tejada reframed the question. "*How* did you know that there was . . . any controversy?"

"I didn't really," Nilo said apologetically. "But Don Pablo was her lawyer, you know, and a couple of weeks ago she came in all steamed up, muttering about changing her will. She was always coming to Don Pablo with one thing or another, but that last time she was hissing and spitting about disowning this one and punishing that one. And then when I heard she'd gone so suddenly, I thought there'd be trouble. So when you came to see Don Pablo, I put two and two together."

"You know she made a will?" Tejada demanded, suddenly intent.

"Not *a* will," Nilo laughed. "At least half a dozen since her husband passed away, poor lady."

Tejada stiffened. How had Pablo Almeida described Rosalia's will? "Some of the bequests are a bit . . . inequitable." And now Nilo was offering confirmation. Then why had his father said that Doña Rosalia died intestate? Perhaps his father was simply mistaken and had assumed the old lady had left no will because if there had been one he should have been summoned to a reading of the document. If there was a will, why had it not been read and published? *Maybe one of the potential heirs she disinherited took the will and is hoping he'll receive a share according to the law if she's presumed intestate,* Tejada thought. With something like horror, he recalled that the only person who had insisted Doña Rosalia was intestate was his own father. *No.* Instinctively he searched for ways to discredit the half-formed accusation. "You don't mean to say she confided in *you* about her will?" he demanded harshly.

"Not about details," the old man admitted. "But she passed the time of day with me when she came in. Maybe she talked a bit more freely than she should have. But she was angry and upset that last time, and Don Pablo's a busy man, so he didn't always have enough time for her." Nilo coughed deprecatingly. "We old folks keep each other company sometimes."

Tejada sighed, defeated. Doña Rosalia had been anything but discreet, especially when she was angry. He could picture Don Pablo tactfully ushering her out of the office, still in midcry, ready to vent her annoyance on whoever happened to be within earshot. "What did she tell you?" he asked.

"She'd fought with Señorita Dani. I don't know what about,"

Nilo answered. Tejada took a moment to translate "Señorita Dani" into the deceased's daughter, his father's cousin Daniela, more commonly known since her marriage as the Condesa de Almagro. Nilo continued. "They were always quarreling, but nothing serious. Just the way mothers and daughters do. But she was *really* angry with Señorito Felipe. She said he'd disgraced the family and was worse than a Red."

Tejada blinked. Although they were actually first cousins once removed, he had always known Doña Rosalia's youngest son as "Tío Felipe." Only fifteen years separated Felipe Ordoñez from the lieutenant whose older brother was even closer to him in age. Tío Felipe had been the good-natured playmate of their childhood and sympathetic counselor of their adolescence. The lieutenant remembered Tío Felipe as a lazily cheerful man, who delighted in shocking the female members of the family by his determined refusal to marry and settle down. Felipe had inherited a controlling share in a profitable sugar refinery from one of his paternal uncles, but he never seemed interested in business. In his youth he had written some poetry, which he freely admitted was terrible but published at his own expense anyway. Although Tejada's mother, along with Doña Rosalia, had delighted in calling Felipe "irresponsible," the charge was not really justified. He lived comfortably but not extravagantly, well within his income, and without being a burden on his family. Although his mother had nagged him from time to time, it was always with considerable affection. He was her youngest child, and he had mastered the art of being lovable. "She was angry at *Felipe?*" Tejada said, disbelieving. "*Why?*"

Nilo shrugged. "I couldn't really figure it out. She had the usual complaints about him." He hesitated. "But she was more. . . more *vicious* the last time. I mean, she always said he was irresponsible and needed to learn that the world wasn't there for his own amusement but . . ."

"She enjoyed saying that," Tejada confirmed.

The old man nodded. "That's right. But this time she was really angry. She was raving about how men like him would bring down the country with their immorality."

Tejada experienced a faint twinge of guilt as he remembered his last meeting with his Tío Felipe. He had been twenty-one and preparing to enter the Guardia. Newly imbued with the ideals of the Falange, he had eagerly preached them to his cousin. Felipe had laughed at him, making a light response about wine, women, and song. With his boy's offended dignity Tejada had flared: "It's people with your attitude who are responsible for the Republic! You'll drink and dance while this country goes to the dogs, and you don't even have the decency to *care* about it!" Annoyed, but still with a pretense of laughter, Felipe had told him to take himself less seriously. They had parted in anger. Now, hearing the echo of his own words in Doña Rosalia's, and able to imagine his own reaction to the certainties of an arrogant youth, it occurred to Tejada that he had been cruel to his uncle. "You think she cut Felipe out of her will?" he asked, finding himself feeling sorry for his cousin.

Nilo nodded. "Absolutely certain. But there was more than that." He lowered his voice. "She was saying she ought to report Felipe to the Guardia." He looked at Tejada and his voice was pleading. "She didn't do that, did she, Lieutenant? I've met Señorito Felipe a time or two, and he's a nice gentleman. He wouldn't do anything wrong."

Tejada took a deep breath and silently thanked God that Rosalia had died before expanding her wild accusations about Reds from her servants to her children. "No," he said. "No, of course not. And even if she had . . . well, the Guardia knew that she was an elderly lady who got a little confused sometimes."

"That's good then." Nilo relaxed. "I'm sorry to be nosy, but as I say, Señorito Felipe's a good man, and when I saw you coming to Don Pablo's I thought maybe there'd been some kind of trouble."

"And I thought you wanted the pleasure of my company," Tejada said wryly.

"That, too, of course," the old man agreed. "And I was curious to meet your wife. I get bored, you know."

"It sounds like there's plenty of drama at Number Five," Tejada remarked with a laugh.

"It's not like being a guardia though," Nilo said wistfully.

The conversation became general again, and a few minutes later they were rejoined by Elena and Toño. The rest of the evening passed pleasantly. It was after eleven when the Tejadas said their good-byes, and Nilo warmly invited them to have dinner with him again whenever they had time.

Away from the bustle of the cafés in the plaza, the streets were dark and silent. Toño walked between his parents, too sleepy to talk much. When they reached home, Elena tucked him in and, returning to their room, and found her husband already in bed.

"That was a very enjoyable evening," she said. "I liked him."

"I thought you would."

Elena frowned at his tone. "Didn't you have a good time?"

Tejada watched Elena undoing her hair and smiled, remembering Nilo's estimation of her. "No. I did. But . . . it's hard being home."

He woke early the next morning, restless. A lingering memory of Nilo made him decide to wear a uniform instead of his vacation clothes, and a shrewd suspicion of what his mother would say about his wearing it made him skip breakfast and head straight for the post. He told himself that since he had a limited amount of time he ought to spend most of it working. When he arrived, his industry was justified. The post was buzzing with activity as the shift changed, and a guardia hailed him as soon as he entered, and directed him to Sergeant Rivas's office.

"Sir!" the sergeant saluted formally. "Good morning. Good to see you so early. What are your orders about the Ordoñez case?

I've detailed two men to search the Casa Ordoñez and more are at your disposal if you need them. And naturally I'll be happy to assist you personally as soon as you give the word."

"I thought you said you'd already made up the duty roster for the week." Tejada wondered briefly if Rivas was also trying to ignore demons by losing himself in his work. He seemed almost unnaturally eager to help this morning. "There's no need to waste men on this. I was really just checking in."

"I've been waiting for you to check in, sir." Rivas saluted again. His face had the expression of a man who is suffering from a toothache. He took a deep breath, squared his shoulders, and prepared himself for a metaphorical dentist's drill. "We received the autopsy report late last night. It seems Doña Rosalia had ingested cyanide. The poison killed her."

Chapter 9

Tejada spared a moment to wonder why he had been so anxious to get to work early that morning.

He asked, with faint hope, "I suppose there's no possibility of eating or drinking cyanide by accident?"

"I'm afraid not, sir. Not seeing how careful she was."

"Suicide?" Tejada knew as he spoke that this was nonsense.

"She was very devout, sir. And, anyway, why would she do a thing like that?"

"Your men are searching the house for a source?"

"Yes, sir."

Tejada thought about what he should do next. No good options presented themselves. "Good work," he said, paving the way for telling Rivas that he had absolute confidence in the investigative skills of the Guardia in Granada and that he would be happy to let Rivas continue to handle the case.

"Thank you, sir." Rivas hesitated. "Sir?"

"Yes?"

"I wondered." Rivas swallowed. "That is . . . your father seemed to feel that we hadn't been as diligent as we might have been, and . . . well, to tell the truth, we probably wouldn't have realized it was murder quite so quickly if he hadn't suggested it and I was wondering—"

"Wondering what?" Tejada demanded sharply. Someone would have to interview Andrés Tejada and ask him why he had believed that his aunt had been murdered. He suspected that Rivas wanted to shift this responsibility to him.

"If you could see your way to breaking the news to him?" Sergeant Rivas finished hopefully. "I'm sure he'll be very upset about the poor lady's death, you see, and I thought maybe the news would come best from a family member . . . to comfort his grief. . . ."

Tejada was able to repress the comment that immediately came to mind, but not the small incredulous snort that went with it. Rivas looked agonized. "I'd take it as a great personal favor, sir."

For a moment, Tejada was grateful Rivas had not mentioned the need to question his father. Then he sighed again. Someone would have to. "I'll talk to him," he said. "But I'm officially on leave. I'll help if I can, but if you don't want the case, perhaps it might fall within the Policía Armada's jurisdiction."

"Thank you, sir." Rivas was relieved. "But Doña Rosalia always called the Guardia. And . . . well, I don't like to let her down again."

"Again?" Tejada raised his eyebrows.

"All those times she said someone was trying to kill her, sir. And now, it seems she was right."

"Maybe," the lieutenant said thoughtfully. "Or maybe not. Do you know anything about her will?"

"No, sir."

"I've found out a little." Tejada briefly summarized what he had learned from Nilo the night before. "But the thing that puzzles me is that no one's mentioned her will having been read. I'd think Daniela and Felipe would be baying for blood by now if they'd been disinherited."

"I suppose someone will have to interview them as well." Rivas looked depressed. "I don't suppose—"

"Why don't you question her household," Tejada interrupted, before the sergeant could frame another request. "I'll deal with her family." Rivas began to express his gratitude. Tejada cut him off impatiently. "Pull the files on all the Ordoñez household. Anything, as far back as we have. And I want written reports of your interviews with the servants on this desk by the end of the day. Find out everything they remember about the night she died. What she ate, what she drank, where it came from, who served it, everything. When was the last time each one saw her alive and did they know of anyone who saw her after that. And your own notes from when you were first called."

"Yes, sir."

"I'll meet you here at eight o'clock, with my information. We can collate our reports and see what we've got."

"Very good, sir."

Tejada turned on his heel. At the doorway he paused. "Oh and Rivas?"

"Sir?"

"Pull the files on all her potential heirs, too."

The sergeant swallowed. "I don't think we have any records with respect to her children, sir. They've never been in any kind of trouble."

"Grandchildren then. The boys at least will have military records." Tejada smiled without humor. "If nothing else, the Guardia keep tabs on their own. You can take a look at my dossier, Sergeant. See what you learn." He was gone before Rivas could think of a tactful reply.

The *churrerías* were still serving late breakfasts in the Plaza de la Trinidad as Tejada made his way back to his parents' home. His steps slowed in the plaza, and on impulse he stopped and bought a coffee. He leaned against the bar, listening to the hiss of the coffee machines and the careless conversations of university students who were probably cutting morning classes. After a moment's thought, he dug out the notepad he always carried in his work clothes and began to write, awkwardly squeezing his elbow close to his body to avoid the newspaper of the man on his right.

To Do:

Interview: Fernando Ordoñez—His father's heir. Estates tied
    up for him?
Daniela Ordoñez (de Almagro)—What was her quarrel with
    her mother? Was she expecting a legacy?
Felipe Ordoñez—Why was Rosalia angry at him?
Andrés Tejada—Why does he believe she was murdered?

To Ask:

1. What do they know about the will?
2. What do they know about poisons?
3. Who do they think might have killed Dna. Rosalia? Why?

He looked at the list with distaste and wondered where he would find Doña Rosalia's children. His father would know, of course. But he disliked the idea of confronting his father until it was absolutely necessary. Ignoring the nagging voice that told him he should interview his father first, he turned south, and headed for the casino. Fernando and Felipe Ordoñez were both almost certain to drop in sometime during the day. With any luck he would catch at least one of them. If they were not there, the employees of the club would know where they could be found.

Granada's casino stood just past the post office, a discreetly dignified nineteenth-century building. Glass doors gave admittance to a marble-floored lobby, under a lofty ceiling adorned by a massive chandelier that seemed out of place in the morning sunlight. He had visited the club a few times with his father as a child and had taken a juvenile delight in listening to the echoes of his tapping shoes on the marble. Tejada crossed the lobby, absently noting that his footsteps still echoed in the empty space, although the rhythm of the echoes had changed now that his stride had lengthened.

A uniformed concierge rose to greet him as he reached the cloakroom. "Good morning, Señor Guardia. Would you like to leave a message for one of the members?"

"That depends. Are either of the Ordoñez brothers here?"

"I believe not, sir, but I can check if you wait a moment," the concierge answered.

Tejada had suspected that neither brother would be at the casino so early, but on the off chance that one of them *was* upstairs, it would be better to catch him off guard. The lieutenant took off his cloak and tricorn. "Don't trouble yourself. I'll go and check." He held out his hat to the concierge, who looked stunned and a little apprehensive.

Tejada waited a moment, and when the concierge made no move, dropped his hat and cloak on the counter in front of the frozen man and headed for the stairs. The concierge came out of his daze and gave a strangled cough. "Er . . . I beg your pardon, officer. But with all due respect . . . the casino is open only to members and their guests."

"I know," said the lieutenant, and continued up the stairs. "My name is Tejada Alonso y León," he added kindly. "Check the membership lists. You'll see it's there."

The casino was nearly empty at this hour of the morning except for a few old men and a pair of youngsters Tejada suspected had not seen their homes the evening before. The young men were agog at the sight of Tejada's uniform and one of the older ones at the bar turned to inspect him, blinking nearsightedly. The lieutenant ignored the boys, but he made his way to the bar. As he reached it, a bald man with an impressively pointed mustache got to his feet and held out his hand. "Good morning. It's Carlos Tejada, isn't it?

"Yes, sir. How do you do?" Tejada had no idea who the man was, but he assumed that they had met in his childhood.

"Well, thank you. And you?"

Tejada answered courteously and inquired as to the whereabouts of his cousins.

"The Ordoñez? Fernando may stop in for lunch," Tejada's companion answered readily. "You are likely to find him at the Suizo at this hour. But we haven't seen much of Felipe lately. Hard to tell where he keeps himself. He used to be at the flamenco clubs a lot, but it's been a while since I've seen him there." He laughed. "You know Felipe. He always knew how to have a good time. But he's getting rather old to stay out all night."

"Thank you. I'll leave a message for them then." Tejada stood to go.

"I'll let Fernando know you'd like to see him. How long will you be in Granada?"

"Until November third."

"And you're staying at your parents'?"

"That's right."

"When did you get in?"

"Tuesday." Tejada allowed a little of his impatience to creep into his tone.

"That's an awfully short visit." The old man shook his head. "Especially since you've been away so long. We hear all about you, you know. Your father told me you were stationed in—Salamanca, was it?"

"Not for some years now." Tejada wished he knew who the old man was. It would have made it easier to take his leave gracefully. At worst, it would have given him a prying question to ask in return so that he would not have to stand and be cross-examined. But the old man's face remained utterly unfamiliar, and since he did not mention his own family, Tejada was left with no clue as to which of his father's many acquaintances the man might be. He endured a leisurely review of his life and his family connections, giving away as little information as possible.

Rivas is probably usefully occupied, the lieutenant thought glumly. *I told him to have the reports by this evening, and at this rate he'll have done everything and I won't have a thing to tell him.* When the old man finally worked his way back to his connection with the Ordoñez family Tejada seized his opportunity. "You mentioned that Fernando might be at the Suizo?" he said quickly. "I think I'll go and see if he's there. It was nice to see you again."

"Likewise. Say hello to your parents for me."

"I will," Tejada lied hastily and made his escape.

Made cautious by his experience at the casino, the lieutenant was careful not to make eye contact with any of the patrons in the Café Suizo. This made his search somewhat difficult as the café was crowded, and any number of people were looking at him. He glanced around cautionely whenever he thought it was safe, but saw no one he recognized. He was about to give up when a voice called, "Carlos! Pablo Almeida told me you were in town!"

With a sinking heart, the lieutenant turned around and found himself within a few feet of the man he was looking for. Fernando Ordoñez Tejada looked like exactly what he was: a prosperous landowner and the head of a respected provincial family. In his late fifties, he was stocky and running a little to fat, but his physical imperfections were concealed by an expensive tailor, who had provided a mourning suit that was appropriate and discreet. He wore a neatly trimmed silver beard, a pair of glasses, and a welcoming expression. He did not look like someone who had recently poisoned his elderly mother for an inheritance. Tejada put out his hand, relieved. "Hello, Tío Fernando. How are you?"

"Well, thanks, and you? Señor Ordoñez turned to the man on his right. "Rafael, did you ever meet my cousin, Andrés's son? Carlos, my associate Rafael Montefrío. Rafael, Carlos Tejada Alonso."

There was another round of courteous introductions, and

then Ordoñez invited the lieutenant to take a seat. Tejada did so, wondering if his idea of interviewing his cousin at the Suizo had been ill-advised. For all his good nature, Fernando Ordoñez appeared to be discussing business with Rafael Montefrío, and he was unlikely to break off an important negotiation to talk about his mother's demise. But luck was with the lieutenant. After ten minutes, Montefrío looked at his watch, and then leaned forward to gather up his briefcase. "I'm sorry, Fernando, I told my foreman I'd be with him by noon, and I won't get out to the country at this rate. But, look, if you think we can go to the ministry with that offer, we will. I'm just afraid that if we go too high they'll relax the duty on imports to keep the ration coupons stable."

Fernando spread his hands and shrugged, but his voice was disgusted. "The refineries will operate at a loss if we go lower. If they want Cuban sugar they can start building more poorhouses, because we'll have to let workers go."

"You've always been best at dealing with them," Montefrío conceded. "As long as we can count on you for the meeting then." He reached for his wallet and was forestalled by a gesture from Ordoñez. "No, Fernando, I insist."

"Your treat next time," Ordoñez said. "I've got this. You won't make it on time if you don't hurry."

"Thanks. I'll see you Monday. Nice to have met you, Lieutenant." Montefrío put on his coat and departed.

"Good man," Fernando commented. "He's the new secretary of the General Association of Sugar Producers. Clever on the technical side, but a bit supine when it comes to dealing with the government." He laughed. "Although I suppose you approve of that, don't you?"

"I only get sugar through the ration coupons, too, you know," Tejada commented. "So I have to trust the government to negotiate on my behalf."

"Stop by our house before you leave Granada," Fernando

ordered with a smile. He tapped his nose. "The railway patrols won't inspect a guardia's luggage."

Torn between irritation that his comment had been interpreted as an invitation to bribery and corruption and the conviction that Elena would greatly appreciate the extra sugar, Tejada said nothing. His cousin filled the silence. "So what are you doing in Granada these days?"

"Looking for you," the lieutenant answered.

"Really? I'm flattered. Any special reason? Aside from the rationing, of course."

Fernando smiled to show that his last comment had been a joke, but Tejada, annoyed, said curtly, "Yes. I'm investigating the death of your mother. We have reason to believe she was murdered."

"Oh, God, Carlos, not her Red delusions again. She was completely insane about them, may she rest in peace. Your father and I made that clear to the Guardia any number of times."

"I've read the reports. They don't appear to be helpful, but we are not speculating on the motivation for the crime at this time."

Fernando took a sip of coffee before answering, watching the lieutenant over the rim of his cup. When he set it down on the saucer he was no longer smiling. "You're serious."

"Absolutely."

Fernando lowered his voice and leaned forward when he spoke. "You think she was murdered?"

"We have compelling proof."

"What kind of proof?"

"An autopsy report. She was poisoned."

Fernando seemed neither angry nor grief stricken, merely perplexed. "But *why*?"

"You tell me."

"Why would someone do that?" Fernando did not appear to have heard his cousin. "You knew Mother, Carlos. Everybody wanted to kill her, but nobody could actually have wanted to *kill* her."

"Someone did."

A pair of businessmen squeezed past Fernando's chair to get to an empty table. Glancing around, he said softly, "Why don't we go somewhere and talk in private?"

"Your sister's," Tejada suggested. "I'd like to speak to her afterward anyway."

Ordoñez nodded and signaled a waiter for the bill. Giving him no time for private thought, Tejada said quietly, "Can you think of any enemies your mother had? Any *real* enemies?"

"Of course not," Fernando responded. "Not enemies of that sort. I mean, she didn't visit us very often because she used to say that she couldn't bear to be under the same roof as Bernarda, but she didn't mean it seriously." The bill arrived and he dug in his wallet for coins.

"How did your wife feel about *her*?" Tejada asked, although he could form a good guess based on his own mother's opinion.

"I suppose a wife is always a bit jealous of her mother-in-law." Tejada started to understand why his cousin was a good negotiator. "But Bernarda was always very respectful of her."

"The few times they were under the same roof," Tejada said with a faint smile as they stood.

Fernando shuddered slightly and leaned toward his cousin with a sudden impulse to openness. "It was just as well they weren't often. We last spent Christmas together three years ago. Bernarda had a migraine until Three Kings Day, and the doctor said it was a wonder Mother's heart hadn't given out under the strain."

"Did she have heart trouble?" They were out of the café by now and crossing the street nearing the post office.

"Well, the doctor said that she shouldn't get excited. But they always say that once you get to a certain age, don't they?"

"Did she take anything for it?" Tejada asked, wondering if it was going to be that easy to find the source of the cyanide. "Pills? Special teas?"

"No," Fernando shook his head, and then, understanding

the purpose of the question, added more carefully, "I don't think so, but I don't know. I didn't see her every day. Why don't you ask her maid?"

Since this was a sensible suggestion, Tejada decided to move on to another topic. "So, she fought with your wife?"

"Not *seriously*," Fernando protested.

"Not seriously," Tejada agreed. "How did she get along with her other children?"

"Felipe and I were always her favorites," Fernando said consideringly. "First and last born, you know. But then after what happened to Ramón and Javier . . ." He hesitated. "It changed her, you know. She was a sweet-natured woman when I was growing up."

"I'm sure of it," Tejada lied.

Fernando sighed, still thinking of his brothers. "Such a waste. They never got the bastards who did it, you know?" He turned on the lieutenant with sudden ferocity. "And now the damn Reds have killed Mother, too! Javier and Ramón weren't enough for the sons of bitches. Now they've killed Mother! You'll get them, won't you, Carlos?"

As far as Tejada could tell, Fernando's emotion was genuine, but he replied coolly, "I thought you said your mother's fears about Reds were delusions? Fantasies that the Guardia was right to discount."

"Obviously, I was wrong, wasn't I?" Fernando snapped. "Why would anyone else kill her?"

"Why would the Reds?"

"For God's sake, Carlos, you served in the war! They don't need a reason."

Tejada felt a flicker of annoyance at his cousin's naïveté. "Right now, they kill for money or to make a point," he said. "And usually we catch them. I don't see what they'd gain from Doña Rosalia's death."

"No one else would gain from murdering Mother!" Fernando shot back.

They walked in silence for a few steps. "What are the terms of your late mother's will?"

Fernando snorted. "You'd know more than I do."

"What?"

"The Guardia have it, don't they? That's what your father told me when I went to see him about it."

Tejada stopped walking. "When was this?"

"A couple of days ago. I didn't like to bring it up until after the funeral, of course, but I knew Mother had made him her executor and I thought—" Fernando became aware that his cousin was no longer walking beside him, but standing stock-still, looking sick. He took the younger man's arm with concern. "Carlos, are you all right?"

"I'm fine. Go on."

"I thought I'd better ask him what he knew," Fernando finished, puzzled. "He told me that the Guardia were holding the will pending an investigation into her death because of all the silly complaints she'd made about Reds threatening her." Fernando grimaced. "That's what he said. 'Silly complaints.' And I told him we should explain to the Guardia what nonsense it had been. God! Poor Mother."

They had reached the Río Genil and were strolling along the park on its banks. It was, Tejada remembered, only a few more steps to the Condesa de Almagro's home. He would have dearly liked time to think over what he had been told. He wanted to be able to sit facing Fernando, to interview him properly, with a notebook in hand. The wind along the river whirled dead leaves along the sandy paths, in sympathy with the random motion of Tejada's thoughts. His heel met one of the leaves in its skittering flight and he crushed it violently, glad to make something stand still.

"What do you know about the provisions of your mother's will?" he asked, trying to pin down some facts.

Unaware of the lieutenant's inner turmoil, Fernando

assumed he was merely following an earlier line of thought. "Not very much. That was why I asked your father. Mother was. . . rather volatile. She changed her will around quite a bit, so none of us ever knew exactly what was in it. Ever since Father died, she'd felt alone and helpless, and she . . . couldn't always handle the responsibility wisely. Here," he added, taking his cousin's elbow. "Dani's house is just across the street."

Tejada was grateful for the arm on his elbow. He felt as if the world were spinning too quickly. "So none of her heirs knew exactly what they would inherit?" he managed.

"Father had left the refinery and some of the land in trust for her lifetime, so that she would be provided for. They'll revert to my sole control now," Fernando answered easily as they crossed the street. "I don't know about the rest. Why does it matter?"

Fernando's blithe ignorance of the obvious was hard to swallow. "Because if no one knew the terms of your mother's will, no one would have been likely to poison her for the sake of an inheritance."

"That's ridiculous." Fernando was impatient. "Anyway, she would never have left her money away from the family."

He rapped on a dark wooden door in a whitewashed wall, broken by a tile proclaiming the name Carmen del Río—river garden. Daniela, Tejada recalled, had always been literal minded.

A maid opened the door and curtsied. Recognizing Señor Ordoñez, she gestured them inside, and they found themselves in a courtyard overflowing with lushly flowering bougainvillea. A small fountain tinkled in one corner. "The *conde* and *condesa* are not home," the maid said. "Would you like to wait?"

"Yes, please." Fernando was obviously at ease. He guided his cousin to a stone bench in the shade of a screen of vines. "We can sit in the garden; it's still pleasant at this time of year. Would you like a drink, Carlos?"

"Just water, thanks." The lieutenant sank onto the bench and placed one palm flat against the stone, glad of its coolness and its unforgiving solidity. He waited until Fernando was sitting comfortably beside him and then he dug out his notebook and a pen.

"You said your mother would never have left anything away from the family. Does that mean her children or would it include," he swallowed, "other family members as well?"

"I don't know, but I'd guess just her children," Fernando said. "And perhaps your father, as well. She was always very fond of him, and he was her nearest relative, after us." He smiled. "I'm afraid there aren't any mysterious heirs with evil designs, Carlos."

Tejada was tempted to retort that Fernando seemed eager to narrow the circle of suspects to himself and his siblings, but the unsettling knowledge about his father's deception kept him silent. His father had clearly lied to Fernando. That suggested that he had lied about Doña Rosalia dying intestate as well. What did the lies have in common? *No one's seen this will,* Tejada thought. *Except Don Pablo, and he wouldn't tell me what was in it. Why? Because knowing the beneficiary would point the finger at Rosalia's murderer? But if the will just divides the property among her children, or even her children and Father, no one would be surprised by it.* The maid brought water, and he gulped it gratefully. Elena had reminded him that his father would not have called for a murder investigation if it could harm him in any way. *But he's breaking the law, no matter what,* the lieutenant thought miserably. *And I'll have to tell him that I know. Oh, God, I'll have to let Rivas do it. But even if Rivas tells him, he'll know I found out.*

Desperately, he tried to think of further questions for his cousin. But the will continued to intrude on his thoughts. "You're sure you have no clearer idea of the provisions of her will?" he asked hopelessly.

"I can tell you about one I saw about a year ago." Fernando sounded exasperated. "But I can also tell you that she's seen Pablo many times since then, and that it's likely to have been completely altered."

"What did her will provide a year ago then?"

Fernando rolled his eyes. "Aside from the land that reverted to me, I also inherited some property in the Alpujarra that she bought right after my father died."

"Houses or land?"

"Both. Some houses in Órgiva and the farms that go with them. I wondered if they'd be good for cane, but there are stable tenants in place and the farms are likely to be more profitable as they are, besides the expense of getting cane to a refinery from the mountains. The nearest refineries are Don Estéban's, on the coast, and I'd be charged for using them."

"Anything else about the will?" Tejada prompted, before his cousin could get lost in musings about the sugar-cane industry.

"No, that was all my share. I was more than happy with it."

"What about the rest of her assets?"

Fernando frowned, fishing for memories of facts that had made less of an impression. "Daniela got all of Mother's jewelry, of course. And some money, with a recommendation that she uses it to buy a little summer place we'd stayed in years ago that she liked. I think there were some small charitable bequests, to the orphanage and to Nuestra Señora de las Angustias, maybe five thousand pesetas altogether. And the rest was divided between your father and Felipe." Fernando smiled. "She must have been angry at Felipe when she drew it up because I think it said something like 'my nephew and my youngest son receive equal shares, even though my son Felipe will probably have spent it all in six months.'"

"Do you know why she was angry at Uncle Felipe?" Tejada asked, remembering his conversation with Nilo.

"She wasn't really angry," Fernando corrected. "Two years earlier she said she was going to leave everything to Felipe because he was such a born fool he'd need it, and the rest of us had enough brains to take care of ourselves. It was just her way of talking. She loved him."

Even allowing for the sentimental gloss that the dead acquire almost instantly, Tejada thought his cousin was speaking the truth. But Nilo had said that Doña Rosalia's affectionate scolding of Felipe had turned into something more serious just before her death. Tejada could not imagine his easygoing Tío Felipe surreptitiously poisoning anybody. But he still asked, slowly, "When was the last time she spoke to you about Tío Felipe?"

"I don't know. I tried not to talk to her about him or Dani. She always ended up making comparisons and—" Fernando paused and Tejada easily guessed that Doña Rosalia's elder son had not come off well in comparison. "And I think it upset her," Fernando finished piously.

Tejada asked a few more desultory questions and then thanked his cousin. He did not bother to ask where Fernando had been the night of his mother's death. He was sure that none of his cousins would have been stupid enough to poison their mother themselves. "I'll need to speak to Tío Felipe, too. Do you know where I can find him?"

"He has an apartment on the Gran Vía, but he's never there. I'll give you the address, if you like."

"Please. And the phone number, if he has one." Tejada flipped over to a fresh page in his notes and held out the book to Fernando.

Fernando frowned in concentration. "It's one-two-four-six, I think. Or one-six-four-two? Some combination like that. I don't use it often. He got rid of his valet a few years back, and since then no one's ever home to answer the dratted thing. Besides, I feel stupid talking into that contraption. I usually just leave a written message with the doorman if I need him."

"Why did he get rid of his valet?" Tejada asked, surprised. He remembered Felipe as a dandy.

"How should I know? I'm not his keeper." Tejada was sure that Fernando Ordoñez's paraphrase was quite unconscious.

"Was he having money problems?" Tejada persisted.

"He shouldn't have been. He has a perfectly comfortable income. Or he would, if he didn't spend it all in cabarets and on every new hobby he took up."

Tejada had a good idea of what his cousin considered a "comfortable income," and he privately thought that one would have to live in cabarets every night of the week for years on end to dissipate it. On the other hand, that was probably what Felipe had done. "Women?" he guessed, as Fernando copied out the address.

"You know Felipe," Ordoñez agreed. "I think lately it's been a flamenco dancer, but I'm not sure. He's always been pretty discreet."

"First rule of a gentleman." Tejada quoted a lecture of his adolescence.

Fernando, recognizing his brother in the mimicry, laughed and handed back the notebook. "He's always been a patron of the arts. Do you remember that actress who—" He broke off suddenly as the door to the hidden garden opened and a lady in a wide-brimmed hat and a black dress stepped through it. She was followed by a clean-shaven man with steel gray hair, who offered her his arm. The lady caught sight of them first. "Hello, Nando. What are you doing here?" She came forward with her hands outstretched.

Fernando rose to greet his sister. "'Morning, Dani." He turned from her to the gentleman who had followed her and added, "Sorry to intrude like this, Alfonso, but it's important. Do you remember our cousin Carlos? Andrés Tejada's son?"

"We met when he was a child." Daniela's husband held out his hand as he spoke. "How do you do, Lieutenant, isn't it?"

"Yes, Señor Conde. Well, thank you." Tejada assessed the man before him as they shook hands. The conde did not resemble Fernando Ordoñez physically, but they shared an aura of contented and self-assured prosperity. Daniela was speaking now, welcoming both men, asking after the lieutenant's family with a mixture of courtesy and genuine warmth. Tejada performed the social conventions with a strange sense of unreality. *What am I doing here?* he thought. *These people are my family. My friends. Good, respectable people. Christians. I don't belong here. I should be up in the mountains with the Reds, doing my job, not bothering them.* He was grateful that Fernando had taken responsibility for breaking the news of Doña Rosalia's murder to her daughter.

Daniela was far quicker than her brother. "Poisoned! Good God, Carlos, you don't suspect one of us?"

"I don't suspect anyone." Tejada was grateful for the condesa's quick comprehension. It made him feel more like he was working. "I'm here to ask if you have any suspicions."

"No, of course I don't! It certainly wasn't one of us. And Mother didn't go out much anymore, so she didn't have many friends."

"The question is who were her enemies?" Tejada pointed out.

"You know what I meant." Daniela was impatient. "She didn't see anyone, really, after our father died. She was too afraid to leave the house."

"Afraid to leave the house?" Tejada echoed, startled. "Why?"

"She was always muttering. Either it was the servants who were in league against her or there was some kind of Red plot to seize the house." Posthumous respect apparently restrained Daniela less than her brother. "It always seemed totally implausible to me."

"Perhaps more plausible than any of us thought." Conde Alfonso spoke pensively.

"A Red plot?" His wife was skeptical.

"Not necessarily, dear. But a disgruntled servant. Someone who felt he'd been cheated of his wages or simply been the butt of her tantrums too often. After all, poison is a cook's weapon." The conde turned to Tejada. "Have you spoken to her household?"

"My men are doing that right now." Tejada had forgotten that he was supposed to be helping the Guardia unofficially. "I wanted to speak to you personally because . . ." Tejada hesitated for a moment. Rivas's words came back to him and served as an inspiration. "I thought it would be kinder to break the news personally instead of leaving it to a stranger."

A faint gleam of humor in the conde's face suggested that he had a good idea of why the lieutenant was breaking the news to Doña Rosalia's family, but all he said was, "If you have any questions for me or my wife we'll be happy to answer them, of course. Why don't we go inside?"

Chapter 10

Sergeant Rivas had passed the casino on his way to the deceased woman's house at around the time Tejada first encountered his cousin. Rivas, accompanied by Guardias Flores and Girón, ignored the portal of the venerable club, as solidly closed to them as the thick-walled gardens in the neighborhood of the Casa Ordoñez. The three guardias were met at the gates by Guardia Medina, whom the sergeant had sent to search the house an hour earlier, along with his partner.

"Nothing yet, sir," Medina reported. "I've asked the servants a few questions, but they clammed up. If you ask me, there's something suspicious about that. Might be worth pulling in a few just to put the fear of God in them."

Rivas was somewhat annoyed at his subordinate's casual advice. Medina had, the sergeant thought, a habit of acting as if he was a child of the corps who had grown up in barracks, instead of the shoeless farmworker he had been. "Your orders were to search, not question the servants," Rivas reminded him. "What have you found so far?"

"All foodstuffs are kept in a pantry in the cellar. They look clean but the cook admitted that icemen come in from the mountains every day, so any evidence could have been smuggled out," Medina reported.

Rivas, who had some responsibility for provisioning at the post, refrained from telling his subordinate that the cook's "admission" was what he would have expected from any house in the city. "What do you mean 'they look clean'?" he asked instead.

"No poison we could find," Medina explained.

It was on the tip of the sergeant's tongue to say that perhaps Doña Rosalia's murderer had done something fiendishly clever like not putting the murder weapon in a bottle clearly labeled with a skull and bones, but he kept silent, unwilling to take responsibility for what might happen if the eager guardia started tasting everything in Doña Rosalia's pantry. "What about outside the kitchen?" he asked, without much hope. "Anything out of place? Any unexpected items? Or things missing that you'd expect to be there?"

Medina hesitated. "Well, she had some really nice jewelry. Bit showy, for a woman her age."

The sergeant suppressed a groan. "Let's take a look at the room where she died," he said, with the uncomfortable feeling that Lieutenant Tejada was going to be unhappy with his report when he wrote it.

Rivas's first thought when he entered Doña Rosalia's study was that, except for her absence and the presence of Guardia Soler, who was methodically emptying a cabinet along one wall, the room was just as he remembered it from the last time he had been there. The plain cream-colored walls were broken in the same place by a crucifix and a painting of the Virgin. The hole in the plaster that Doña Rosalia had been convinced was a peephole for tiny cameras was still plugged by a piece of putty painted black. (Doña Rosalia had insisted on painting the plugged hole black so that no light could get through to the camera, just in case.) The bookcase sat in the corner as always, although the ranks of books looked somewhat disordered, because the diligent Guardia Soler had removed all of them in his search but then replaced them carelessly. The rolltop desk by the window was still open, as it had been when Doña Rosalia had sat in front of it the afternoon of her death and rambled on at the sergeant about plots. He remembered returning late that night, to find the old woman's corpse sprawled at the desk. The dinner tray that had presumably contained the cause of her demise had been cleared away, and the spilled wine sopped up, but an attentive observer could still see a faint reddish stain soaked into the blotter on the desk. A ghoulish witness might have romantically attributed the stain to Doña Rosalia's life's blood, but Rivas, familiar with the color of dried blood, knew that the pale pinkish blot had almost certainly come from the contents of her wineglass. Still, he looked at it with a somber respect. He suspected that the poor lady had knocked it over in her death throes. (The medical examiner had kindly appended a brief list of the symptoms of cyanide poisoning to the autopsy report Rivas had skimmed that morning, and convulsions were listed as a "possible side effect.") The window that faced onto the courtyard was open. That was another discordant note. Doña Rosalia had disliked opening the window because it made her feel unsafe. Sergeant Rivas looked out of it and realized simultaneously that the view was an exceptionally good one and that he had never seen it before. He mentally forgave Medina and Soler for opening it. He had always assumed that the room was stuffy. He saw that it could be quite pleasant. Guardia Soler had nodded at the sergeant when he entered, and continued emptying the cabinet. Now he spoke. "We went through her bedroom first, sir. She had a lot of little bottles. Perfumes and smelling salts and suchlike."

"We've impounded them and ordered them analyzed," Medina put in, unwilling to let his partner steal the limelight.

"Good work," Rivas said, since he knew it was expected. Something about the room—about the position of the books or the arrangement of the candlesticks—was wrong, but he could not think what it was.

"It might be a good idea to ask the servants if she was carrying a particular bottle of smelling salts when she died," Soler said thoughtfully. "Because it's hard to see how the food could have been tampered with."

"Why?" Medina demanded, truculent. "The cook or her maid had access to it, and they're obvious suspects."

"But they'd have to be very stupid to think they could get away with it," Rivas pointed out. He remembered a little unhappily that pretty Luisa had been responsible for taking Doña Rosalia her meals. Then he brightened at the thought that this gave him an excellent excuse for a prolonged interview with her. He ran his eyes around the room again, trying to pinpoint what was different about it and wondering if it was just his imagination.

"*Hel-lo.*" Guardia Soler's soft exclamation of triumph interrupted the sergeant's train of thought. Soler turned to face his commanding officer, holding a half-empty wine bottle. "I think we should analyze this as well, sir."

Rivas nodded. "Good thought. When you're finished here, take anything that looks like it might have contained poison back to the post, and then come back. I'm going to talk to the servants." The wine bottle had come from a highly polished mahogany cabinet, almost invisible under a stack of papers. Rivas remembered wondering on his previous visits if Luisa was responsible for polishing the expanse of dark wood. It was odd that he remembered seeing more of the wood than he did now. He glanced back at the desk where Doña Rosalia had sat for the majority of their interviews and a memory of loose sheets of paper floated across his mind. The desk was clear now. That was what was different: the clean desk and the messy cabinet. Soler and Medina had probably gone through the desk searching and moved any documents on it out of their way. Rivas wondered if he should rebuke his men. "Have you found any papers?" he asked abruptly.

Guardia Soler looked puzzled. "What kinds of papers, sir?"

"Papers with writing on them," Rivas snapped.

Medina now saw an opportunity to gain credit for diligence. Screened by Soler, he quickly scanned the documents lying on the cabinet. "There are some household accounts here, sir," he volunteered. "And what looks like a letter to a foreman in the Alpujarra. Unsigned. Probably you should ask her secretary about that one."

The sergeant nodded, and decided that it was not worth reprimanding his men for moving the papers. At least they had been careful enough to read them. He left orders for them to search the rest of the room then went downstairs and made himself comfortable in one of the parlors that he remembered from previous visits. Then he asked Guardia Flores for a list of the staff. "There's four in all, sir," Flores reported. "Two maids, the cook, and a sort of caretaker-manservant type. But they say that two women come in a few times a week to help clean, and Doña Rosalia hired outside laundrywomen, too."

"Get their names and addresses," Rivas ordered, not that he thought the information would prove helpful. "And stay with them until we call them. Note if they say anything to each other. Girón, get me Doña Rosalia's personal maid—María José, I think it is—and then stay here and take notes on the interviews."

"Yes, sir." The pair saluted and left.

A few moments later, Guardia Girón returned, shepherding María José before him. Rivas had met Doña Rosalia's maid in the past and even exchanged a few words with her, but he knew very little about the woman who had silently watched Doña Rosalia berate him for years. He greeted her courteously, not denying their previous acquaintance, and she rewarded him with a watery smile. She was dressed in mourning for her mistress, and Rivas was stunned to see that she looked like she was actually grieving. The sergeant had a maiden aunt who had fed him sweets in his childhood and was perpetually in mourning for some family member or other, who looked rather as María José did now. Since he had been fond of his aunt, he did his best to be polite.

Doña Rosalia's maid answered his questions readily. Her full name was María José García Caló, and she was fifty-eight. (She answered his question about her age with considerably less embarrassment than he asked it.) She had lived in Doña Rosalia's household for thirty-four years. Yes, the señora had been a bit nervous since her husband had passed away ("You'd know about that already, Sergeant."), and she was sometimes irritable, which was only to be expected in a lady of her age, but she had been a good employer and a good woman. No, the señora had not had any enemies, although she had been very frightened of the Reds, and of course there was no saying what the Reds might do.

"She was a good lady." María José brought her handkerchief to her eyes and vigorously rubbed tears out of them. "She went to mass at Las Angustias every day, rain or shine. And she was good to us. All of us."

"You mean she was a good mistress?" Rivas prompted.

"Yes, sir. Always generous and considerate." The maid wiped her eyes again.

"I did meet her several times," the sergeant reminded María José, a little acidly. "Generous and considerate" were not words he would have used to describe the late Rosalia de Ordoñez. "She struck me as a lady with a temper."

María José gave him a look of red-rimmed disapproval. "You only met her when she was upset. I don't deny that she could be a bit sharp tongued sometimes, but that was only to be expected with all that she suffered from the Reds. First her poor sons and then her grandsons. Then her husband. And now they've finished her off, too." The maid began to weep noisily into her handkerchief.

If Sergeant Rivas had been given to reflection, he might have thought it ironic that despite the death of its owner he was still tactfully comforting a hysterical woman in the Casa Ordoñez. Since he was not, he simply made an effort to keep his eyes from rolling, and said, "Do you have any idea how the Reds could have administered poison in her own home?"

"She always said they were cunning," María sobbed.

Rivas took pains to choose simple words and spaced them out as he would have spoken to a child. "The kind of poison that killed her works very fast. Do you know what she ate or drank the night she died?"

To his astonishment, María José pulled herself together and proceeded to be helpful. "Luisa always brought her a tray in the evenings. But it couldn't have been anything from that."

"Why not?"

"Because as often as not she'd make Luisa taste everything on the tray. And on days when she was agitated enough to send for you she was sure to do that. And Luisa wasn't even sick."

Rivas frowned and made a mental note to ask Luisa if she had acted as a taster the night Doña Rosalia had died. "What exactly was on the tray? Wasn't there anything that could have been partly poisoned, so that tasting a portion would not have affected Luisa?"

María José thought for a moment, interested now, and trying to remember. "There was ham. And a bit of tortilla. And a few pieces of bread. I suppose only one of the pieces of bread might have been poisoned." She caught her breath. "Blessed Virgin, you don't think that it was only luck that Luisa wasn't killed as well?"

She crossed herself, and Rivas had to suppress the urge to follow her example. The kind of killer who would risk an innocent life to strike his victim down—not that Doña Rosalia was not an innocent life, too, the sergeant reminded himself—was the lowest kind of vermin and would be difficult to catch. "There's nothing else she could have eaten that evening?"

"She didn't call for anything." María José was positive.

"What about smelling salts?" Rivas asked. "Or any kinds of pills or medicine?"

"She wasn't one for taking pills. She was always afraid they'd be tampered with." María José's eyes filled again, and for a moment the sergeant was afraid she was about to relapse into tears.

"Smelling salts?" he asked hastily.

Doña Rosalia's maid sniffed contemptuously. "The señora never felt faint. She was a marvel for her age."

"But she had a large collection of them?"

"Gifts from her daughter. Señorita Dani was always giving her presents for invalids, as if she thought her mother *ought* to be sick because she was elderly. The señora told her again and again not to waste her money on foolishness, but Señorita Dani can be stubborn."

Rivas nodded understandingly. His own mother had made the last years of his grandfather's life miserable by inquiring kindly after rheumatism the old man had always claimed was nonexistent. Rivas asked where the food for Doña Rosalia's last meal had come from, but María José was vague on such details. Luisa or Fulgencio would be able to help him more, she suggested, since their business was in the kitchen. He thanked her for her time and dismissed her, with a caution that she should not leave the neighborhood until the investigation was finished. She stood to go, mopping her eyes, and urged the sergeant to find the soulless Red who had murdered the señora.

Although Rivas disliked the idea that he had wrongly dismissed the notion of a Red conspiracy against Doña Rosalia, he could not at the moment see any more plausible motives for her death. He had half suspected that poison had been the desperate last resort of one of the unfortunates who had been forced to deal with Doña Rosalia on a daily basis, but there was no question that María José's grief was genuine. Apparently Doña Rosalia had only shown him her worst side. It occurred to him that Lieutenant Tejada had not mentioned whether Doña Rosalia had made any provision in her will for her household. Perhaps she had but the amounts involved might seem to one of her blood kin too small to recall. Perhaps the lieutenant had not spoken of it because all the Tejadas provided for their servants in their wills, and he had not thought it worthwhile to mention such routine bequests. Or perhaps the old woman in front of him was out of a job and had no hopes of a new one. It was a strong reason to have wanted Doña Rosalia to live and might partially explain her grief.

"What will you do now?" he asked, partly as a sergeant, and partly merely from personal curiosity.

She smiled, flattered by his interest in her welfare. "I don't know. I imagine the house will be Don Fernando's. It's for him to decide. If he pensions us off, I can always go and live with my daughter."

"She lives in Granada?"

"Oh, yes. She's married to a cobbler on Recogidas. Such a nice boy. She was brokenhearted when she heard about the señora. She grew up in this house, you know."

Rivas watched her go, thinking that it would be a shame if Don Fernando threw a loyal servant out into the street. Perhaps he could speak to Lieutenant Tejada about it. He was tempted to see Luisa next, but he decided to save her interview until the end and sent for Doña Rosalia's cook, Fulgencio, instead.

Five minutes with Fulgencio Lujo taught the sergeant that María José's sentiments about her mistress were not universally shared by the household. Fulgencio's main emotion on being interviewed by the Guardia appeared to be nervousness. He certainly was not bowed down by grief. "Doña Rosalia was a good lady," he said in response to the sergeant's question. "But if I had a cent for every time I've seen a good meal thrown across the room . . . I'll tell you there were times when I almost cried."

"Do you think her fears about Reds were reasonable?"

"Doña Rosalia—may she rest in peace—was not a reasonable person," Fulgencio said firmly. "Even before her husband died. For instance, Sergeant, *you* must know that ever since the war it's been difficult getting real coffee and white flour and so on."

Rivas nodded, and the cook continued. "I had to use substitutes. Now they may be very nutritious, Sergeant, but they don't taste the same and it's no use saying they do. So I experimented with recipes. I was creative. I invented new dishes that could have been served in the finest hotels in Paris!" The sergeant frowned and Fulgencio added hastily, "Or Rome! *Before* the war. I don't mean to boast but some of those meals were miracles, considering the ingredients. Miracles!"

"Doña Rosalia didn't appreciate your efforts?" Rivas guessed.

"If it wasn't the taste, it was the expense," Fulgencio agreed gloomily. "She *knew* that food prices were going up, and she wouldn't let me economize, and then she complained that the household accounts were wasteful. I *told* her that unless she was willing to settle for fewer eggs in her tortillas the costs would keep rising. There's a perfectly *good* egg substitute that isn't nearly as expensive. But she kept complaining that it tasted funny. And if I tried a new dish without her permission, or even a little substitution . . ." The cook rolled his eyes.

"She threw it across the room?"

"She'd burst into tears and claim I was trying to poison her. Once the top of the salt shaker came off and the soup was too salty. She almost had hysterics. I was a poisoner who was in league with God knows who!" Fulgencio threw up his hands in exasperation.

"Someone did poison her, though," Rivas pointed out.

"Not me," the cook said firmly. "You can test everything in my kitchen, if you like, Sergeant. But I wouldn't have been able to get poison past Doña Rosalia. And I don't think you'll find she was poisoned by anything she ate."

"You're very confident," Rivas said, although he had a sinking feeling that Fulgencio would not have boasted of his kitchen's purity if there were any trace of poison to be found. "What makes you so sure?"

"Because she made Luisa taste everything on her meal trays," Fulgencio said simply. "It was nice in a way. Luisa's got a good palate, and she reports back to me on how things turn out."

Rivas exchanged glances with Guardia Girón. If Luisa confirmed what both Fulgencio and María José said about her acting as a taster, they could absolve the dinner. "What about what she drank?" he asked. "Was she as fussy about that?"

"No." Fulgencio shook his head disapprovingly. "I've been in houses where the wine mattered more than the food. But Doña Rosalia never cared what she drank. Homemade *costa* with whitefish, albariño with steak. She just didn't care. After her husband died—" He shut his mouth abruptly.

Rivas prompted, "After Señor Ordoñez died?"

"She just didn't care."

It was patently not what Fulgencio had started out to say. Rivas said, "She must have had something to drink that night. I responded after María José found her, and there was a wine stain on her desk."

"I didn't send up any wine." Fulgencio looked worried now.

"Where did she get it then?"

The cook took a deep breath. "I . . . I think she got it out of her cabinet."

Rivas remembered Guardia Soler's find and felt a prickle of excitement. "How long had it been there?"

"I don't know." Fulgencio shifted in his chair. "A few days, maybe a week."

"And what was it doing there?"

The cook sighed. "Look, Doña Rosalia was an old lady. She usually ate up there, and she spent a lot of time in that room, too. She didn't like always calling for us, because we weren't fast enough for her. She kept a bottle of wine and a couple of glasses in that cabinet so she could have a drink when she wanted one. She didn't drink much at a time, so a bottle would last her for a while. And like I said, she didn't care about the taste, so she could leave it open."

Rivas leaned forward. "Who put the wine there?"

"It depended. Sometimes she would call for a new bottle to be bought when she needed one, and Luisa or María José would bring it. Sometimes one of the cleaning women might find the old one empty and they'd let me know and I'd give them one to replace it."

"And who had access to that room?"

Fulgencio, who understood all too clearly the drift of the questions, opened and closed his mouth several times without answering. Finally he said cautiously, "That was Doña Rosalia's private room. She didn't like people going in and out of it whom she didn't know."

"Who did she know?"

The cook hesitated. "Look, just because someone had access to that room doesn't mean—"

"I'll be the judge of what it means," Rivas interrupted.

"María José," Fulgencio said unwillingly. "And Luisa. And the cleaning women. And maybe some of her visitors."

"Who were her visitors?"

"Nobody much besides you, Sergeant. Her nephew came to see her every week or so, and sometimes one of her children would drop by."

"So anyone who wanted to poison her would have had to suborn one of her servants?" Rivas said slowly. "Assuming someone from outside *did* want to poison her."

"Hey, you don't think that *we'd* do anything like that!" Fulgencio did not hide his alarm.

Rivas remembered his last question to María José. "What are you going to do now?" he asked, deliberately ignoring the cook's protest.

Relief made Fulgencio voluble. "It depends on Don Fernando, I suppose. We haven't heard anything from him, but the house must be his now. If he wants a cook I'll gladly stay with him."

"And if he doesn't?"

Fulgencio shrugged. "I trained in Paris," he said with some pride. "I've worked at the Hotel Alhambra Palace. I can find a job if I need to."

Rivas thanked the cook and dismissed him. "Who's next, sir?" said Girón after he had ushered out Fulgencio.

"Alberto Cordero, I think," Rivas replied, following his plan to save Luisa for last. "I want to know if he had access to that wine bottle."

The guardia obediently left to get Cordero. When he returned, the difference in atmosphere was obvious. Alberto opened the door himself and entered speaking over his shoulder to Girón. ". . . go up to the Sierra myself if I can't find a decent contractor, and that's the last thing I want to do in winter!" Alberto turned and nodded sociably as Girón entered. "Hello, Sergeant. Sorry to bother you again."

The words were familiar. Alberto had used them at least half a dozen times at the post, ever since he had understood that Rivas did not take the threats against Doña Rosalia too seriously. Rivas looked at the man who had carried Doña Rosalia's alarms to the Guardia, wondering if the corps had seriously misjudged him to be an innocuous messenger. "Not a false alarm this time," he said dryly.

"No, sir."

Alberto was more subdued than Fulgencio but he answered the sergeant's questions readily, without María José's emotional digressions. He confirmed what the sergeant already knew: that he had worked for the Ordoñez family for twenty years and had been Doña Rosalia's caretaker, responsible for minor repairs in her house and for dealing with contractors in case of major repairs. He had acted as a secretary and helped her oversee her lands and investments. Interested by the man's role as secretary, Rivas asked for details of who had visited Doña Rosalia in the days before her death.

"Besides you, you mean?" Alberto asked, with a faint smile. "Her nephew came the morning before she died. But he didn't stay long. And before . . ." He wrinkled his nose in thought. "I think her youngest son, Felipe, came a few days earlier. He's not around too often, so it made an impression. And, of course, Señorita Amparo."

"Who's she?" Rivas asked with interest.

"Señorita Amparo Villalobos de la Sierra," Alberto explained. "She was engaged to marry Doña Rosalia's grandson Jaime."

"And why did she visit Doña Rosalia?" Rivas demanded.

"She always comes—always came—on Sunday afternoons." Seeing that the sergeant looked puzzled, Alberto elaborated. "She's worn mourning since '38, as if she had been Señorito Jaime's wife. She's stayed very close to the family, especially Don Fernando's wife. And since Doña Bernarda didn't get along with her mother-in-law, Señorita Amparo used to come on Sundays to visit to do Doña Bernarda a favor."

"A substitute daughter-in-law?" Rivas said, thinking that Jaime Ordoñez Tejada must have been a man of considerable charm to make his former fiancée devote her Sundays to his grandmother so many years after his death.

Alberto shrugged. "One of the 'eternal brides,' you know."

Rivas nodded. Too many young women still wore mourning for the men they should have married. "Would you have the dates of Señorita Villalobos's visits, and of Felipe Ordoñez's?" he asked.

"I'm afraid not," Alberto was apologetic. "Our lady didn't keep a date book if it was just family. But Amparo Villalobos came every Sunday. And I'm nearly positive Señorito Felipe was here before that."

"What about business dates?" Rivas said, without much hope.

"I can show you the book, but I can tell you now that I probably didn't write anything in it," Alberto said frankly.

After demanding the location of the book, Rivas sent Girón to get it. Alberto seemed embarrassed that the schedule was not more comprehensive. "Honestly, my job might have been better filled by two men," he volunteered. "I wasn't trained as a secretary. But the señora didn't like new people, and after Señor Ordoñez died it fell to me."

Rivas nodded and thought about that statement while he waited for Girón's return. When the guardia entered, carrying a red leather date book, the sergeant said casually, "You must have a spent a lot of time with Doña Rosalia?"

Alberto shrugged. "A fair amount, I suppose."

"In the room where she died?" Rivas raised his eyebrows.

The man nodded, apparently unsuspicious. "Yes. She spent most of her time there, you know."

"You must have gotten to know that room very well."

"What do you mean?"

Rivas leaned forward slightly. "You passed hours there with her, working. You both must have gotten tired. Maybe thirsty. Didn't she ever offer you a drink?"

Alberto laughed. "Are you joking, Sergeant? The señora didn't drink with her servants. She'd pour wine for herself. I could damn well wait."

"Pour wine for herself?" Rivas desperately hoped his voice was neutral.

"Yes, she kept a bottle up there. It must have been vinegar half the time considering how slowly she went through it—" Alberto stopped abruptly and flushed scarlet, suddenly understanding that he had walked into a trap.

"Never shared any of it, did she?" Rivas said, satisfied. Alberto was silent. "And you could have walked in there any time, for some repair to the cabinet where it was kept, say, and moved the bottle—"

"But I didn't!" Alberto interrupted. "I'd have no reason to, Sergeant!"

"You were practically her man of business," Rivas purred. "She depended on you. Surely she made some provision for you in her will? A generous one, maybe?"

"No! That is, I don't know! But I don't think so. I never had anything to do with her will!" Alberto's words tumbled over each other in his desperation to be believed. "Look, Sergeant, I had a good life here with Doña Rosalia. A decent salary and pretty light duties. The sorts of things an elderly lady needed a man to take care of. But Don Fernando has his own secretary, who does a lot of the things I did for his mother. He'll likely pension me off. I'd be crazy to kill her!"

"If you're innocent, you don't have anything to worry about," Rivas said, his tone of voice making the words less comforting than they might otherwise have been. "That's all for now, but don't leave here without permission."

Alberto, who had already risen to his feet, froze unhappily. "You mean I have to stay in the city? But I can't. I'm scheduled to look at one of Doña Rosalia's properties in the Sierra. I was just telling Guardia Girón—"

"It will have to wait," Rivas said and added with a faint smile, "or perhaps Don Fernando can designate someone to go in your place."

"But I had a pass to go to my sister's in Málaga afterward!" Alberto protested. "It's been worked out for months."

"It will have to wait," Rivas repeated, wondering a little why Alberto was making foolish objections. He must know that they were useless. Exactly why did Alberto want to leave the city? "What's so urgent?"

"Well, not the business exactly." Alberto flushed. "But it's hard to get permission to travel to other provinces, you know. And I haven't seen Dulce in years. She's asked me to stand god-father to her son."

"Very touching," Rivas said. "You'll have to hope we finish the investigation quickly then." He signaled to Girón, who held the door open and shepherded the reluctant Alberto through it.

When the door had closed behind Alberto, Rivas turned to his subordinate. "What do you think of Alberto's story?"

Girón considered. "He knew about the wine. And taking care of the house like he did, he would have been able to lay hands on poison likely."

"And he's anxious to get out of the city," Rivas agreed. "But it made sense what he said about being better off with the lady alive."

Girón nodded. "Yes, sir. But that's true for all the servants. Except, perhaps, that cook. But maybe they didn't think ahead."

Rivas was about to respond to this when the door opened again and Luisa entered, eyes on the ground, and hands twisting in front of her in her apron. "Good afternoon, Sergeant."

Rivas smiled at her. "Sit down," he said, doing his best to sound like a friendly elder brother. "We're going to have to ask you some questions, but if you answer them truthfully nothing bad will happen to you."

"Yes, sir." Luisa sat on the edge of her chair, knees tightly pressed together, eyes still downcast.

Rivas, who had been secretly looking forward to the interview, was disappointed. The girl answered his questions, but she volunteered no information, and it was difficult for him to get her to look at anything other than her folded hands. She admitted that she had been responsible for taking Doña Rosalia all of her meals. In response to his gentle questioning, she confirmed what Rivas already knew: that she worked as a maid, cleaning the house, and also assisted Fulgencio in the kitchen. She confirmed that Doña Rosalia had frequently asked her to act as a food taster.

"Did she ask you the night she died?" Rivas asked casually.

Luisa frowned for a moment, remembering. "I think so. Yes,

yes, she did. There was ham that evening, the same as the stock you'd tried earlier."

Rivas, who was less than pleased by the thought that he had eaten at a table where poison had perhaps been prepared, spoke a little more harshly. "What about drinks? Did you taste the wine you brought up?"

"I didn't bring up wine with the meal," Luisa said.

"Oh, what did she drink?"

The girl hesitated. Then she said, "She kept an open wine bottle in the cabinet in her room, and drank from it when she wanted."

"And who brought up those bottles?"

For a moment, Luisa's eyes flickered to his face. Her voice shook a little as she said, "Usually, I took a freshly opened bottle of wine up to her with her lunch when she needed a new one. She would recork the bottle and leave it in the cabinet until it was empty, a few days later. Then she'd leave the bottle and the used glasses on a tray for me to take downstairs, and I'd bring up more wine with her next meal."

It has to be the wine! Rivas thought, triumphant. At least he would have one definite thing to report to the lieutenant that evening. His voice was once more gentle as he asked, "What will you do, now that Doña Rosalia is dead?"

Luisa looked startled, and the sergeant guessed that she had not considered this question. "I don't know," she said, sounding rather forlorn. "Look for work, I guess. I haven't thought."

"How long have you worked for Doña Rosalia?" the sergeant asked, aware that she had been there as long as he had visited the Casa Ordoñez, but unable to guess how many years she had previously spent in sevice there.

"Five years now. Since I was fourteen."

It was more disinterested pity for a young girl cast adrift in the world than a professional interest in the answer that made Rivas ask. "Was this your first job?"

"Yes, sir."

"And your family? Could they take you in now?"

Luisa blushed. Then she said quietly, "I have no family. I was placed here by an orphanage."

"I'm sorry," Rivas said honestly. "But I'm sure Don Fernando will give you a reference."

"Thank you, sir," the girl whispered.

Rivas asked a few more questions and then closed the interview with a friendly smile and an assurance that all would be well. Girón apparently felt sorry for the girl also. He put a comforting arm around her shoulders as he held the door for her. Rivas suppressed a flicker of envy.

Chapter 11

Tejada's interview with Daniela Ordoñez and her husband was not very productive. Daniela confirmed that her mother had been in the habit of making and changing wills and added that she was unsure of the provisions or even the date of the latest one. Since, unlike her brother, the bulk of her inheritance depended on her mother's whim, she was considerably more interested in the topic than he had been. She recounted the fluctuations of her inheritance with some bitterness of spirit and ended up by saying that she thought her mother's mental state was close enough to unbalanced to provide grounds for a legal challenge to any will. Tejada, who was starting to wonder why anyone would bother to poison a woman who was apparently both elderly and insane, was depressed by Daniela's stance. Then she went on, "And what is this nonsense about the Guardia keeping the will during the investigation? I could understand it if the property couldn't be disbursed until the case was closed, but her heirs have a right to at least know what her last wishes were!"

"I'll speak to Sergeant Rivas about that this evening," Tejada promised truthfully, thinking with a twinge of discomfort that he would probably have to speak to his own father about it first.

He thanked his hosts for their time and cooperation and left the Carmen del Río. It was nearly lunchtime, and the day had warmed. He dawdled along the Paseo del Salón and heard the

clock strike the half hour in the bell tower of San Basilio de
Escolapios across the river. The bells were followed by an explo-
sion of shouting boys from Escolapios. A few solitary ones, who
were either hungry or eager to escape, ran across the bridge,
book bags flying behind them, hurrying toward home and
lunch. But most milled around outside the school, blocking the
Paseo de los Escolapios, the older ones roughhousing or searching for friends and the younger ones being collected by mothers or nannies. Tejada was about to turn away from the paseo
when he heard a shrill cry. "Carlos!"

He turned toward the call instinctively and saw that one of
the boys on the bridge had made a megaphone of his cupped
hands and was yelling. "Carlos! I need that book back today!"

A sandy-haired boy of about fourteen, who had just passed him,
came to an abrupt stop. "I'll bring it to Religion!" he yelled back.

Tejada had the odd sensation of being caught in a landscape
where the passage of time was a myth. The bells had always rung
that way for dismissal of the morning session and always would.
The first class of the afternoon session for the upper school had
always been Religion, and at four o'clock, when the bells rang
again, Father Diego, who taught the class, would forever look
over his spectacles and make sure that Carlos and his classmates
were in their seats and orderly. The lieutenant's uniform and
thirty-five years and the memory of his wife and child were a
dream, and the only true thing was the automatic lift of his
heart at being liberated from Escolapios and the knowledge
that he was free for the brief walk between the school and his
home. He watched the boys who ran across the bridge and disappeared into the streets, looking into their faces and half
expecting to recognize them as his classmates.

A soccer ball bounced in front of him, and its owner, racing
to retrieve it, cut across Tejada's path and nearly bumped into
him. "Oh! Excuse me, sir! I'm so sorry!"

The child's timid politeness broke the spell. Tejada looked at the youngster and saw a boy nearer Toño's age than his own, not a hauntingly almost familiar contemporary. "That's all right. But be careful of cars on the way home."

"Yes, sir."

Tejada turned away from the school and walked along the Acera del Darro, noting absently that it seemed to be a street like any other, with no hint of the river that had flowed there in his childhood or the massive construction site he remembered from his last visit to Granada. It was now a broad, straight avenue, as wide as the Gran Vía. The houses along it were modern apartments, with glass windows facing the streets, rather than elaborate villas hidden behind blank walls. It was the sort of street that looked right in a modern, forward-looking city. Tejada found it relaxing. It was comforting to know that he and his city had both definitively changed with the times.

It was a few minutes before two o'clock when he reached his parents' house, and his precarious sense of contentment evaporated as he glanced at the clock in the hallway and confirmed that he was in time for lunch. Checking the clock was a familiar action (although he could have sworn that it was necessary to glance *up* at it), and its very familiarity brought back his nagging sense of dislocation. *Lunch first*, he thought. *Then I'll find out about the will. But there's no need to spoil a family meal.*

Tejada went directly to the dining room. Elena met him on the threshold, looking relieved to see him. "Good, you're back early. There's a problem I wanted to ask you about."

"Can I at least get a welcome before someone dumps another problem in my lap?" Tejada snapped.

"I'm sorry, darling. Welcome home." Elena kissed him on the cheek.

"Home," the lieutenant said dryly, "is in Potes."

Elena kept one arm around him and lightly stroked his forehead. "What's the matter?"

"Everything." Tejada leaned forward and kissed her on the

lips, careless of who might come into the hall. "Everything is a royal mess, and thank God you're here."

He was about to kiss her again when there were footsteps behind him and his father's voice said cheerfully, "Carlos! I'm glad you're back in good time today. Are you making any progress with the investigation?"

Elena, who had one arm around her husband, felt him go still. She was frightened by his tone as he said quietly, "Yes. I've learned quite a lot today. I'll tell you about it after lunch, if you like. But I'd like to eat first."

"Fair enough," Andrés Tejada agreed.

When they discussed it later, Elena claimed that the lunch that afternoon had been quite good. At the time, Tejada felt as if Doña Rosalia's killer had laced the food with some slower-acting poison. Everything he ate tasted like sand, and there was a knot in the pit of his stomach that tightened into an outright cramp by the end of the meal. Neither the lieutenant nor his wife could ever recall anything about the conversation, although they were divided as to whether that was because everyone had been so quiet or because it had been such a supremely awful experience that they had suppressed all memories of it.

It was with ambivalent relief that Tejada stood up at the end of the meal, pushed back his chair, and said to his father, "I wanted to tell you what I've found out about the case. And I actually hoped to ask you a few things as well. Do you think perhaps we might go into your study?"

"That sounds like a good idea." Andrés Tejada rose also, and the two men excused themselves.

Tejada regretted his choice of venue as soon as they entered the study. His father naturally took the wing chair behind the broad desk, and the lieutenant was forced to pull up an armless gilt affair from between two of the bookcases that was clearly meant more for ornamental purposes than for sitting. Andrés Tejada opened a desk drawer and drew out a cigarette case and lighter as his son wriggled on the little chair's hard cushion, vainly attempting to find a comfortable position. "Smoke?"

"Thanks." The lieutenant took the cigarette with infinite relief, and then regretted allowing his father to offer it to him, too late.

Andrés Tejada smiled reminiscently. "It's funny to offer you a cigarette. It seems like only yesterday you and Juanito were sneaking them out of the drawer and hoping I wouldn't notice." He leaned back and exhaled. "What did you want to tell me?"

The lieutenant took a deep breath and decided to go through the day's revelations in chronological order. "We received the autopsy report today. It appears that you were correct."

"Correct about what?" Andrés Tejada looked puzzled.

"The cause of Rosalia Tejada's death was cyanide poisoning."

"*What?*" Fortunately, Señor Tejada had been holding his cigarette in his hand, so his jaw was free to drop open. "Are you joking?"

The lieutenant raised his eyebrows. "What's startling about the use of cyanide? It's quick, it's effective, and it's relatively easy to obtain."

"Well, I didn't mean the cyanide! That is, I meant—" Andrés Tejada got a grip on himself. "I meant it's a shock to hear that she was murdered."

His son frowned, confused and unsettled. "You were the first to suspect she had been murdered," he said, and was unable to prevent himself from thinking, *A clever killer might try to disguise his guilt by demanding an investigation that he was sure would take place anyway. And if he was a little too clever—or troubled by his conscience—he might not realize that he would have been able to get away with murder, that there would have been no investigation otherwise.* He clamped down on this thought, horrified. His father could have had no reasons to kill his aunt, he assured himself.

"Suspicion is different from proof," Señor Tejada pointed out. "I thought something didn't feel right. But, still, it's horrible to have it confirmed."

"In any case, it brings us to the question of motives for murder." Fear and embarrassment made the lieutenant's voice brusque.

"My God, yes," his father agreed. "You don't suppose there was anything in all those conspiracies she was terrified of? I would have said all her servants were trustworthy, but I suppose now you'll have to look at their political sympathies."

"Yes. There are, also," the younger man swallowed, "more personal reasons for murder."

Andrés laughed. "In this case, I can't see a jealous lover!"

"I meant her will."

Señor Tejada stopped leaning back in his chair. "You asked me about that earlier." His voice was guarded now.

"Yes. I'd like the truth this time."

"Carlos!"

The lieutenant stubbed out his cigarette and spoke in a flat monotone, staring at the ashtray. "Two witnesses have independently confirmed that you were her executor, and two others have speculated that you were also a beneficiary. You lied to interested parties and claimed that the Guardia had taken possession of your aunt's will."

"Damn Fernando!" Andrés interjected.

The lieutenant continued without drawing a breath. "One witness told me in so many words that you knew the terms of her will, which is more than anybody else seems to. What do you know about the will, and why have you been lying about it?"

Andrés Tejada took a deep breath and then said slowly, "I'm sorry. I shouldn't have misled you. I know Aunt Rosalia made a will, but I don't know where it is."

The lieutenant made a disbelieving noise. "You don't know where it is? That's the best you can do?"

"I'm sorry, Carlos, but it's the truth. Pablo Almeida told me it was missing, and I told Fernando and Daniela the Guardia had it to buy a little time in which to look for it. I was hoping that no one would ever need to know it had been mislaid."

"You searched for it?" Tejada demanded, with the vague feeling that he should be very angry.

His father sighed. "I went over Aunt Rosalia's rooms with a fine-tooth comb. There was nothing. If your men find it I'd be more than grateful if you'd pass it along, Carlos."

"Did you see this will before it disappeared?"

Andrés looked embarrassed. "No, but Pablo told me the provisions. I can tell you what's in it, if you like."

"If it wouldn't be too much trouble."

The older man frowned at his son's tone and said a little sharply, "Daniela and Felipe have been disinherited, but I'll thank you not to tell them that before we have paper in hand to prove it. Fernando and I are the heirs."

Tejada stared at his father, incredulous. "You expect me to believe that the will you've been lying about makes *you* a major beneficiary but has just vanished?"

"If I give you my word, yes."

"And what exactly has your word been worth so far in this case?"

"Don't take that tone of voice with me, young man!"

Something snapped. Tejada raised his head and met his father's eyes, furious. "I'm here as an officer of the Guardia Civil, investigating a murder. At your request, I might add."

"That gives you no right to be disrespectful!"

"When was the last time you saw Rosalia de Ordoñez alive?"

"Carlos, this is ridiculous!"

"Señor Tejada." He was now past caring about gathering information. "If you continue to avoid my questions I will have to ask you to accompany me to the post."

Andrés Tejada's fists hit the desk with a crash as he stood and leaned across it. "How dare *you* accuse me of murder?" he hissed.

The lieutenant met his father's eyes without flinching. A part of him that was not much older than Toño wanted to cry, *Because I am part of this family, too! As much as Juan Andrés! And you are my kin and I am tired of being the only one with blood on my hands!* But he only said stiffly, "I am not accusing anyone. I'm doing my job."

"Carlos, I have been *very* patient with you." Andrés Tejada's voice was low and venomous. "I never opposed your 'job' or your marriage, or any of the other damn fool things you've done. I have given you every advantage, and not once have I reminded you of your obligations to this family. If you choose to throw away every worldly advantage, I will not object. But I am responsible for your soul, Carlos, and I will *not* let you break God's commandment to honor thy father."

"Do you think that one's more important than 'Thou shalt not kill?'" Tejada retorted, uncomfortably aware that this was a commandment that could be legitimately broken in wartime and that even since the war he had occasionally interpreted it liberally.

Andrés Tejada raised his hand and started to swing. Almost before his arm moved, his wrist was caught in a painfully tight grip. "Attacking an officer is an offense that carries a prison term," his son warned.

The two men's eyes locked and held for a moment as each read the other's face as if in a magic mirror that kept expressions identical, but changed the viewer's age by thirty years. Finally, with a contemptuous gesture, Andrés jerked his arm out of his son's hold. "Get out of here, *Lieutenant*," he whispered, and the last word was an insult.

Carlos stared in disbelief at his own arm, still hanging in the air. He let it fall to his side, took a step backward, and dropped his eyes. "I'm sorry, Father." His father did not reply, and he added, "I shouldn't have spoken that way to you. I . . . I beg your pardon."

"I expect you have things to do at the post," his father said coldly.

"Yes, Father." The lieutenant's voice was barely above a whisper.

"I suppose your zeal has its uses. Find Aunt Rosalia's killer. But don't come and talk to me about the case until you can tell me who the guilty party is. Is that understood?"

"Yes, Father." Years of experience and some shred of dignity made the lieutenant add, "Do you want me to look for Doña Rosalia's will also? Since it's missing?"

"You might as well make yourself useful," Andrés snapped. "I would ask you not to mill around making scenes with Daniela, Fernando, and Felipe, but apparently that's impossible. But, for the love of God, try to remember that your actions reflect on your mother and me."

"Understood." The lieutenant stared at the floor of the study. "I . . . excuse me."

He fled from his father's presence, shaking with what he told himself was humiliation. He had conducted himself unforgivably; he had been arrogant and stupid and had not even gained the information he needed. He had been a bad son and a bad guardia. And woven through his shame, like scarlet threads through black, was an all-encompassing fury: against himself, his father, Doña Rosalia, Rivas, and all of Granada. He considered going to find Elena, but she had warned him that there was another problem waiting for his attention, and he was in no mood to act as a shield between her and his mother. Instead, he let himself out of the house and headed for the post. If Rivas was back already, so much the better. If the sergeant was still occupied, he could take the opportunity to call Potes and find out what was happening at his command in his absence.

The siesta was not yet over, and the streets were still silent and deserted. In Potes, where the weather was cooler and days were shorter, the siesta ended earlier, and the lieutenant found himself longing for the green forests of the north. He half hoped that Rivas would not be available when he reached the post. He needed to talk to Mojica.

He was meditating whether he could condense his orders to his sergeant in Potes into a telegram or whether a long-distance phone call would be justified when he turned the corner into the Calle Duquesa and reached the post. The guardia on duty saluted him. "Sergeant Rivas is in his office, Lieutenant. He left orders that he was available as soon as you wanted to see him."

Concealing his disappointment, Tejada thanked the guardia and sought out Rivas. The sergeant was bent over his desk, several sheets of paper spread before him, chewing his pen, when Tejada entered. "The reports, sir," he explained, after greeting the lieutenant. "You wanted them written by this evening. Of course, if you'd prefer them orally, now . . ."

"No, write it all down," Tejada said, relieved. "I should write up what I've found, too, and then we can compare notes." Writing a report was a sane activity. And far better than having to discuss his interviews with the sergeant right away. He took a seat at a small typewriter table in the corner and dug out his notebook.

"Very good, sir." Rivas in turn stifled his disappointment. He hated paperwork. But at least the lieutenant wasn't shirking his share. "Stationery is in the top drawer on the right."

"Thanks."

The two men wrote in silence for perhaps an hour. Then Rivas coughed and said, "Excuse me, sir. But if you'd like me to type this up we'll have to switch seats."

Tejada, who was just finishing his description of the interview with Daniela Ordoñez and her husband, decided that the report of his session with his father could wait. "No," he said. "Hold on a minute and let me finish this. Then we can talk about what we've found."

Rivas, whose typing was of the loud and careless kind that led to frequent errors, and who tended to accompany the clatter of the keys with a variety of oaths, preferred to type in private anyway. "As you wish, sir," he agreed.

Tejada finished his paragraph and then swung around to face the sergeant. "All right," he said. "What have we got?"

"I've talked to the servants, and there are men searching her room, but I don't know if we've made much progress," Rivas admitted. He summarized his morning's work for the lieutenant, referring only occasionally to his notes. "We'll see if Medina and Soler find anything else, but I'm betting it was the wine," he finished.

"Mmm." Tejada had been skimming the medical examiner's report as the sergeant spoke. "The room where she died had been cleaned up, you said?"

"Yes, sir. That same evening." Rivas flushed uncomfortably. "No one suspected anything but natural causes, sir." He did not feel it necessary to add that he had been the one to authorize a weeping María José to clear away the tray, mop up the obscenely spilled wine, and begin the process of making her mistress decent for burial.

"There was no sign that it had been searched by someone?"

"Not really." Even in the midst of his preoccupation Tejada heard the nervousness in the sergeant's voice. "My men weren't looking for signs of a search, of course. There'd been no orders, so they might have"—Rivas swallowed—"overlooked it."

"Or moved things." Tejada supplied the words Rivas was too embarrassed to say. He sighed. "It's probably not important. And if it was the wine, it could have been any of the servants."

"They all knew about her wine storage, sir. Didn't bother to deny it." Since the lieutenant was still pensive, Rivas added, "I don't think any outsider could have gotten at that bottle without attracting attention. Doña Rosalia didn't share it with her guests. But one of the maids could have gotten to it while cleaning the room. Or Cordero, if he went to get something in that cabinet. And the cook just had to sprinkle something into the wine when he sent it up, newly opened."

"There would have been more wine in the bottle if it were a fresh one," Tejada pointed out.

"Unless she had accidentally spilled some of it," Rivas countered.

"I suppose, if he'd been desperate, this cook, Lujo, could

have gotten at an open bottle even if it were upstairs," Tejada conceded. He paused. "Do you think he did?"

The lieutenant's tone was sharp, and for a moment Rivas was uncertain whether he was being reprimanded or genuinely asked for an opinion. When Tejada's polite silence convinced him of the latter, he said slowly, "Not really. He didn't like Doña Rosalia. He practically said so. And he's the only one who'll be able to find another job easily. But I don't know that he had any reason to *kill* her. He could just have left. That's the problem with all of them, really. What Cordero said is true: they had secure, easy work, and they weren't going to go hungry while she was alive. None of them gained from her death."

"Unless someone else made it very worth their while," Tejada said, disliking his own thoughts. Rivas diplomatically remained silent. After a moment, Tejada tossed the folder he had been reading onto the desk. "What about this Cordero?" he demanded, postponing the discussion of his own interviews with the sergeant. "You said he seemed overanxious to leave the city."

"Well, I suppose if the man was looking forward to seeing his sister, he might be disappointed," Rivas said. "But he was awfully insistent. Too urgent, if you know what I mean."

"I know exactly." Tejada smiled briefly. "Did he give you his sister's name?"

"Dulce."

Tejada snorted. "Suppose you make a phone call to the post in Málaga, and ask them to check if there's a Dulce Cordero who recently had a baby and who has a brother in Granada," he suggested.

Rivas looked at the lieutenant with new respect. "Yes, sir. Good idea." He hesitated. "Do you want me to do that now, sir?"

"No time like the present."

Tejada tapped a pen absently against a folder as Rivas made the call. The sergeant had gained a good deal of information, and he seemed to know how to organize it. It would be only reasonable

next to tell Rivas what he had learned about Doña Rosalia's will
in the course of the day and examine who would benefit enough
from her death to bribe a servant to poison her. Rivas had to wait
for the call to go through, and, when he was finally connected,
explaining the particulars of his request took some time, but the
delay was too short for Tejada.

"Fine, thanks. *Arriba España.*" The sergeant hung up the
phone. "They've never heard of Dulce Cordero but they'll
check it out and call in a couple of days, as soon as they have the
information." Tejada nodded but said nothing, and after a
moment the sergeant asked, "What now, sir?"

Tejada pulled himself together. "Even if we find a motive for
Cordero," he said, "we still don't know how he got hold of
cyanide. It's not the sort of thing you leave lying around the
house."

"In the movies, spies always keep cyanide capsules behind
their teeth to commit suicide," Rivas offered, half embarrassed.

"Well, did you look in Cordero's mouth?" Tejada snapped,
annoyed.

"No, sir." The sergeant was chastened. "But I meant if someone bribed the servants to kill her, he was maybe the sort of person who could get hold of that kind of capsule."

"And what sort of person would that be?" Tejada's voice
would have stopped a charging bull. Rivas flinched. "Well?" The
lieutenant demanded.

"I . . . I don't know, sir." Rivas gulped and blushed. "I thought
maybe a Red. It's just that she was always talking about the Reds
trying to kill her and I always figured it was nonsense—begging
your pardon, Lieutenant—but if they're the sort of people to
have cyanide, I think maybe I was wrong." He floundered to a
stop, looking unhappy.

Tejada let out his breath. "It's an idea," he said, consciously
trying to make his voice sound neutral instead of relieved. "And
I'm sure that you can obtain cyanide easily enough if you know

where to look. Let's assume that any of them had the opportunity and the ability to kill her."

"And the motive?" Rivas hazarded, reassured by the lieutenant's tone.

"Let's see if Cordero's story checks out. If it doesn't, we'll pull him in and get a motive out of him. He's got no reason to protect whoever hired him."

Rivas nodded, satisfied, then made a mistake. "Who do you think hired him?"

Tejada went still. "I don't—" he began, intending to say that he did not have the faintest idea.ˑ

The office window was open, and the faint breeze carried the sound of childish voices and scuffles. The Falangist youth were preparing to parade on their way back to school. The chaotic noises of the schoolboys died suddenly. There was a little silence and then someone in the plaza below shouted, "All right, on three. One, two, THREE!" and the words to "Cara al sol" filtered into the room along with the afternoon sunlight.

"—know what's happened to her will, but there's something fishy there," Tejada finished slowly, as the wavering soprano voices died away in the distance.

Rivas remembered the lieutenant's last words to him that morning and took pains to avoid Tejada's eyes. "Oh?"

Tejada looked past the sergeant, to the pattern of sunlight on the wall. "You should be aware that I may not be the best person to head this investigation," he said quietly.

Rivas's silence was a confirmation of the statement. Tejada took a deep breath and began to tell the sergeant what he had learned from his interviews that morning. He did not give any details with respect to his meeting with his father, and Rivas did not ask for them. When he had finished, Rivas said cautiously, "It seems to me, sir, that the important thing is who poisoned the lady. Not who may or may not have taken her will."

"You don't think they're the same person?" Tejada asked sardonically. "It makes more sense than phantom Reds."

"Not really," Rivas said, and was surprised to hear his own voice sound soothing. *A man like him shouldn't join the Guardia*, the sergeant thought. "It sounds to me like someone who didn't like Doña Rosalia's will would have just had to wait for her to change it. Stealing it and then killing her doesn't make any sense. And if it was only stolen *after* the fact, by someone who was desperate, then it was someone who didn't know in advance about her murder."

Tejada was dimly aware that the sergeant was tactfully trying to tell him that his father was probably guilty of fraud but not of murder. He did not find this theory particularly comforting. "What about someone who *did* benefit from Doña Rosalia's will but knew that she was likely to change it?" he countered.

Rivas sighed. "We don't know exactly what's in the will?"

"The only person who admits to having seen it is her lawyer."

"That would be Señor Almeida?" Rivas confirmed. The lieutenant nodded and Rivas added, "You know him, sir?"

"He's my godfather."

"You don't think he might cooperate if you asked him as a personal favor then?"

"I asked him at our first meeting," Tejada said.

"But we had no evidence then that Doña Rosalia had been poisoned," Rivas urged. "Surely he'd be amenable to influence?"

"Maybe if you dragged him down here and put him in a cell where he could hear the firing squads at work for a few mornings," Tejada said consideringly.

Rivas swallowed, his sympathy for the lieutenant severely lessened by the lieutenant's lack of empathy for his own position. "He's a personal friend of the mayor, sir."

"Then I'm out of ideas," Tejada snapped.

The awkward silence that followed this statement was broken by the entrance of Guardia Medina, breathless and excited.

"Sir!" He saluted to Rivas, and then gave Tejada a hasty half bow. "It was a Red plot! They killed Doña Rosalia because she'd uncovered a conspiracy!"

"What do you mean, 'a conspiracy'?" Rivas replied, embarrassed and furious that Medina had broken the news in front of the lieutenant.

"Are you joking?" Tejada demanded at the same instant, his voice harsh with the effort of hiding his relief and hope.

Faced with two apparently angry superior officers, Medina deflated rapidly. "Of course, it might not have been," he muttered. "But we found this in the bottom of the cabinet." He held out a crumpled sheaf of papers, which had obviously been rolled into a tight cylinder at one point and still curled upward at the edges.

The lieutenant took the papers, smoothed them out, and saw that they were actually a pamphlet, crudely printed on cheap newsprint. Large black letters across the top of the cover page proclaimed the title: OUR STRUGGLE. In smaller letters he made out "July 1945." Below that was a drawing of a peasant carrying a hammer and sickle, drawn in the blocky style popular ten years earlier, and a series of headlines: THE LAST FASCIST GOVERMENT OF EUROPE, OUR BROTHERS IN FRANCE, and THE CALL TO ARMS. His lip curled, and he held out the paper to Rivas without comment.

The sergeant scanned the pamphlet and gulped. "Jesus," he murmured, wondering desperately if Lieutenant Tejada would report him to his superiors for incompetence and struggling with a horrible feeling of guilt for having ignored Doña Rosalia's fears. To gain time, he began to leaf through the pamphlet.

"I think we can assume that my aunt was not the one reading OUR STRUGGLE," Tejada said. Only years of training enabled him to keep his face and voice expressionless. He wanted to run and leap and sing with relief. His aunt's death *had* been the result of Communists' actions. He could go back to dealing with the kind of people who read Communist propaganda and talked about the workers of the world and who could be exterminated like vermin, and forget about his father and his family's friends. "Any guesses as to who in the household might have procured the latest issue?"

"Cordero," Medina spoke confidently. "I never liked his looks. And that cook may be in on it, too. I say we bring them in and give them a working over they won't forget."

"Well?" Tejada pointedly ignored Medina and turned toward the sergeant.

Rivas had quickly skimmed the articles about the liberation of France and Russia's solidarity with the Spanish people, but a smudgily printed headline, TRAGEDY AND TRIUMPH IN THE ALPUJARRA, had caught his eye. He had started reading it more closely and become almost deaf to Medina's voice. Tejada's sharp question jolted him back to the present. He felt nauseous. He raised his eyes from the pamphlet with relief, but could not bring himself to face his superior. Some shred of self-preservation made him turn to Medina and say, "Is Soler still in the house?"

"No, sir, he's working on his report."

"Get him," Rivas ordered, desperate to get Medina out of the room.

Medina saluted and left. *Slimy little bastard*, Rivas thought, with unaccustomed violence. Then he was submerged once more in panic. *This is grounds for court-martial*, he thought. *Oh, God, Doña Rosalia* warned *me. Shit, how do they* know *all this?* He became aware that Lieutenant Tejada was speaking. "Don't feel too bad. A little of that stuff always gets through. They have presses even up in the mountains, you know."

"We need to know who was writing this." Rivas spoke hoarsely.

Tejada shrugged. "Someone in a café in Paris, probably. The interesting thing is why it turned up in the Casa Ordoñez."

For a moment, Rivas was tempted to accept the lieutenant's reassurance. But he knew that the situation was too serious for that. He shook his head. "This wasn't written in Paris," he said. "It contains details of a major operation our antiterrorism people carried out last spring. With names and places."

Tejada took the pamphlet back from Rivas and read the passage indicated.

> On the morning of May 23, cowardly and brutal Fascist spies blockaded the exits of the home of the valiant fighter known as El Tuerto and set fire to it. El Tuerto's companion, Adela Colón, 43; her daughter, Linda, 20; son Marco, 15; and grandson, Miguel, 2, were burned to death under the gaze of these soulless and pitiless monsters. El Tuerto himself escaped miraculously and has once more sworn allegiance to the People's Cause which will give him vengeance.

Tejada raised his eyebrows. "The stuff about this El Tuerto is accurate?"

Rivas nodded. "You didn't get his description, sir? I thought it went out to all the posts in Spain."

"In May I was preoccupied by other things." Tejada retorted. "And we have local boys to worry about."

"That's not the worst of it," Rivas admitted. "Keep reading. The part about Suspiro del Moro."

Tejada followed the sergeant's shaking finger and read.

> . . . this village stands as a shining example of the liberation that will soon come to all of Spain. On the morning of June 16, its citizens rose up against their oppressors and, supported by Republican troops, disarmed the local Guardia Civil and Fascist authorities and meted out justice to greedy overseers. They set up a fair government . . .

"True?" Tejada demanded, understanding Rivas's nervousness for the first time.

"Well, they didn't really set up much of a government," the sergeant mumbled.

Tejada winced. "How long did they have control of the town?"

"Two weeks." Rivas decided to get the worst over with as quickly as possible. "It's a small post there, because we thought it was a quiet area. They stormed the post, killed two of the guardias, and imprisoned the rest. Then they shot a couple of overseers and then . . . well, not much really, as far as we can figure out. They distributed a lot of leaflets like this one, which didn't do them much good because most of the people up there can't read. So they put on a couple of propaganda plays and brought in a doctor from somewhere to give the kids checkups and set all the locals babbling about how the town should have a clinic. And then the army took care of it. They'd raided the Guardia's ammunition depot, though, so they were pretty well armed and there were a couple dozen casualties."

"How many men were needed?" Tejada asked, remembering the Valle d'Aran and desperately wishing that he had time to call Potes and find out how things were at the post.

"About six hundred, sir."

"And how many bandits were captured?"

"Four. And another ten killed. We think the rest got away."

"Was it in the newspapers in Granada?"

Rivas frowned. "Two inches, on the inside page. 'Bandits hold town hostage,' 'Guardias Slain.' No details. But this—" He gestured helplessly to the pamphlet. "This looks like it was written by someone who's read our reports. Or was actually there."

Tejada smiled suddenly. "Alberto Cordero asked to go up to the Sierra just now, didn't he?" he demanded. "And, as I recall, Doña Rosalia owned property around Órgiva."

Rivas, who had been too upset to think clearly, heard the satisfaction in the lieutenant's voice and felt his own brain start working again. "Maybe we should check the dates of his visits," he suggested, returning Tejada's smile.

"Maybe you should invite him down to the post and ask him."

The door opened before Rivas could respond, and Medina and Soler entered. Rivas listened to Soler's report with barely concealed impatience, and then ordered the pair of guardias to go back to the Casa Ordoñez and arrest Alberto Cordero.

When the door had closed behind Medina and Soler, the sergeant turned back to Tejada. "It'd be a rare thing if it turned out that your lady aunt was right after all this time, wouldn't it?"

"Very strange," Tejada agreed, lighthearted.

Neither man dreamed of admitting his wild relief to the other. Rivas knew he should feel guilty that his carelessness had perhaps cost Doña Rosalia her life, but even in death, with her worst fears on the point of being confirmed, he could not think of her as anything but a nuisance. It was, he thought, providential that her murder had provided a clue to a dangerous source of propaganda.

Tejada knew that he was abandoning his investigation of his father's role in the disappearance of Rosalia's will too easily but, naturally, subversive propaganda had to come first. *Please let it be Cordero*, the lieutenant thought. *Please, please, something neat, for once.* He shared an easy camaraderie with Sergeant Rivas as they pored over the medical examiner's report, knowing that Rivas felt the same way. "I wish there was something here about where you can get cyanide," Tejada said. "It might help to have a line on Cordero when we bring him in."

"Do you want to question him?" Rivas asked, with less resentment than he would have dreamed possible a few days earlier.

The lieutenant shrugged. "Not if your people know what they're doing. We deal with a lot of bandits in the north, but you must also, if they're active in the Sierra."

"The worst is in the Axarquía over toward Málaga, thank God," Rivas admitted. "We can handle him. But I was thinking, sir, if you didn't mind not being present for the interrogation . . ."

"Yes?" Tejada asked, with renewed tension.

"We're just across the street from the university," Rivas said humbly. "I thought if you had contacts there, you could ask someone about where to find cyanide."

"Good thought." The lieutenant relaxed and looked at his watch. It was a quarter to six. "I'll go over now and see if the library's still open."

He left the sergeant's office feeling infinitely better than when he had entered it. The familiar rush of energy that accompanied a suspect identified and an arrest put a spring in his step. It was an incredible relief to be dealing once more with smugglers and bandits. This was the work he was used to—hard and dirty, with opponents worthy of his cunning.

The University of Granada backed onto the plaza where the Guardia Civil had their headquarters. Tejada hurried around the corner humming the tune the children had started singing. The guard in front of the arched entryway saluted him. "Can I help you, sir?"

"Is the library open?" Tejada asked. "I want to look something up."

"First floor. Up the main staircase and you can't miss it."

The guard gestured. Tejada thanked him and moved lightly up the broad marble steps. The building was set around a large interior courtyard, and the stairs curled around the court, leading to a covered patio above. A number of students were leaning on the railing, looking down into the courtyard and chatting. A few of them ducked their heads and murmured to each other when they saw the lieutenant making his way through the building. Tejada ignored them.

The library was open, although not crowded. The air inside was warm and had the dry dusty smell of old paper. Tejada made his way to a battered central desk, where a lone man sat at a high swivel chair. Behind him rose a cliff of card catalogues higher than the lieutenant's head. The man in the chair froze as Tejada approached, as if immobility would grant him invisibility. The lieutenant stood in front of the desk for a moment, waiting for the man to speak. The man stared down at the surface of the desk. Finally, Tejada coughed. "Are you the librarian here?"

"Yes, sir." The man looked at him with hunted eyes. "I was approved by the director." He fumbled for a moment and then flipped open a wallet. "See?"

Tejada glanced at the librarian's ID and noticed that the man had shown him a membership in the Falange, instead of an official identity card. *Lukewarm to the Movement,* the lieutenant thought. *Probably barely kept his job after the war.* "I need information on cyanide," he said simply. "How can I find it?"

For a moment the librarian blinked stupidly. Then he pulled himself together. "Toxicology? The medical school would have more on that than the general collection, I'm afraid. But we could look it up." He swiveled in his chair and then stood, lifting one of the card catalogue boxes to shoulder height and placing it on the desk.

"I'm not so interested in the medical aspects," Tejada said as the librarian began to flip the cards with an impressive combination of delicacy and speed. "I want to know how you find it or make it. I can look under poisons or toxicology while you check there," he added as the librarian continued his search.

"Yes, sir." The man obediently swung the drawer around so it was facing the lieutenant. "It's in alphabetical order, and if you see a book you want you just copy the number in the corner here—"

"I know how a card catalogue works," Tejada interrupted. "Suppose you look under poisons." He reached the place he was looking for and added, "Or a good encyclopedia might help."

"Yes, sir. Are there any cross-references?" The librarian spoke over his shoulder as he pulled out drawers.

"Amyl nitrite, cyanosis, hydrocyanic acid, poisons," the lieutenant read promptly. "What is amyl nitrite?"

"I don't know. Just a minute." A researcher's curiosity was beginning to override his nervousness. He scurried out from behind the desk to a row of reference volumes along a low shelf on the opposite wall. After a moment, he selected one, and opened it. Tejada, patiently copying titles and call numbers that looked as if they might be useful, ignored him. He was recalled from his work a few minutes later by the librarian's voice.

"This article might help a little, sir. It says amyl nitrite is the only known antidote for cyanide. But it's only effective if given immediately."

"Interesting," Tejada admitted. "But not what I was looking for. Does it say anything about how an average person might *get* cyanide?"

"Used in electroplating, tanning, and the 'cyanide process' of ore extraction," the librarian read aloud. "Also found naturally in the pits of cherries, apricots, plums, and other plants of the genus *pranus.*"

Tejada abandoned the card catalogue. "Perfect. Let me see that article."

The librarian rose, leaving the encyclopedia open to the correct page. Tejada sat down and after a few moments took out his notebook and began to copy parts of the article verbatim. The librarian retreated to his desk and replaced the abandoned drawers. The silence descended again, broken only by the scratching of the lieutenant's pen and the occasional creak of the swivel chair. Half an hour later, Tejada closed the book and stretched, feeling as if he were coming up for air. The librarian looked over at him. "Did you find what you needed, sir?"

"A good start, in any case. Thanks for your help."

"It was nothing." If Tejada had not been armed and in uniform, the librarian would have asked him why he wanted the information. Even as it was, he was tempted to crack a joke about wanting to poison someone. But he only smiled and assured the lieutenant that it had been his pleasure to be helpful.

When Tejada returned to the post, he found that Sergeant Rivas was still interrogating Alberto Cordero. "He was being difficult, Lieutenant," Guardia Medina explained, in response to Tejada's question. "If you know what I mean."

Tejada looked at Medina's leer with dislike. "Knows how to keep his mouth shut, does he?" he said shortly, reflecting that if Guardia Medina had known how to keep his own mouth shut, Doña Rosalia's death would never have given rise to a long distance phone call to Potes.

"He doesn't have too many teeth left," Medina confided. "But don't worry, Lieutenant. We'll get a confession out of him."

"Interrogate a lot of guerrillas, do you?" Tejada asked, with the irrational feeling that he was being patronized. He was torn between a desire to say that the guerrillas in Potes were far tougher and better organized than anything in the south and a feeling that this particular boast might reflect poorly on his own skills as a commander.

"Not too many," Medina conceded. Because he was a more accomplished boaster than the lieutenant, he added, "They know what happens when we catch them here, so there aren't too many."

The clocks began to strike the hour. Tejada was not anxious to go home, but he had no desire to remain in Medina's company, and he could not shake the nagging feeling that Alberto Cordero's ties to the Reds were irrelevant. On the other hand, if one member of Doña Rosalia's household had been sympathetic to the Reds, another might be as well.

"Anything the sergeant finds out about the bandits in the Alpujarra is all to the good," he said. "But let's try to remember the point here."

Medina was instantly grave. "Yes, sir. We all want to find out who killed your lady aunt, sir."

"Tell Sergeant Rivas to check the family connections of all the rest of her household," the lieutenant ordered. "You never know."

Swelling with importance, Medina promised to deliver this

order to the sergeant. Tejada waited for him to leave the office, and then wrote a note to Rivas, giving the same order, in more detail, in case Medina messed it up. He put the note on the sergeant's desk where he was sure to see it and then left the post with the satisfaction of a job well done. His feeling of accomplishment peaked as he stepped out of the post, ending the day's work. Unfortunately, it waned steadily as he walked back to his parents' house. As he reached their home, it occurred to him that he was going to have to face his father across the dinner table. He would almost have been willing to change places with Alberto Cordero for the evening. But not quite.

Chapter 12

Tejada's precipitous departure that morning had left his wife the pleasure of a solitary breakfast with her in-laws. The evening with Nilo had put Elena in a good mood, though, and she was able to answer with smiling calm when Doña Consuela asked if Elena wanted her to babysit for Toño for the morning. "You must want to go shopping, dear," her mother-in-law added. "I'd be happy to take care of him."

"It depends on what Toño wants to do," Elena said sweetly. "He's not used to being left without me. But I *would* like to look up an old friend here." She was certain that her mother-in-law had intended a veiled reference to her wardrobe, and she managed to take a certain pleasure in blunting Doña Consuela's attack, although she knew that any acquaintance she admitted to having exposed a new flank to the enemy.

"Surely you'll want Carlos to go along if you're visiting friends." Doña Consuela was bland.

"I try never to interfere with his work," Elena lied politely. "And Cristina is my friend, not his. If you have a directory of the city, perhaps I could borrow it? I'm sure I can find my way."

Doña Consuela frowned. "If you have to see this . . . *person*"—her tone made it clear that she thought Elena was lying about the gender of her acquaintance—"Juan Andrés will accompany you. It's not appropriate for you to be wandering around the city by yourself."

Juan Andrés looked up, not at all pleased. "I can't, I have business today, Mother." It occurred to him that this was an ungracious comment and he added to his sister-in-law, "Of course I can show you the way, if you can find your way back."

Elena nodded at him and smiled, acknowledging but excusing his rudeness. Relieved, he smiled back.

"If this person lives in a safe neighborhood," Doña Consuela interjected, pursing her lips. "Elena doesn't know the city. She could easily find herself in a bad part of town."

"What would *you* like, Toño?" Elena spoke quickly, determined to avoid leaving her son to his grandmother's tender mercies.

Her son was unenthusiastic about both plans. "If you went out, would you come back soon?" he asked, with a glance at his grandmother.

"I don't have to go," Elena said hastily. "Or you could come with me."

"To the toy store?" Toño asked.

"If you want. And there's a lady I used to know whom I'd like to see."

The little boy wrinkled his nose. "I'll stay here. You can go visit the lady. Unless you *want* me to come," he added generously.

"No, no, we can both stay here," Elena reassured him, resigning herself to another interminable day with her mother-in-law. She would have liked the chance to talk to Cristina and find out what had become of the funny, unconventional girl she had known, but it was not fair to drag Toño on expeditions he did not enjoy, and she was not going to leave him with Doña Consuela.

"Maybe I could stay with Alejandra?" Toño suggested. "I like Alejandra."

"I think she is in school now," Elena pointed out gently.

Unexpectedly, Elena's sister-in-law spoke up. "What about Alejandra's mother, Carmen? She used to take Marta and Paco out to the park when they were little. She could take Toño for you for a few hours."

Doña Consuela glared at her elder son's wife. "Rosa, most women don't like to leave their children with people who aren't family."

Rosa glared back at Doña Consuela, solidarity with a fellow daughter-in-law temporarily overriding her dislike and distrust of Carlos's wife. "I thought Elena might like to know that there's someone trustworthy to take care of her son," she shot back, emphasizing the word *trustworthy* a little more than necessary.

"I don't have to go visiting today," Elena said, in a vain attempt to keep the peace. "I can take Toño out to the park myself, but I'll introduce him to Señora ... err ... Carmen after breakfast so he'll know her for another time."

She drained her coffee, willing Toño to eat quickly so that she could escape from the breakfast table. Rosa, with renewed helpfulness, volunteered that Carmen could be found in the kitchen and Elena hurried her son out of the room with the excuse of going to meet Alejandra's mother.

The kitchen was a narrow, stuffy room with an enormous black stove in one corner, noisy with the clatter of plates. Isaura, the Tejadas' maid, was dumping used breakfast dishes in the sink as they arrived. At the far corner by the stove, a squarely built woman wearing an apron was polishing a set of silver. Both women looked up as Elena and Toño entered and stopped what they were doing. Isaura spoke first. "Señora Fernández? How can we help you?"

Elena felt awkward. "I wondered if"—she hesitated, uncertain what to call the quiet woman in the corner—"if Carmen—Señora Llorente—would be willing to look after my son for a few hours when she's free. Rosa—my brother-in-law's wife—suggested it."

Carmen set down the sugar bowl she was holding, wiped her hands on her apron, and came forward. "Of course, Señora. It would be a pleasure." She squatted to be at eye level with Toño and added, "Hello, Señorito. I'm sure we'll have a good time together."

Elena looked down at the kneeling woman and saw threads of gray in the straggling hair. A memory rose in her throat like bile: a chestnut-haired mother, kneeling in the school playground on a golden September morning and tightly hugging her little girl, saying cheerfully, "I'm sure you'll have a good time in second grade, Aleja."

Toño inspected Carmen. "Are you Alejandra's mama?"

(Elena had memorized the class list the night before and she had been able to smile at the shy little girl and say, "You're María Alejandra, aren't you? And this must be your mama?")

"Yes, Señorito. It's Carlos Antonio, isn't it?"

("Yes, Señorita Fernández. I'm Carmen Llorente.)

"Mostly people call me Toño."

("My name is Aleja, Señorita.")

Elena closed her eyes for a moment. When she opened them, Carmen had risen and was facing her with no trace of recognition. *I'm sorry*, the lieutenant's wife thought, longing to say the words aloud. *I didn't think it would turn out like this.* But she was no longer a young teacher in a public school in wartime Madrid, and the omnipresent smell of burning buildings and sound of distant cannon fire no longer made even strangers confide in each other like friends. "Do you think you could take care of Toño this morning?" she asked.

Carmen Llorente hesitated a moment and then said quietly, "Of course, Señora. You can drop him off here any time. But . . ."

Elena looked up, hoping that the pause meant she had been recognized. Isaura began to run water over the dishes, and Carmen spoke so that the other maid could not hear. "Can I speak to you alone, Señora? Just for a few minutes. I need to ask you something."

Elena did not reply immediately. Isaura turned off the faucet. "If you take Toño for the morning, I'll be back in time for his

nap," Elena said slowly. "But maybe you could help me put him
down for his nap after lunch, so you know his routine for next
time?"

Carmen let out a silent breath. "That would be fine." A smile
flickered across her face. "Just let me put these away, Señora,
and I'll be ready to take care of the little one."

Elena nodded. She kissed her son good-bye and left him in the
kitchen with an oddly hollow feeling. She had never left Toño
with a strange babysitter before. She was proud that he was such
an outgoing child, of course, but she had expected that he would
be a little more worried about being left behind. Her memories
of teaching in Madrid came to her aid. Carmen had been one of
many parents who hugged their children tightly and watched
with hurt eyes as their children scrambled away to explore their
new classroom and meet classmates. Elena had always been slightly insulted by the parents who obviously hated to leave their children in her care. Now she understood perfectly.

She went in search of a city directory. Andrés Tejada provided Elena with one, warning her that it was not up-to-date. There
were four Encinases listed in the directory: Enrique, María
Isabel, Osvaldo, and Ubaldo. Elena tried to remember the
names of Cristina's parents and siblings. She was fairly sure that
Cristina had spoken of an Ubaldo. Consulting a map, she saw
that Ubaldo's address seemed close to the Tejadas' home. She
set off without specifying her destination, after assuring her in-
laws that no escort was necessary.

A very few minutes' walk convinced Elena that she had been
wise not to tell the Tejadas where she was going. She found her
way back to Puerta Real easily, but as she turned into the sunlight and began to head uphill, the neighborhood changed
abruptly. The street was almost a parody of the landscape around
Potes. It ran up a narrow valley, so steep as to be almost a gorge,
that would have been impressive had it been left in its natural
state. But where the bubbling Deva in Potes ran plentifully

between unspoiled ledges, the Darro was little more than a
trickle among muddy rocks, strewn with garbage from the
dilapidated buildings clinging precariously to either side of
the cliffs. It had more the appearance of a sewer than a river.
A number of the houses clinging to the hillside looked as if
they had been damaged by cannon fire. Elena, instinctively
glancing upward to see where artillery could have attacked
from, saw the yellow bulk of the Alhambra looming above her.
From this angle, the ancient fortress looked more menacing
than picturesque.

Tiny alleys leading up, away from the river, were darkened by
laundry crisscrossing the streets. Something about the shadowy
figures lurking in the alleys made Elena avoid eye contact with
them. *Paseo de los tristes*, Elena thought. *The path of the grieving.
The street's well named.* She could feel herself attracting curious
stares. She was too well dressed and walked too purposefully to
belong in this part of town. She was unwilling to draw more
attention to herself by consulting a map, so she contented herself with carefully checking the street numbers and hoping to
reach her destination soon.

She was becoming nervous when she saw the number she was
looking for on a heavy wooden door in a blank wall on her left
unbroken by windows. It was sheer luck that she had not walked
past it. Wondering if this had been such a good idea after all,
Elena rapped on the uninviting entrance.

Somewhat to her surprise, the door swung open after just a
few moments. "Yes? Can I help you?"

For a horrified instant, Elena feared that the woman facing
her was Cristina. Then her common sense reasserted itself. War,
starvation, and suffering had aged many people prematurely,
but the lines bitten into faces that should still have been young
were harder and sadder than the gentle wrinkles of the woman
who had opened the door. The woman's hair, caught up in a
bun, was still thick, although frosted lightly with age. But the

features, build, and coloring all strongly suggested the laughing student Elena had known. She smiled. "Señora de Encinas?"

"Yes?"

Elena hesitated, uncertain how to introduce herself, although she was now sure that she had found the right address. "My name is Elena Fernández. I was a student in Madrid, in the early thirties. In the school of education."

Cristina's mother smiled. "You're a teacher then? Come in." She stepped back, welcoming Elena with a gesture. Elena followed her into a tiled courtyard with a practical-looking well in the center. A stone bench had been set under a lime tree. Señora de Encinas led her guest through the *carmen* into a sitting room open to the courtyard. The room contained a pair of easy chairs, a low table, and an ironing board in one corner. "Please, sit." Elena's host indicated a chair and moved toward a cabinet along one wall. "It's so good of Ubaldo's friends to remember him."

"I was interested in Señor Encinas's work," Elena said. "But actually I was a friend of Cristina's. I was in Granada and I thought I'd look her up."

"Oh!" Señora de Encinas had drawn a tray out of the cabinet drawer and had apparently been rummaging for something to put on it. Now she left the tray sitting on the cabinet and turned around, her face completely expressionless.

Elena recognized the woman's set look. With a sinking feeling that was all too familiar she said, "Cristina and I lost touch a few years after we graduated. I didn't know if she was . . . still here. But I wanted . . ." She said nothing, hoping that Cristina's mother would offer some information. The older woman said nothing, but her eyes shut for a moment.

"I'm sorry," Elena whispered.

"Thank you, dear." Señora de Encinas was obviously a woman of grace and control. Her voice was steady as she took the chair opposite Elena. "There was no way for you to know. Cristina . . . passed away nine years ago."

The war and its aftermath had given Elena enough experience with the need for unexpected condolences to enable her to match her hostess's self-control. She apologized for the intrusion and offered her sympathy with a fluency born of agonizing practice. The rules for the situation were clear: you did not ask for any information about the cause, or time, or place of death, in case dwelling on such details was shameful or dangerous for the family; you did not mention your own losses; and, above all, you did not cry, because once your tears started they might never stop.

Señora de Encinas was unwilling to speak of her daughter, but she was warmly, almost eagerly polite to Elena. She spoke willingly about her son, Félix, and his wife, and about her grandchildren. Then she asked about Elena's connection with Cristina. She seemed almost desperate to hear stories of the girls' years at the university. Elena found herself digging out old memories of exams and classes, of heated political debates and hopeful ambitions. When she mentioned that Cristina had spoken of her father's work as a teacher, her hostess looked pained for a moment. "Ubaldo was the commissioner of public education for two years," she said quietly. "But his life's work was really the Home."

"The home?"

"The Home for Indigent Children of the Albaicín," the older woman explained. "It wasn't just an orphanage. It was a place for abandoned children as well and a free school for the poorest. Ubaldo was so proud that it was the first of its kind that wasn't run by the church."

"It sounds like a wonderful idea." Elena's voice was gentle.

"We provided vocational training for the older ones and a clinic." Señora de Encinas spoke with obvious pride. "We were just expanding into basic health care for the community."

"You were involved with Señor Encinas's work as well?"

"I'm a trained nurse." The older woman smiled. "I was the director of the clinic."

Elena felt a slight catch in her throat at this unexpected vision of marriage. It was partly envy of the easy equality that Señora de Encinas seemed to share with her husband that made her cruel enough to say, "Was Cristina—?"

"No," Señora de Encinas shook her head. "We would have loved to pass along the clinic to Cristina, but she was a surgeon. She had just earned a post at the university hospital here. Ubaldo was sorry she wasn't interested in the home, I think, but I was so proud of her. I'd wanted to be a doctor, but when I was a girl it wasn't possible. . . ." She trailed off, her eyes tear bright.

Elena silently watched her grief, remembering a friend—had it been Cristina or someone else?—from her years at the university saying exultantly, "Nowadays we can do anything!" Cristina's mother took a deep breath and spoke almost steadily. "After—the government changed—we thought maybe it was for the best. The church had never liked our work, but we thought, since Cristina wasn't involved with the home, they'd have nothing against *her*. We'd hoped . . ." She closed her eyes and remembered that she was speaking to a stranger, albeit a sympathetic one. "We've been very lucky," she finished piously. "Ubaldo is up for parole soon. He has friends who've interceded for him. And Félix and his family are doing well."

Parole, Elena thought. Ubaldo Encinas must be nearly seventy. If he had been arrested at the outbreak of the war as a city official, which seemed likely, he had spent nearly ten years in prison. *And they're the lucky ones.* Señora de Encinas was asking her now about her own life, with kind courtesy. Elena was accustomed to embarrassment about her husband's profession, but now she found herself admitting to the bare fact of marriage and motherhood almost regretfully. *We were going to do so much more*, she thought. *To be so much more.* Horrified at her own disloyalty to Toño and Carlos, she crushed her thoughts and began looking for a graceful way to end the visit.

Elena had just risen to her feet and begun her farewells when the door to the courtyard opened and a boy of about sixteen came toward them with hurried steps. Señora de Encinas presented him. "My grandson, Baldo. This is Elena Fernández. She was a friend of your aunt's in Madrid."

Baldo supported the introduction as well as could be expected for a shy adolescent. His grandmother explained that he was currently employed as a delivery boy and messenger for *El Ideal*. "And he hopes to be a reporter soon." His presence delayed Elena's departure, but only by a few minutes. When she again began to leave, Baldo spoke up, a bit nervously. "I could go with you a little ways, Señora. Since you're new to the city. And maybe show you some of the sites. This is a very old neighborhood. Very historic."

Elena had no particular desire for an escort, and her visit to the Encinas family had depressed her, but she did not want to hurt Baldo's feelings, or injure his grandmother's. She accepted with as good a grace as possible and set out with Baldo by her side.

The boy was silent as they left his home, and Elena was beginning to think that he was going to be too shy to make good his promise of showing her the sites when he coughed and said, in a slightly furtive tone, "Señora Fernández, can I ask you something?"

"Of course." Elena liked children, even older ones, and she smiled at him encouragingly.

He gulped and fell into step beside her. "You—you said you were a friend of Tía Cristina's?"

"That's right."

"Do you—" The boy turned a deep shade of red. "Do you know anything about her? About what happened to her?"

"Only what your grandmother told me." Elena was puzzled.

"What did she say?" His voice was sharp.

"She didn't tell me much." Elena frowned, seeking a gentle way to remind the boy that asking for details was against the unwritten code.

Baldo hesitated. "Could . . . could you help me find out what happened to her?"

"Surely your family—" Elena began.

"*They* all say she's dead," the boy interrupted. "But *I* know she's not." Seeing that Elena looked skeptical, he plunged on. "Look, there wasn't ever a funeral or anything. No body. No news from the police."

Elena opened her mouth to explain to him that all over Spain people were waiting for a body or official notification that would never come and found she had no words to tell a grieving boy the truth. "Sometimes in wartime—" she began, seeking for one of her husband's phrases.

"It wasn't *like* that!" There was almost a sob in Baldo's voice. "Look, I know you mean you think she was shot up by the cemetery walls, like Julián's dad and the mayor and all those others, but listen, she *knew* they were coming. The night she left, I woke up because I *heard* my parents and my grandparents arguing about it. And Grandpa was saying she hadn't done anything wrong and she shouldn't run, and Grandma was crying, and I wanted to get up and get a drink of water, because I hoped they would stop yelling. But I was too scared to get out of bed. And then the door opened." Baldo closed his eyes, as if reliving the scene. "And Tía Cristina was there. She was dressed like she was going out to make a house call. And she just stood there in the doorway for a second, outlined, and I sat up in bed. And then she came over and hugged me and said she had to go away for a little while but that I should be a good boy and she would come back. Then she left." Baldo swallowed. "And they didn't arrive looking for her until a few hours later. So I *know* she got away."

Elena's memories of Madrid were very near the surface and she realized unwillingly that Baldo was the age of many of her students. *How many of them lived through that?* she wondered. "*Be a good boy and I'll be right back.*" *How many of them are still waiting?*

"After all these years," she murmured, "don't you think she would have sent you a message?"

"Maybe she went to France." Baldo's face lit up as Elena tacitly conceded his version of his aunt's disappearance. "Maybe she couldn't write until now. But now that the war's over . . ."

Elena knew it was a fool's errand. Her friend was dead, and it was wrong to let the boy think anything else. But Cristina had been a vivid, laughing, daring personality, and it was difficult to imagine her vitality snuffed out, decomposing in an anonymous lime pit along with countless others. Perhaps she *had* managed to stay one step ahead of the Fascists who had sought her death—either for her politics or because she was a woman who had dared to trespass in a man's profession. Elena doubted that the Guardia had accurate records of everything that had taken place at the outbreak of the war. Too many people were too invested in forgetting what had happened. But it would not hurt to try. "I . . . know someone who could look at the official records," she admitted. "I'll try to see what I can find out."

Baldo gave a sigh of relief. "Oh, thank you, Señora. Thank you so much. But you won't tell my parents or my grandparents, will you? They get angry when I mention it."

"No," Elena promised. "I'll try to let you know directly."

"You can leave a message for me at *El Ideal*'s offices," Baldo offered. "And listen, one thing that might help, if you can really look at the records. Find out what happened to Dr. Esteban Beltrán."

"Esteban Beltrán," Elena repeated. "Who's he?"

"He was a doctor at the same hospital as Tía Cristina," Baldo explained. "And he came to dinner a few times, and he used to bring bonbons. I thought they were for me when I was a kid, but I remember my mother joking with Tía Cristina about 'your friend Esteban' and I thought maybe he really brought them for her, because they were . . . well, close. So maybe if *he* went abroad, she went with him."

Elena sighed. Baldo had worked out an entire fantasy, perhaps even complete with little cousins he had never met. She did not know whether it would be kindness or cruelty to confirm for him that the aunt who had passed him candy from her lover and the man who had courted her were both long dead. But she had given her word. "All right. I can't promise you anything. But if I find out anything about Cristina or about this Dr. Beltrán, I'll let you know. Where are *El Ideal*'s offices?"

Baldo gave her directions with almost feverish eagerness, and then added, a little apologetically, that he needed to run back to work. "I had to run a message to the Calle Elvira, and I wanted to check in on Grandma on the way back," he explained. "But if I'm away too long they'll wonder."

"Run then," Elena commanded. "It would be a shame to jeopardize your career when you have the makings of such a fine journalist."

Baldo flushed. "What do you mean?"

"You're good at research," Elena explained.

"Oh. Thanks." The boy scuffed his heel. "I guess. But someday I want to write, you know. Really write, I mean. You think I can still do that, even though I didn't finish school?"

"Absolutely." Elena spoke without hesitation. "Now run."

Baldo ran, after a final thanks that encompassed her assistance in finding out Cristina's fate and her encouragement of his literary ambitions. Elena returned to the Tejadas' home thoughtful. Her husband would be less than pleased to hear about her morning, and he was likely to firmly negate any request to check the Guardia's records for mention of Cristina Encinas. In Potes she would have been able to speak to the parish priest, and if he had been unable to help he would have leaned on the mayor, who was his cousin. But here in Granada she could only act with Carlos as her proxy. And he was likely to tell her to let well enough alone. *He won't want me upsetting his mother by knowing "that sort of person,"* she thought with a flash of anger. *He won't want to get the Guardia involved, even if definite word could put an end to a family's private hell.* Her annoyance at her husband's probable opposition made her more and more sympathetic to Baldo.

Chapter 13

Elena arrived a little before lunch, anxious to discuss the question of Cristina Encinas's fate with her husband, but he was distressed and annoyed when he returned to his parents' home, and Elena had no chance to speak to him alone before he disappeared into his father's study after the meal, and then hurried back to the post. When she went to put Toño down for his nap after lunch she found Carmen Llorente waiting for her.

Elena had temporarily forgotten Carmen's request to speak to her, but confronted by the woman's silent reminder she reluctantly put aside her worries about her promise to Baldo Encinas. Carmen observed Elena as she prepared Toño for sleep, never offering assistance, but wordlessly picking up the toys the little boy had left out in his room, and straightening the clothing that Elena had carelessly folded. When Elena left the child's room, Carmen followed her, head respectfully bowed. "Thank you for agreeing to see me, Señora."

Elena winced. She remembered Carmen talking to her with the friendly superiority of an older woman and a mother addressing a younger, unmarried one, and Carmen's present punctilious formality depressed her. Carmen saw her involuntary wince and added hastily, "If you're tired now, Señora, you can send for me at any time. I do appreciate the favor."

"No, no, we can talk now." Elena wistfully recalled a grim November afternoon during the war when Carmen and Aleja had shared a crowded streetcar in Madrid with her. "Sit, *hija*," Carmen had commanded her, pointing to the only available seat. "You're on your feet all day running after the kids."

"And you're not on your feet?" Elena had retorted. In the end, Aleja had taken the seat.

Now, listening to the maid's polite deference, Elena realized she had been foolish to hope that Alejandra's mother would refer to their previous acquaintance. None of the Tejadas knew that Alejandra had been Elena's student long before the lieutenant had taken responsibility for her after he had murdered her aunt. They did not know that Carmen had been a Red, although perhaps they suspected something. Carmen doubtless hoped for anonymity in her new home. *Besides,* Elena thought sadly, *I betrayed her. I married a man who destroyed everything and everyone she loved, and then tried to soothe his conscience by making her his dependent. At least he has taken care of her though, and she never had any reason to think well of* him. *But she used to believe I was different. Why should she or Alejandra ever want to lay eyes on me again? Why should Baldo or his grandmother trust me? I've become one of Them.*

Elena wondered a little nervously what the older woman wanted to tell her or ask her. Perhaps Carmen merely wanted Elena to relay a message to the lieutenant.

"Why don't we go into my room?" Elena suggested, since the other woman seemed hesitant how to begin. "We can sit there, and no one will disturb us."

"Thank you." But even when they were sitting with the door closed, Carmen was still unable to begin. "Maybe the lieutenant would be the one to speak to, actually, Señora. But since I saw you . . . and besides Aleja always liked you."

"Aleja?" Elena asked.

"Yes." Carmen took a handkerchief from her pocket and began to nervously tie knots in it. "The lieutenant's been so good to Aleja. Paying for her schooling all these years. At the same school as Señorita Marta and everything. She's had so many opportunities. More than she would ever have had without his help. It's just that now . . ." She paused, and Elena, who had gained some experience of the problems of schooling, half guessed what was coming next. She remained sympathetically silent, and Carmen continued, "She's going to be fourteen this May. I haven't said anything, because I didn't know if Lieutenant Tejada had thought about it, but . . ."

"She can study for the baccalaureate," Elena assured her. She knew that her husband would pay for the rest of Alejandra's education without a murmur, but should she be proud or ashamed of the reason he would do so. "And university is free for war orphans, if she has the grades."

"University!" Carmen's laugh was half a sob. "Oh, God, her father would have been so proud of her. He wanted his daughter to have a high school degree and work in an office. There was a stationery store with a typewriter in the window on the Ronda de Atocha, and he used to push her carriage past it every Sunday and say, 'Someday my baby is going to know how to work that thing.'" She hastily unknotted her handkerchief and brought it to her eyes.

"She'll learn." Elena put one arm around Carmen's quivering shoulders, and prayed that she was telling the truth. Alejandra's education, Elena realized, would purchase not only her husband's peace of mind but her own. "It's no problem. You shouldn't have worried."

Carmen shook her head. "No. It's Aleja that's the problem. She says she won't study for the baccalaureate. That she wants to get a job when the school year's over."

"What?" Elena was confused. "But why?"

"She says school is useless." Carmen looked down at her hands. "That it's all lies and fairy tales and has nothing to do with the real world. And that she hates it." Elena stared, incredulous, remembering Alejandra's glee at memorizing the times tables before anyone else in the class, her enthusiasm for history, and her eager interest in science. For a split second it seemed to her that the most evil outcome the Civil War had not been the death and destruction that had engulfed Aleja's world, but the extinction of her love of learning. Then the world came back into perspective, and Alejandra was once more an incredibly lucky girl to have a place to live and enough to eat. Carmen was still talking. "I've reasoned with her, pleaded with her, even screamed at her. But it's no good. She hates school and she won't go back. 'I was working at her age and why shouldn't she? There's no point in going to school anyway,'" is what she says.

"Do you want me to speak with her?" Elena asked.

"Would you?" Carmen spoke with pathetic eagerness. "You're educated. You even went to university. You can tell her that it's a good thing for a woman. She could become a teacher, like you. Or a nurse. Tell her she shouldn't throw away her opportunities."

She can become a teacher, Elena thought. *And then marry, and then become . . . like me. Or not marry, like Cristina. A Fascist's wife or a nameless grave. Why should she listen to anything I say?* "Of course I'll speak to her," Elena said. "But . . . I assume her grades are all right?"

"She gets Bs and Cs," Carmen reassured her. "She failed History last year, because she said she didn't like the teacher, but she's made up the work." Elena winced. Alejandra had been an A student in the midst of bombardment and starvation in Madrid. She felt her confidence ebb further as Carmen added, with painful honesty, "The thing is, she's refused to attend mass for the last quarter. The sisters have said that they'll expel her if she doesn't start going next semester. And they say that she's sullen and uncooperative in all her classes. Can't you urge her to at least go to mass?"

Elena's discomfort grew to alarm. She had been proud of teaching in a completely secular school but she had always believed that religion was a matter of private conscience, and that a student's private beliefs should be respected. (This attitude had in fact led to arguments with her more vigorously anticlerical colleagues during the war years and still provided fuel for a running debate with Father Bernardo in Potes.) The idea of convincing an unwilling student to attend mass was repugnant to her. "I don't suppose another school . . ." she began doubtfully.

Carmen shook her head. "It's the same everywhere, Señora."

Elena bowed to the inevitable. "I'll speak to her."

"Now?" asked Carmen. "She should be upstairs."

Elena hesitated. She would have liked a chance to ask her husband for ideas on how best to approach Alejandra. But in the face of Carmen's desperation, Elena knew there was only one thing to do. "I can't promise anything," she said, rising. "But I'll go and have a chat with her."

Carmen and her daughter shared an attic room, up a flight of stairs that was steep enough to make Elena breathless. She paused a moment on the landing to catch her breath before knocking. "Come in!" Alejandra called.

Elena squared her shoulders and then pushed open the door. She was standing in a room with a sloping roof, illuminated only by a skylight. The open door brushed against the foot of a neatly made single bed pushed against the wall in one corner of the room. Alejandra was leaning against the headboard of the other bed, with a textbook braced against her raised knees to form a makeshift desk. Her book bag and other textbooks were lying on the bedspread in front of her. The girl's eyes widened when she saw who it was, and she put aside her textbook and pen, and slid off the bed to bob a curtsy. "Hello, Señora Fernández. Did you need me for something?"

"Not exactly," Elena hesitated. "Can I come in?"

"Yes, please sit down." Alejandra gestured to her mother's bed in the corner, the only other available seat. "How is Toño?"

Elena smiled. "Well. He's taken to you. And your mother."

"He's a very nice little boy." Alejandra spoke with warmth as well as politeness. "It was a pleasure to take care of him."

Elena thought that she saw an opening. "Do you like taking care of children?"

Alejandra nodded. "I used to babysit for Señorita Concha, when she was little. And Isaura's little nephews come to visit her sometimes."

"Have you ever thought of doing it for a living when you grow up?" Elena asked.

"Being a nanny, you mean?" Aleja smiled. "I'd love to. But Mama says I'm too young. Maybe if the lieutenant spoke to her—"

"I think you are young to be a nanny," Elena interrupted hastily. "But I was thinking a few years into the future. How would you feel about becoming a teacher?"

Alejandra's face went still. "No, Señora. I don't think I'd like that. I wouldn't want to be a nun."

"Not all teachers are nuns," Elena pointed out.

Alejandra shook her head, and the lines running downward from her mouth were as deep as carved marble. "No. Too much school."

"You used to like school," Elena dared to remind her.

"I was a kid then. A stupid kid. Besides"—Aleja's voice had been harsh, but now it quavered—"school was different then."

Elena dropped her eyes and studied the pattern of the bed-spread and the textbooks lying on top of it. They were well worn, probably bought secondhand, and had the scuffed edges that books owned by children mysteriously acquire. But she knew that they could not be more than a few years old. The Movement had reformed the education system, and no text-book with a whisper of anything contrary to the Regime's poli-cies had survived the purges. No textbook and no teacher. She remembered the giddy excitement of her first year's teaching. Her classmates and colleagues had been intoxicated by the dream that all Spanish children would graduate from high school. They had been sure that they were teaching the first generation of children who would grow up free of calcified superstition, class restrictions, and fear. Elena remembered her own amazed, half-terrified delight at the reading primers that told stories of boys who sold newspapers in the morning before going to school, the histories that celebrated Averroes and Maimonides, and the science textbooks with pictures of Elizabeth Blackwell and Marie Curie. *History of Spain: Imperial Glories* read the title of the textbook lying by Alejandra's feet. The cover showed a conquistador in armor, brandishing an out-sized cross, with a missionary and a palm tree in the background. Elena remembered joking with other teachers that it would be impossible for her students to imagine what Spain had been like before the Republic, no matter how good the history textbooks were. "They'll just have to listen to us old folks," someone had said, and the group, five new graduates, none of them more than thirty, had all laughed. With a chill, Elena remembered that two of the people who had laughed with her then were dead and another was in prison.

"It was different," she agreed softly. "But that doesn't mean it's all bad now, does it?"

Aleja shrugged and nudged aside *MORAL AND CATHOLIC DOCTRINE FOR GIRLS.* "It's all right for rich girls, I guess. Something to do before they get married. But I'm not a señorita."

"That's foolish," Elena said, annoyed. "You don't need to be a señorita to get an education. And a good education *certainly* isn't only designed to get you a husband!"

"The sisters say it is," Aleja pointed out.

"They're wrong."

"Well, I don't like school, and that's that."

"Do you like work so much?" Elena retorted.

Again the shrug. "It's all right. At least it's something real. And I'd be helping out Mama."

"You're not worried about your mother paying your fees, are you?" Elena asked, with sudden hope.

"No, I know she doesn't." Aleja was impatient. "And it's very good of you and the lieutenant, Señora. But I'm just not a book-ish person. I don't want you to waste more money."

Elena had hoped to convince Alejandra that continuing her schooling was an opportunity worth attending a few masses, even if she was not a believer, but it was obvious that Alejandra was ready to deny that school represented any kind of opportunity. Elena repressed a strong desire to cry.

"You know your mother doesn't feel this way?"

"I know."

Aleja's voice was careless, almost insolent. The set of her jaw dared Elena to argue and provoke her into open impertinence. Any reference to her refusal to attend mass, Elena realized, would only give Aleja an opportunity to show contempt and defiance. Elena sighed and rose, admitting defeat for the time being. "I'm sorry you feel that way," she said, aware of her own dignity and embarrassed at being put on the defensive by a child. "Your mother asked me to speak to you about your schooling. She thinks you're making a mistake, and so do I."

"It was good of you to ask," Alejandra said in a parody of grown-up manners that made Elena want to shake her.

"Perhaps we'll talk about it again," Elena said. "I'm sorry for disturbing you."

She retreated to her room, shaking with fury and grief. Aleja had been such a sweet, bright little girl, curious about every-thing, never stupidly antagonistic. She was cutting off her nose to spite her face, and yet . . . and yet Elena knew that she herself would not have been able to bear reading the pap that consti-tuted the lessons in Alejandra's current textbooks. *Maybe she needs a father's influence,* Elena thought. *Maybe she'd respond better if Carlos talked to her. And maybe she'd spit in his face.*

Elena spent a long afternoon with her mother-in-law, chafing at the forced inactivity. To her annoyance, her husband returned late from the post, and there was no chance to talk to him before dinner either. *It's all very well for him,* she thought. *He can disappear all day, without so much as a word, and then complain that everything's a mess when he comes home!* Andrés Tejada had telephoned to say that he was dining at the casino with friends. His absence did not notably improve the atmosphere as far as Elena was concerned.

After Elena had put their son to bed, her husband asked, "Do you want to go for a walk? I need to get some fresh air."

Elena was tired, but the idea of talking freely outside the confines of his parents' house was extremely attractive. "I'd love to."

The streets were cold and silent at night, undisturbed by cars or pedestrians. The occasional streetcar screeched down the Gran Vía, incongruously bright and noisy in the calm. The temperature was near freezing and a brisk wind was blowing. Elena shivered and was not surprised to see her breath turn into golden mist as they passed under a streetlight. Tejada put an arm around her. "Cold?"

"A little."

"Sorry."

Their footsteps echoed in the silence. Elena could feel the lieutenant's tension. "Are you all right?"

Tejada sighed. "I suppose. We made some progress today. Found some Communist propaganda hidden in Doña Rosalia's house, and have a good idea which member of her household it came from."

"Do the guerrillas operate here, too?" Elena asked.

"*Bandits* operate all over Spain." Tejada automatically corrected his wife's terminology.

"But nothing about who might have killed Doña Rosalia?" Elena asked. She was unwilling to debate with him.

"Well, we've arrested the man we think is responsible for the pamphlet. If we're lucky, Rivas will get a confession out of him." Elena shivered again. "And I practically accused my father of murder," Tejada added, keeping his voice conversational.

Elena stopped dead, not fooled by his flippant tone. "What?"

"How was your day?" Tejada evaded her question. "You said you had something to tell me at lunch."

"Carlos, what did you just say about your father?"

"You first."

"I've had a long day, Carlos," Elena cautioned him.

"Dear God, so have I!" he retorted.

"What happened?" Elena asked.

Slowly, Tejada summarized his morning for his wife. Under her gentle prompting, he rehearsed the majority of his interview with his father, knowing that she would tell him that talking about it would make him feel better. Frequently Elena was right, but in this instance repeating the scene made him feel worse. But at least it was nice to have someone to hold hands with as he relived the low points of his day. "What about you?" he asked, seriously this time, when he had finished an account of his day. "You said you'd met with a problem?"

"Yes. Actually another one has arisen since we talked." Elena was apologetic. "But neither of them have to do with Doña Rosalia."

"Thank God for that!" Tejada managed to smile. "What is it? Is Mother being horrible to you?"

"Not even that," Elena smiled too. "My problems are a missing person and an obnoxious child. Which do you want to hear about first?"

"The missing person. Children are your job, not mine."

Squelching her annoyance at this casual assumption (which under normal circumstances she would have admitted as perfectly accurate), Elena told him about her meeting with the Encinas family and about Baldo Encinas's request for information about his aunt. Tejada was silent while she talked, and she had the uncomfortable feeling that he disapproved. Or possibly he was simply abstracted, still worrying about his own day.

In fact, because he wanted to think about something besides Doña Rosalia's murder and his confrontation with his father,

Tejada gave the problem his full attention. "I can check the files if you like," he said mildly, when Elena had finished her story. "And I'll write a formal request on the Guardia's letterhead, too. But you won't get a reply to that within the next ten days. You'll have to mail any information you get to this kid."

Elena, who had been tense with defiance expecting a refusal to become involved, gave a little gasp and remembered why she had married Carlos Tejada. "Do you think she might have actually gotten away?" she asked, his startling cooperation making her hope for other, greater miracles.

Her husband sighed and squeezed her arm. When he spoke, his voice was gentle. "You do understand that I'll only be able to find out if your friend ever saw the inside of a jail cell?"

Elena nodded without looking at him. She was aware of the possibilities. If Cristina had been taken straight to a place of execution there would be no record. "Will you ask about this friend of hers, Beltrán, too?" she pleaded.

"Of course."

There was a little silence. Tejada wished, not for the first time, that his wife had less unconventional acquaintances. But he had known the shock of discovering the deaths of friends and contemporaries, too, and it was as much sympathy for his wife as a desire to forget about her Red friends that made him say abruptly, "What about the other problem? The obnoxious child?"

"That was this afternoon." Elena explained her meeting with Alejandra. Here his reaction was exactly what she had foreseen.

"She has to attend mass," Tejada said. "The sisters are only insisting on it for her own good."

"I think she's avoiding it because she wants to be expelled from school," Elena explained.

"She's much too young to make any decision like that," said Tejada, remembering his glimpse of Escolapios earlier in the day and thinking that more than one boy there might decide to start

boycotting religious observances if that were a way to avoid
school. "If Carmen wants her in school, then she stays in school."

"She can flunk out if she tries hard enough," Elena reminded him dryly. "Or be expelled for her behavior."

"And break her mother's heart? I don't think so," Tejada
retorted. "I won't let her get away with that. And I'll tell her to
her face, if you like."

"Yes, but she says she hates school," Elena protested sadly.

"So what?"

"You can't tell her how to feel!"

"Maybe not," the lieutenant said grimly. "But I can damn well
tell her how to act." Elena had her doubts, but she did not
argue, recognizing that her husband's mood was still fragile.
They walked in silence for a while in a wide loop, Tejada automatically guiding them toward the house. The breeze was at
their backs now, whipping Elena's skirt in front of her, and plas-
tering the lieutenant's cloak to his legs. Elena leaned back
against the wind. Tejada noticed that her weight on his arm was
less. "It's funny," he said in a meditative tone.

"What?"

"I was thinking about the first night I walked you home. In
Madrid."

Elena closed her eyes. On the night he referred to she had
been cold and hungry and terrified. He had been confused and
angry and grieving for a friend. Neither of them had enjoyed the
walk. "It's the wind," Tejada continued apologetically. "And being
in a city street that's so quiet like this."

"I know," Elena said. "I was remembering it, too."

Chapter 14

The next morning Elena was awake before Tejada. "What are you going to do today?" she asked as she brushed out her hair.

"I don't know." The lieutenant sat and watched the hypnotic strokes of the brush, wishing that he did not have to get up and face the day. "If we're lucky, Alberto Cordero will have confessed last night."

"To what?" Elena demanded, sardonic.

The lieutenant sighed. "Murder? Contacts with the bandits in the Alpujarra? Both?"

"Aiding and abetting military rebellion?" Elena snorted contemptuously. That was the standard charge brought against the losers of the Civil War.

"I'm sure Mother would be very interested to know all about your friends in Granada, you know," Tejada said, annoyed.

Elena swung around. "You wouldn't!"

"Are you going to keep giving me a hard time about Cordero?"

"That's blackmail."

"Of course. 'We're soulless oppressors who profit from the sweat and blood of the people,' remember?" Tejada quoted the pamphlet.

Elena laughed reluctantly. "Do you really think he's guilty of anything?"

"What difference does it make what I think? He admits it or he doesn't," Tejada retorted, hiding his own unease.

Elena bent her head to start separating her hair into three strands for braiding. "So do you think you'll have time to talk to Alejandra today?" she asked.

He could not see her face, but he knew that her question was malicious. She disapproved of the standard methods of interrogation and was deliberately reminding him of a time when they had failed. "I'm sure Rivas hasn't hurt him," he said defensively. She made another derisive noise and he added, "Not seriously."

"And what if he *hasn't* confessed?"

Tejada shrugged. "I'll keep interviewing other suspects, I suppose."

"Your cousins again?"

"I haven't talked to Tío Felipe, yet. And there's this girlfriend of Jaime's, too."

"Why would she be a suspect?" Elena demanded.

"I haven't the faintest idea, but she visited Doña Rosalia regularly, and she could have poisoned her."

"So you'll probably be out all day today again?"

The lieutenant was torn between a desire to shield his wife from his mother and an instinct to avoid his father. Self-preservation won. "Probably," he admitted, adding as a sop to his conscience. "But I'll make sure to find out about your friend and this Beltrán as well."

"Thank you." Elena sounded more grateful than her husband had expected and he guessed how worried she had been about asking him for help.

Guilt about her lack of trust in his sympathy combined with guilt about abandoning her. He sought something to make her happy. "I'll take the day off tomorrow, and we can take Toño up to see the Alhambra," he suggested. "He'll enjoy that. And maybe Alejandra can come, too, and we can have a chat."

"It's a good idea," Elena agreed, tacitly giving her husband permission to flee the family mansion for one more day.

As it happened, flight was barely necessary. Andrés Tejada came late to the breakfast table and hid behind a newspaper for the ten minutes he was in his son's company. When Tejada left for the post he was still feeling a little guilty about abandoning his wife, but tremendously relieved that his father had not made a scene.

Rivas met him at the post, looking excited. "Málaga called half an hour ago. Dulce Cordero is in prison. Her husband is wanted in connection with the law against banditry and terrorism. He's believed to be a smuggler, with contacts in Granada."

Tejada drew a long breath. "What has Alberto said so far?"

"Not a word," the sergeant answered. "He won't admit to his own name."

"Guilty as hell," the lieutenant translated.

The sergeant nodded. "Clearly. I think mostly he's holding out on us with respect to his brother-in-law. I'd like to keep interrogating him about that." Rivas was ready to add that guerrilla activity was obviously the most important thing to worry about when he remembered that Lieutenant Tejada had a personal interest in solving Doña Rosalia's murder. Of course, a real guardia would understand that the banditry and terrorism were the important charges. But the lieutenant was a Tejada. "We can charge him with Doña Rosalia's murder, too, if you like," Rivas offered.

For a moment Tejada was tempted to agree. It would be a successful end to the case. Cordero would be garroted for the murder of his employer, and the newspapers would print an article about a dangerous Red who had taken advantage of an elderly lady's kindness. The lieutenant would be able to go back to his father and present him with Doña Rosalia's murderer, and Sergeant Rivas would not need to visit the Casa Ordoñez again. Elena could have her vacation in Madrid before they had to return to Potes. *There's a good chance Cordero is guilty,* Tejada thought wistfully. *He had the opportunity, and he could have gotten hold of poison. So what if he didn't have a motive? Reds don't need one. So what if someone else paid him to kill her? The fact is, he's still the guilty party. And if we get him on terrorism charges, he's a dead man anyway.* But there were degrees of guilt, and if Alberto Cordero had been hired by someone else, the lieutenant wanted to know who that person was. Even if it was a family member. Especially if that person was a family member.

"Let's hold off on that until we get the lab results as to the wine and find a motive," he said. "I have another week here anyway. I can work on the case to make it tighter."

"Yes, sir." Rivas was a little surprised that Lieutenant Tejada had rejected the opportunity to close the case quickly and quietly. "Of course, the disposition of Doña Rosalia's estate isn't really our business in the normal course of things," he reminded the lieutenant gently.

Not unless it has to do with her murder, Tejada thought. "I know," he said. "Don't worry about it, Rivas. I was just going to speak to Felipe Ordoñez today and the girl . . . what was her name, Villalobos?"

The sergeant shuffled through the papers on his desk. "Yes. Amparo Villalobos. We don't have an address for her. But she first came to our attention in Alberto's statement, and anything he's said is suspect now, isn't it?"

"Anything anyone has said is suspect," Tejada corrected. "But I can't think why Cordero would have lied about her being a regular visitor to the house. And if she befriended my aunt, she might have an idea about who would want to kill Doña Rosalia and why."

"We don't have her father's name or her second surname," Rivas said. "Might be hard to find her in a directory."

"If she's known to my cousin Fernando, I can ask him," Tejada replied. "Where's his file?"

The sergeant blinked. "His file, sir?"

Tejada scowled. "I told you yesterday to pull the files on all of Doña Rosalia's potential heirs. I need to check his address. And phone number, if possible."

"Yes, sir." Rivas gulped back his startled question as to why the lieutenant did not know his own cousin's address. After all, Lieutenant Tejada had been stationed far from Granada for a long time. "I'll get it."

He left the office and returned within a few minutes with the addresses and phone numbers of both of the Ordoñez brothers. Mollified, Tejada thanked the sergeant and then dialed Felipe's number. There was no answer. He tried Fernando. A servant answered. The lieutenant gave his name, and after a few moments Fernando Ordoñez came on the line. "Hello? Carlos?" Ordoñez spoke a little too loudly, spacing his words carefully as if he was unsure of being understood. "Is that you?"

"Yes, Tío Fernando, it's me." Because Rivas was still in the office Tejada did not roll his eyes. He remembered that his cousin had never liked technological innovations. "I was wondering if you could tell me the address of Amparo Villalobos."

"Amparo? Why do you want to speak to her?"

"Because she was a regular visitor of your mother's."

"Yes, she's a good little soul. Bernarda's always been grateful to her. She lives over on Tablas. Down toward the hospital."

Tejada did roll his eyes this time. "You don't have an exact number?"

"I know where it is. Bernarda might have it." If Fernando Ordoñez had been twenty years younger he would have asked the lieutenant to hold the line while he found the address. Since he had never mastered the intricacies of a device he disapproved of and did not trust that his caller would remain on the line if he put the receiver down, he added loudly, "But if you want to see Amparo, why don't you drop by this morning? She'll likely be visiting Bernarda soon."

"Thank you. I'll do that."

"See you soon, then?"

"Yes, see you soon. Good-bye, Tío." Tejada broke the connection and turned to Rivas. "I'm going to go over to Fernando Ordoñez's house to try to interview Señorita Villalobos there. I'd like to try to find Felipe Ordoñez as well. He doesn't seem to answer his phone."

Rivas glanced at his watch. "It's ten-thirty, sir. He might be at work."

Tejada considered telling the sergeant that if Felipe Ordoñez was out of bed—much less doing any sort of work—at ten-thirty in the morning he had changed greatly. "I suppose anything's possible," he said. "I'll try to report back here this afternoon."

"Yes, sir." Rivas's tone became official. "Would you like to work with a partner, sir? Guardia Medina has no duties for the day."

Tejada was grateful Rivas had mentioned Guardia Medina as his option for a partner. He suspected that Rivas wanted Medina out of the way. He also suspected that the sergeant did not realize how well Tejada knew Medina. "No, thanks," he said. "I'm visiting as a family member. I'd like to keep things informal."

"Very good, sir. What are my orders?"

Tejada considered for a moment. "Keep working on Cordero. If he's holding out information about the bandits he may have given himself a twenty-four-hour deadline. They do sometimes, you know. See if he says anything about Doña Rosalia when he cracks."

"Yes, sir."

"And why don't we try to run checks on *all* of Doña Rosalia's household. No one suspected Cordero of anything like this. Some of the others might have surprises in their pasts as well."

Tejada headed for Fernando Ordoñez's home. It was a cold, cloudy day, and the few pedestrians on the streets walked quickly. *Not the sort of day to tempt anyone to take a stroll*, Tejada thought, and then remembered his cousin Felipe with inexplicable unease. Felipe going to work in the morning was laughable. Felipe out of bed on a cold October morning was unheard of. Of course, Felipe in a bed other than his own was entirely probable, but it occurred to the lieutenant that neither his family nor his friends nor members of the casino appeared to have seen Felipe Ordoñez lately. "Spending all his time in flamenco bars and cabarets" was the general verdict. It was *possible* that Felipe was merely enjoying himself in private, but Tejada could not help thinking it was a little strange that a man who was—the thought came as a shock—nearly fifty should disappear into anonymous bars and brothels so completely and so soon after his mother's funeral.

Felipe, Tejada recalled, was the one person who had not shown any interest in Doña Rosalia's will. His father had said that in his Aunt Rosalia's missing will, Felipe had been disinherited, but he had said the same thing about Daniela, and she was most certainly interested in the contents of her mother's will. And Fernando Ordoñez had mentioned that his younger brother had dismissed his valet several years ago, as if money were a concern to Felipe. Surely it was odd that he had not inquired about his inheritance. Unless he already knew that he had been disinherited. But he would only know that if he knew the provisions of Doña Rosalia's most recent will. *Which has disappeared,* Tejada thought. *Like Felipe.* He could not think of any reason Felipe Ordoñez would wish to disappear, but he had to admit that his cousin's lifestyle would make such a disappearance easy. But perhaps someone else had wanted to make Felipe disappear. Tejada felt a sinking in his stomach. He knew from previous experience that it was easiest to get away with murder if no one was likely to search for the victim. *He's probably just fine,* Tejada thought. *But I've got to find him to make sure. Disappearing like this is too much of a coincidence. And if he's disappeared, it damn well has something to do with his mother's death.* Then, with a flash of something that he decided was anger because it was too sharp and bitter for sorrow: *And if Alberto Cordero masterminded Tío Felipe's disappearance as well as Doña Rosalia's murder, I'll join the Communist Party!*

Fernando and Bernarda Ordoñez lived in a spacious townhouse just off the Puerta Real. The lieutenant was evidently expected. A butler showed him into a guest parlor immediately, barely stopping to ask if he was Carlos Tejada. Fernando Ordoñez and his wife both rose to greet their guest. Perhaps because of Fernando's dislike of the telephone, they had evidently heard nothing of the lieutenant's dispute with his father, and they were affectionate in their welcome. After urging Tejada to sit, offering him coffee and refreshments, and lamenting that they had not met earlier in his stay, Bernarda de Ordoñez, who had not seen him for many years, asked the usual run of questions and then said, "Fernando tells me you want to meet Amparo."

Tejada explained again his reasons for wishing to see Señorita Villalobos and added, "I understand she's remained very close to you?"

"Yes, it is as if she were poor Jaime's widow," Bernarda agreed. "And honestly, Carlos, I wish that she had been. I can't think of a girl I would rather have had for a daughter-in-law."

"It must be a comfort to her that you feel that way," Tejada said. He wondered if Elena was spending the morning with his mother.

"We're all sorry she never became part of the family properly," Fernando agreed. Bernarda blinked back tears. "The youngsters wanted to get married before Jaime enlisted, but the Villaloboses thought they were too young. And we thought so, too, God forgive us."

Fernando cleared his throat noisily, and Tejada looked at the ground, embarrassed by the couple's emotion. "Anyway," Fernando spoke briskly into the pause, "Amparo's like a daughter to us and always will be. We'd even like to see her married, a sweet girl like her."

Bernarda nodded. "Yes, it breaks my heart to see her in black. She was just twenty when we lost Jaime. Just a child still. I was so pleased when Fernando said you wanted to meet her, Carlos. But of course I'd forgotten that you're married. You'll have to bring your—Elena, isn't it?—to meet us."

"I'd love to," Tejada lied, with a flash of alarm. "I gather it would be possible to interview Señorita Villalobos here?"

"Yes, I telephoned her and asked her to come over today," Bernarda confirmed. "She usually visits anyway, but since you had asked specially, I invited her. She said she'd be here by noon at the latest."

"Thank you." Tejada turned to Fernando Ordoñez. "There is one other thing. You haven't heard from Tío Felipe by any chance?"

"Not since yesterday," Fernando replied. "But I haven't been looking for him. Why don't you leave a message with the concierge at his apartment building? Or at the casino?"

"I will," Tejada said, thoughtful. "Don't you have any way to contact him in an emergency?"

"Not if he doesn't answer his blasted telephone," Fernando said. He glanced at the clock and stood. "I'm sorry, Carlos, but I must leave. I have an appointment at eleven-thirty. It was good to see you again."

Tejada stood also and offered the older man his hand. "Likewise. Thank you for your help."

"Anything, if it will help catch the man who killed Mother," Fernando answered. He moved toward the door, adding, "If I see Felipe, I'll tell him you're looking for him."

The lieutenant made small talk with Bernarda for a few minutes. It was easy to bring the conversation around to Doña Rosalia. Fernando had told his wife about his conversation with Tejada the preceding day, and Bernarda was deeply shocked by the news that Doña Rosalia had been poisoned. The lieutenant knew this because she said so within ten minutes of her husband's departure. "Poor soul." Bernarda shook her head. "To die alone like that, without confession."

"She lived alone as well," Tejada pointed out.

"I always said that was very unwise." Bernarda pursed her lips. "She was an elderly lady, and she could have suffered an accident very easily. And besides—she became confused in her mind sometimes, and she should have had her family around to care for her."

"Really?" Tejada said, trying to decide whether Bernarda's opinions were the result of posthumous piety or whether her husband had grossly misrepresented her relationship with her mother-in-law. "Did she not want to live with you?"

"With us?" Bernarda looked startled and faintly alarmed for a moment. "Goodness, no. She never liked this neighborhood. And it would have broken her heart to leave her husband's home. No, no, that was out of the question. But," she lowered her voice and leaned forward a little, "I really do think Felipe behaved very badly to her."

"Felipe?" Tejada repeated, stunned. "What should he have done?"

"Moved back in with her, of course," Bernarda said, as if surprised that the answer was not obvious. "He doesn't have a family or business or a house to take care of. And at his age, living in a bachelor apartment is really ridiculous. The house would have been perfect for him. It was his childhood home, and it really did need a man to make sure that it was kept up properly."

Tejada gritted his teeth to prevent his jaw from dropping. "You don't think residing with his mother might have . . . interfered with his independence?" he managed, thinking how lucky he was to live in a blizzard-swept, Red-infested place like Potes, out of reach of family machinations.

Bernarda laughed. "Really, Carlos, he's not a university student. Wild oats are one thing, but a man his age should take some responsibility for his home and his family. If he wasn't going to get married he could at least have cared for his mother."

Swamped by a wave of pity for Felipe, Tejada suddenly wondered how much of the family shared Bernarda's attitude and how much pressure they could bring to bear on a man in Felipe's position. Probably not enough to make him commit murder. But perhaps enough to make him want to disappear.

The clock chimed a quarter to twelve, and Bernarda added easily, "Fernando and I had hoped for a little while that Felipe might think of our Amparo. She was always so good to Doña Rosalia. Sometimes I think she was at the Casa Ordoñez more than I was. She would have been a good companion for both of them."

"Señorita Villalobos?" Tejada blinked and did some rapid mental arithmetic. "But Tío Felipe must be twice her age!"

"Age doesn't matter so much for a woman in Amparo's situation, almost a widow," Bernarda said, a little primly. "Amparo's always been very mature and serious minded. And Felipe is so youthful. He could certainly make himself attractive to a girl like her if he tried."

Ingrained good manners prevented Tejada from saying that he thought the Pyrenees would become flatlands before Felipe made an effort to attract a girl who was a virgin at twenty-seven. He leaned forward, afraid that his thoughts might show in his face. Bernarda, misinterpreting the gesture, raised the tray of cookies sitting beside her. "Would you like another?"

"Thank you." Tejada took a cookie to cover his embarrassment, holding it gingerly by the edges to avoid spilling confectioner's sugar. He ate quickly, wondering what on earth had possessed Bernarda to imagine that her brother-in-law might marry her late son's fiancée and worrying absently if he could surreptitiously lick his fingers to avoid having them remain sticky with sugar. It was real sugar, too, although that made sense, considering Don Fernando's business. Sugar. . . . "Villalobos and Rioseco!" he exclaimed suddenly.

"What?"

"Amparo Villalobos," Tejada amplified, forgetting about his

sticky fingers. "She must be related to the Villaloboses of Villalobos and Rioseco? The refinery corporation?"

"That's right." Bernarda nodded, pleased that Tejada was once more relating to the world of Granada's elite. "Except that the Riosecos are out of the business now. It's just Amparo's father."

"Her father must own some very desirable lands," Tejada suggested, understanding now why the Ordoñezes were so anxious to have Amparo marry into the family.

"I suppose so." Bernarda was uninterested. "I know Fernando's mentioned that we share a boundary with them. And Jaime and Amparo were very excited about uniting the estates."

"Real love match then?" Tejada commented. He recalled his cousin Jaime as an insufferable monarchist, whose fervent belief in a lost age of chivalry was matched only by his constant need for money. He had once commented to a friend that it was a shame Jaime had been born too late to die in a fruitless quest for gold in South America and be made a duke for his pains. He had remembered the casual slur when he learned of Jaime's death in combat in '38 and felt guilty. Now he remembered it again and was struck by its appropriateness.

"Oh yes." Bernarda was apparently unaware of any irony. "Well, when you see Amparo you'll understand why all the boys were in love with her. If you'd been here in those years, you would have been yourself."

The door opened and spared Tejada the effort of responding to this dubious assertion. "Señorita Amparo," the servant announced without formality.

The woman who entered the room behind him was in fact a notable beauty. Her hair, visible beneath an elaborately draped mantilla of black lace, was blond and ringletted, its fairness in striking contrast to her enormous dark eyes. Considerably shorter than the lieutenant, she had a good complexion and a figure that even Felipe Ordoñez would have stopped to look twice at, elegantly swathed in black silk. As joined to these advantages was one of the largest dowries in Granada, Tejada could well believe that she had been much sought after. She came forward now and kissed Doña Bernarda affectionately, greeting her and asking after her concerns with the familiarity of a frequent and welcome visitor.

"And this is Carlos," Bernarda said, turning her guest to greet the lieutenant. "He asked to meet you especially."

"A pleasure to meet you." Amparo put out her hand, smiling. Tejada kissed it, because she obviously expected him to, and murmured something polite. "You're here because of poor Doña Rosalia, rest her soul, aren't you?" Amparo continued when they were once more sitting.

"I'm afraid so," Tejada agreed. "I wonder if I could ask you some questions, Señorita?"

The lieutenant had used the formal you, although Amparo, following Doña Bernarda's lead, addressed him as *tu*. She noted his formality, but answered easily, "Of course. However I can help."

"You visited Doña Rosalia the day before her death?"

The girl's eyes clouded. "Yes, I think so. Or perhaps two days before. I went often." She hesitated a moment and then added quietly, "My days are empty now. I had time."

"What did you talk about?" Tejada asked.

Amparo misunderstood the question. "Everyday things. The way the house was running, how the weather would affect the garden. Sometimes we reminisced about Jaime or his cousins. Sometimes about her late husband. I suppose you could say we lived in the past, but it was a comfort to her. And to me."

"The last time you saw her," Tejada clarified. "Do you remember talking about anything in particular?"

"No, I don't think so." Amparo shrugged. "She was worried about one of the maids slacking off, I think. I brought her some fresh apples, and we talked about how the fruit season was almost over."

Little Red Riding Hood taking a basket of fruit to Grandmother,

Tejada thought. *And not a wolf in sight, damn it.* "Do you know if she had any enemies? Anyone who would try to kill her?" he asked.

"No." Amparo was emphatic. "No, I can't think of anyone who would do such a wicked thing."

"Who were her friends?" Tejada asked, without much hope.

"She didn't go out very much. Her husband's acquaintances still called occasionally, but she didn't"—Amparo hesitated—"really enjoy that. She was upset by strange people. I think she was shy, you know. She liked it when I came or Felipe or Don Fernando or your father, because she was used to us. But . . . well, she didn't really like to have many visitors, poor lady."

It was an unusually charitable interpretation of Rosalia's behavior, but still recognizable. "Did you know that she had made a number of complaints to the Guardia Civil?"

"Oh, yes." Amparo smiled. "She used to talk about the sergeant sometimes after he'd been to see her. I think she enjoyed *his* visits as well. But, of course, he couldn't come if she didn't make complaints."

Tejada swallowed a smile and made a mental note to tell Rivas that he had been the high point of an aristocratic lady's social life. His opinion of Amparo's intelligence increased. The girl had a combination of tact and insight that might be useful. "The last time you visited her," he said carefully, "do recall her eating anything?"

"Oh, we never ate when I was there," Amparo replied. "Doña Rosalia always had her meals at the same time and never when there were visitors present. She preferred to dine at home, alone. She didn't like eating out at all. It was one of the reasons she didn't go out much."

"What about drinks? Did she offer you a glass of anything, for refreshment?"

"No." Amparo shook her head. "In the summer she would offer a glass of water sometimes, but that was all. And that last time, nothing."

"You were very good to spend so much time with someone who wasn't really a relation," Tejada said. "Why did you?"

Amparo blushed at such a frank question. Then, looking at the ground, she said. "I felt sorry for her. And . . ." She took a deep breath and the lieutenant had the impression that she was summoning words from memory. "I don't intend to marry now. I have no children. I was glad to do something useful."

Coming from a sixty-year-old widow, the words would have been heartrending. Coming from an undeniably beautiful twenty-seven-year-old, Tejada found them a little odd. He understood—or thought he understood—why Fernando Ordoñez was anxious to remain close to a sugar heiress who was the daughter of a major colleague and rival. But he could not understand Amparo's apparent determination to remain close to her fiancé's family. He could only imagine that she had been deeply in love with his cousin Jaime. The lieutenant personally could not comprehend Jaime inspiring that kind of devotion in anybody, but he supposed a well-bred young woman might feel differently. "That's very kind of you," he said.

Amparo looked embarrassed. "Not really." She paused. "Do you have any other questions?"

Tejada considered. "Not really," he echoed with a faint smile.

The smiled emboldened Amparo. "Then would it be very improper for me to ask you what you've found out so far? Don Fernando told me that his mother had been killed, but he didn't say how."

"She was poisoned," Tejada said. Bernarda, sitting beside Amparo, made a face.

Amparo flinched. "Was it . . . quick?"

"Yes," Tejada said quietly. "Very quick. She probably didn't suffer."

"No time for a priest," Amparo murmured. She crossed herself and Bernarda followed suit. Tejada again had the odd sensation of watching a child playing a part, imitating a much older woman's gestures. He remembered what Bernarda had said about Amparo being mature for her years. She was certainly grave and serious, but her widow's black and measured gestures paradoxically made her look young for her age. The lieutenant found himself thinking of her as a child, instead of a woman within ten years of his own age.

"I'm sorry to distress you," he said.

"I understand."

Tejada turned to his hostess. "Thank you for letting me spend so much time here."

"Please, feel at home." Bernarda gave the standard reply with grace, but was startled when the lieutenant rose.

"I'm sorry," Tejada apologized. "But I'm working. Thank you again, Señorita."

Amparo smiled at him and stood also. "It's nothing. Especially if it helps you catch the man who killed her." She, too, turned to Bernarda. "Forgive me for running away, but Papa is having visitors for lunch, and he likes me to be there. May I call Sancho and ask him to pick me up from here?"

"Of course, dear." Bernarda kissed the girl's cheek and then added, "But you have time to walk if you like, don't you? Carlos, can you take Amparo home, so she doesn't have to bother with a chauffeur?"

Tejada choked back annoyance at Bernarda's casual assumption that his work could be put on hold indefinitely. He was severely tempted to ask why a young woman in full possession of her limbs needed a chauffeur or an escort to travel a few kilometers in her home city in full daylight. But what he said was, "It would be a pleasure." His wife and perhaps a few of the more perceptive members of the Guardia in Potes would have been able to tell that he was lying, but it was not obvious to the two ladies in Granada.

Amparo accepted the lieutenant's escort with the ease of a girl who never walked alone. When they reached the street, she linked her arm through his with the automatic trust of a child. Tejada, who was accustomed to walking quickly, did his best to shorten his stride, and make polite small talk. "Your wife isn't from Granada?" Amparo asked when the conversation was in danger of dying.

"No."

She waited for him to expand on the topic, and then said, "I haven't seen her at the casino dances in the evenings."

"No, our son is too young to leave alone," Tejada answered tactfully, suppressing his wife's opinion of the casino and most of its members.

"Oh, I see. But she must be very lonely here, if she doesn't know anyone. I would love to meet her." Amparo hesitated. "And, of course, your little boy."

"That's very kind of you," Tejada said, so grateful that Amparo had thought of his wife's comfort in Granada that he did not stop to think whether Elena would like the girl. "Is there a good time to call on you?"

"This afternoon?" Amparo suggested with a smile. "Say around seven o'clock? I would love to see you as well, but I imagine you may be busy. I've taken up far too much of your time already."

The lieutenant courteously denied that she was taking up his time and wondered again at her strange mixture of innocence and insight. Her portrayal of Doña Rosalia's difficult personality, though kindly, was accurate, and her concern for Elena's friendless state in Granada suggested a fair amount of empathy. Yet she acted and sounded like a girl barely out of her teens. He decided that she must be exceptionally sensitive to things relating to the emotions. Either that or she was trying to act stupider than she actually was. But that made no sense. Women were emotionally sensitive, and she was just unusually feminine, he concluded.

He left Amparo at the door to her home and, after a glance

at his watch, worked his way back to the Gran Vía. He still had time to see if Felipe Ordoñez was at home before returning to the Tejada villa for lunch. Felipe's building was a modern, characterless apartment house on the west side of the street, slightly farther from the center of town than was fashionable. He was about to ring the bell to summon a concierge when a woman in a maid's uniform with her arms full of packages, trailed by a boy and girl within a year of Toño's age, fumbled for her keys and opened the door. She disappeared up the stairs with the children scampering on either side of her, and Tejada, who had entered in their wake, inspected the mailboxes in the half dark of the hallway.

"Can I help you, sir?" The concierge was young, perhaps thirty. He moved with a brisk step that suggested the military to the lieutenant. The young man saluted with his left hand as he noted Tejada's uniform, and the lieutenant saw that his right arm was missing from the elbow down.

"I'm looking for Felipe Ordoñez Tejada. Do you know the apartment?"

"Ordoñez Tejada? Yes, sir. Second floor, front. But he's not in."

Tejada inspected the concierge. "When was the last time he was in, do you know?"

The young man considered. "I haven't seen him in a few days, now that you mention it. You might ask the night man. He comes on duty at seven."

"Has his mail been picked up?"

"As much as usual, but that doesn't mean anything." The concierge was interested and clearly making an effort to be helpful. "He has a cleaning woman come in three times a week, and she picks up the mail, as often as not. He doesn't ever get more than a few letters."

"Can you remember exactly the last time you saw him?"

"Today's Friday." The concierge frowned in thought. "Not yesterday. The day before? Or no, no, it was Tuesday because he came back with a package and told me to take a sniff, and the market had coffee on Tuesday."

It was the lieutenant's turn to pause and think.

"Why are you looking for him, sir? He's not wanted for anything, is he?" The concierge spoke with eager interest.

"What? Oh, no. No, he's not wanted." Tejada hesitated, wondering whether to acknowledge a relationship with Felipe. "I'd just like to ask him a few questions," he said instead. "Do you suppose I could leave a note?"

"Yes, of course, sir." The concierge seemed disappointed. He paused and then added hopefully, "We do have keys to the tenants' apartments, sir, if you wanted."

Second rule of a gentleman: always knock, Tejada thought, remembering another of Felipe's precepts with amusement. Felipe would be livid at the thought of a guardia civil searching his apartment. Tejada could practically hear his cousin's indignant protest: *For goodness' sake, Carlito, you can't go grubbing through another man's private possessions with no valid reason.* Entering Felipe's apartment without his permission was an impertinence. The appropriate thing to do was to snub the concierge for his prurient curiosity. "Thanks," he said. "If you have the key, I would like to take a look around."

Chapter 15

The concierge would undoubtedly have enjoyed staying and helping the lieutenant with his search, but Tejada thanked the man, took the key from him, and firmly shut the door in his face. At first glance, Felipe's apartment was exactly what the lieutenant would have expected. The youngest of the Ordoñez siblings shared his family's good taste in real estate. The apartment was spacious for a single man, with a living room that faced onto what—when the shutters were open—were probably French doors leading to a princess balcony overlooking the street. The furniture was relatively modern and, though not new, was comfortable and of good quality. An electric chandelier hung from the ceiling. Tejada glanced at the shutters and then decided that throwing them open would attract unnecessary attention. He hunted for a light switch, and the shadows gave way to a yellow glow as he flicked it on.

He probably would have noticed something wrong sooner if he had searched the apartment in natural light. The faintly musty smell would have seemed out of place with the shutters folded aside and the windows flung open. The cleaning woman was conscientious, and the rooms were not noticeably dusty, but everything was too neat. There was no ice in the icebox and no bread or fruit or perishables. The kitchen was empty of foodstuffs, except for a half-empty can of coffee beans, an unopened container of sugar from the Ordoñez refinery, and several tins

of evaporated milk. There were no half-smoked packs of ciga-
rettes in the empty ashtrays, and no books or folded newspapers
by the bed. The worn cake of soap in the dish by the bathroom
sink was bone dry, and there were flecks of rust on the razor that
lay beside it.

It was like seeing an apartment put on show, Tejada thought.
There were just enough realistic touches to prove that the place
was not brand-new, but the minor clutter of daily living was
absent. He opened the bedroom closet. It was empty, except for
a single suit, a dinner jacket, and an old overcoat that had obviously seen better days. No shoes or sweaters or bathrobes. The
dresser drawers held a clean shirt and a few changes of under-
wear. It was the clothing one might expect to find in a pied-à-
terre in a foreign city, not the wardrobe of a primary residence.

Tejada shoved the drawer closed. It creaked loudly in the
silence. He grimaced. Felipe Ordoñez had perhaps lived here at
one point, but clearly he was no more than an occasional visitor
now. The address was a convenient place to pick up messages
and perhaps to make the odd phone call or spend the night, but
nothing more. Felipe had not told his family that the apartment
was no longer where he lived, although Fernando had perhaps
guessed. So where was he? *At home,* Tejada thought uneasily, *when
a man disappears, he's taken to the mountains.* He was sure that had
not happened to Felipe. Aside from the fact that his cousin had
always been utterly uninterested in politics, he could not really
picture the lazy, pleasure-loving Felipe as a guerrilla. *You haven't
seen Felipe in years,* a voice in his head cautioned him. But none of
Felipe's friends or family had described any change in him. *He
wanted them to think he still lived here,* the voice countered. *He might
have let them keep thinking a lot of things.* The lieutenant shook himself. This was ridiculous. Felipe Ordoñez had no reason to lead
a double life, and certainly had never had any reason to become
a Red. And even if he had become one, he would have had no
reason to kill his mother. But why *had* he disappeared then?

The lieutenant went back into the dim living room and surveyed it, searching for some clue to the owner's whereabouts. The room was almost aggressive in its lack of personality. The walls were bare of paintings. No photographs stood on the coffee table or bookcase. Tejada remembered one of his wife's theories about the keys to people's personalities and went over to examine the books on the bookshelves.

They, too, had the faint aura of displaying a persona rather than a personality. They were almost too well selected and well arranged. There was a handsomely bound double-volume history of Granada. The collected works of Angel Ganivet. A translation of Irving's *Tales of the Alhambra*, and a few books about the history of flamenco and classical guitar. The shelves looked like a display in a bookstore labeled "Touristic Interest." There was no fiction, and none of the books showed any signs of wear. Only the bottom shelf offered a ghost of the Felipe that Tejada remembered. There were several copies of Felipe's own slim volume of poetry and those of a number of other better-known contemporary poets. Antonio and Manuel Machado peaceably shared shelf space, along with Sánchez Mazas, Rosales, and— the lieutenant raised his eyebrows—Rafael Albertí and César Vallejo. At the end of the shelf was a folio, its slightly worn red tapes tied in neat bows. The lieutenant levered it out and opened it with care, wondering what his cousin had prized so much.

As he lifted the flaps, Tejada felt the weight in his hand shift and found that not one but several smaller books had been wrapped in the stiff cardboard. He caught one as it almost slid out of his hands and righted it automatically. Then he looked at the cover. *Poeta en Nueva York por Federico García Lorca.* "Shit," he said softly.

Tejada set the folio down very gently and inspected the other books inside it with hands that trembled although he hardly knew why. The books were all by Lorca. There was an Argentine edition of *Bodas de Sangre* and two older books, the *Poema del Cante Jondo* and the *Romancero Gitano*. Unlike everything else in the bookcase, the last two books showed signs of much use. *He just liked the poetry. But someone who didn't know him wouldn't realize that he was never political,* Tejada thought, brushing away cobwebs of unease. *That's why he put these books away like this. Besides, they're probably first editions. They might have value abroad.*

He opened the *Romancero Gitano*, searching for a date to confirm his hypothesis. It was a first edition, but scrawled across the title page was an inscription:

31 October 1928

To Felipe, friend and fellow poet,

Ever yours,

Federico

A suspicion brushed against the lieutenant's mind with the delicacy of a mosquito alighting. He opened the *Poema del Cante Jondo*. The inscription here was simpler: "*Mi querido Felipe, un abrazo, Federico.*" My dear Felipe, an embrace, Federico. The suspicion bit and drew blood.

Tejada stared at the words and fought nausea. He closed the book gently, and picked up the ones he had dropped. Very gingerly, he aligned the edges of the books once more in the folio and retied the tapes, meticulously trying to knot them in exactly the spot where the red silk had been chafed thin from an earlier knot. He worked slowly, knowing that if he altered so much as a hair of his cousin's arrangement he would be overcome by sick fury and would rip the mocking inscription to shreds and most of the apartment with it. *Un abrazo, Federico.* Felipe had been his friend and guide and mentor. Felipe had demystified sex and soothed the worst torments of adolescence with the sympathetic words, "For God's sake, Carlito, of course you're normal. You just need to get laid." *Ever yours,*

Federico. He had admired Felipe. His dashing cousin who all the girls had been in love with, and who had courted all of them, extravagantly and without intent or preference. *Un abrazo. Ever yours.*

Tejada shoved the folio back into the bookcase and sat back on his heels, trembling. He was sick to imagine that Felipe would ever . . . He avoided the words. *Sick.* Probably Felipe was just living a double life because he was a Red. He hoped. The sound of a key in the outside lock surprised him and he scrambled to his feet, vibrating with tension. There was the muffled noise of someone crossing the foyer, and the lieutenant froze, indecisive. Then a round-faced, clean-shaven man of about fifty walked into the room, stopped dead, and said. "Who the—? What the hell are you doing here?"

Tejada stared at his cousin, too anguished to speak. Felipe Ordoñez took a step closer. "Carlos? It's you, isn't it? How did you get in? You gave me a scare there for a second."

"The concierge has a key," Tejada said tensely. It took all his self-control to keep from backing away.

"He also takes messages," Felipe retorted. "And he could have told you I wasn't in."

"I know. But you'd disappeared. I didn't know what to think."

"That's a fine comment from a man who's visited his home twice in fifteen years," Felipe said. "Well, I'm here now. I ran into Nando at the casino and he told me you were looking for me. What can I do for you?"

Tejada took a deep breath. "I'm here to ask you some questions regarding the death of your mother." He gestured stiffly to a chair. "Would you sit down, please?"

"You're too kind." Felipe gave an ironic half bow. "You might offer me a drink while you're at it. It is my house."

The lieutenant's hands balled into fists at his cousin's mockery. Felipe saw the convulsive gesture and added soothingly, "I'm sorry, Carlito. I'm not used to being"—he paused and smiled—"interrogated by the Guardia. Sit down and I'll try to answer any questions you have."

Torn between an absurd desire to berate Felipe and a resolve to behave with icy professionalism, the lieutenant sat on the edge of a chair. "You visited your mother shortly before her death?" he rapped out.

"Yes."

"Well?" Tejada snapped. "Go on. What for? I thought you were being cooperative."

"I was her son," Felipe said gently. "Visiting your aged parent is considered good breeding in some circles."

"So you just dropped in?" Tejada asked, his voice heavy with sarcasm. "No special reason?"

Felipe drew a deep breath. When he let it out again, his voice was hard. "No, as a matter of fact, she had asked to see me. To be exact, her man Alberto had left a message for me here, several days earlier. I naturally complied as soon as I could."

"So you admit you know Alberto?"

"What do you mean admit?" Felipe snapped. "Of course I know him. I know the entire damn household, better than I need to. I don't know what you're driving at, Carlos, but you'd better just spit it out. I have a date for lunch and I don't want to be too late for it."

Even in his fury, Tejada knew that Felipe's acquaintance with Alberto Cordero was no great matter. He shifted course. "Why did your mother want to see you?"

Felipe hesitated. Then he said, "I'm sorry, Carlos. But I really don't think that's any of your business."

"You quarreled, didn't you?" Tejada accused.

"Are you asking or telling?" Felipe's mouth was a thin line.

"She was furious with you. She cut you out of her will."

"You've been very busy playing detective, haven't you?" Felipe's mocking voice barely masked real anger.

"More than that." Tejada was too upset to stop, although he

knew that he had no proof, only a terrible knot in his stomach and a miserable wish that he had never left Potes. "She threatened to turn you in to the Guardia. To expose you to the world. You had to kill her, didn't you?"

"*What?*" Felipe's jaw dropped. "Carlos, I don't have the faintest idea what you're talking about."

"She must have found out you—*you!*" Tejada swallowed and sank backward into his seat. "Oh, God, Tío, how *could* you?"

Some of Felipe's anger had already turned to puzzlement, and now his voice was tinged with concern as he said, "Look, Carlos, I'm sorry if I was short with you just now. But I really don't understand what it is I'm supposed to have done. Mother was a damn irritating woman sometimes, and I'll admit we had a bit of a fight the last time I saw her, but I certainly didn't kill her."

Tejada stared at the floor, longing to believe that he was mistaken, but afraid to hope. "I found the books," he said softly. "The ones autographed by Lorca."

Felipe paused. "You're thorough," he said, and the mocking edge was back in his voice. "Look, I know you probably don't approve. A lot of people don't, which is why I keep them out of sight. But the fact is, he was a good poet, and—I'm sorry, Carlos— he was a friend of mine."

"A friend." Tejada echoed bitterly.

"Yes, a friend." Felipe was defiant. "I'm not going to lie and pretend we never met just because it isn't fashionable to admit to knowing him anymore. And what's more, *Lieutenant*, if I hadn't been in San Sebastián that summer, I would have gone to the commandant when he was arrested."

"Because you were such good *friends*," Tejada said.

"Yes. So what?"

"You pervert!"

"I beg your pardon?" Felipe stared. Then he said slowly, "Carlos, are you trying to say that you think I'm a fairy?"

Tejada said nothing, but looked at his cousin with pleading eyes. To his astonishment, Felipe laughed. "I don't see what's funny," the lieutenant said stiffly.

"Your incredibly poor judgment!" Felipe snorted. "Jesus, Carlos, you've known me for how long? And on the basis of two inscriptions you suddenly decide I was one of poor Federico's boyfriends? My God, I should give you a clip on the ear!"

"It wasn't just the books," Tejada muttered sullenly, although Felipe's ringing denial had made him feel a little better. "I knew your mother disinherited you in at least one of her wills and about your fighting with her. I knew about Tío Fernando and his wife still nagging at you to marry. And it's obvious you're not living here. This is a cover for something, but I couldn't think what. I knew you got rid of your valet so I figured you were having money problems, and then, when I found the books, I thought maybe—blackmail."

Felipe sighed. "Oh, hell. I'm sorry, Carlito. I guess if you look at it like that it doesn't sound so crazy. I . . . look, you're here as a guardia, right? Not just my little cousin?"

Tejada smiled briefly. "Yes."

"All right, then." Felipe heaved himself to his feet. "I guess I can't expect you to just believe me out of hand. I can explain everything, but I think it will be simpler if you have lunch with me. Can you come now?"

"I'm supposed to be at home," Tejada said dubiously.

"With your parents? Call them and tell them you ran into me and I invited you out." Felipe gestured toward the telephone.

Tejada hesitated. If he was right, Felipe was a cold-blooded poisoner. But he did not see how even the most diabolical villain could slip poison into a restaurant meal with no advance preparation. And he could always refuse to eat or drink anything suspicious. Tejada looked at his cousin and realized with something like sadness that there was no way Felipe could physically overpower him. With a faint sense of shock, the lieutenant remembered that he had stopped his own father's hand, forestalling a blow. And Felipe was a small man and no longer young. With an effort, the lieutenant recalled past kindnesses and reminded himself that Felipe deserved the chance to prove that he was not . . . *not like Lorca*, Tejada thought, shying away from the word in disgust. "All right," he said.

He called his parents and then, before Felipe could comment, picked up the phone again and called Sergeant Rivas. He left a message at the post, saying that he was going to interview his cousin over lunch and expected to be back at the post by five o'clock. His cousin raised his eyebrows at the second message. "Insurance?" he inquired sardonically.

"Just scheduling," Tejada said with embarrassment.

"After you." Felipe bowed and gestured, making no attempt to move close enough to Tejada to touch him.

They passed out of the building under the curious gaze of the concierge and crossed the Gran Vía in silence. Tejada thought at first that his cousin was heading for a small restaurant on the Calle Elvira that he had patronized in other times, but Felipe crossed the Calle Elvira as well and began to climb a steep cobblestone-covered alleyway, narrow enough that the lieutenant could lay his palms flat along the windowless walls on either side. The buildings pressing in on them were crumbling and decrepit, with no visible house numbers. Number plates would have been useless anyway. The alley was too narrow to have a name.

"Where are we going?" Tejada demanded, suspicious.

"Into the Albaicín." The path was curving upward, and the steps had been set into the pavement at irregular intervals. Felipe was moving quickly, and the brevity of his reply might merely have been due to a lack of breath.

"You don't say!" Tejada retorted, and Felipe gave a breathless grunt that might have been a laugh.

"I'll explain when we get there."

Tejada did not press him further, but he was glad that he had called Sergeant Rivas. The Albaicín was the oldest quarter of the city. The dark twisting maze of streets crouching on the hill beneath the ruins of the old Moorish walls was avoided by respectable people. The Reds had built barricades here in '36 and resisted the Movement in bloody street battles, assisted by the hordes of Gypsies and the lowlifes that inhabited the overcrowded slum.

They reached a slightly wider street, perhaps wide enough for a car to enter, if any ever tried to in this neighborhood. Barefoot children with ragged clothes that were too small even for their skinny bodies were playing in the gutters, the smallest of them cheerfully shouting obscenities that the lieutenant had not spoken above a whisper until his university days. Young men who should have been at work lounged in doorways, smoking and observing the street with tired eyes. The children quieted at the sight of Tejada and Felipe and ducked into doorways or behind piles of garbage. The lieutenant heard a few mutters as they passed. "Fascist pig." "Fucking tricorn." He stiffened.

"Keep walking," Felipe said quietly. "No sense starting something." Oddly, the muttered warning made Tejada feel better. Felipe had not spoken with fear or glee, but rather with a sort of embarrassment, as if he felt responsible for the jeers but was disapproving. The lieutenant did not think his cousin would speak that way if he was leading a victim into a trap.

The upper part of the Albaicín boasted impressive views of the Alhambra on the opposite hill. Perhaps because of the prospect, this neighborhood was not as poor or as dilapidated as the area leading up to it. The streets were still narrow and the houses shabby, but they were clean and the few people out of doors appeared to be hurrying about their business in what struck the lieutenant as an orderly fashion. A woman leaning out an upper window to hang her laundry saw them, and gasped. "Don Felipe! Blessed Virgin, are you all right?"

"Fine, thanks." Felipe looked up, shading his eyes with his hand, and added a phrase in a language incomprehensible to the lieutenant. She laughed, responded in the same tongue, and drew her head in.

Tejada stopped walking and stared at his cousin. "What was that?"

"Nothing. I just told her you were family."

"What *language* was that?"

"Calé. Gypsy. I've picked up a few words from Lili."

Tejada fell into step beside his cousin. "You speak the Gypsies' language?"

"Not well," Felipe said modestly. "But when I got interested in flamenco I started spending a lot of time in the Gypsy caves, and I got tired of not understanding what everyone was saying behind my back."

"Who's Lili?" Tejada asked, remembering that Fernando had said something about his younger brother being involved with a flamenco dancer. *Please, dear God, let him say she's the woman he's been staying with,* he thought, but the prayer lacked the urgency it would have had half an hour ago.

"The person we're going to meet." The road forked, and Felipe unhesitatingly dived down the narrower of the two paths, adding over his shoulder, "I'd appreciate it if you didn't mention this place to the rest of the family, unless it's absolutely necessary."

Tejada nodded and followed his cousin with some curiosity. They were not quite in the neighborhood of the Gypsy flamenco bars yet. And the neighborhood was too inconvenient to house the exclusive brothels that Felipe had patronized in his youth. All in all, Felipe seemed out of place in these surroundings. The roof of the house on one side had been seriously damaged by what looked like cannon fire and ill repaired, but the walls were scrupulously whitewashed. The sheets hanging out of the windows to dry were threadbare but there was no garbage in the little alley. The whole place had an air of shabby respectability, and Tejada did not associate either adjective with his cousin.

"Here we are." Felipe stopped in front of a heavy door with the number twelve painted on it in black. Tejada expected his cousin to knock, but instead Felipe dug in his pocket and produced a ring of keys. He fitted one into the outer lock and shoved open the door.

They were in a *carmen*, but a far humbler one than the elaborate ornamental gardens belonging to Felipe's mother or sister. This was simply a cobblestone-covered courtyard with some raggedy bougainvillea clinging to one wall and a well in the center, around which someone had placed a few clay pots of begonias. A whisk broom was lying against one wall and a dented washtub sat beside it, tangible reminders that the courtyard required constant upkeep. Felipe turned unhesitatingly and unlocked an interior door. "It's the second floor," he explained, beginning to climb a narrow staircase, lit only by the light that filtered through tiny windows.

Tejada followed, wondering with one half of his mind about their final goal and with the other about whether the alarming creaks emitted by the wooden steps signaled some structural instability in the building. They passed the door to the first landing. It was closed. As they reached the second landing, the smell of tortilla began to seep into the darkened stairwell. Felipe opened the door to an apartment, calling as he did so, "Hi, Lili! I've brought a guest."

Tejada's first impression was of a darkened foyer. He heard the clatter of pots in a nearby kitchen, and then a shrill voice saying, "Marianita, *no!*" Then he was standing beside Felipe in a long, low room cluttered with books and toys. A dark-eyed girl of perhaps ten with a toddler on her hip was about to deposit the child into a playpen. She looked up and smiled at Felipe, and then froze as she saw the lieutenant in his cape and tricorn and regarded him with suspicious eyes.

Felipe smiled ruefully at the child. "Hi, sweetie. Don't be scared. This is your cousin, Carlos. Carlos, this is my daughter Maya, and the baby is Mariana."

For a moment the lieutenant and the little girl regarded each other with mutual shock. "Aren't you going to say hello to your cousin?" Felipe prompted.

"Hi," Maya murmured at the same instant Tejada responded, "Hello, Maya."

Awkwardly, Tejada leaned forward and kissed the little girl's cheek. The baby, who had taken advantage of Maya's distraction to lever herself up onto the rail of the playpen, now wriggled over the edge and took a few toddling steps toward the two men. "Hi!" she said distinctly, smiling happily in anticipation of praise for her cleverness and stumbled into the lieutenant.

"Marianita!" Maya snatched her sister back, cheeks flaming. "Oh, I'm so sorry, Officer!"

Tejada laughed, still unsure of himself but relieved by the ordinariness of the scene. "It's all right. Why don't you call me Tío?" he suggested and heard the echoes of Felipe's words in his own.

She nodded, but said nothing, still shy. Tejada put Mariana back into her playpen. "And this is Lili and Pepín," Felipe said, sounding both relieved and approving, as the lieutenant straightened. "Lili, my little cousin, Carlos."

Tejada turned to see a woman coming out of the kitchen with a boy of about Toño's age clinging to her skirts, who was observing him carefully. It was difficult to estimate her age. Childbearing had probably broadened her figure, and there were lines carved in her dark face and threads of silver as well as hennaed red showing in her hair, but the lieutenant guessed that she was near his age. She checked for a moment at the sight of his uniform, and then came forward, wiping her hands on her apron and holding one out. "A pleasure to meet you. It's Lieutenant Tejada, isn't it? Andrés's son?"

"Yes. Likewise." Tejada glanced sideways at Felipe, looking for cues as he shook hands.

Felipe ignored him and squatted to be at eye level with the little boy. "How is the king of the household this afternoon?"

"Good." Pepín emerged from behind his mother and was rewarded by being picked up and thrown into the air. "I set the table all by myself, because Marianita was fussy," he added with pride, when he was once more safely in his father's arms.

"I knew there was a reason we kept you around," Felipe said. "Listen. Your cousin is going to have lunch with us. Can you set another place all by yourself or do you need Amayita to help you?"

"I can do it!" Felipe set Pepín down, and the boy scurried back into the kitchen, intent on proving himself useful.

"Maya, put the baby in her chair before she gets out of her playpen again," Felipe ordered. He smiled at Lili, slid an arm around her, and murmured, "Give us ten minutes."

"It'll take that long to make salad anyway," she answered.

When Lili and the children had returned to the kitchen, Felipe turned back to his guest. "Questions, Lieutenant?" he asked sardonically, gesturing toward the couch.

Tejada sank down gratefully, and then immediately started up. He removed the square block caught between the cushions, put it on the floor, and seated himself again more carefully. He was silent for a moment, unsure what to ask first. This cluttered apartment certainly explained the empty rooms on the Gran Vía, and Felipe's dismissal of his valet made sense in the light of the expenses of three children, but Lili's existence raised almost more questions than it answered. "Tío Fernando said you were having an affair with a flamenco dancer," he said finally.

Felipe smiled and sat beside his cousin. "He's right in a way. Lili was one of the best dancers in Granada. She could *really* dance, you know. She didn't just look pretty and shake her ass. Although with a body like hers . . ." He trailed off, contemplating a fond memory.

Tejada blinked, trying to reconcile the image of the matron-
ly figure he had just seen with Felipe's warm praise. He was
unable to manage it until he considered that Maya might
resemble her mother. He mentally aged Felipe's daughter ten
years and discovered that Lili had probably been beautiful.
"She doesn't . . . er, dance now?" he hazarded. It was a measure
of his confusion that he was genuinely uncertain of the answer.

"Oh, no. She says she's out of practice. She still sings, and
sometimes we'll do a little *sevillanas* when her people come over
and there's a decent guitarist. But it's hard for us to go out in
the evenings because of the kids."

"Her people come over?" Tejada said faintly, wondering what
kind of affair Felipe was conducting. It was unlike him to social-
ize with his mistresses' families, and Lili had seemed uncommon-
ly well informed about the Tejada and Ordoñez families as well.

"Her cousins and their husbands. Lili's an orphan, actually,
but the Gypsies take care of their own, you know, so she's never
lacked for family."

Tejada swallowed. "She's a Gypsy?"

"Of course. The best flamenco artists always are."

"And how long have you been . . . involved with her?" Tejada
asked, longing to demand what exactly the involvement consisted
of, and why Felipe was so positive that the children were his own.

"You don't need to use that tone of voice," Felipe said mildly.
"It got serious a little before Maya was born. I found Lili a room
near a doctor when she was pregnant, and she wasn't used to
being alone so I ended up spending a lot of time with her and
one thing sort of led to another."

"How old is Maya?" Tejada asked, dazed.

"She'll be ten at Christmas."

Pepín appeared in the doorway. "Papa! Lunch is ready."

"Coming." Felipe rose, and Tejada followed him into the
kitchen.

The room was warm and lit by electric bulbs. A long narrow

table against one wall held five plates, and Marianita was wriggling in a high chair in the corner. Lili and Maya passed around slices of tortilla and pieces of bread. Felipe opened wine and offered a glass to the lieutenant. Tejada drank and noticed with amusement that the wine was good, a vintage Cáceres, that seemed out of place with the setting. The drink was a faint reminder of the expensive tastes of the young Felipe whom Tejada remembered. Conversation was stilted at first, made awkward by the stranger's presence. Tejada complimented Lili on the meal, and she thanked him politely, but with reserve. "Have you been settled here long?" he asked, remembering the end of his chat with Felipe.

"Since just after the war ended," Lili answered. "It's a miracle we found it when housing was so short."

"San Miguel found it for us," Maya interjected, smiling mischievously.

Both her parents and Pepín laughed, as at a familiar joke, and Lili explained. "We were living in a tiny studio, and Maya desperately wanted her own room. When she was four we took her up to San Miguel Alto during the pilgrimage, and she insisted on lighting her very own candle to the saint. We had been talking for a while about having another baby, and we thought maybe she had decided to pray for a baby brother or sister. But when her papa asked her, she said she had prayed for her own room."

"We found an apartment right after that," Maya pointed out, triumphant. "And I had my own room until Mariana was born, so San Miguel listened."

"A skeptic would also say that I knew the landlord," Felipe added.

Tejada laughed. "My wife and I have lived in temporary quarters since our son was born, and I've been promised a new barracks for the last six months. Maybe we should start lighting candles also."

"It couldn't hurt," Maya said.

"How old is your son?" Felipe asked at the same moment.

"Four and a half."

"Close to Pepín's age," Lili commented.

"No, it's not," Pepín interjected with disgust. "I'm almost six."

"Practically ancient," his father agreed with a smile.

The conversation continued—aimless, casual, and friendly. Tejada found himself more relaxed than he had been since arriving in Granada. He spared a moment to feel guilty about abandoning Elena, and then reflected uneasily that it would be awkward to explain his cousin's domestic arrangements to her. When the meal had been cleared away, Pepín was shooed off to nap, grumbling, and Maya disappeared into her room, murmuring something about a book she wanted to finish. Felipe took his guest back into the living room, and Lili picked up Mariana and carried the baby into the master bedroom. Within a few moments, the sound of a flamenco lament rearranged into a lullaby emerged from the bedroom. Felipe looked smugly at Tejada. "Doesn't she have a great voice?"

"I suppose," Tejada said, a little embarrassed.

Felipe leaned forward, resting his elbows on his knees, and spoke seriously. "You understand now why I'm not down on the Gran Vía much, and why I don't have much spare cash, don't you?"

"I guess so," Tejada nodded slowly. "But . . . I'm sorry, Tío, I still don't know why Doña Rosalia was so angry with you, or what you went to see her about."

Felipe sighed. "I was hoping you wouldn't ask about that."

Chapter 16

"You know I have to ask." Tejada regarded his cousin steadily. "I know, I know. You always did take yourself too seriously." Felipe smiled wryly. "Look, Carlito, I was hoping you'd understand after you met Lili and the kids, and saw all this." He waved one arm, an expansive gesture that took in the battered furniture, the abandoned playpen, the faint smells from the kitchen, and the song from the bedroom. "That this is important, you know? That I'm not just—" He paused and his mouth twisted. "Not just being irresponsible and self-indulgent. I didn't *mean* to get this involved with Lili, but I am, and nothing can change that now and I'm not sorry for it!" he finished defiantly.

"I didn't say anything," Tejada pointed out.

"I know." Felipe let out a breath and smiled. "But Mother and Dani have said more than enough. Even Nando thinks I should get married and settle down, and not spend all my time and money on my mistress."

"They know about Lili?" Tejada asked, surprised.

Felipe shrugged. "Nando knows in a general sort of way that I have a couple of kids to provide for. I haven't told him that I'm basically living here. I never told Dani or Mother details, of course. They just assume that I'm out with a different girl every night of the week, and that it's high time I got married." He grimaced.

"Was that what your mother called you about?" Tejada guessed. "Getting married?"

"Got it in one," Felipe nodded. "She and Nando had hatched this ridiculous scheme for me to marry that little girl Jaime was engaged to."

"Amparo Villalobos," Tejada said. "Tía Bernarda mentioned it to me."

"Then I imagine you've heard all the arguments," Felipe said dryly. "She's beautiful, virtuous, and not so young that she wouldn't look at me. And since Rioseco flitted, her father's rich as Croesus."

"Flitted?" Tejada repeated, momentarily distracted. "What do you mean?"

"You haven't ferreted that out yet?" Felipe laughed. "You should listen more to old gossip. One of the Rioseco boys— Miguel, I think—was arrested at the beginning of the war. One of the ones who disappeared 'without official news,' as you people say. Don Ramiro sold out the business at a loss, and the rest of the family moved to Cuba."

Nilo's voice echoed in the lieutenant's memory. "*Folk guilty of nothing more than belonging to the wrong party. . . . He was like his father. A real gentleman.*" For a moment he had the obscure feeling that the Rioseco family's misfortune was tied to something in Alberto Cordero's statement, but he could not think what. He regretfully dismissed the possible connection. It would be too easy to pin everything on Cordero. He wondered when Amparo and Jaime had announced their engagement. "So now Amparo's father is looking to become Villalobos and Ordoñez?" he asked.

"And Nando wouldn't mind being Ordoñez and Villalobos." Felipe nodded. He became more serious as he added, "I don't mean that Amparo's part of all that. She's a nice kid, and she was damn near crazy when Jaime died. But I can't marry her."

Tejada remembered Amparo gravely crossing herself and

wondered what she would think of a husband who lived with a mistress and three bastard children. "No, I don't think you could. Is that what you told your mother?"

Felipe shrugged. "More or less. I tried to put it down to the age difference, and then to my liking my freedom, but she was more persistent than usual and—" He broke off, looking uncomfortable. "I mean, God rest her soul, Carlos, she was my mother and I shouldn't speak ill of her, but she got me so *irritated*. Talking to me as if I were five years old and telling me that she wanted grandchildren before she died! I tried to tell her that my sister and brother had already provided her with enough grandchildren to field a soccer team, but she wanted grandchildren from *me!* And then—well, she was my mother, and I shouldn't have done it. But I'd just come from registering Pepín for school next year, and when she started going on about it I just—" He stood abruptly and crossed the room. "I had a copy of this in my wallet," he said, his back to Tejada, and his voice muffled as he opened a writing desk and rummaged in one of the drawers. "I finally took it out and told her to stop worrying about grandchildren."

He held out a creased paper to the lieutenant. Tejada unfolded it and read a declaration by the parish priest of San Nicolás certifying that the firstborn son of Felipe Ordoñez Tejada and Liliana Soto had been baptized into the Christian faith with the name José Felipe on December 4, 1939. Tejada considered how Doña Rosalia was likely to have reacted to such an announcement. "She was upset?" he guessed.

Felipe, who had been pacing nervously in front of the lieutenant, stopped walking and snorted. "There's an understatement! She told me I was crazy to give my name to another man's bastard. I told her that Pepín was neither a bastard nor another man's. She wanted to know how I knew, and I ended up explaining about Maya and Mariana."

"Explaining?" Tejada raised his eyebrows.

Felipe gave a reluctant smile. "Well, throwing them in her face maybe. But I was pretty angry by then."

"She threatened to disinherit you?"

Felipe nodded and resumed his pacing. "And said some things about Lili that I'd rather not repeat. I . . ." He trailed off. The lieutenant waited. "I was pretty angry."

Tejada looked at his cousin's face and wanted to let the matter rest. But one thing was still unexplained. "I don't see what she could have threatened to go to the Guardia with," he said honestly. "You're not the first man to have a—a friend like Lili. Or the last."

Felipe took a deep breath. "There was more to it than that. She said that until I told her I was ready to marry Amparo, Nando was her only son, and that I could forget about any inheritance of hers ever going to . . . to the illegitimate children of a woman like Lili." He winced, and Tejada guessed that Doña Rosalia's original phrasing had been something along the lines of "to a Gypsy whore's bastards." Felipe kept speaking in a low rapid monotone, as if anxious to finish his confession. "I yelled at her that I didn't want a penny of her money, and that I'd marry Lili before I let anyone speak about her or my children like that. She said I wasn't serious, and when I told her I was, she—" Felipe glanced toward the bedroom and lowered his voice almost to a whisper. "She said she would lodge a denunciation against Lili for lewd public behavior and have her arrested as a streetwalker."

"Did you think she would actually do it?" Tejada asked, privately thinking that Rivas would have been unlikely to waste time and money tracking down anyone accused by Doña Rosalia.

Felipe dropped into the chair opposite him and leaned forward. "Yes. Oh, I know, she pestered the life out of the Guardia about all sorts of things, and they might not have done anything, but this wasn't like one of her Red plots. She had Lili's name and surname thanks to my stupidity, and—" He choked slightly. "Do you know what they do to the women accused of being prostitutes outside of the licensed brothels? They lock them up in the convent of San Antón and shave their heads and take away their children!"

"Well, in some cases that might be for the best," Tejada pointed out.

Felipe glared at him. "Oh, really? We had a neighbor who used to help Lili with Pepín when he was small. Her husband was killed at the barricades in '36, damn fool, and left her with two babies. She was mostly a seamstress, but when money wasn't coming in she worked the streets a little on the side. She was arrested in a sweep one night, and the next day they came and took away her boys and put them in an orphanage because they were 'of an unknown father and unfit mother.' She got out six months later, all skin and bone and bald as a baby, and when she found out that her kids were gone—my God, I never want to hear a woman make noises like that again. I swear to you, Carlos, I spent a month carrying all my kids' birth certificates in my wallet so I could go and get them out of an orphanage if I had to. I was scared every time Lili went out to do the shopping until —" He stopped abruptly, his fists clenched. "I could have *killed* Mother!"

"Did you?" Tejada asked softly.

Felipe looked up at his cousin, startled. "No. No, I didn't. But, God forgive me, I was glad when I learned she was dead." He smiled a little crookedly. "I don't suppose you'd know if she actually changed her will, would you?"

"You mean you don't know?" Tejada asked.

"I was damned if I was going to go to Nando and beg for information," Felipe retorted. "I didn't hear anything, so I assume that I'm not one of her heirs. Which is another example of my stupidity, because we could have used the money."

"I haven't actually seen the will," Tejada said carefully. "But it looks that way."

Felipe sighed. "Well, if Nando gets my share maybe he'll be resigned to my not marrying Amparo."

"Maybe." Tejada glanced at his watch. It was a quarter to four. He would have been happy to drop the subject, but Felipe's own words—*"You're here as guardia, right? Not just my little cousin"*—made him ask, "The last time you saw your mother, did you have anything to eat or drink with her?"

Felipe stared at his cousin, disconcerted by the change of subject. "I don't remember. She probably offered me a glass of wine. She used to drink this god-awful stuff that had been open so long it was nearly vinegar—" He broke off. "Wait a minute, Nando told me she was poisoned. You think I put something in her wine!"

"We don't have a source for the poison yet," Tejada said.

Felipe looked at him through narrowed eyes. "What was she poisoned with then?"

"Cyanide."

Felipe put one hand to his face. "Oh, shit. Cyanide's what they use in gold plating and all that jewelry stuff, isn't it?"

"Yes, that's right," Tejada said, remembering his afternoon in the library, but surprised that Felipe was so well informed.

"Well, I'm screwed," Felipe said. "Lili's brother-in-law is a jeweler. We've visited his workshop a couple of times and had to hold onto the kids the whole time for fear they'd go sticking their noses into something poisonous. So I guess that gives me—what do they call it in detective stories?—means, motive, and opportunity."

Tejada nodded. "On the other hand, if you were arrested, you'd leave Lili and the children more vulnerable than ever, and I don't think you'd want that."

Felipe smiled. "For a guardia, Carlos, you're pretty intelligent."

"I hear that a lot," the lieutenant said. He stood up. "Thanks for lunch, Tío. And for answering the questions."

"You're welcome." Felipe stood also. "I'll see you out."

"Please thank Lili for me as well," Tejada moved toward the door of the apartment, accompanied by his cousin.

"I will. I'm sure she'd want to say good-bye, but it's hard to get Marianita to sleep, and I don't want to disturb her. Here, the bolt's tricky." Felipe stepped in front of the lieutenant and twisted the lock before shoving the door open and ushering him down the stairs.

In the courtyard, Tejada turned to face his cousin. "Thanks again. And sorry about searching the apartment and, well, everything really. Sorry about everything."

"It's all right." Tejada watched his cousin nod gravely and wondered if Felipe guessed that the apology extended to their last conversation fifteen years ago as well. He hoped so. Felipe held out his hand. "Come again, if you have time."

Tejada grinned, pleased his apology had been accepted. He was about to agree enthusiastically when Felipe added, "And bring your family. I'm sure Pepín would like to meet his cousin. And I'd like a look at this girl you've been hiding up north."

Tejada was already nodding, and he felt a certain embarrassment as he said, "I'd love to come, of course. But . . . well, Elena and Toño may be busy. That is, I don't know if they'll be able to."

Felipe laughed softly, but his voice was sad as he said, "Still true-blue, aren't you, Carlos? I had the idea from your parents that maybe your wife wasn't the sort of convent-bred señorita who'd mind visiting Lili. But if you feel that way—"

"Oh, no, of course not," Tejada interrupted, flushing because he *did* feel that way, but he was old enough now to know that he was hurting his cousin's feelings.

Felipe sighed. "Would it make you feel better to know that Lili and I are getting married next weekend?"

Tejada's jaw dropped. "You're joking!"

Felipe frowned. "No. I thought it over after that yelling match with Mother, and I decided it was the best way to protect Lili and the kids in case someone threatened them. And then, after

Mother died and I was thinking about her will, I realized that if something happened to me, Nando and Dani would fight tooth and nail to prevent Lili getting anything more than a pittance. So Lili and I talked it over and we agreed. It's at San Nicolás next Friday, if you'd like to come."

"You don't think that's a little . . . extreme?" Tejada said. "I mean, your family will have a fit, you know."

"I can imagine." Felipe grinned suddenly. "I was there for some of your mother's palpitations after your honeymoon. I'm can't remember whether her favorite adjective for your wife was 'red' or 'scarlet.'"

"But at least Elena was never a—" Tejada remembered, barely in time, that he intensely disliked it when anyone made comments about his wife, and that Felipe might feel the same way. "—a dancer," he finished.

Felipe went still. "I told you before," he said, "Lili really could dance. She was a dancer and that's all she was." Tejada said nothing, but his skepticism showed in his face, and Felipe added, "I'm not saying she was a virgin when we met. She had a past, but so did I. And it's in the past."

"And that doesn't bother you?" Tejada said, more astonished than censorious.

"Look." Felipe's voice was half rueful and half amused. "When Maya was seven months old I went to San Sebastián for two weeks, for a vacation. I'd been there a week when the war broke out, and I couldn't get back to Granada until the air base was secured. Even then I had to pull a lot of strings to get on a flight as a civilian. Lili didn't have a phone, and I couldn't write because the siege had cut off the mail. There were stories about the Reds taking over the Albaicín and bombing the city, and casualties, and God knows what all. I damn near went crazy with worry. I spent Maya's first birthday in a hotel room by myself, not even knowing if Lili or my baby were still alive, getting drunk. I finally got home in the middle of January, and when

Lili opened the door to the apartment and saw me we just walked into each other's arms and cried. I haven't spent more than a couple of nights away from her since then. I haven't been with another woman. I spend a night on the Gran Vía sometimes, and I have trouble falling asleep because she's not there. Being without her bothers me."

"But now that your mother is dead, there's no one who would come between you," Tejada said, and then mentally kicked himself for reinforcing Felipe's motive for murder.

"And what happens if I'm hit by a streetcar tomorrow?" Felipe said, with no sparkle of laughter in his eyes or voice. "I've acknowledged the children, and my will is in her favor, but can you see Pablo Almeida defending Lili's rights against Nando and Dani?" Tejada hesitated, and Felipe added vehemently, "You go down and take a look at the orphanage on the Cuesta del Chapiz. It looks like something you people use for prisoners. Half the poor brats in there are the children of Reds who are dead or in jail. I'm not taking a chance on my kids ending up in a place like that because some smart-ass lawyer manages to twist things around to imply they aren't mine."

Tejada hesitated, thinking about the lengths he would go to to protect Toño, and then held out his hand to his cousin. "Congratulations," he said quietly. "We'll visit, if we have time."

Felipe took his cousin's hand and clapped him on the shoulder. "Thanks, Carlito." His voice was husky, and Tejada was suddenly sure that protecting the children was only an excuse for his marriage to a Gypsy dancer, an excuse Felipe made perhaps even to himself. "It . . . it would mean a lot to Lili if you came again with your Elena."

"We'll try," Tejada said, thinking about bringing Elena and Toño through the narrow stinking streets, past the urchins— whom Toño would probably want to play with—and the hostile lounging young men.

He shook hands with his cousin again, opened the courtyard

door, and stepped out into the street. As he turned to close the door behind him, he saw his cousin heaving the abandoned washtub onto his shoulder and heading back toward the stairs. Friday afternoon must be Lili's wash day. Tejada pulled the door shut, regretting his last glimpse of Felipe. His cousin had strained slightly to pick up the washtub, and the dull metal was sure to leave a mark on Felipe's shirt. He had looked like one of Potes's more prosperous farmers: poor, but not starving; vigorous, but starting to feel his age and complain a bit of aches and pains in the cold weather.

For a moment the bare planks of the door transformed themselves into a red curtain before the lieutenant's eyes, and he remembered being twelve years old and allowed to go out to the theater with Tío Felipe, resplendent in evening dress. He remembered goggling at the inevitably bare-shouldered and beautiful girls, diamonds flashing in throats and ears, and the intense embarrassment of having them kiss him on the cheek as if he were a baby and coo how cute he was, as Felipe laughingly introduced him: "This is my little cousin, Carlos." And then the vision disappeared, replaced by Lili wiping her hands on her apron, and the lieutenant knew that the debonair young man who had taken him to the theater was lugging a washtub up a flight of dark stairs to a cheap apartment, to a woman who would probably kiss him on the cheek and remind him that he had promised to fix the blinds this weekend.

Tejada was not sure whether the laughing young dandy or the middle-aged head of a family was the better man. He knew that he would have found a man of Felipe's age who still chased after chorus girls and went out drinking until dawn both distasteful and faintly ridiculous. But he had loved his big cousin, although it had been a love tinged with disapproval by the end of his adolescence, and he left the Albaicín with the irrational feeling that the Felipe he had once known had died. He looked at his watch, wondering if he had time to stop and see Elena before going back to the post. He wanted to tell someone about his meeting with Felipe and about Felipe's incredible plan to marry a Gypsy, but telling a member of the Ordoñez family was out of the question, and even telling Sergeant Rivas seemed like a betrayal.

It was after four. Remembering his phone call to Rivas, he decided to go straight to the post. He did not take the most direct route back because he could not remember Felipe's exact path through the Albaicín's winding alleys, but he did not worry about getting lost. To get out of the Albaicín you just had to keep heading downhill. Sooner or later you hit the solid ground and solid citizens of the plain. He reached the post a few minutes after four-thirty and asked to see Rivas.

The sergeant was not in his office. Tejada waited for a few minutes, and then decided to make good his promise to Elena. He found Captain Vega's office and asked to see the records relating to arrests made in the summer of 1936, explaining that he was looking for information about two specific people. The captain very nearly laughed in his face. "In '36, Lieutenant? You've got to be kidding. Between the militias and the army and overcrowding, half the people who went through here were never processed."

Tejada explained that he was fulfilling a request from his wife, and that merely checking whatever files were available would be sufficient. Vega nodded comprehension. "If you want to go through the motions to satisfy her, you're welcome to. Here, I'll write an authorization to take to our archivist."

Tejada thanked the captain and left with a brief note addressed to Corporal Méndez, instructing the corporal to let Lieutenant Tejada inspect the arrest and transfer records for 1936 and requesting that he give the lieutenant any necessary aid and assistance in locating files. Tejada checked that Rivas was still not back in his office, left a note on his desk, and headed for the archives.

The archives of the Guardia Civil were located at the seat of the civil government next door. Granada's municipal government was housed in an impressive mansion with an echoing entrance hall and a flight of marble steps. A dark and narrow stairwell concealed below the curving stairs leading up to the main floor went down to the archives in the basement. Tejada headed into the depths of the building with a reminiscent smile, remembering his youthful curiosity about what happened in the hidden parts of grand public buildings, like lifting a rock in a forest to see all the little creatures wriggling beneath it in the damp leaves.

Very little seemed to be wriggling beneath the municipal government building. The Guardia's archives had been placed to one side of the cellar behind a heavy set of swinging doors, which squeaked as he pushed through them. He found himself confronting a man in a corporal's uniform who was sitting at a small table, working on a crossword puzzle. Behind the table rose wall upon wall of filing cabinets, arrayed in straight rows like an army. The man looked up, and light gleamed off his glasses. He stood. "Can I help you?"

"Are you Corporal Méndez?"

"Yes?"

Tejada handed over the captain's letter, along with his own identity card, and inspected Méndez as he peered at both pieces of paper carefully. The corporal was one of those men whose age is difficult to guess because they look much the same at sixty as they had at thirty. Heavyset and running to fat, Méndez had thinning hair and a neat little mustache. He looked more like an interrogator than an archivist. The impression was dispelled when he spoke. "The summer of '36, sir? I'm sorry, I doubt I can be very helpful. We did try to keep things filed, but there was so much disorder. . . ." He sighed.

"I'm looking for information on two people," Tejada explained. "The first one is Encinas. Cristina Encinas."

"Then your best bet is to see if they have dossiers, rather than combing through all the old arrest records. Why don't we take a look? This way, sir." Méndez heaved himself to his feet and padded down one of the corridors of filing cabinets with Tejada behind him. "Here we are: García, N. to Evoras." He pulled out a drawer and began to riffle through the folders. "Guerrero, Gutierrez, Gutierrez . . . Encinas! Encinas Arriaga, Ubaldo, Encinas Rosado, María Isabel, Encinas Zapatero, Osvaldo. . . . I'm afraid those are the only ones. No Cristina."

Tejada sighed. "Oh, well. Thanks. The other name is Esteban Beltrán."

"We can look him up, too, if you like, sir," the archivist agreed. "But what sort of information were you looking for about this Cristina?"

"Anything we have. Which seems to be nothing."

"Not necessarily nothing," Méndez corrected. "She doesn't have a separate file, but she might be cross-referenced. Do you know her second surname?"

"No," Tejada said, wondering how Elena had managed to leave out so basic a piece of information. But the boy she had mentioned was called Baldo, he recalled, and might have been named for his grandfather. So he ventured, "Her father is probably the Encinas Arriaga you mentioned."

"Fine, we'll start there then." Méndez spoke with unmistakable enthusiasm.

"Look," Tejada interrupted. "I haven't got that much time. Why don't we check and see if Beltrán is here, and then I can look at his file while you search for information on Cristina."

"Fair enough."

Méndez hurried toward another filing cabinet, moving with surprising grace for such a big man. Luck was with the lieutenant. Beltrán Monteroso, Esteban, was neatly filed between Barba and Berrios. The file was thick enough to be promising. Leaving the lieutenant at his table, with a pad and the pencil he had been using for the crossword, Corporal Méndez returned to scanning the archives for references to the elusive Cristina.

Forty minutes later, the lieutenant had read the entire Beltrán file and filled a page with notes. He was just about to seek out Corporal Méndez again when the archivist returned. "Your Cristina is María Cristina Encinas Rosado," he said, sounding pleased. "Thirty-three years old, MD from the University of Madrid, appointment to the surgical staff at the University of Granada medical center, February 1936."

Tejada nodded. "That's the woman. Any arrest records?"

The corporal shook his head. "Nothing definite, sir. But she's currently listed as 'missing' in her parents' files."

"Do you think she's in hiding?" Tejada asked. "Abroad?"

"It could be," Méndez sighed. "But a lot of doctors were picked up in the first months of the Movement. *We* kept records, of course, but the militias—" He clicked his tongue, a prim gesture at odds with his appearance. "Amateurs, you know."

"Is there any way to find out more definitely if she's alive?" Tejada reflected as he spoke that he had so far found out nothing about Cristina that he had not already known.

Méndez considered. "If she's in hiding you might find more about her by looking in the files on the bandits' activities. They need medical attention after their attacks, and we do sometimes try to trace them through medical supplies bought, or doctors we think are sympathetic. A lady doctor might attract enough attention to be put in a report. If she's abroad you might look at her family's correspondence and see if they've received anything from her. But her death will be hard to confirm."

Tejada was tempted to ask where the files regarding bandits' activities were kept, but a glance at his watch told him that Sergeant Rivas was probably waiting for him. *Besides, Méndez will want a reason for undertaking such an extensive search,* he thought. *And I can tell him what? That my wife was friends with the woman?*

That's hardly a good enough excuse for wasting his time. He had opened his mouth to thank the archivist for his help when Méndez said, "This other guy you wanted, what was his name?"

"Esteban Beltrán Monteroso."

"What's his connection to the lady doctor?"

"Colleagues. Possibly romantically involved. Disappeared around the same time."

"I'll take a look in his file, too, if you like," the corporal offered. "I might see some connections there. And maybe look up the hospital's records and check out their families. There are a few places. Can I get back to you in a day or two?"

"That would be wonderful," Tejada said, surprised. "But I don't want to put you to too much trouble."

"I like doing research," Méndez answered. "And I think I remember Beltrán's name from somewhere. I'll see what I can dig up."

Tejada offered his heartfelt thanks and returned to Rivas's office to wait for him, satisfied that he had done his duty to Elena. The sergeant entered within a few minutes. "Good afternoon, Lieutenant," Rivas saluted. "I received your message. Were your interviews productive?"

Tejada shrugged. "Yes and no." Rivas waited in inquiring silence, so he summarized his meeting with Amparo Villalobos and his lunch with Felipe Ordoñez, suppressing his discovery of Felipe's copies of Lorca, his own momentary suspicion that his cousin had been the poet's lover, and Felipe's incredible plan to marry a Gypsy. Rivas listened to the lieutenant, looking increasingly depressed.

"It's an awfully good motive," the sergeant said sadly, when Tejada had finished. "And he had access to cyanide, too. This could get very messy."

"You don't think Felipe's guilty?" Tejada protested, alarmed. Rivas maintained a tactful silence and the lieutenant added, "His motive is thin, and he told me himself about the cyanide.

He didn't have to, and there's no way we would have known of his access to it otherwise!"

The sergeant hesitated. Then he squared his shoulders and said, with the air of a man determined to do an unpleasant duty, "His motive is better than anyone else's: his mother was threatening a woman he was in love with. And if we had investigated and found out about this girl's connections to a jeweler, his failure to come forward with the information would have looked very suspicious."

"Next you'll be saying it was suspicious that he knew about the open wine," Tejada snapped.

He had the satisfaction of seeing Rivas blush and cough. "The wine. Yes. We got the lab analysis today."

Something in his tone made the lieutenant look at him sharply. "Don't tell me?"

"It's perfectly healthy, Lieutenant. No one had tampered with it," Rivas admitted sheepishly.

"The smelling salts?" Tejada demanded.

"Good for reviving fainting ladies, sir." The sergeant made a weak attempt at a joke.

"The food samples?" Tejada asked with some desperation.

"Sorry, sir."

Tejada sighed. "Oh, well. We'll find out how it was administered eventually. Has Cordero talked?"

"A little, sir." Rivas was not noticeably cheered by this reference. "Well?"

"He admits that he was trying to contact his brother-in-law, but he won't say where the brother-in-law is. He's still insisting he's never seen the propaganda before and has no idea how it got there."

"Did he say anything about Doña Rosalia?" Tejada demanded.

Rivas looked miserable. "Just that he would never have been fool enough to kill her because look where it landed him, and he'd like to lay hands on the idiot who did." He paused to see if

Tejada was going to say anything and then added, almost in a whisper, "I'm sorry, sir. But I'm afraid he might be telling the truth."

"It's always annoying when they do that, isn't it?" Tejada wondered what would happen to Maya and Pepín and baby Mariana if Felipe was arrested for murder. "It makes it so hard to get them to change their stories."

Chapter 17

Tejada and Rivas discussed the matter further, but came no closer to a solution. Nor did they reach a true accord, although Rivas did not openly challenge his superior officer's judgment again. The lieutenant knew that Rivas would have pursued Felipe Ordoñez further, and he was torn between anger at the sergeant's stupidity and a sneaking fear that Rivas might be right. They parted after agreeing that Alberto Cordero should be transferred to the Guardia in the Alpujarra, who were more familiar with the sites and people involved, for further questioning regarding the guerrillas.

Tejada searched for his wife when he reached home and found her sitting with his mother, discussing opera. To be exact, his mother was explaining why the Princess Eboli's solo in *Don Carlo* was the high point of the act, and Elena was listening with a smile as glazed as a piece of porcelain. She greeted him with almost visible relief. "Carlos! How was your day?"

"Interesting," Tejada said briefly, leaning over to kiss her on the cheek. "And yours?"

"Lovely. Your mother was kind enough to take me shopping this morning." Elena clasped his hand in welcome, and then gripped it as if she were drowning. "And then at lunch we talked a little about ways I could keep myself occupied in Potes."

Tejada squeezed her hand in sympathy, pleased that he had the means rescue at hand. "I hate to interrupt your discussion," he said, glancing at the clock, "but I actually have an invitation for you. For seven o'clock."

"Oh, really?" Doña Consuela was suspicious. "I thought your wife preferred to make her social calls alone."

Elena dug her fingernails into her husband's palm. The warning made him bite back his angry response and say instead, "I saw Amparo Villalobos today, and she was kind enough to invite Elena and me to visit her this evening."

"Amparo?" Doña Consuela relaxed. "How sweet of her. But she always was a lovely girl. Such a shame you weren't in Granada after Jaime died. She was simply devastated, and I'm sure you would have been a comfort to her."

Given his own opinion of Jaime and Amparo's evident estimation of her fiancé, Tejada could not help thinking that his mother was wrong, but now he said simply, "Well, I took the liberty of accepting the invitation. Would you mind a walk, Elena?"

Elena was already on her feet. "I'll go and check on Toño."

"He's napping?"

"No, he wanted to play with Alejandra." Elena looked briefly amused.

"I'd hoped he would get to know his cousins a little better," put in Doña Consuela. "But Elena indulged him, even though I wasn't sure it was a good idea."

"I don't think Toño's at the age where we need to worry about him playing with the housemaids yet," Tejada said, deliberately being provocative.

He took Elena's arm and steered her out of the room before his mother had time for more than an outraged gasp. His wife turned to him, smiling faintly. "You shouldn't have said that."

Tejada looked sheepish. "I was afraid she would volunteer to come with us to Amparo's."

Elena laughed. "No fear of that. She's glad to be rid of me. Let's see if Toño wants to come along."

The little boy declined the invitation to visit Amparo. The

lieutenant and his wife set off for the Villaloboses' house. On their way, Tejada briefly explained his meeting with Amparo and her history. Elena listened with interest, but after his family's exclamations, Tejada found her brief expression of sympathy for Amparo's plight perfunctory. "You worked over lunch," Elena commented. "What *else* did you do today, besides see this little girl?"

"I tracked down Tío Felipe," Tejada admitted uncomfortably.

Elena sensed restraint in his tone. "And?"

Tejada opened his mouth to spill all of Felipe's startling secrets, and then closed it again. Elena was unlike any of the other women in his family. She would probably not be shocked by Felipe's way of life. After all, she had known plenty of Reds who did not even believe in marriage as a sacrament. But did the fact that she had a tendency to immorality give him the right to speak to her as if she was a friend or colleague rather than the wife whom he was obliged to protect and honor? He hated the way his mother behaved toward Elena, but wouldn't telling Elena about Lili be treating her with another form of subtle disrespect? He shrugged. "He's still Felipe," he said lightly.

"What's that supposed to mean?" Elena said tartly.

"Nothing. Just that he's always been unconventional and he still is." Tejada spoke quickly, a little frightened by her tone.

"Unconventional how?" Tejada identified the tone in his wife's voice as suspicion.

"Well, by not marrying and settling down," he floundered, knowing that any other respectable woman would have understood by now that he did not wish to discuss Felipe's lifestyle and drawn the appropriate inferences without embarrassing him. He felt a flash of guilt at the trite phrase, as if he was lying. "Settling down with a nice girl," he amended truthfully.

Elena raised her eyebrows. "You make him sound as if he's living secretly in a pirate's lair and smuggling opium," she commented.

Tejada laughed and remembered that he loved Elena because she made him laugh. She smiled back at him the way she did when they were at home, and he relaxed. "He's living in the Albaicín with a Gypsy dancer and three kids whom he thinks are his," he said.

"Three?" Elena repeated. "This must be a long-standing relationship then?"

"It looked very permanent," Tejada agreed, and described Lili and the children to his wife. As he had expected, she was unfazed by their existence. When the lieutenant finally added that Felipe intended to marry Lili, Elena laughed.

"So he's finally able to legalize things now that his mother's dead!"

"I'm sure that's not what kept him from marriage this long," Tejada lied. "It's a very serious step. Not something he would rush into."

"You did!" Elena pointed out.

"You and Lili have nothing in common!" Tejada shot back, genuinely annoyed. "You never agreed to live in sin before marriage!"

"I never had much of an opportunity," Elena retorted. "You weren't so frightened of your mother."

Tejada would have argued the point further, but they had reached the Villaloboses' mansion, and there was no time for further discussion. He knocked and a maid admitted them and showed them into a sun-drenched room, where Amparo was waiting for them. The lieutenant spent the few moments in the hallway quashing the thought that Elena, as well as Rivas, assumed that Felipe wanted his mother out of the way.

Amparo greeted Tejada warmly and was politely happy to meet Elena. The lieutenant noticed that the girl's manners toward his wife were less natural than toward him. In spite of her age and unmarried state, Amparo seemed anxious to be received as an equal, a concern that made her act a little overly gracious. Knowing Elena's ability to put people at their ease,

Tejada expected Amparo's initial manner would be quickly overcome. So he was surprised when Elena made no attempt to respond to the girl's friendliness. Poor Amparo smiled and chattered in vain. Elena did not thaw. Tejada, who had assumed the women would want to talk together and had resigned himself to being superfluous, found that he was taking a much larger role in the conversation than he had anticipated.

"So you're living in Cantabria," Amparo said, during a lull in the conversation. "I've never been there, but I've heard it's beautiful."

"If you like mountains," Elena agreed.

"I love them. I've always been glad that my window looks out at the Sierra."

"Then you would probably like Potes," Elena admitted. "Although you might find it a bit dull in the winters. We don't have Granada's glittering society."

Amparo looked down. "I don't go out very much anymore. Ever since my fiancé . . . I haven't wanted to. But at least I'm able to be useful here."

"Really?" Elena's surprise was a little more excessive than courtesy dictated. "I know you're a great comfort to Jaime's family. What else do you do here?"

"A little charitable work." Amparo was modest. "I've been involved with subscription drives for the hospital and for our war widows. And I'm a member of the ladies' auxiliary of trustees of the orphanage." She caught Tejada's approving eye and smiled. "We had a meeting this afternoon actually, or I would have invited you to visit me earlier."

"Do you do a lot of work for the orphanage?" the lieutenant asked, positive that an interest in children's welfare would gain Elena's approval if anything would and remembering Felipe's vehement denunciation of the way Granada cared for its children.

"We have fundraising drives for the children several times a year," Amparo explained. "And then there are several benefits for the poor things as well. Right now we're focusing on a Christmas spectacle for them."

"But you don't actually go to the orphanage?" Elena clarified. Her voice was quiet and courteous, but Tejada sensed her disgust.

"Oh, yes. The committee visits once a month, to meet with some of the older girls." Amparo cast her eyes down. "They need to be prepared against temptation when they go out into the world. So many of them . . . fall to sins of the flesh."

"How much is a housemaid's salary?" Elena demanded, her voice low but acid.

Fortunately, Tejada had anticipated her reaction and spoke loudly at the same moment. "I'm sure you do very valuable work." He kicked his wife's ankle.

"Yes. We're very grateful you found time in your busy schedule to see us," Elena said sweetly. "We really shouldn't keep you any longer."

"Oh, no, you're most welcome," Amparo protested.

Elena rose, inexorable. "That's kind of you, but our son will need me."

Amparo gave way gracefully. "I do hope to see you again soon."

She accompanied them to the door, and Tejada, feeling his wife's rudeness and anxious to make amends, invited her to visit them with more warmth than he really felt. Elena turned on him as soon as they were well away from the house. "Why on earth did you invite her to visit?"

"Because you practically spat at the poor girl!" Tejada retorted. "There was no need to be so abrupt with her."

Elena sniffed. "Prissy little señorita. 'I don't go out very much anymore. Ever since my fiancé . . .'" She mimicked Amparo's voice cruelly. "What a hypocrite!"

"Elena!" Tejada was shocked. "The girl's in mourning!"

"In heat, you mean," Elena retorted.

The lieutenant stared at his wife. "What?"

"That girl needs to find a husband, and soon, or she'll suffocate from her own piety," snapped Elena.

Tejada laughed to cover his unease. "There you're wrong. I'm sure other people have wanted to marry her. But whatever else you say about her, she was in love with my cousin."

"But she'll take you as a consolation prize," Elena said.

"Don't be silly!"

Elena suddenly leaned on his arm, so heavily that he slowed his steps and looked down at her, concerned that she was ill. She looked up at him through her lashes and then blinked slowly several times. Tejada stopped walking and frowned. "Are you feeling all right?"

"Of course." Elena straightened and spoke briskly. "I'm just showing you how she was looking at you the whole time we were there."

"That's not—" Tejada began, and then remembered Amparo clinging to his arm on the walk back from the Ordoñezes'. "That's a little exaggerated, don't you think?" he finished.

"No." Elena was definite. "She was looking at you as if you were a tall glass of iced lemonade and she was very thirsty."

The lieutenant's laughter this time was unforced. "You're just jealous."

"Of course I am," Elena agreed comfortably. "Would you want me not to care?"

Tejada thought about this for a few steps. "No," he said. "I'm glad you care. But you have no reason to be jealous, you know."

Elena gave his arm a friendly squeeze. "I know."

"I'd hoped you would like her," Tejada apologized. "It seemed like a way to get you out of the house and away from my mother while we're here."

"It was a nice thought." Elena was soothing. "And probably Amparo is a perfectly nice little girl. She just needs to learn that she can't make eyes at other women's husbands."

"And to look for someone her own age," Tejada agreed. "Although all of my family have been throwing her at Tío Felipe."

"Poor Lili," Elena commented. "Now why didn't you take me to visit *her*? Or weren't we invited?"

Tejada coughed. "Well, Tío Felipe invited us. But not Lili. And I wasn't sure . . ."

Elena read his pause. "For goodness' sake, Carlos, you take me to meet a little slut who bats her eyelashes at every presentable male, and then try to avoid a perfectly respectable woman just because she doesn't have a marriage license?"

"It's not a very good neighborhood," Tejada defended himself. He knew better than to argue over Elena's definition of "perfectly respectable." She would only become temperamental. Besides, Lili really did seem more like a respectable housewife than a kept woman.

"The Encinases live nearby!"

"And a bit of a climb."

"More than from Potes to Argüébanes?"

"All right," Tejada capitulated. "We can go tomorrow, if you like. You should see the Albaicín after seeing the Alhambra really."

"I thought we were taking Alejandra to the Alhambra tomorrow?"

"Sunday, then," Tejada offered.

When they reached home they sought out Alejandra and Toño, and found them deep in an engineering project. The lieutenant reclaimed his son, and then asked Alejandra, a little awkwardly, if she would like to accompany them to see the Alhambra the following afternoon. Alejandra hesitated. Toño put his arms around her waist. "You'll come?" he wheedled.

Alejandra patted his head and exchanged a smile of grown-up complicity with Elena. "Of course I'll come, if you want me to."

Tejada was pleased for his wife's sake that Alejandra had agreed to go with them to the Alhambra, but as the hour of their excursion approached he had a premonition that she was going to be difficult. When she joined them the next day after lunch she was obviously in high spirits, and it made him smile to see how much Toño enjoyed her company. He elected to hold her hand instead of that of either of his parents so the Tejadas were free to walk arm in arm through the crowds of Saturday afternoon strollers on the Calle Mesones.

"They're sweet together, aren't they?" the lieutenant commented as Toño laughed at something Alejandra had said. Elena nodded and smiled. "It would be nice to have a little girl maybe," Tejada added thoughtfully.

"Do you think he'd be as gallant to a younger sister?" Elena's voice was teasing.

"Of course." Tejada instantly defended his son.

Toño's gallantry was worn out shortly after they reached the Plaza Nueva and began the steep climb up to the Alhambra. His steps began to lag along the Cuesta de Gomérez, and shortly after they entered the green calm of the park around the Alhambra he trotted back to his parents and asked them to fly him. "Maybe on our way back," Tejada suggested. "You're getting too heavy to fly uphill."

"But I'm tired," Toño protested.

Finally, Tejada swung the little boy up onto his shoulders. Toño rode along clinging to the lieutenant's tricorn and inspecting the view with renewed interest. They entered the palace complex through the Puerta de la Justicia, where the lieutenant set his son down and Alejandra amused herself by trying to read the inscription to the Catholic monarchs.

Toño enjoyed climbing on the nineteenth-century cannons in the plaza, and he liked the square red walls of the Torre de la Vela and the ancient fortress complex. But he was less interested in the delicate palace of the Nasrids, and it was here that Alejandra and Elena wanted to linger, exclaiming over the filigreed detail and the calm reflecting pools. Tejada found himself drawn farther and farther away from his wife and their guest as Toño hurried through the famed halls.

It was not until they were out in the gardens of the Generalife that the lieutenant had the chance to strike up a conversation with Alejandra. Toño was deeply impressed by the carp in the reflecting pools and plopped himself down on the path to inspect them. Alejandra sank onto a sunny bench nearby, looking relieved to rest. The lieutenant sat beside her, wondering how to begin. Before he could think of a good opening, Toño looked up. "I'm thirsty."

"We'll get you an ice later," Elena said, taking a seat on the other side of her husband.

"The Moors must have often had ices in this garden in the summer, if they were as pleasure loving as everybody says," Alejandra commented.

"I imagine ice carriers could have brought ice down from Mulhacén then as well as now," Tejada agreed.

Toño stood up and came to loll against his father's knees. "And maybe they had hot cider in the winter?" he suggested.

"It doesn't get cold enough for apples here." Tejada shook his head. "Although I suppose they might grow up in the Sierra." He smiled. "At least the Moors here could see what snow looked like up in the mountains."

"You mean it doesn't snow here in the city?" Toño asked, wide eyed.

"Once in a while," Alejandra answered him. "But only a few flakes, and they never stick. Not like real snow." She sighed.

Tejada smiled at her. "Do you know the story of the Moor who tried to bring snow to Sevilla?"

She shook her head. "Tell!" Toño commanded.

Tejada lifted his son onto his knees and began to retell a half-remembered legend from his childhood. "Once upon a time, there was a Moorish prince who fell in love with a slave girl. He decked her with jewels and silks and brought her trinkets from the ends of the earth. She fell asleep to the sweetest music his musicians could make, and the air of her rooms was perfumed with roses and jasmine. But although she had everything her heart desired, she languished."

Tejada paused for poetic effect and to think what came next. "What's 'languished' mean?" Toño asked.

"She was unhappy. The prince saw this and asked her what was wrong. Now his love was a northern girl, from a distant land of long, white winters. 'I miss my home,' she said to the prince. 'I miss the snow.'

"'The snow?' the Moor said, puzzled, for he had never seen snow.

"The girl tried to explain what a snowstorm looked like, until she began to weep. 'I miss the smell of pines and wood smoke. I miss running to a frosted window on a morning cold enough to see your breath in and seeing the land turned white with snow.' The prince pleaded with her, but it was no use. She would only reply, 'It never snows here.'

"For many days the prince was thoughtful. Then he had an idea. He called together his gardeners and ordered them to scour the countryside for blossoming almond trees. Then one night, as his love slept, he ordered all the almond trees planted outside her window. In the morning, the wind began to blow, and the blooms whirled through the sunrise in a gentle blizzard. The prince woke the girl and led her to a shuttered window. He threw it open. 'Look, my love,' he cried. 'I have brought you the snow.'"

Toño considered the story. "That's stupid," he said at last. "Almond blossoms aren't like snow. They're not cold."

Tejada was amused. "I think the point is the lengths a man will go to for the sake of a woman he loves," he said.

"So, the girl was happy then?" Toño asked.

"I assume so. If she wasn't, at least he could feel he'd made every effort."

"He could have set her free."

"What?" Tejada said, startled.

"If the almonds didn't work," Toño persisted with the inexorable logic of a four-year-old, "he could have set her free so she could go back home."

Disconcerted, the lieutenant looked to Alejandra for support, but she said nothing. He smiled down at Toño. "You're too young to understand," he said indulgently. "He couldn't set her free because—because of politics."

"Oh," Toño nodded, satisfied.

"I think he was cruel to her," Alejandra remarked. "Showing her something that looked like snow but wasn't, to make her realize how far out of her reach her homeland was."

"I'm sure that wasn't the intention!" Tejada protested.

Alejandra gave a very adolescent shrug. "Then he should have thought it out better." Her voice held a trace of defiance.

Tejada turned to his wife. "What do *you* think?"

Elena was silent for a moment before replying. "I think it depends on what the girl thought," she said at last. "And I think the problem with the story is that it doesn't say."

"I bet she was unhappy." Alejandra was truculent.

"I'm no good at arguing literary subtleties," Tejada said, joking although he was annoyed by Alejandra's tone. "You're probably right."

"Of course I'm right." Alejandra was firm.

Toño, bored by the discussion, wandered a few steps away to another bench that presented interesting climbing possibilities. Elena followed him, with a significant glance at her husband. Tejada took a deep breath and followed the opening he'd been given.

"You're good at arguing about the meaning of stories."

Alejandra shrugged again. "All right, I guess."

"You must get good marks in composition."

The gaze Alejandra turned on the lieutenant carried the full weight of a teenager's contempt for a clumsy adult. She said nothing.

"Do you like literature?" Tejada asked, feeling vaguely ridiculous. Still the unflinching, disgusted gaze. "You've been so kind to Toño, telling him about history, I thought perhaps that was your best subject."

"I hate history."

"So you like literature best?"

No response.

"Surely you don't like science and mathematics best? That would be very unusual for a girl."

Still stony silence.

Tejada's discomfort began to turn to anger. No chit was going to give him the silent treatment. "What are your grades like?"

"All right."

The lieutenant abandoned subtlety. "So what is this nonsense about your refusing to attend mass?"

Shrug.

She had always been a stubborn little person, Tejada recalled. "I asked you a question," he said harshly. "I expect an answer."

Alejandra raised her head and met his eyes, clearly intending to be defiant. For a moment she held his gaze, and then her lashes dropped again. When she spoke, her voice was a mumble. "I don't believe in all that stuff."

Tejada opened his mouth to reply, and then shut it again. He was sure she was lying. She must be lying. But he was unsure how to say so. Who ever asked if someone *believed* in the rites of the church? The point was to practice them. Except of course, the point *was* to believe in them. He remembered Elena's words: "You can't tell her how to feel." His own reply came back to him, and he unconsciously used the argument his wife had intended to use: "If you don't go, you'll be expelled."

Shrug.

"It's for your own good. And only for a few more years. But it's not worth losing your chance of an education for the sake of a silly principle."

"I don't need more education. I'm old enough to work."

Tejada leaned forward to catch her sullen mutter and suddenly saw her as she had been six years ago when they first met: a wounded, starving, pathetic little creature, ready to resist him with all of her pitifully small strength. He made out her words now with the frustration of a man who liked his antonyms clearly defined: black and white, good and evil, truth and falsehood.

She was old enough to get a job. Many girls no older than she were already maids or laundrywomen, and children half her age worked as shepherds and cowherds in Potes, and as messengers and street vendors in Madrid. But the lieutenant knew that the baby curves of their faces hid hollow bellies. He knew how easy it had been to seduce the servant girls of his adolescence, if seduction was the right word for what happened between a hungry fifteen-year-old who earned a peseta a day and tried to send money home to her parents and a bored señorito whose weekly pocket money exceeded her monthly salary. He looked at Alejandra. Her face was as grave as an adult's, but she held her body as rigidly as the frightened child she had been in Madrid. He half wanted to put an arm around her shoulders and reassure her that he would protect her. He wholly wanted to shake her until her teeth rattled for being such a stubborn little fool.

"You're old enough to *work*," he said honestly, "but you're not old enough to earn a living."

"I can help out my mother."

"She doesn't need your help." Tejada saw her draw a breath to retort and added quickly, "Right now. She wants you to stay in school. And if you become a nurse or a teacher you can help her more later."

"I don't want your charity." Her words were choked.

"It's not charity," the lieutenant denied.

"What is it then?"

"Keeping a promise I made when you were a child," Tejada said shortly. He had no intention of discussing the circumstances of his promise with an insolent adolescent. "I said I'd take care of you, and I'm going to. You're going back to school in the autumn, and that's final."

Alejandra raised her chin. "You're not my father. You can't tell me what to do!"

"You think if you were working you'd be able to talk that way to your boss?" Tejada snapped.

Alejandra lowered her eyes. "Sorry," she muttered. "But I remember my father a little, you know." Her voice was trembling, but it still held a hint of belligerence. "He was a Red."

"I know."

"They say . . . *things* about the Reds in school."

"I know."

"When I was little I told the sisters that what they were saying was wrong. They've hated me ever since."

"I'm sure that's not true," Tejada replied, although he thought it was more than plausible. If she showed her teachers the same attitude she was showing him it was a miracle she was passing any of her classes.

"I don't care if he was a Red." Alejandra was crying silently. "He was my *father*."

Tejada was embarrassed by her emotion. He looked for something to say and came up with a platitude. "It's to your credit you feel that way."

"That's not what they say in school!" Alejandra's voice was choked, but she impatiently waved away the handkerchief the lieutenant offered her. "They say the Reds were pigs. And that they d-did terrible things. And th-that we're *lucky* General Franco led the National Movement to s-save S-Spain and th-they *talk* about the girls who have relatives in prison."

"Are there many?" Tejada asked, surprised.

"No." Alejandra shook her head and rubbed her eyes with the back of her hand. "Just two others. And they're friends but everybody whispers and points at them behind their backs and the sisters give them the lowest marks even though one of them is smart, and anyway they're not like me either and I hate them. I *won't* go back there after June! I *won't!*"

"Be reasonable," Tejada said, angrily because he found himself feeling sorry for her. "What other choice do you have?"

"I'll get a job!"

"As what?" The lieutenant was contemptuous. "A maid? A nanny? With no experience and no references? Girls ten years older than you are *with* experience are looking for positions. You don't have a hope!"

"I'll find something." Alejandra was dogged. "I don't care if it isn't anything grand. I just don't want to keep going to school."

"It's not a question of what you want." Tejada was once more in control of himself. "It's a question of what your elders decide is best for you."

Alejandra stood up and faced Tejada. "Then I'll refuse to go to mass so the sisters won't take me back."

"You'll be taken to mass, whether you wish to go or not." Tejada spoke with deadly calm.

Alejandra's eyes narrowed. "They can't make me go to confession." She hissed, "I'll just sit there and won't say a word. And . . . and I'll *gag* if they make me take communion."

"You do that and I'll take a strap to you!" Tejada threatened, forgetting that he was only planning to be in Granada for another week.

"That's what you people do, isn't it?" she shot back.

"You ungrateful brat!" Tejada sought words and found that he had raised his voice without being aware of it. His wife and son had heard him and were heading back to the sunny bench, looking concerned. He took a deep breath as they approached. They drew up and stood for a moment in a frozen tableau, Elena frowning at her husband and Toño staring at his father, his eyes enormous. Then Toño moved to put his arms around the girl's waist.

"Don't cry," he said, with a little catch in his own voice. "Please don't cry, Alejandra."

"Oh, Aleja." Elena put one arm around the girl's shoulders. "Oh, sweetie, I'm so sorry."

Surrounded on all sides, Alejandra was unable to pull away. She settled for hunching her shoulders and shrinking inward away from Elena's embrace. "I'm not crying." She patted Toño's head, her voice shaking. "I'm all right, Toño." She turned to Elena. "I'll be all right."

"Let's go home," Tejada said. "We can talk about this later."

Chapter 18

"Why not find the girl a decent apprenticeship with a seamstress or something?" Felipe Ordoñez suggested.

"Because I want her to stay in school," Tejada replied with a scowl that even he knew was sulky.

The two men were sitting in a café in the Plaza San Miguel Bajo, watching the afternoon sunlight play across the facade of the church of San Miguel. Tejada had sent a message to his cousin the preceding evening, suggesting that they meet at a restaurant for lunch after mass on Sunday. Felipe, recognizing that the lieutenant was attempting to compromise, had agreed and suggested that Tejada bring his family to San Miguel.

Tejada had been unsure of the wisdom of taking his wife and son to the Albaicín to meet Lili and her children, but to his somewhat rueful surprise, an instant sympathy had sprung up between Elena and Lili. Maya and Pepín had apparently been briefed in advance, and they were immediately kind to "our cousin Toño." Now that the meal was over, the children were racing around the square playing hide-and-seek. Lili, holding a sleeping Mariana on her lap, was carrying on a low-voiced conversation with Elena. Tejada and his cousin were chatting, and the lieutenant, in an effort to avoid discussing Doña Rosalia's death, had confided his difficulties with Alejandra. "It's not what her mother wants either," he added, defensive.

"I'm not saying you're wrong." Felipe was soothing. "But if the girl wants to get expelled she'll manage it. And you ought to have something for her to do. She doesn't have a father, you say?"

"War orphan," Tejada replied briefly.

"Well, then, with no money and no father, she's not likely to marry soon," Felipe said. "So you'll have to figure out what to do with her eventually."

"You'd want that for Maya?"

"Maya's parents can support her until she marries. And Maya will have a dowry," Felipe pointed out. He frowned. "At least, she will if I can manage it. You're sure there's no word about Mother's will, Carlito? I talked to Nando yesterday and he was downright cagey with me."

"I thought you said she'd disinherited you." Tejada avoided the question.

"I thought you said that." Felipe gave his cousin a shrewd look. "Is this something I'm not supposed to talk about?"

Tejada hesitated. Then he said, "I haven't seen her will. I'd talk to Pablo Almeida if I were you. He knows what's in it, but he's not telling the Guardia."

"And you think he'd tell me?" Felipe laughed. "Pablo doesn't approve of me, Carlito. Too much of a stuffed shirt."

"I'm afraid I can't help you," Tejada said, feeling guilty although his response has been absolutely truthful. "I'm sorry."

"It's all right."

The two men sat in companionable silence for a little while. Then Tejada said, "I went to see Don Pablo when I first came. And I ran into old Nilo."

"Who?" Felipe leaned back in his chair, his eyes on Pepín and Toño, who were chasing each other around the fountain by the side of the church.

"You must remember him—the porter, an ex-guardia, walks with a cane." It had not occurred to Tejada that other people might value Nilo less than he did. He summarized his meeting with the ex-guardia to Felipe and ended up describing their evening together. "We both liked him, didn't we?" he finished, with an appeal to his wife.

Elena looked across the table. "Who? Nilo? Yes, a nice man. A sad story about his wound."

"What happened to him?" Lili asked, and Elena recovered much of the ground Tejada had already gone over. She explained the circumstances of Nilo's injury and present employment a little more fully, and Lili clicked her tongue in sympathy.

"He's lucky Pablo bought that building before the city seized all the Rioseco properties," Felipe commented. "Any connection of the Riosecos would have been out on his ear if the government had confiscated it after that business with Miguel."

The lieutenant made an annoyed noise. "You can't fault him for his loyalty. And it's not as if he's responsible for the family. He was just one of their peasants."

"*I* know that. I'm not faulting him," Felipe said. "But you know what politics are like."

"*Their* peasants?" said Elena pointedly, at the same moment.

"Don't argue." Lili shook her head at Elena with a faint smile. "It isn't worth it."

Tejada was exasperated. "This city is impossible! You can't do business that way, stigmatizing everybody because they might be related to somebody who was a Red once upon a time!"

Felipe was still mild. "If it makes you feel any better, I don't do business that way. I bought some of the Rioseco lands that adjoined mine, and I haven't dispossessed anyone. But I know of people who *were* dispossessed, because some of them ended up asking my foreman for work. And Nando's, too, come to that."

Tejada exchanged glances with his wife, half ashamed that he suspected he agreed with her and half relieved that someone at the table understood his feelings. Life in Potes would have been impossible if everyone with blood relatives among the Reds was excluded from civil affairs, much less everyone who had at one point or another come into contact with them. Besides, he had the odd feeling that Felipe had never actually *met* any of the people he had been too kind or too sensible to throw out of their jobs and homes. "I suppose Nilo is lucky then," he said.

"Weren't the Riosecos the ones who had that cottage on the coast we stayed at when Pepín was teething?" Lili asked, tactfully turning the conversation.

"No, Ramiro just recommended the place, he didn't own it," Felipe corrected, and the discussion moved on to other things.

To Tejada's surprise, the subject of the Riosecos recurred the next day in a different context at the post. The lieutenant arranged for Alberto Cordero's transfer to the Málaga Guardia Monday morning and sent Rivas back to Doña Rosalia's house to continue searching for possible sources of poison. When the sergeant did not return by lunchtime, Tejada went home for another joyless meal with his parents. His father was present, and Tejada could not help wondering if anyone else noticed that he addressed no comments to his younger son.

Tejada ate silently and rapidly. When he was finished, he pushed back his chair, muttered an excuse, and fled back to the post, leaving his plate lying abandoned on the dining-room table. Sergeant Rivas had not yet returned. Tejada settled himself in the office to wait and spent an inordinate amount of time worrying about what to do about Alejandra. The sergeant finally arrived a little before five, looking relaxed, and greeted his superior officer with the utmost good humor.

"I'm glad you had a good day, Rivas," Tejada said. "Would you like to share your progress?"

Rivas sensed that the lieutenant was in a bad mood and added apologetically, "I'm sorry I took so long, sir. But I ended up staying at the Casa Ordoñez until lunchtime, what with one thing and another, and then Luisa—Luisa Cabrera, the cook's assistant—offered me lunch, and Fulgencio's always been a good cook, so I stayed, and I think I found out something interesting, sir."

"Oh, yes?" Tejada was neutral. The sergeant might have found something interesting, or he might be covering for his own laziness.

"I had a bit of a chat with Luisa," Rivas explained. "And it seems Doña Rosalia bought some land in the Alpujarra a few years back."

"I know," Tejada nodded, and then two pieces of information connected in his brain and he added, "It's not anywhere near Suspiro del Moro, where the bandits took over, is it?"

"No, sir. It's just outside Órgiva. It's a little place called Tíjalo. The point is, she bought it from Ramiro Rioseco, when the family went abroad."

"I'm not following you," Tejada said, skeptical.

"I remember the Rioseco case a bit," Rivas explained. "It got some publicity and, of course, we went carefully, because they were a prominent family. The original denunciation against Miguel Rioseco was lodged by Doña Rosalia's husband."

Tejada went still. "Had he wanted to buy the land earlier?"

"We have no record of that. But the fact is he denounced the Rioseco boy, and his widow—your aunt—bought a parcel of their land."

And Felipe bought another parcel, Tejada thought but did not say aloud. *And Fernando is trying to merge with Rioseco's old partner.* "Did any of the family stay in Granada?" he asked.

"A couple of the married daughters, I think. It might be worth checking out, sir. Especially in light of Doña Rosalia's . . . worries about Reds."

Tejada snorted. "You think she worried because she had a guilty conscience?"

"Oh, no, sir." Rivas was shocked. "After all, if the Rioseco boy was lukewarm to the Regime, her husband did the only thing he could have done."

Tejada could not tell if Rivas was genuinely certain of Miguel Rioseco's guilt, unwilling to admit that the Guardia had made a mistake, or gently pulling his leg. He decided it was not important. Something that the sergeant had said nagged at him. He tried to think what it was. "This land in the Alpujarra," he said slowly. "Was Rioseco using it for sugarcane?"

"I don't know." Rivas was puzzled by the lieutenant's question. "I'd guess not. Doña Rosalia didn't, and there aren't refineries nearby."

"Have you ever visited this place Tíjalo?" Tejada asked, certain that there was something about the land or the location that was important. Something Felipe had said, perhaps, about the tenants of the Reds being dispossessed? But if Felipe and Nando had not blacklisted the former dependents of the Riosecos, there was no reason their mother should have done so.

"No, sir." The sergeant frowned and then added, "If you think it's important, sir, I'll check the records and see if any of the men come from that area."

"I can't think why it would be," Tejada admitted, and let the half-formed association vanish. "But it might be worth finding out which of the Rioseco family connections are still in Granada."

Rivas nodded. "Of course, the daughters who stayed were married to respectable people," he said. "I don't think they'd be involved with murdering the poor lady for revenge. But Miguel Rioseco was in with a bunch of hotheads, and perhaps one of them—"

"It's possible," Tejada agreed. "The only question is why *now*? After all, Rioseco disappeared in '36, right? And the family went abroad . . . when?"

"Not until after the war," Rivas said quickly. "The fall of '39. It took some time for them to sell off their lands."

"Then why would someone wait all this time, until the man who had lodged the accusation against Miguel Rioseco was dead, for vengeance?" Tejada wondered. "Doña Rosalia retired from the world after her husband died. She would have been much harder to reach now than in '39. Why wait so long?"

"Maybe it was someone who'd just found out she had bene-fited from the denunciation." Rivas liked his theory and was unwilling to give it up. "Or maybe they found out she'd changed her will and were hoping to throw suspicion on her own family to mislead us."

Once again, Tejada had the feeling that he was overlooking something, coupled with an unpleasant suspicion that he would dislike whatever pattern finally emerged. "I suppose anything's possible," he said. "Why don't you check out friends of Miguel Rioseco's. If you get me a list I can interview them tomorrow."

"Yes, sir." Rivas was approving. "And we can make a list of the Riosecos' dependents as well."

Tejada hovered in the office for a little while longer, looking for something to do, uneasily aware that he was in Rivas's way. Finally, when the sergeant began to work on patrol duties utter-ly unrelated to the Ordoñez case, the lieutenant reluctantly excused himself and returned to his parents' home. He found his mother sitting with Amparo Villalobos. Both women greeted him warmly, and Doña Consuela informed him that "dear Amparo" had been waiting, hoping to see him. "Or your wife, of course," Amparo added tactfully. "It was such a pleasure to meet her the other day."

"I'm sure she's sorry to miss you," Tejada lied. He had been about to ask where Elena was, but he was unwilling to give his mother further ammunition against her. He was tired and dis-couraged, and the only thing he wanted to do was find Elena and lean back in a comfy chair and tell her about his day, but he resigned himself to socializing for a little longer.

His mother and Amparo made polite conversation and the lieutenant answered, feeling surly and gauche as he had felt long ago, before joining the Guardia. At twenty-one, one of the

Guardia's attractions for him was that its members were not called on to make conversation with young ladies. After a few minutes, Doña Consuela rose. "I'm sorry, dear. I have to talk to Isaura about the supper. You won't mind staying here with Carlos for a few minutes, will you?"

Amparo assured her hostess that she would be happy to converse with Carlos, leaving him no opportunity to say that he, too, had urgent business elsewhere. After Doña Consuela left them, a little silence fell. Amparo smiled timidly at the lieutenant. Tejada remembered what his wife had said about her batting her eyelashes. Covertly inspecting Amparo now, he decided that Elena was imagining things. There was no way that a girl as beautiful as Amparo, with one of the largest dowries in the city, was going to waste her time flirting with a married Guardia. The girl coughed and then said, blushing a little, "Have you made any progress? About Doña Rosalia?"

"We have several leads," Tejada replied automatically.

"I think it's wonderful of you to come and help us," Amparo offered.

"I couldn't do less," Tejada replied with perfect truth. "And I don't know how helpful I've been so far."

"Oh, just knowing someone's *here* and in charge is reassuring," Amparo said quickly. "Not that I don't think Sergeant Rivas is doing a wonderful job, but . . ."

Tejada was annoyed. He liked Rivas, and he understood that Amparo was patronizing him. "I tend to agree with the Guardia's policy of having officers serve far from their homes," he told her.

She spoke hastily, knowing she had offended him. "I meant—well, someone so competent. Jaime spoke of you, did you know? He admired you so much."

Tejada, whose recollection of his last meeting with his cousin Jaime involved an acrimonious political debate about the monarchy, kept silent. Amparo smiled as if at a tender memory. "I know he fought with you and probably said all kinds of awful things when you argued, but he always said to me that at least you were sincere. And that you had the courage to follow your convictions and try to do something real. And I"— she hesitated and her voice caught—"I find sincerity and courage comforting at the moment."

The lieutenant's annoyance faded. If what Amparo said was true, Jaime Ordoñez had paid him perhaps the only compliment worth having and certainly the only plausible one a Carlist would ever give a member of the Falange. "I'm glad he thought I was sincere," he said. Then, afraid he appeared ungracious, he added, "I'm honored by your trust. I'll do the best I can."

"I'm sure you'll succeed" Amparo said softly. "You've done so well so far." She met his eyes and Tejada saw that her own were filled with tears.

"Are you all right?"

"Oh—yes." She blinked them away, impatient. "It's just . . . you're so like Jaime. Jaime as he would have been, if he'd lived. And it's so *maddening* to think of a life wasted that way."

Tejada was embarrassed by her grief. He turned rapidly to the doorway as he caught a flicker of movement in his peripheral vision. "Toño!" he exclaimed with relief. "What are you doing here?"

Thus hailed, Toño entered. "Mama's talking to Carmen," he explained. "And I was bored." He eyed Amparo. "But you're busy, too."

"Oh, no," Tejada denied hastily. "Come and meet Doña Amparo. She's your—well, nearly your cousin by marriage."

Amparo wiped her eyes and received Toño with the hungry politeness of a woman denied children. Toño submitted with his usual good grace to being hugged, kissed, asked how old he was, and having his size and beauty exclaimed over. Doña Amparo did not ask interesting questions, but Toño had found that most adults did not. It puzzled him that she seemed sad when she said, "I wish I had a little boy like you at home!" Usually ladies laughed when they said that to him.

Tejada watched Amparo play with Toño with proud fondness. It was obvious how much she liked the boy, and he found himself more and more in sympathy with her. When he thought of her tragic loss, his good will was tinged with pity. He remembered that even Felipe Ordoñez had said that Amparo had played no part in her family's schemes, and decided that Elena's reaction to the girl must have been a remnant of her ridiculous inverted snobbery. Or perhaps just one of those strange instant dislikes that sprang up between women for no good reason. He agreed readily when she looked up at him and said wistfully, "You will bring Carlos Antonio to come and visit me soon, won't you?"

When she had received his promise of a visit, she made her farewells, kissing Toño good-bye and leaving in a flurry of silk and perfume. Tejada turned to his son, ready to amuse him. "Well, what did you think of Doña Amparo?"

Because the lady was Papa's friend, Toño made a conscientious effort to be pleasant. "She smelled nice."

The lieutenant laughed. Toño's observation was accurate. Amparo carried with her the scent of a *carmen*, filled with sweet flowering trees and fountains. "She did," he agreed. "Do you think we should try to buy a bottle of her perfume for Mama for a Christmas present?"

"No!" Toño was shocked and definite.

"Why not?"

"Because then she wouldn't smell like Mama," Toño said. Surely Papa did not want Mama drenched in a sickly sweet odor that would block out all the other good home smells of soap and pines and wood smoke.

"I suppose you're right," his father admitted. Elena seldom wore perfume. It would have been silly to wear it at home, and there were no theaters or casinos in Potes. Perhaps a small vial accompanied by a promise of another trip to Santander, or even Madrid, would make her happy. "What kind of scent would smell like Mama then?" he asked.

Toño considered. "Apples," he said at last.

"Apple blossom, you mean?"

"Apples or apple blossom." The little boy was judicious. "Mama likes apples. And she doesn't like almond cakes."

"I know," Tejada said with a smile. "Why should she?"

"Doña Amparo smelled like almonds," Toño said logically.

Tejada blinked. *Almond trees!* he thought. *And Amparo keeps asking about the case. And if she always smells of almonds, no one would think to notice it if*—He dismissed the thought instantly. "Come on, Toño. Let's go see if your cousin is using his ball," he said, laughing at himself for his vague suspicions. But he abandoned the idea of buying perfume for Elena.

Tejada did not see his wife again until the family gathered for dinner. She smiled at him but was quiet throughout the meal, speaking only in an undertone to Toño and silently bowing her head in response to Doña Consuela's glittering hostility. Juan Andrés Tejada and his wife spoke only to each other and their children, and Tejada's father was once more absent, dining with friends at the casino. The lieutenant occasionally joined in his mother's conversation with his wife, but neither woman welcomed his contribution to their covert war of wills, so he ended up speaking little. He was not particularly bothered by his own silence. He could not remember ever having much to say for himself at family gatherings and at university, and later, in the Guardia's barracks, he had gained the reputation of being friendly but not sociable. Active conversation while eating was a tradition in his wife's family and he had adapted to it readily, but now he was more troubled by Elena's unnatural stillness than his own. He disliked seeing her unhappy.

Elena did not linger after eating, but rose and bore Toño away.

Tejada was just moving to follow her when Isaura entered. Doña Consuela turned on her. "What is it, girl? No one called for you."

"I beg your pardon, Señora. But there's a message for Señorito Carlos. From the post. I thought it might be important."

"Thanks." Tejada was already moving toward the door as he spoke.

His brother's voice detained him. "Is this a written message, Isaura?"

"Yes, Señorito."

"Then I suggest you give it to Señorito Carlos here, so that he can have coffee with us." There was a faint edge in Juan Andrés's voice. Isaura curtsied and withdrew.

"I wasn't really planning to have coffee."

"A drink then," Juan Andrés insisted, glaring at his younger brother. As Isaura opened the door a second time, bearing a sealed letter, he added sharply, "Sit down, *hermanito*."

Tejada sat and looked at the envelope. It was from Corporal Méndez. He slid a thumb under the flap and was once more forestalled by his brother. "I've been meaning to ask your advice about the land in the Vega," Juan Andrés said, switching seats to sit closer to his brother and proceeding to embark on a monologue that summarized the expenses and profits of the Tejadas' major holdings in mind-numbing detail. The lieutenant would have let his mind wander, but every time his older brother caught him glancing longingly at the letter from Méndez he would slip in a question that demanded a reply.

Juan Andrés's wife and children murmured their excuses and left the table within a few minutes. Doña Consuela was made of sterner stuff. She maintained her seat and watched her sons with an eagle eye until Juan Andrés said, "Actually, we should really check the accounts. They're in Papa's study, I think. Come on, Carlos."

The lieutenant allowed his older brother to steer him out of the room and turned toward his father's study with the usual sinking sensation in his stomach. Juan Andrés continued talking until they were safely in the study with the door closed behind them and then said, "All right, Carlito, give. What's happening between you and Papa?"

Tejada was startled. He had some affection for his brother, but he had always assumed that Juan Andrés was a basically self-centered individual. It had not occurred to him that Juan would sense the trouble between him and his father. "Nothing," he said. "What do you mean?"

"You haven't said a word to each other for the past three days," Juan Andrés retorted. "And he's been eating out every evening to avoid you. What have you done to him?"

"I haven't done anything," Tejada snapped, annoyed. "Why shouldn't he spend the evening with friends? He doesn't need to dance attendance on me like a guest. I'm family, too, you know."

"Well, you could start acting like it then!" Juan Andrés said. "You spend all your days at the post, and on the week-end you and Elena disappear for hours together. You even arrange to have mail delivered to you after dinner so you can slip out!" Tejada began an angry retort but his brother cut him off. "I don't know what you said to Papa, but he's been looking sick lately. You upset Mother, you treat Papa and me like objects of your investigation and the house like it's a damn hotel, and then you have the nerve to claim your rights as a family member!"

"I'm here to conduct an investigation," Tejada reminded his brother. "I have to spend most of my time at the post. And I certainly don't 'arrange' to have letters delivered. My job doesn't have fixed hours." With a stab of bitterness, he added, "We can't all be gentlemen of leisure, like you."

"Oh, don't pull that crap on me, Carlito!" His brother was impatient. "You *chose* the Guardia and damn near broke Mother's heart doing it. The martyr's role doesn't work for someone who picked it like a spoiled brat."

Tejada's nostrils flared. His brother's words were too near the truth to debate. "I'm sorry I haven't been living up to your standards," he said quietly. "I'll try to be nicer to Father, if you think I haven't been."

Juan Andrés nodded, satisfied. "Good. Try hard." Seeing his brother's still face, he punched him lightly in the shoulder and added, "Come on, *hermanito*. I'm just looking out for you. For Papa, too. You're both too stiff-necked."

Tejada forced himself to nod and smile. "Thanks, Juan. I— I'm going to go check on Toño."

Tejada found the door to Toño's bedroom closed. No light seeped out under it. He opened the door carefully and peered into the darkness. After a few moments, he made out steady breathing. The boy was already asleep. Tejada closed the door softly, wondering with aching sadness if Toño would grow up to avoid his company and think of him with contempt.

The door to his own bedroom was also closed, but the light was on. Elena was sitting up in bed, reading. She put the book aside and smiled at him. "How are you?"

"Tired."

"Long day?"

"Just a lot of stupidities." He recounted the scene with his brother and felt his own suppressed anger lessened and diluted by her indignation. By an association of ideas too nebulous even for him to understand, he proceeded to a summary of his day: the departure of Alberto Cordero, Sergeant Rivas's prolonged absence at the Casa Ordoñez, and the possible motives of the Riosecos. Elena asked questions, exclaimed, shared his unease and amusement. Even her quiet sympathy for Alberto Cordero was a relief. It was an echo of the faintly aggrieved disapproval that hung over him after every successful operation in Potes, when farmers and storekeepers eyed him balefully, knowing that he was only doing his job, but still blaming him for the loss of sons, fathers, and brothers. It tasted like home.

As usual, Tejada was unable to articulate his gratitude to his wife. But it was with a special pleasure that he pulled the half-opened letter Isaura had delivered to him from his pocket. "Corporal Méndez sent me this just after you left," he said. "It looks like he's found some information about your friend."

Elena was grateful but she felt a knot in her throat. Her husband was holding out the envelope but she was afraid to take it. "Could you read it?"

Tejada raised his eyebrows at her. "You wanted to know."

"Baldo wanted to."

The lieutenant put an arm around her shoulders and squeezed gently. "If Méndez has bad news, will you tell him?"

Elena closed her eyes. "Yes. I've promised to. And not knowing . . ."

The lieutenant nodded without speaking and opened the envelope. There were several papers folded together. He riffled through them and saw that two appeared to be copies of bank statements. The third was a cover letter. He scanned it and felt a sudden bubble of lightness in his chest. Elena heard his sharp indrawn breath. "Well?"

Tejada read aloud, not trusting himself to paraphrase.

> Esteban Beltrán Monteroso escaped from a transport to Viznar on August 2, 1936, along with two others when a flat tire was being changed. He was presumed to be in the mountains with the bandits. There are no arrest or transfer records available for Cristina Encinas Rosado.
>
> However, three weeks ago, Félix Encinas Rosado's account received a wire transfer of five hundred pesetas from Credit Lyonnais (see first attachment). Five hundred pesetas were also transferred to the account of Dr. Beltrán's mother, M. Mercedes Monteroso, from the same Credit Lyonnais account

(see second attachment). Said account is held jointly by a
married couple M. and Mme. Montrose. This seems like an
obvious French form of Dr. Beltrán's second surname and in
light of the suspects' former association . . .

"Thank you, thank you, Carlos!" Tejada got no further with
his reading. Elena sprang at him, laughing and crying at once.
He closed his arms around her, savoring her joy. It was rare
enough that his job brought tears of happiness.

"Take it easy," he commanded, smiling. "Baldo's parents must
already know where the money came from. If they haven't told
him yet, there's a reason."

"I suppose," Elena admitted. "But still, I'll speak to them
tomorrow. I have to. Oh, Carlos, thank you."

"It's nothing." Tejada was seized with a sudden burst of artic-
ulateness. "I like to make you happy. Because it makes me
happy."

And that was the key to much of his life, he thought a little
later after they had turned out the lights. He had married her
because he had felt an almost unbearable urge to protect her
and would have cheerfully killed or died to make sure that she
was safe and happy. And her happiness was still the key to his
own. Staying in Granada had been difficult so far partly because
she had been so miserable.

It occurred to him that he had asked nothing about her day
and that she had volunteered nothing. They had been talking
about other things. He wondered uncomfortably if he was really still the one who protected her or if sometime during their
marriage their roles had become reversed and she had become
the guardian of what might loosely have been called his soul or
perhaps simply his sanity. It was a disturbing revelation, and he
comforted himself that in times of *real* danger he was still the
strong one.

As if to offer confirmation of his shaky self-sufficiency, his memory sweetly offered the name of the little place near Órgiva that Sergeant Rivas had mentioned: Tíjalo. And then suddenly he remembered the name of another little place near Órgiva and why it was significant, and the dual memory had the force of simultaneous thunder and lightning. He shivered and clung to Elena, once more dependent on her half-acknowledged strength. Sleep was a long time in coming.

Chapter 19

Tejada woke the next morning with a stuffy nose and an ache in his throat that he hoped was an infection but suspected was only unresolved sadness. He was gentle and deferential to his father at breakfast, so much so that Elena looked at him with concern and questioned him with her eyes. He avoided her gaze, unwilling to drag her down into the murky depression that had enveloped him.

Elena wondered how late he had fallen asleep the night before. She was worried when he refused to meet her eyes, and her worry grew into outright alarm when he said softly to his father, "I'd like to go over to the post now if it's all right with you. I think we're close to an arrest of Aunt Rosalia's murderer. Perhaps I'll be able to make an entire report to you this afternoon."

"Really?" Andrés Tejada's tone was one shade short of disbelief. "That's good news. Who did it?"

Tejada swallowed. "I'm not sure yet. That is, I think I know, but I don't have proof, and I don't want to lay blame until I'm positive."

"This afternoon then." His father spoke with such good grace that Tejada wondered if Juan Andrés had taken him aside as well.

"Thank you." The lieutenant's voice was barely above a whisper.

On other days he had gulped his coffee with barely decent haste and hurried away to the post, determined to escape, but today Elena thought he dawdled. He expressed interest in his mother's plans for the day and complimented his sister-in-law on her earrings. He asked his brother about land in the Vega and devoted his entire attention to the response. The lieutenant's nephews and niece had left for school, and his father and brother had departed for work before Tejada finally pushed back his chair, kissed his mother and his wife, and headed for the post.

He walked slowly, and the careful serenity he had cultivated for his family blew away in the morning wind. He stopped in the Plaza Bib-Rambla and looked at the *churrería* next to Pablo Almeida's office. He could stop there and have a coffee before going to the post. Or stop and talk to Nilo once more informally, for old times' sake. He sighed. Any delay would only make his errand more difficult. But still, Tejada stared at the doorway to Pablo Almeida's offices for a long time without moving. Finally he rang the bell. Nilo greeted him with a salute and a broad smile. "Come in! Come in! How are you? Are you here to see Don Pablo?"

As soon as the old man spoke, Tejada regretted stopping. It would have been better to go on to the post. Better to have spoken to Sergeant Rivas. But it was too late now. "No." Years of experience kept his voice even. "I'm here to see you."

"Really? Again?" Nilo still smiled, but he was a little confused by the grim note in the lieutenant's voice. "That's kind of you. I'm afraid I can't offer you more than a chair. . . ."

He gestured to a wooden seat by the stairs. Tejada ignored the gesture. "I wanted to confirm a few things with you. Jesús del Rioseco found you a place here, is that correct?"

"Yes, sir, that's 'correct.'" For a moment, Nilo mimicked Tejada's formal tone. Then he smiled. "Don't forget how to speak *andaluz* way up north, son."

Tejada paid no attention to the old man's digression. "Your family were tenants of the Riosecos, and you yourself were stationed in Órgiva, correct?"

"Right." Nilo looked uncertain now. "Why? What's the matter?"

"Near Tíjalo?"

"That's right." Nilo was surprised. "I didn't know you knew the area." He shifted on his cane, wishing that he could sit down but unwilling to be impolite, although the lieutenant showed no sign of taking the empty chair.

"Who bought the Rioseco land there when the family went to Cuba?" Tejada rapped out.

The old man shrugged. "I don't know. I haven't been back since I was wounded. And my girls aren't there either, so I don't get much news."

"You knew the Rioseco family had left the country though?"

"Yes." Nilo was somber.

Tejada took a deep breath. "Why did they leave?"

Nilo shook his head as if to clear it, his eyes on the younger man's face. "It's all ancient history," he said gently. "Don Jesús was a fine man and Don Ramiro as well. He just had some bad luck."

"What kind of bad luck?" the lieutenant pressed.

Nilo closed his eyes for a moment. "Don Ramiro lost his oldest boy during the war," he said finally. "They say it broke his heart."

"Not in combat." Tejada's voice was harsh.

"No." Nilo sighed. "I know you wore a blue shirt before it was fashionable. But not everybody did you know, son. Miguel del Rioseco—"

"Was a Red," Tejada finished brutally.

Nilo shook his head. "He wasn't anything. He was just a kid, barely out of university. They say he wanted to be a professor, but his father wouldn't let him. He—" The old man became aware of Tejada's scrutiny and broke off. "He wasn't even arrested by the Guardia," he finished, his voice shaking. "It was one of the militias. His mother said he recognized two of them."

"How do you know what his mother said?"

"Because his father came to me to ask if I still knew anyone in the Guardia." Nilo reached for the chair and then lowered himself into it, sounding very tired. "It was a bit like that revolution the Falange was always talking about. The head of the Riosecos coming to ask an old man like me for help."

"You felt sorry for him." Tejada respected Nilo's need to sit, but regretted that he had not taken the chair earlier when it was offered. He, too, was tired. The ex-guardia nodded without speaking and Tejada continued. "The Riosecos had done everything for you. And you watched them lose everything they had because of an accusation brought by a man whose family bought the land they'd owned in Tíjalo." He saw Nilo's eyes widen and guessed that the old man had known who had lodged the denunciation. "Doña Rosalia chatted with you about her will," the lieutenant continued, his voice relentless, although he was avoiding Nilo's eyes now. "She must have told you about purchasing lands in the Alpujarra. Lands bought cheaply, because the owners were desperate to sell. You saw her every time she came to change her will; a bitter, cranky, obnoxious old woman who'd gained from the Riosecos' loss. You must have hated her."

"No," Nilo said softly. "The poor lady wasn't right in her mind after her husband died. I didn't hate her." He waited to see if the lieutenant was going to respond and then stretched out one hand, not quite touching Tejada's elbow. "Why are you raking up the past, kid?"

If his voice had been less gentle, Tejada would not have been angry. But the old man spoke as he would speak to a frightened child, not to a colleague—*and a superior officer!*—Tejada thought, indignant. "My aunt was poisoned," he said sharply. "You have a good motive. And you questioned me about the case even before we had established a cause of death. You're a suspect."

The lieutenant met Nilo's eyes squarely as he spoke to show that he had no compunction about making such an accusation. So he was able to see the dawning horror on the old man's face;

he remembered the expression for the rest of his life. "Well?" he demanded sharply. "Aren't you going to deny it?"

Nilo said nothing. He merely looked at Tejada with wide rheumy eyes. The lieutenant saw that he was trembling and did not know if it was from fear or anger or merely old age. "I wanted to speak to you privately," he said, wishing that Nilo would say something. "Sergeant Rivas is drawing up lists of the Riosecos' dependents, and I wanted to talk to you before he did."

"Thank you, Señorito. That's kind of you." Nilo's voice was barely above a whisper. "But Sergeant Rivas knows me."

"You had no way of tampering with her food," Tejada said, with the vague feeling that he was carrying both sides of the argument. "And, of course, you were a guardia. That speaks in your favor. But I wanted to be the one to tell you."

"Sergeant Rivas knows me," Nilo repeated.

"Oh, well, then. . . ." Tejada felt vaguely ridiculous. It would have been so much better if Nilo had been offended or angry or disbelieving or even frightened. *Anything* rather than hurt. "I'll try to come back to say hello if I can."

He raised his hand in a wave, and Nilo gestured vaguely in reply. "You're always welcome, Señorito."

Tejada left the Plaza Bib-Rambla shaking with a fury that even he knew was irrational. It wouldn't have been so bad if Nilo had only been *angry*. Maybe he was just a very calculating murderer who knew that as a former member of the Guardia, with no evidence to link him to Doña Rosalia's house, he was unlikely to be prosecuted. Tejada clung hopefully to the thought that perhaps Nilo really was a murderer until he reached the post.

Rivas, who had been at work for some while already, greeted him cheerfully. "Here's the information on the Rioseco girls," he said, holding out a folder to the lieutenant without bothering to rise from his desk. "And here's a list of Miguel del Rioseco's friends, those who are still around and not active members of the Movement."

Tejada took the second folder automatically. "What about the family's dependents?" he asked hollowly.

"Bit harder, but we're working on it. I want the list to be comprehensive," the sergeant explained.

Tejada took the only free seat in the office. "I can add one," he said quietly. "An old man from the Alpujarra. He owed the Riosecos everything and made no secret of it. And he knew Doña Rosalia and knew the terms of her will. He knew she'd changed it to disinherit her children, which might give . . . someone else a good motive for her death. And odds are he'd know enough about poisons to manage to obtain cyanide."

"Great!" The sergeant was enthusiastic. "Could he have slipped cyanide to her somehow?"

"Probably not without the cooperation of someone in her household," Tejada admitted. "But I don't think that would have been impossible, do you?"

"No. Whoever did it would have used one of them," Rivas agreed. "Likely Alberto, since he could be blackmailed. So, who's our suspect?"

Tejada's lack of sleep was catching up with him. He rubbed his eyes with the heels of his hands. "His name is Nilo Fuentes. He's the porter at the Plaza Bib-Rambla, Number Five."

"*Nilo*? Nilo Fuentes?" Rivas was incredulous. "Not Nilo the cripple?"

"That's the one."

"B-but—" The sergeant frowned, searching for a way to remind Tejada of the obvious. "Nilo's a *guardia*, sir. He couldn't—"

"He was stationed in Órgiva until he was wounded," Tejada interrupted. "Jesús del Rioseco found him work. He knew the family well. *And* knew that Rosalia de Ordoñez had bought up their land in the Alpujarra and had just changed her will."

"I know where Nilo was stationed," Rivas protested. "But, sir, he spent nearly twenty years in the Guardia. He had an exemplary record. He—"

"Had means and motive," Tejada finished.

"Nilo Fuentes is a *guardia*," Rivas repeated, inarticulate.

Tejada met the sergeant's eyes and read dislike and contempt and bewildered hurt there. He thought of his father saying, "How dare *you* accuse me of murder?" and of his older brother saying, "You have the nerve to claim your rights as a family *member?*" He thought of an old commanding officer in Madrid saying to him with exasperation, "The man's an officer, Tejada. I can't go around making accusations like that against him." He thought about Nilo Fuentes telling him he had done well for himself. "I'm a guardia, too," he said. "And I told you to pull my file for investigation also."

"I know, but—" Rivas made a last desperate attempt. "Well, that was a formality, sir, wasn't it? And Old Nilo—he's not like you, sir. He's never been anything *but* a guardia. It was his whole life."

Tejada had the odd feeling that this was a variant on an old conversation. A *real* guardia was incapable of murder. A *real* member of the family was incapable of murder. He wondered for an insane instant if somewhere in the mountain cottages where the maquis' contacts lived, an indignant peasant had ever told the story of a family member's arrest, exclaiming that a *real* Red didn't commit murder, and if a wild-eyed bearded anarchist with a machine gun had ever felt an urge to throw back his head and howl at the moon when he heard the words. "I've already spoken to him," he said. "He denies everything. But add him to the list and keep in mind we're dealing with someone clever who knows the Guardia's procedures.

"At your orders, Lieutenant. If you'll excuse me." Rivas saluted stiffly and left. Tejada propped his forehead on his hands and sat motionless in the silent office and wondered if Nilo would ever believe how sorry he was. He wondered where Rivas had gone. Doubtless he had to attend to lots of other business. Or perhaps he had gone to speak to Nilo, to tell the old man that a crazy señorito who thought he was a guardia had accused him of murder.

Rivas returned half an hour later and handed him a list of the Riosecos' former employees and servants. The list was long and the annotations brief. Nilo Fuentes's name had been added in at the bottom by hand. The sergeant had followed orders punctiliously. "Would you wish to investigate these personally, Lieutenant? Or should I detail men to do it?" Rivas was cold and formal.

Tejada stared at the typewritten list and the names swam before his eyes. *Damn Medina to hell,* he thought. *Why did he have to drag me down here? I don't know any of these people. I'm supposed to be on leave.* "I doubt I could efficiently question all of them," he said. "Why not divide up the list and send a couple of pairs of men to interview them?"

"At your orders, Lieutenant."

Tejada pushed himself to his feet, disgusted with the sergeant, with Granada, and with himself. "You don't need me for this, Sergeant," he said dryly. "An arrest of any of these people would not be likely to upset my family. Why don't I just get out of your way for the day?"

"You've been very helpful, sir." Rivas was contrite now. "And you're right about Nilo Fuentes. I was just a bit surprised, but you're right; he has a motive. We'll question him."

"I don't think he's guilty," Tejada said, not at all sure if he was telling the truth. *I hope he's not,* he thought. *God, I hope he's not. And if he's not, I'd give anything to have everything I said to him this morning unsaid.* He excused himself in spite of Rivas's guilt-ridden politeness and left the post.

What's wrong with me? he thought, emerging into the sunlight. *I've jumped to too many conclusions in this case. I'm flailing around blindly and with each new hunch I think I've uncovered a plot.* Even the thought of returning to Potes within the week depressed him. He did not want to go home with the case unsolved and his

father's angry contempt hanging over him. The idea of returning to his parents' house empty handed after his boast to his
father depressed him, but he had excused himself from Rivas's
presence too firmly to return to work.

He stood watching the pigeons perched on the statue in the
Plaza de la Universidad and wondered where Elena and Toño
were and what they were doing. Elena, he thought, had actually
believed that his father was happy to see him. She had naively
believed that her father-in-law was interested in finding his aunt's
killer, rather then engaged in concealing a missing will. That sort
of innocence was typical of her. The sort of idealism bordering
on idiocy that had made her a Red. Tejada stopped, ashamed of
his anger at his wife. He had married her of his own free will,
knowing that she was a Red. It would have been simpler, perhaps, to marry a girl approved by his parents, but he had chosen
Elena, and it was wrong to lament his choice. Still, for a moment,
he imagined what it would be like to marry someone like
Amparo Villalobos. It would not have been so bad. Amparo was
pretty, gentle, submissive . . . *rich*, said a cynical voice in his head.
Not the girl to take well to life at a rural post. He pictured Amparo in
the Monday market in Potes, weaving her way among the cattle
driven down from the mountains and bargaining with hardheaded Cantabrian peasants. The vision would have been horri-
fying if it had not been so irresistibly funny.

Not that Amparo had never dealt with peasants, the lieutenant reminded himself, in fairness. She took an active part in
running her father's household, and she was interested in the
orphanage and all sorts of other charities. And she was not
unintelligent. It occurred to the lieutenant that Amparo was the
one person he knew who was closely connected to both the
Ordoñez and Rioseco families. She might well know other people who had been acquainted with both. He thought for a
moment and then turned and walked back toward the post and
the Calle Tablas. He did not want to see his father or Rivas.

Señorita Villalobos might be a useful person to interview instead.

He was a little uncertain of his reception at the Villaloboses' townhouse, but he was in luck. Amparo was at home and willing to see him alone. She asked after his family with her usual grace and was politely sorry that Elena and Toño had been unable to accompany him. She smiled when he explained that he had come from the post. "You've been working too hard," she remarked. "You only have a little time here. You ought to spend some of it with your family."

"I've had enough chance to catch up," Tejada said, thinking that his father and brother would probably be more than happy to see the back of him.

"With your parents, perhaps. But I know Fernando and Bernarda are sorry they haven't seen more of you. And I'm sure Felipe would like to see you as well."

"Felipe and I have talked," Tejada answered, thinking ruefully that Felipe might be the one family member who was not actively angry with him at the moment and knowing that Felipe's goodwill would probably not survive an investigation by Sergeant Rivas.

"How is he?" Amparo frowned gently. "I've seen almost nothing of him since his mother's wake. He looked terrible then, poor man."

"He seems to be bearing up," Tejada said vaguely, wondering involuntarily if Felipe's distressing appearance at his mother's funeral had been due to a guilty conscience.

"Poor Felipe," Amparo sighed. "I always think of him laughing, and then to see him like that . . . he was devastated. You know, for all his frivolous ways, I think he was devoted to his mother. And now that she's gone . . . it wouldn't surprise me if he settled down and got married."

Tejada reflected with amusement that Amparo's instincts about Felipe's conduct were sound, although her guess as to his motivation was faulty. "I think it's very likely," he agreed gravely.

"I wonder whom he'll pick?" Amparo smiled. "I remember all the girls being wild about him in my young days. I imagine he'll be a great catch."

Tejada thought of Lili and was unable to keep a straight face. "I'm sorry," he apologized when he was once more appropriately sober. "It was you referring to your 'young days' like that, as if you were an old matron."

Amparo looked down, coloring a little. "Thank you, Carlos. I do forget sometimes that . . . that other girls think of time differently. I meant before I met Jaime. Do you know," her color deepened, "I was half in love with Felipe myself when I was a girl."

Blushing, her long lashes shading her cheeks, she was very beautiful. The scent of almonds hung around her like a floating veil and reminded the lieutenant of his son's comment. Remembering Toño, he also remembered Elena and unwillingly heard an acid voice that sounded like his wife's saying, *Jaime's inheritance must have been bigger than Felipe's. But she'll take what she can get, now that Jaime's gone.* "I'm sure his family would be happy if he brought someone like you home," he said, and then regretted the comment. He had been thinking of Bernarda and Fernando when he spoke, but as he said the word *family,* he remembered the last time he had seen Felipe and felt guilty, as if the gentle compliment was a betrayal of Lili and her children.

"That's kind of you, Carlos." Amparo met his eyes, openly flattered. "I've sometimes thought we could be . . . companionable. Of course, Jaime was the only man I could ever love but Felipe's not young anymore. He needs someone to take care of him."

"Was that why you stayed in contact with his mother?" Tejada asked bluntly.

"Partly," Amparo admitted. "Of course, it was mostly as a favor to Bernarda, but both she and Doña Rosalia . . . well, they spoke of Felipe sometimes. They worried about him."

Embarrassed, the lieutenant looked for a way to turn the discussion. No graceful way presented itself. "I'm afraid we haven't made much progress toward finding Doña Rosalia's killer," he said apologetically. "But I wondered if perhaps you could help me."

"Of course. Anything I can do."

"I imagine you must have known your father's partners?"

Amparo looked blank. "My father doesn't have partners."

"His former partners, I should say," Tejada corrected himself. "Ramiro del Rioseco and his family."

"Yes. I met Don Ramiro a few times." Amparo was composed but guarded.

"And his children?" Tejada asked hopefully.

"Really, we weren't social acquaintances," Amparo explained with a hint of apology in her tone. "My father invited Don Ramiro to the house a few times, but I didn't know his family well. I don't believe his sons took much interest in the business. And his daughters were all older than I."

She lied well, gracefully and without self-consciousness. But her words were clearly nonsense. The firm of Villalobos and Rioseco had been venerable in the lieutenant's childhood. The two families were tied together by generations of shared business transactions and a few intermarriages. Tejada wondered why she bothered to deny what was common knowledge in all of Granada. Unless no one admitted to knowing the Riosecos anymore. He remembered Felipe saying, "I'm not going to lie and pretend I never knew him." But Felipe had always been unconventional. "I heard Miguel del Rioseco got into trouble a few years back," he said experimentally.

Amparo pursed her lips. "Yes. Poor Miguel was always foolish. Led around by the nose by all sorts of people."

Tejada blinked. His own opinion was not substantially different, but it was odd to hear it articulated in such a soft voice by a delicately pretty girl. She was startlingly hard underneath her fragile femininity. *Elena wouldn't say something like that*, he thought, disapproving. "Did you know any of his friends?" he asked aloud. "Anyone who was upset at his death."

The girl raised her chin. "*I* didn't know people like that."

"I'm sorry," the lieutenant apologized. "I meant did you know *of* them? You see, we have reason to believe one of them might have resented Doña Rosalia for his death."

"Oh, I see." Amparo softened instantly. "You mean one of those murdering cutthroats might have held a grudge against the poor lady and taken revenge on her? How terrible! Just like those Red plots she was always frightened of!"

That was the problem. The idea of a mysterious Red nursing a grudge *was* too much like one of Doña Rosalia's hysterical fantasies. It didn't fit reality. "Did she ever mention anyone Miguel del Rioseco would have known when she talked about these plots?" he asked, not quite daring to hope that it could be so simple.

Amparo frowned in thought. "No. No, I don't think she ever spoke of anyone in particular. It was the Reds in general she was frightened of. But I know that she knew some of the Riosecos' friends. Miguel was friendly with the Santos Vicentes. His older sister Paloma married Enrique Santos Vicente, and I know Doña Rosalia knew Señora Vicente."

Tejada took out his notebook and jotted down the name, making a note to direct Rivas's attention to it. Amparo, flattered by the attention, became voluble. "She probably knew the Rodríguez Martín family, too, but they're good people. They wouldn't have anything to do with the Riosecos after that business with Miguel. And I can't think how Doña Rosalia would know him, but Miguel was always running around with a boy— What was his name? Something foreign—Marco? No, Max! Max something. They met one summer in San Sebastián, and then this Max stayed with them for a while. He was a university student, I think. He was trouble."

"Can you recall a surname?" Tejada pressed gently, scribbling as he spoke.

Amparo shrugged, helpless. "I never met him. I just know Don Ramiro worried that Miguel was making the wrong sort of friends."

"And Doña Rosalia never mentioned him?"

"Oh, no. He wasn't the sort of person she would know."

"Then what brought him to mind?" the lieutenant asked, genuinely curious.

Amparo took her time answering the question. When she spoke, her voice was thoughtful. "I suppose he just seemed to be the sort of person who might do such a terrible thing. And I know he wasn't in Granada during the war, so I don't know what might have happened to him."

"You're sure there was no one Doña Rosalia herself mentioned?" Tejada asked again.

"I don't think so. I can't remember." Amparo turned large and appealing eyes on the lieutenant. "I never thought I'd be answering questions like *this*. The last time I saw her she seemed so . . . normal. So much herself." She brought her handkerchief to her eyes. "What kind of animal would do something like that to her?"

Her last words mocked the lieutenant's suspicions. *What kind of animal?* He thought. *And I've accused my family. My old friends. The people I've trusted since childhood.* He looked down at his notebook, flipping through the pages to avoid her eyes. A starred entry from several days earlier flashed before his eyes. "Nilo says she was angry at her children." He remembered Nilo giving the information, eager to help, in good faith. He remembered Nilo as he had last seen him. "She didn't seem upset or worried about anything?" he asked.

"Not especially. I can't imagine why she would have been." Amparo's soft voice changed pitch ever so slightly.

Tejada noticed the change. He remembered how easily Amparo had denied knowing the Riosecos. He suspected she was lying, but it might have been merely the type of polite fiction that had made Fernando's wife claim she was very fond of her mother-in-law. It was likely that Doña Rosalia had thrown a tantrum, and the young woman might now be ironing her last memory into a smoother and kinder shape. "Did she ever mention her will to you?" he asked.

"N-no. No, I don't remember that."

Amparo's eyes flickered. The lieutenant had seen the same flicker in the eyes of a guerrilla when he was confronted with a photograph of a comrade's body. *Got her*, Tejada thought, with satisfaction. And then, puzzled, *But why would she lie? She's not an heir.* "I suppose she must have made one," he said experimentally.

"I wouldn't know. I was never really interested."

A faint memory penetrated Tejada's depression like a sunbeam in a fog. He opened his mouth to frame another question and then paused. He didn't have much evidence, and he had already accused too many people needlessly. "I couldn't expect you to be," he said sympathetically. "I'll try to pursue this Max, although it will be difficult without a surname."

"I'm sure you'll track him down." Amparo spoke with warmth.

Tejada chatted for a few more minutes, barely paying attention to what he was saying, and then stood up. "I'm afraid I've taken up too much of your time."

"Not at all. It was a pleasure to see you." Amparo stood as well. "You will give my regards to Felipe, if you see him?"

"Yes, of course." Tejada hesitated. "Do you have plans for this afternoon?"

"No, none at all. Why?"

The lieutenant paused for an instant and again remembered Nilo. *Better to talk it over with Rivas.* He thought. *Better to let Rivas handle it entirely, if possible.* "I was just thinking that I might try to bring Elena and Toño over," he lied smoothly.

He said farewell to Amparo as gracefully as possible and hurried back to the post. Rivas was out, but Guardia Medina was on desk duty. Tejada reminded himself that it was better to take Rivas into his confidence before acting on a hunch. Then he counted to ten. Then he waited for half an hour in the sergeant's office. Rivas did not return. Tejada began to pace. An hour. An hour and a half.

The sergeant finally arrived a little before two o'clock. "Can I help you, Lieutenant?" he asked, the polite words barely masking his impatience.

Tejada nodded. "I wanted to ask your opinion. And then, if you don't think I'm crazy, I want four men and a search warrant."

Chapter 20

Rivas hoped his expression did not reflect his feelings. Lieutenant Tejada had seemed like a serious and competent officer. The lieutenant's tendency to ignore the political realities of Granada was only natural for a member of his family and a man who had not visited the city for many years. Tejada had been refreshingly down-to-earth. Rivas had been disappointed but unsurprised by the lieutenant's refusal to consider his cousin Felipe as a serious suspect despite overwhelming evidence the day before. But he was disgusted by Tejada's scurrilous charge against Nilo Fuentes. It was one thing to try to exonerate your own flesh and blood. It was another to try to throw the blame onto a member of the corps. A man should have loyalty. "My opinion of what, sir?" he asked.

"I think I know where Doña Rosalia's will is," Tejada said and summarized his meeting with Amparo Villalobos. "I can't prove she took the will," he finished. "But she was close enough to Doña Rosalia to know where it was kept, and she has an interest in seeing that Felipe Ordoñez isn't disinherited."

It was nice that the lieutenant no longer seemed intent on bullying poor Nilo, Rivas thought, but unfortunately he had swung back to the other extreme of offending powerful interests. "Don Fernando gets all the land anyway," he pointed out, skeptical.

"Yes, but Felipe bought land from the Riosecos in his own

name," Tejada explained. "Amparo's father must have taken a hit when the Riosecos pulled out of Villalobos and Rioseco. If his firm can regain those lands through Amparo's husband, they'll be back where they were before the war."

"Then she doesn't need the will," Rivas argued.

Tejada shook his head. "She doesn't *need* it," he agreed. "But Felipe would have inherited a nice amount of cash from his mother. Even he admitted to me that it would have come in handy. She probably just saw the will and grabbed it, trying to do Felipe and herself a favor."

"Just saw the will?" Rivas repeated. "You don't think that Doña Rosalia kept her important documents locked up? She was a"—he coughed and rephrased his comment out of respect for the lieutenant's relationship to the dead woman—"a very careful woman."

Long experience had taught him that complaining about subordinates to their officers often backfired, so Tejada resisted the urge to tell Rivas that Medina and Soler had made such a mess of Doña Rosalia's apartment during their initial search that it was impossible to tell whether Doña Rosalia had kept her important documents in any sort of order at all. "It *is* just a theory," he repeated patiently. "But according to the reports, Doña Rosalia saw Felipe on Friday, changed her will on Saturday, and saw Amparo that Sunday." The lieutenant took a deep breath and forced himself to speak openly about one of the more painful pieces of the puzzle. "Nilo—Guardia Fuentes—said she was so angry that she was fuming to *him* about Felipe after she changed her will. And Amparo was her confidante, practically the only person she trusted. Don't you think Doña Rosalia might have mentioned her will—or even shown it—to Amparo when she visited the next day?"

Rivas was unwillingly impressed. The lieutenant's theory made sense. On the other hand, it was sure to make powerful enemies for the Guardia, and it did not bring them perceptibly closer to Doña Rosalia's murderer. "It doesn't tell us who killed her," he reminded Tejada.

"Maybe not," the lieutenant agreed. "But it's one less thing to worry about." He did not admit to Rivas that he wanted to find the will because he wished to have something concrete to present to his father. He did not even admit to himself that his father would probably care more for the recovery of the will than the capture of his aunt's killer.

Rivas thought for a moment. He had no desire to offend the Villalobos family. But if the lieutenant was set on his course then Rivas might as well try to make sure they were the only family offended. "Do you think Doña Rosalia could have found out that Señorita Villalobos stole her will?" he asked. "If she confronted the girl, it might be a motive for murder."

Tejada blinked. "It's a possibility," he said. "But I can't really see Señorita Villalobos committing murder. She'd have to find poison and a way to administer it."

"She was a frequent visitor," Rivas pointed out. "She must have known Doña Rosalia's habits as well as anyone." He hesitated and then added, "And she might have had an accomplice."

"I don't think so." Rivas took the words as a reproof, which was a mistake. Tejada was genuinely thoughtful. "She doesn't strike me as the sort of girl who gets along well with the servants."

Because he liked Tejada, the sergeant took a risk. "I didn't mean in the house. But if you're right, Lieutenant, she and Señor Ordoñez had a shared interest."

Tejada opened his mouth to deny that Felipe would ever collude with Amparo, and then shut it again. He had not told the sergeant about Felipe's plans to marry Lili because he felt that it was not Rivas's business. But without that crucial piece of information, Amparo and Felipe seemed to be obvious allies. "My Tío Felipe will never marry Amparo," he said quietly. "So he wouldn't hatch this kind of a scheme with her."

Rivas sighed. The lieutenant apparently still had a blind spot where his cousin was concerned. "Señor Villalobos is likely to be very offended if we search his house," he said instead.

Tejada nodded. "I know. But I doubt a very thorough search will be necessary. I don't think I showed too much interest in the will this morning. We will probably find it if we just look in her room."

Rivas made a face. "Oh, great. I'm sure the gentleman will be less offended if we leave the public rooms alone and just go through his daughter's private possessions."

Tejada thought about going back to Amparo's house and demanding to search her room. He winced mentally. "Tell Señor Villalobos that he can be present the entire time," he said.

"What do you mean, tell him?" Rivas's amused grimace turned to an expression of horror. "You're the ranking officer, sir!"

"I know," Tejada said dryly. "And I'm pulling rank. I've interviewed Señorita Villalobos twice, *and* spoken to the Ordoñez and Tejada families. I don't need to do everything. You take four men and go find that will."

"But *why?*" Rivas was aghast.

"Because," said Tejada, remembering Elena's estimation of Amparo, "if my wife finds out that I went through Amparo Villalobos's bedroom, my marriage will not survive the strain."

Rivas was eighty percent certain that the lieutenant was joking, but he could not think of a way to contest the order. Lieutenant Tejada *had* been very obliging about interviewing the more difficult suspects in the Ordoñez case, and the sergeant could not blame him for wanting to avoid a confrontation with Señor Villalobos. "Yes, sir," he said miserably, wondering if his superiors would accept the argument that the entire thing had been the lieutenant's idea if Señor Villalobos lodged a complaint.

"You might take Medina with you," Tejada suggested generously. "He's always struck me as a very tactful man."

Rivas, who was by this time thoroughly damning Medina's bright idea of calling in Lieutenant Tejada, kept his face blank with a skill that showed his own tact. "Perhaps you'd like to go through the reports on all the Riosecos' connections while we're out, sir," he suggested woodenly.

"I'll do that," Tejada agreed. Something in his tone suggested that the sergeant was dismissed. Rivas left the post with the picture of Tejada comfortably appropriating the sergeant's desk.

Rivas would have been somewhat relieved to learn that Tejada's apparent ease was an illusion. The lieutenant was unable to keep his mind completely off what was happening at the Villaloboses' mansion. He dutifully reviewed the files of the Riosecos' old servants and dependents and the surviving friends of Miguel del Rioseco. They were extensive and dull. He found the servants pathetic and the young men who had been Miguel's friends annoying. It took him an hour to work through the first pile of folders. He had to suppress a groan as he turned to the second. He reached the end of the Riosecos' dependents' dossiers after reviewing three and half piles. The last half of the fourth pile was composed of members of Doña Rosalia's household. Alberto's—by far the fattest—had been transferred with him to the Axarquía. Because there was nothing else to do, Tejada began working through the remaining folders.

The topmost file belonged to Luisa Cabrera. It was thin, containing nothing more than copies of a birth and baptismal certificate, a blurry carbon copy of the admission form to the Orphanage of Granada, dated in April of 1939, and a form letter addressed to Doña Rosalia from the father confessor of the orphanage stating that Luisa Cabrera was of good moral character and well qualified to be a maidservant. Tejada flipped through it and then picked up Fulgencio Lujo's file.

The cook's folder was substantially heavier, providing evidence of a longer and more eventful life. According to Fulgencio's birth certificate, he was a native Granadino, born in 1904, the sixth son of a trolley-car driver. He had finished primary school and begun an apprenticeship in the kitchens of the

Guzmán Vega family. He had been issued a passport and a visa to France in the summer of 1923. The visa had been renewed over the following six months and the occupation given was "student." Fulgencio had applied for a new identity card on his return to Spain, and along with his application was a letter on heavy stationery embossed with the double-headed Hapsburg eagle that was the symbol of the Hotel Alhambra Palace, confirming that Fulgencio Lujo was gainfully employed as a sous-chef at the Palace. The Palace had provided Fulgencio with references five years later when Don Antonio Ordoñez Guzmán hired him. He had worked at the Casa Ordoñez ever since. It was possible, Tejada thought, that Fulgencio still had connections among the Guzmán family's far-flung web of dependents, but he could not see any reason why any of the descendants of Doña Rosalia's in-laws should have wanted to kill her. He remembered Doña Rosalia's son-in-law saying, "Poison is a cook's weapon" and wondered if any of Fulgencio's culinary studies had included helpful information about why cooking crushed apricot pits was highly inadvisable.

Tejada closed Fulgencio's folder with a sigh and picked up María José García's. Although the maid was older than the other servants, the file on her was brief. He skimmed through the information about her date of birth, her family, and her few employers. She had never left Granada and had never been in trouble of any sort with the law. He flipped over the last page and saw, puzzled, that a prison record for someone named Luis Romero had been slipped into the maid's file. He read it for a few minutes and discovered that Romero had been charged with church burning and murder connected with service in the Red army during the war. He had been sentenced to twenty years' hard labor outside Madrid in the spring of 1939. For a moment, Tejada thought that the record had simply been misfiled. Then he looked back at María José's family information. She had married Luis Romero on June 12, 1905. A daughter, Catalina, had been born the following year.

Tejada felt his muscles tense for a moment, the way they did when something was on the verge of being worked out. He searched for Guardia Girón's notes on Rivas's interview with María José. The sergeant had put them in his desk drawer, and it took Tejada nearly twenty frustrating minutes to find them. As far as the lieutenant could tell, María José had not mentioned a husband during the interview. But at the end of Girón's notes were the scribbled words: "May go live with daughter now (daughter lives on Recogidas, married)."

The lieutenant considered for a moment. He still thought it would be impossible to completely cut out of civic life all the people who had family ties to Reds. But that didn't mean people with close family ties who were involved in a murder investigation shouldn't be carefully watched. He stood up and went in search of the post's archives. An identity card had been issued for Catalina Romero García, married to one Arturo Perea three years previously. The address given was Recogidas 28. Tejada copied the address and then left word for Sergeant Rivas that he would return shortly.

Stores were just starting to close for the siesta when he reached Recogidas 28. It was at the outskirts of the city—a tall, narrow building, sandwiched in between similarly characterless neighbors. A boy of about fifteen was rolling down the shutters of a store with a sign that read: ARTURO PEREA. SHOES REPAIRED. Tejada stood on the sidewalk and watched the boy close the store. The boy cast a few nervous glances at him, but said nothing. When the shutters were closed, Tejada spoke up. "You work for Arturo Perea?"

"Y-yes, sir." The boy turned white.

"He lives here?"

"Y-yes, sir."

"Can you take me to him?"

The adolescent's Adam's apple bobbed desperately as he attempted a reply. Tejada waited for the youngster to stutter out an affirmative and then silently followed him through the narrow doorway beside the shuttered store and up a dark flight of stairs. The boy stopped on the first landing. Tejada could hear a babble of voices and a radio turned up loudly enough to sound clearly in the dim hallway. The boy knocked hesitantly. Nothing happened. He turned back to Tejada apologetically. The lieutenant raised his eyebrows. The boy turned miserably back to the door, and hammered on it.

"Coming!" The radio was turned down and the door swung open, revealing a woman of perhaps forty with a baby on her hip and a child clinging to her skirts. "What *is* it, Paco?" she demanded impatiently. "Arturo told you—" She stopped, taking in the silent shape behind the boy.

"*He* wants to speak to Señor Perea," Paco muttered, jerking his head toward the lieutenant.

"Oh." The woman went still.

Paco, taking advantage of the little silence, slid between the lieutenant and his employer's wife and scuttled down the stairs and out into the street. Tejada advanced on the woman. "Señora Romero?"

"Yes?" She backed up, effectively allowing him into the apartment.

"Who is it, Catalina?" a male voice called. They reached the living room, and a prematurely bald man, obviously the head of the household, stood to greet them. He looked somewhat alarmed at the sight of the lieutenant.

"Señor Perea?"

"Yes, Señor Guardia. Can I help you?"

"I'd like to speak to your wife actually. About her parents."

Catalina looked distressed, but Arturo Perea was just annoyed. "Oh, for God's sake. We've been through all this a dozen times. Catalina's never had anything to do with her father. Hasn't even seen him since she was a baby."

"Arturo—" Catalina stretched out one hand toward her husband but he waved it away.

"No, I'm sick of it. We're law-abiding people. Why should my wife be persecuted because a no-good scumbag ran out on her and her mother when she was a kid? My wife's papers are in order and so are mine, Señor Guardia. And we don't know anything about that man. There's nothing to say."

"I actually wanted to ask about your mother-in-law," Tejada said mildly.

"Oh." Perea looked embarrassed. "Well. That's different then."

The living room was cramped, and the only place to sit was a stained sofa. Tejada took the seat, although it had not been offered. He looked up at Catalina Romero, pointedly ignoring her husband. "Your mother and her husband are not close then?"

"Close?" Catalina laughed bitterly. "He took off when I was three. She didn't hear from him again until the Republic was declared. He wanted a divorce, now that one was legal."

"Did she grant one?"

"Of course not!"

Tejada considered a tactful way of asking why Catalina's mother had not accommodated her husband. After a moment's thought he gave it up as impossible. "Why? Do you think she still had feelings for him?"

Catalina drew herself up and sniffed. Had Tejada known María José, he would have recognized the sniff. "My parents were married in a church, Señor Guardia. My mother is a Christian woman."

"It must have been very difficult for her when you were young," Tejada suggested.

Catalina frowned at him, suspicious. Members of the Guardia had come to question her about her father in the past. None of them had ever shown the slightest concern for her mother, except as a possible link to Luis Romero. "She managed fine."

Tejada said nothing for a long minute. The radio played an

incongruous bolero in the background. "It must have been difficult for her to find work. Did her employer know that she was married? And had a child?"

"Of course." Catalina's suspicion was giving way to puzzlement. "I lived with my mother, growing up. How could she not have known?"

"Doña Rosalia had no objection?" As he spoke, Tejada realized that he must have visited the Ordoñez house as a child when Catalina Romero had lived there. She was only a few years older than he. He tried to remember her as a girl, but he could not picture any faces from Doña Rosalia's household. The only childhood memories he had were of furniture at eye level and sad-eyed daguerreotypes that he had secretly found frightening.

"You know about Doña Rosalia?"

"I'm investigating her death."

Catalina laughed briefly. "Did Mother tell you that my father had something to do with it?"

Tejada, who had by now mentally written off the visit as a waste of time, suddenly focused on Catalina intently. "No. What makes you say that?"

"Because she wouldn't put anything past him," Catalina said dryly. "She's said for years the Reds weren't to be trusted because of what he did to her. She's right enough about that, but I don't think my father would ever come back to Granada. He's had more than enough of us." Her lip curled. "He hasn't even bothered to write since before the war."

Tejada opened his mouth to say Luis Romero had been in prison for over five years and then closed it again, uncertain if telling Romero's daughter that would be kindness or cruelty. "Thank you for your time," he said instead.

He left Señor Perea and his wife openmouthed, wondering why the Guardia had come to question them and then departed so gently and quickly. He walked back to the post feeling vaguely depressed once more. The Pereas, with their loud radio and louder denials, had not left a pleasant impression. He thought about Catalina Romero, too angry to know or care if her father was in prison or simply forgetful of her, and about Amparo Villalobos, too well bred to know or remember Miguel del Rioseco or the other young men who had been Reds before the war. He thought about María José, nursing a grudge for years against Reds in the person of the man who had left her and her daughter. If Catalina was telling the truth—and the lieutenant believed she was—María José had good reason to be actively grateful to Doña Rosalia. That made her a bad suspect.

He skirted the Civil Government building and turned onto the Calle Duquesa, deep in thought. *One* of Doña Rosalia's servants had to have been at least an accomplice to her murder. Alberto had denied it even under torture. María José had no motive. That left only Fulgencio and Luisa. And neither of them had any visible motive for murder. So they had agreed to help someone else, who *did* have a motive. Someone who one or both of them trusted. Someone whom they thought could and would give them an ample reward for poisoning their mistress. Tejada was positive that he already had enough information to figure out who the *someone* was and which of Doña Rosalia's servants had been suborned. But the information refused to arrange itself into a neat pattern. It was a maddening feeling, like beginning a sentence and then forgetting what you intended to say.

A guardia hailed him as he reached the post. "Sergeant Rivas is waiting for you in his office, sir."

Tejada abandoned the irritating conundrum and headed for the sergeant's office, bracing himself for a fresh wave of disappointment and disapproval. Rivas was standing behind his desk when the lieutenant entered. "Sir." He saluted formally.

Tejada sighed. "You searched the Villaloboses' place?"

"Yes, sir."

"I'll take responsibility for it with the brass and Señor Villalobos," Tejada said, his voice apologetic.

Rivas smiled and picked up a manila envelope lying on the desk. "No need, sir," he said, holding it out to the lieutenant. "I believe this is your lady aunt's will. Properly signed and witnessed at the offices of Pablo Almeida. October 4, 1945."

Tejada stretched out his hand, but it was not until his fingers closed around the thick paper envelope that the reality of the sergeant's words sank in. "You found it?"

"In Amparo Villalobos's desk, under a pile of scented notepaper." Rivas allowed himself a slightly broader smile.

Tejada stared at the envelope in his hand, half triumphant and half puzzled. "She hadn't destroyed it?"

"No, sir. She said it was given to her for safekeeping."

Tejada snorted. "So she naturally proffered it as soon as she was asked to do so by the proper authorities?"

"Not exactly!" The sergeant shuddered. "She had violent hysterics when we asked to search her room."

"I trust she's over them?" Tejada opened the flap of the envelope and slid out the will.

"I believe so, sir." Rivas coughed. "All things considered, I thought it best just to inform Señor Villalobos that we had found what we were looking for and leave him to . . . er . . . comfort her."

"She may have to prolong her hysterics for a while then," Tejada said absently. "Villalobos has a reputation for having a temper."

After a moment's thought, Rivas decided he was grateful the lieutenant had withheld that information about Villalobos. He shifted from foot to foot as Tejada silently scanned the will. The lieutenant seemed absorbed. After a moment, Rivas coughed again. "Is there anything unusual in it, sir?"

"No," Tejada said slowly, although the first page confirmed Doña Rosalia's spleen against her daughter and Felipe. "Nothing that was unexpected." He skimmed through the vitriolic condemnation of Felipe's irresponsible and immoral lifestyle and tried as best he could to take comfort in Doña Rosalia's final disposition of her liquid assets: "To my nephew and executor, Juan Andrés Tejada León, who maintains the honor of the Tejadas and has ever behaved with the consideration and kindness that my own children have never shown me." He wondered how much money the will was worth to his father.

"I suppose we'd better take it over to her lawyer then," the sergeant said, after an awkward moment. "After all, it's really nothing to do with the Guardia."

Tejada nodded and slid the will back into its envelope. The dry paper resisted his touch for an instant and then slipped downward so fast that it gave his index finger a paper cut. He pinched the envelope between thumb and forefinger, leaving a tiny smudge of blood on one corner. *I've got it*, he thought. *This is what Father called me from Potes to get, and I've found it. I can go home now and be proud.* "I'll take it over to Don Pablo," he said aloud.

If he had been less preoccupied, Tejada would have noticed that Rivas was looking a little sour. In the sergeant's opinion, sending other men to search a place like the Villaloboses' and then hogging the credit for finding what other men had looked for, was a pretty shabby trick, and bad for esprit de corps to boot. Typical of a señorito. "I hope *your* morning was productive," Rivas said with a touch of malice.

Tejada shrugged. "Not very. I went through the files and managed to cross a few names off the list, I think." He summarized his research and his trip to Arturo Perea's home.

Rivas softened a little during the lieutenant's recital. Señorito or no, Tejada was genuinely conscientious, and at least he didn't shirk boring work. He nodded when Tejada mentioned his opinion about a servant's collusion. "Maybe we should just pull them in and question them until one cracks," he said.

Tejada nodded. "Might not be a bad idea."

"You think we should go now?" Rivas glanced at his watch.

Tejada saw the glance and guessed what it meant. "After lunch," he said. "I told my family I'd be home for the meal. I'll drop the will off on my way, and we can meet back here."

"Of course, Lieutenant. At your orders."

The sergeant coughed. Tejada raised his eyebrows. "Is there a problem?"

"No, Lieutenant. It's just . . ." Rivas hesitated.

"You had other work to do this afternoon," the lieutenant guessed.

"Of course, if you think there's any risk of flight we can go right away," Rivas said quickly. "But I did wonder if perhaps tomorrow morning . . . "

"Fine." Tejada tucked the will under his arm, said farewell to the sergeant, and left the post, mildly astonished at his success and wondering why he did not feel more cheerful. Another quick glance at his watch made him decide to go directly back to his parents' house. He could drop the will off with Don Pablo on the way back to the post. And his father would be happy to see it. Tejada walked home, imagining his father's relief, and carefully not remembering that he would have to pass Nilo on his way to Pablo Almeida's office.

Chapter 21

Tejada was at a loss as to what to do with the will when he reached home. He did not want to walk into the dining room brandishing it, but he was wary of putting it down lest it get lost again. He headed for his bedroom and then, after a moment's thought, unbuttoned his jacket and slid the envelope along his chest. Elena entered the room as he was rebuttoning his coat. "Carlos? What are you doing?"

He explained, a little shamefaced, and Elena laughed. "So that's what you wear next to your heart instead of the Virgen del Pilar? I should tell Father Bernardo!"

"Stop!" Tejada protested, his chest crackling slightly. "If you make me laugh I'll crumple the envelope."

"Why can't you just leave it here?"

"Because I'm not taking responsibility for it getting lost *again*."

The lieutenant's voice was still light, but Elena did not press the question. She wondered for a moment if he realized that his excessive caution suggested he did not trust his own parents' integrity. "How did you find it?" she asked.

Tejada summarized his morning briefly, avoiding his encounter with Nilo.

"I *knew* Amparo Villalobos was a sneaky little hussy." Elena spoke with satisfaction. "Did you arrest her?"

"Of course not."

"Why not?"

"We recovered the will," Tejada pointed out. "There's no harm done, after all. And she didn't kill Doña Rosalia."

Tejada suspected that Elena was not perfectly satisfied with this information, but she was intent on other matters. She sat down and gestured for him to sit as well. "I visited Cristina's mother again today."

"Oh?" With a victory of his own to enjoy, Tejada was less pleased with his wife's tendency to visit the relatives of convicted criminals, but he was unwilling to condemn her.

"She says that Félix hadn't told Baldo anything because he wasn't sure who Montrose was. He and his wife had known about Dr. Beltrán's transfer order, you see, but they didn't know he'd escaped."

Tejada nodded. "Transfer order" had been a euphemism for taking prisoners out into the country and shooting them "while trying to escape." It had been logical to assume that Esteban Beltrán was dead. "They didn't think it was odd that Beltrán's mother received money also?" he demanded.

"They didn't know about it. They haven't been in contact with her. With Señor Encinas in prison it's—well, it looks bad for them to meet."

"Well, I'm glad you took good news to Señora Rosado," Tejada said, preparing to dismiss the subject.

"She was *very* happy," Elena assured her husband. "She couldn't stop thanking me. And she told me to thank you as well, when I explained how I'd found out."

"Did she?" Tejada raised his eyebrows, wondering how genuinely grateful a Red's wife would be to any guardia civil.

"Oh, yes."

There was a little pause, and then Elena cleared her throat and said. "Actually . . ."

"Yes?"

"Well, actually, she wondered if you'd be willing to do the family a favor." Elena saw her husband frown and hurried on before he could stop her. "The thing is, Baldo's parents want him to go on with his education, and they feel that he's been marked out here, being from a Red's family, you know. They say there aren't many opportunities for him, and he's a bright boy. He's sixteen now, and his parents were hoping that if Esteban—or Cristina—were alive and doing well enough to send money, that maybe they could get Baldo to France to stay with them. It would be such an opportunity for him."

"They would have to get in touch with the Montroses, wouldn't they?" Tejada demanded.

"Of course," Elena agreed. "Baldo's father has already asked the bank to find the address of M. Montrose, and he's got a letter all ready to send. But if Cristina and Esteban—if it *is* Cristina and Esteban—agree to take the boy, he'll need a passport. So his grandmother was wondering if perhaps you could help with that. You know, with the avowal that he's not politically suspect? And if you knew any priests here, to find one to vouch for him as well?"

Tejada relaxed. Nobody received a passport without a declaration from the police and the parish priest stating that they were politically and spiritually healthy. Practically speaking, no one received a passport without intervention of some kind. "Sure," he said. "He should fill out the application now, before he gets any nearer the age for military service. They might not even like to give it to someone who's already sixteen."

Elena nodded, both relieved and grateful. "Shame he isn't a couple of years younger," she commented.

"He's lucky to have relatives abroad," Tejada said. "I'll ask Felipe about a priest to sign the declaration. I take it he hasn't been in any kind of trouble?"

"Oh no. Señora Rosado says that his parents have been sending him to mass and communion every week since they got the wire transfer."

Worth it to attend mass for the sake of a passport, Tejada thought.

Of course, if he gets to France, his people there won't make him go. A shame, really. That's the age when you really need to be forced. The lieutenant remembered his own horror of confession at sixteen with nostalgic amusement. It was always most agonizing when you did not have any really grave sins to confess. *At least we can make him go through the rites for a few more months for the sake of his future.* "It's a pity we can't send Aleja with him," he said lightly. "That would solve her problems with school too."

He had meant the words as a joke, but Elena sat up, shocked. "So far from her mother!"

"I wasn't serious. Besides, why should Encinas and Beltrán want to take on another kid who's no relation of theirs?"

Because that's what being a Red means: being closer to strangers than you are to your own brother, Elena did not answer. *And because Cristina's father made taking on strays his life's work. Because they only got to France due to a lot of strangers who risked their lives to help them and now they'll help a stranger as payment.* "No reason, really," she admitted. "But I think they'd do it."

"Even if it meant another mouth to feed?" Tejada asked. Elena gave him a reproachful look and he added defensively, "Well, why should *I* pay for her to run off to be with a bunch of subversives?"

"Because you promised," his wife retorted.

Tejada shook his head, the strain of the day starting to tell on him. He was tired of people twisting his words into false meanings, and his voice was sharp as he said, "Absolutely not. I promised to take care of her, and I'll see her raised a good woman and a good Spaniard. That *is* taking care of her, whatever her family might think." He made an emphatic gesture, and the hidden will rustled.

Elena caught the noise of the folded envelope and frowned. There was something Carlos was not telling her about his morning, she guessed. Something that made his temper short and his eyes tired. "Never mind," she said soothingly. "Come on, we're late for lunch." She retrieved Toño from Alejandra on her own, unwilling to rouse her husband's demons by having him cross paths with the girl. The lieutenant waited for them docilely, and they headed for the dining room together.

Tejada met his father across the table wondering why he did not feel more triumphant. Andrés Tejada greeted his younger son graciously. "Is your investigation making any progress, Carlos?"

"A little. Not nearly as much as I had hoped." Elena, watching her husband, saw his hand stray toward the hidden will and clutch briefly at his chest as he spoke. "But I believe I've found something of interest to you, Father."

"I'm always interested to hear about your work." Andrés Tejada might have spoken in the same voice to Toño about electric trains.

"We know you've always encouraged him." Doña Consuela's tone made it clear that her son's current plight was the fault of his father's reckless encouragement.

The lieutenant looked at his plate. "I know. I've always been grateful."

Only until Friday, Elena thought. *Only three more days until Friday.* Carlos sometimes annoyed her by his arrogance. But it was painful to watch the self-assured man she knew dwindle into a quiet shadow. He ate quickly, speaking only when he was spoken to, like a well-brought-up little boy. Fortunately, Toño had learned a new story about El Cid and was anxious to tell it to his father. The lieutenant listened intently to the child's careful recitation of "*Afuera, afuera Rodrigo*" and even managed to sound like himself in some of his responses.

When the meal was over, Tejada stood and turned to his father. "If I could see you in your study, Father?"

Andrés Tejada raised his eyebrows. "Of course."

The lieutenant silently followed his father out of the room,

uncomfortably aware of the last time he had demanded a similar audience. Andrés Tejada obviously shared his awareness. He
sat at his desk and opened a cigarette case without offering one
to his son. "You've found Aunt Rosalia's killer?" he demanded
without preamble.

Tejada shook his head. "I'm afraid not. But we have found this."
He opened his jacket and drew out the will. "I believe it's what you
were looking for," he added, with the lightest tinge of sarcasm.

Andrés opened the envelope, frowning, scanned the document, and then smiled, suddenly cordial. "It certainly is! Well
done, Carlos! How did you find it? And where was it?"

Tejada shrugged and explained in some detail, although the
explanation gave him no pleasure. His father was warmly sympathetic and eager, prodding him frequently with questions.
"Well," he said finally. "That puts any question of Amparo and
Felipe's marriage to rest! I always thought Fernando and
Bernarda were fools to push it anyway. Felipe's so crazy there's
no telling what he'd do if he married the chit."

"I don't think he'd marry her under any circumstances,"
Tejada said, feeling an obscure desire to defend his cousin.

"No, he never had the sense he was born with," Andrés
agreed amicably. "I wouldn't be surprised if he's got a girlfriend
stashed away somewhere and thinks marriage would interfere
with his little friend." He remembered, too late, that he was
speaking to his son and added hastily, "Of course, any decent
man treats his wife with consideration. . . ."

"Which doesn't mean he's a stone-cold saint," the lieutenant
finished.

"Exactly," Andrés agreed with relief, privately thinking that it
was rather nice to finally be able to treat Carlos as a grown-up,
and that it was a shame the boy had not arrived at this realiza-
tion in time to escape from a disastrous marriage. He did not
notice the faint curl of the lieutenant's mouth or guess that the
words were anything other than completely sincere.

Tejada held out his hand. "I told the sergeant I'd take the will over to Pablo Almeida this afternoon, on my way back to the post." He held his breath, half wondering if he would have to invoke the power of the Guardia to retrieve the document. He relaxed as his father readily returned the envelope to him.

"Well done, Carlos. I'm sure that you'll find poor Aunt Rosalia's murderer soon, too. We can't let people get away with murdering family members." Andrés spoke with genuine warmth.

Tejada nodded, made a respectful reply, and escaped. It was odd, thought Andrés Tejada as the door closed behind his son, that Carlos could be so competent in many ways and such a fool in others. But after all, the boy was still young and could learn. And he had apologized properly for his initial disrespect.

The lieutenant headed for his own room. There was a bad taste in his mouth, compounded of the sour remains of his lunch and something that tasted like bile or grief. He wanted a cigarette and he wanted to hide and to hold Elena and pour out his foolishness about Nilo, and he wanted more than anything to go home, to where the problems were simple and clean-cut: maquis vs. guardias, Reds. vs. forces of law and order. His room was empty and he guessed that Elena was reading to Toño before the boy's nap. There was a cigarette pack lying on the night table by the bed, but to his annoyance he discovered that it was empty and remembered, too late, that he had smoked the last one the preceding evening. All the tobacconists would be closed for the siesta already. He had three days before he could go home. Three days to find a killer.

Desperate to wash the bitter taste out of his mouth, he turned to the pitcher of water and glasses sitting on the side table. He picked up the handsome cut-glass pitcher and poured himself a drink with relief. A few chips of ice tinkled into the glass, and he took a long swallow with relief. *Fresh from the wells of the Alhambra,* he thought, remembering the cry of the water carriers in his childhood. He smiled a little, wondering if there were still water carriers anywhere in the city. Perhaps up in the Albaicín, where Felipe and Lili lived. He himself could only vaguely remember a time when his family had not had running tap water during their winters in the city. He had a faint memory of his father lifting him up and saying, "Look, Carlito, turn the faucet," and being startled by a noisy rush of liquid, but the novelty had worn off too quickly to leave a lasting impression. He wondered if Alejandra was the one responsible for leaving a fresh pitcher of water in his room every day. He had noticed it on his first day back in Granada and thought ruefully that his parents were treating him as they treated guests. It was a piece of foolishness, to provide a pitcher of water when you could walk down the hall to the bathroom and get a glass from the tap yourself. A waste of good ice and water, too, to have to change it every day regardless of whether it was used. Today was the first day he had used it and he doubted that he would finish the pitcher, but still it would be emptied out and replaced fresh tomorrow. Something to keep poor Alejandra busy.

Tejada frowned at the thought of Alejandra. He would have to speak to her again before they left and explain to her that he would not allow her to throw away her future for the sake of some idiot desire to remain a true member of the *lumpen proletariat*. Perhaps, he thought dryly, he should simply let Alejandra try to become a maid for a few months and bear the pious injunctions of charitable ladies like Amparo Villalobos who concerned themselves with the morals of orphaned servant girls. It might make her more eager to return to school with the Sisters.

The thought of a confrontation between Alejandra's monumental sullenness and Amparo's relentless sweetness made the lieutenant smile for a moment. He took another swallow of water, still smiling, and then choked suddenly. Did you arrest Amparo? Elena had asked. Why not? Tejada had assumed that

Amparo had neither the skills nor the temperament for murder. But if she had been only the one giving the orders . . .

He settled himself at the table and began to write out his suspicions in his notebook. They gained form and clarity as he scribbled. There was no proof, but for once proof would be easy enough to come by. He had covered half a page by the time Elena entered the room. "I was just talking to Carmen—," she began.

"Read this," the lieutenant interrupted, handing her his notes.

Elena glanced at her husband's face, and read. "It's weak."

"It makes more sense than anything else."

"It could as well be Felipe, by this logic."

"That's ridiculous." The lieutenant spoke sharply, although the unpleasant thought had occurred to him, too.

Elena sighed. "What are you going to do?"

"I don't know." Tejada grimaced. "Rivas said he had other work this afternoon. But he wants to pull in the servants tomorrow and question them. We may get something that way."

Elena never really forgave herself for what she said next. But the leaden unhappiness of Alejandra and the Encinas family were gnawing at her self-possession, and she knew that her husband would not focus his attention on their plight until he had finished the case, and that he would feel no compassion for them as long as he looked so drawn and miserable. She wanted desperately for him to finish the case successfully so that he could offer his help to the families of her student and friend. And perhaps even more than that, she wanted to go home and forget about their nightmarish time in Granada. An extra day loomed large in her mind, so she encouraged him to hurry. "Why don't you go over this afternoon and see if you can find anything out? Rivas won't mind."

Chapter 22

Elena's words might have had no effect if Tejada had not been restless also. He nodded. "After the siesta then."

The next few hours had the feeling of killing time. The lieutenant sat and doodled because he had nothing to write but was too tense to rest. Elena reread a book she had read before. The clock ticked, and Tejada longed for a cigarette. They spoke little, each hoping that the other was relaxing. Finally, at five, the lieutenant started up. "I'll see you in a few hours," he said, leaning over to kiss his wife on the cheek. "Wish me luck."

"Luck to whoever's cause is best." Elena gave him the ritual response she used in Potes, and he laughed, a brief snort of recognition of the formula rather than a genuine response to the joke.

It was a cool, windy evening, and the low sun turned one side of the buildings gold, leaving the other side of the street in shadow as he left his parents' house and headed toward the Casa Ordoñez. Fire-trimmed clouds scudded across the sky, and the air smelled incongruously of spring. Tejada glanced at the side-lit buildings and then frowned. He hated the shortened hours of light around All Saints' Day.

There was a pair of bored guardias on duty outside the Casa Ordoñez. They were standing on opposite sides of a door directly across the street, a few yards away from the doorway on either side. They were widely spaced enough to be inconspicuous, too widely spaced to chat easily with each other. Tejada mentally gave Sergeant Rivas credit for good discipline and training. The pair saluted when they saw him. "Can we help you, Lieutenant?" one of them asked.

"I just wanted to interview the servants again. Are they in?" Tejada asked.

"The women, sir. The cook went out a few minutes ago. Medina and Soler are tailing him."

"Fine." Tejada thought for a moment. "Stay alert. I'll call if I need backup."

"At your orders, sir."

The lieutenant crossed the street and knocked on the door. An elderly woman in a maid's uniform opened it. "Can I help you, Señor Guardia?"

Tejada inspected the woman in front of him and remembered the cobbler's family on Recogidas. "María José García?" He watched her nod, her expression open and friendly, and wondered if she knew—or cared—that her husband was in prison. "I wanted to speak to Fulgencio and Luisa."

"Fulgencio went out to dinner with friends." She stepped backward as she spoke, admitting him to the house. "But Luisa's here, and he should be back soon. Is it about poor Doña Rosalia?"

"Yes." Tejada remembered that Rivas had said María José was genuinely grieved by her mistress's death. "We hope to find her killer soon."

"God willing," María José said. She led him across the courtyard into the kitchen without nervousness or deference. "You're new to the post?" She spoke over her shoulder casually, as she would have spoken to an equal, and the lieutenant guessed that she did not know his surname.

"A temporary transfer," he said, simplifying.

The kitchen was a cavernous, old-fashioned room. The huge sink in a corner was the only concession to modernity, and the single tap proclaimed the absence of hot water. Cabinets and cooking implements hung along the walls like the trophies and spears adorning a hunter's great hall. There were no chairs around the long central table of much-nicked wood, but María José dragged a tall stool from the corner for the lieutenant. "Luisa's probably up in her room," the maid explained. "But I can go and get her if you'd like to see her now."

"Please." Tejada sat quietly until the door swung shut behind María José and then stood up and roamed around the room. It was a space with many doors. One opened onto the courtyard and another onto the alley behind the house, which stank strongly of rotten vegetables. The third led into the interior of the house, via a dark winding hallway to the rooms more cherished by the Ordoñez family. He wandered into the pantry, a long narrow strip of space barely more than a closet, wondering if the poison that had killed the mistress of the house had been stored here, among the gleaming glass jars of spices. It seemed likely. He returned to the kitchen and scanned the wine racks below the cabinets on one wall. They were dusty and half empty. The sort of wine rack that would make Felipe—or Fernando, to whom they now belonged—wrinkle his nose in disgust.

The squeaking of a door alerted Tejada, and he hurried back to his place on the stool as Luisa Cabrera entered the room. "You wanted to see me, sir?" She bobbed a little curtsy as she spoke.

"Yes." Tejada hesitated a moment, inspecting her. She was pretty, taller than average, soft haired, and copper skinned. Had she been lively or even self-assured, she would have been beautiful. But something in her soft voice and downcast eyes reminded the lieutenant of Alejandra. Perhaps it was the downward tilt of her lips, not a seductive pout but an unconscious gravity that sat oddly on such young features. He tried to think of a way to frame his question so that she would give him the answer he wanted. "I wonder if you could describe your duties here? When

Doña Rosalia was alive?" He deliberately kept his voice gentle, speaking as he would have spoken to a daughter. She was only a few years older than Alejandra, after all.

She nodded and spoke without looking up. "Mostly I was Fulgencio's assistant. I would have liked to learn to cook really well. But I also cleaned the house and helped with the laundry. Whatever was necessary, really. I've only started helping Fulgencio lately."

"You didn't receive special training as a cook at the orphanage?"

She looked up, startled, and blushed painfully. "No, sir. I was hired as a maid. It's just that Fulgencio's been very good to me. He says I might make a good cook." Her blush deepened and spread across her neck as she added wistfully, "I studied chemistry in school once. I was good at it. Cooking's like that."

For a moment, Tejada wished irrelevantly that Alejandra was present to hear the girl's words. Then he returned to the matter at hand. Luisa's tone when she spoke of Fulgencio had given him an idea. "You know we haven't found the source of the poison that killed Doña Rosalia yet," he said. "But it's logical to suppose that it was in something she ate. Do you have any idea how the cook might have tampered with her food?"

Her eyes went wide with fear. "Fulgencio wouldn't do that! He's a good man. Besides, I ate everything she did that night. She asked me to! I told the sergeant that! You can't think Fulgencio would—"

"What about what she drank?" Tejada interrupted.

Luisa, brought up short, frowned slightly. "She drank wine. María José told me I could put it away after . . . after the sergeant told her it was all right."

Tejada nodded. "We've analyzed the bottle. There was nothing in it but wine."

"It can't be that either then." Luisa gave a little sigh of relief.

"But you know, I started wondering this afternoon why we had assumed that the wine bottle we analyzed was the same as the bottle Doña Rosalia drank from. The room was cleaned up afterward. And nobody took an inventory for over a week after she died. It would have been perfectly simple for someone to open another bottle, dump half of it down the sink, and then replace the old bottle with it. No one would know. You see what I mean?"

"I guess so." The girl's voice was barely above a whisper.

"Can you remember what kind of wine Doña Rosalia was drinking that evening?" Tejada asked gently.

"I-I don't remember." Luisa looked troubled. She waited for him to continue and then added, "I'm sorry, sir."

"It's all right." Tejada was soothing. "Perhaps Fulgencio will know. When he returns, I'll ask him." He waited a moment to allow the full import of the words to sink in and then said, "Tell me about the orphanage."

The girl forgot her shyness and stared at him. "The orphanage?" she repeated, in a tone that suggested he was insane.

"How much time did you spend there?"

"Just a year."

"Long enough to study chemistry, though?"

"No." The girl's face went still. "That was . . . before. In another school. We just learned sewing and catechism in the orphanage."

"You must have been grateful to find a place here," Tejada suggested.

"Yes, sir," she answered dully.

Tejada took a deep breath. "And perhaps a few charitably inclined ladies helped you? Came and spoke to you before you went out into the world? Offered you comfort and advice? Congratulated you on your good luck, perhaps?"

"Yes, sir." There were tears in Luisa's eyes, but she spoke like an automaton.

Tejada saw her swallow convulsively, and there was nothing feigned about the pity in his voice. "God knows Doña Rosalia wasn't the easiest woman to live with. And she probably threw her charity in your face whenever she felt like it, didn't she? No one who knew her could blame you for feeling like killing her. And then Señorita Villalobos asked you to, didn't she?"

"No," the girl whispered, but Tejada swept on, gentle and insistent.

"You were fourteen when you came here, weren't you? And Señorita Villalobos was only a few years older and practically a daughter of the house. And she'd been kind to you when you had nothing, and maybe she was still kind to you. Did she offer you a reward for helping to poison your mistress? Or promise to take you on as a servant afterward?"

"No." Luisa's voice was steadier now, and she met the lieutenant's eyes. "No. Señorita Villalobos never asked me to do anything."

"Don't be a heroine," Tejada said quietly. "It isn't worth it."

"She never asked me to kill the señora."

"I don't blame you, you know. And if you tell me exactly how she was involved I can protect you." Tejada knew, to his grief, that the first statement was true and the second one false. If the servant girl had been the only one involved, he would have cheerfully let Doña Rosalia's murder go unsolved. But she had been a pawn for Amparo Villalobos—or *someone*, Tejada amended, unwilling to name Felipe even as a possibility—and finding the true killer mattered to him. Unfortunately, there was no way one of the great ones of the city would fall without taking Luisa down as well. He could protect her from torture, but she would likely be garroted for her role in her mistress's death, regardless of any intervention by the Guardia.

"She wasn't involved." There was a suggestion of gritted teeth in Luisa's stubborn reply.

"Who then?"

Silence.

"They're not worth your loyalty," said the lieutenant sadly. "Last chance. Before we go back to the Calle Duquesa. So I ask you again. Who paid you off?"

Luisa had quivered like a plucked string at the word "loyalty." Now she practically spat the words, "No one paid me off! I don't take bribes from any of you!"

"You killed her on your own then?" Tejada asked, sarcastic.

Luisa said nothing. The lieutenant sighed and moved forward to take her elbow. "Come on. I'm taking you back to the post. We'll find out who put you up to it there."

The young woman stood like a statue as he approached, but when his hand closed around her arm she jerked free, suddenly furious. "No one put me up to it! She deserved it!"

Tejada blinked. He had considered Luisa's stubbornness the result of one of two possibilities: either she was both loyal and brave or else he had once more been completely wrong. Now it occurred to him that he might be asking the wrong question. He tried a simpler one. "Why?"

"She lied to me." Luisa faced him, shoulders straight, head raised, eyes blazing. "She let me think my mother was dead. For five years, she let me think that!"

The lieutenant frowned. "You came here as an orphan."

"Fucking bullshit!" The words were little less than a scream. Tejada's jaw dropped at the obscenity, and he wondered what had happened to the silent, demure maid who had entered the kitchen only a few minutes ago. Luisa continued before he could speak, "My mother's alive! And maybe my brother, too! They couldn't come and get me after the war because they were in prison, but they're alive!"

"Couldn't come and get you?" Tejada asked, wishing he had done more research on Luisa's apparently blank past.

"When I came back. From Almuñécar." Luisa saw his bewilderment and added, "It's a town on the coast."

"I know where it is," Tejada snapped, annoyed because he disliked feeling incompetent. "What does it have to do with you?"

"There was a children's camp there." Luisa's voice was as hard as his own. "Before the war. When charity was something the government did, instead of leaving it to ladies like Señorita Villalobos. The city sent eighty of us—workers' children, from the Albaicín mostly—to the seashore for two weeks. You had to have good marks in school, and then it went by lottery. I won. And they sent us"— her voice melted around the edges—"to Almuñécar. On July 17, 1936."

Tejada felt a sudden nausea. The Movement had sounded the call to arms on July 17. A few days later, Granada had been in the hands of the Falange. He remembered Felipe's story of being stuck in San Sebastián at the outbreak of the war. And San Sebastián had quickly joined the forces under General Franco. But the lands along the coast had remained Republican until the bitter end. And to move a child through a war zone . . . "How long were you trapped with the Reds?" he asked quietly.

"I wasn't *trapped!*" Once again, Luisa spoke angrily. "The anarchists found foster homes for all of us, after a few months. Sancho and Aurelia are the best people I've ever known. They took care of me like their own daughter! Aurelia didn't want to give me up, even after . . ." She swallowed, before continuing, her voice thick with tears. "They came and took Sancho away. A few days after Almuñécar surrendered. But then the Guardias came and took me away, too. They put me in a truck with a lot of others and drove us back to Granada because they said the city had negotiated for our release. They didn't even let us say good-bye. And when we got back, the kids who didn't have family members to pick them up were taken to the orphanage. They told us our parents had been killed by the bombing."

Unwillingly, Tejada remembered the end of the war and Alejandra as a young child screaming hysterically, "Mama! Mama!" Felipe Ordoñez's injunction sounded in his ears: "Go take a look at the orphanage on the Cuesta del Chapiz." He put his arm around Luisa's shoulders, a gesture of comfort rather than detention. She ignored him, reliving a private nightmare. "I thought they'd all died when the Albaicín was shelled. I met someone at the orphanage who told me he'd *seen* my father killed in street fighting. I thought Mama and Currito must have been killed then, too. I didn't mind too much. And then I got a job here, and it was all right, except I missed Sancho and Aurelia. But then . . ." She began to cry too hard for further speech.

The lieutenant handed her a handkerchief, oppressed by his own pity. "Then?"

Luisa noisily blew her nose. "Then a few months ago Doña Rosalia got angry with me for some stupid thing and told me that if I didn't try harder she'd never intercede for my family. I thought it was just her craziness. But she kept saying it. And l-laughing at me. S-saying I thought she was just a crazy old woman but that she knew perfectly well that my mother and brother were still in jail and that I'd better behave if I wanted to see them alive again."

"She was mad," the lieutenant said softly. "You must have known that."

Luisa swallowed. "I get the first Sunday of the month off." She scrubbed at her eyes angrily. "On my last free day I went to the prison and saw Mama. She'd thought I was dead. And then, when I came back . . . " She trailed off, but the lieutenant was wise enough to remain silent, listening. "I took the señora her dinner, like always. She asked me where I'd been, and I didn't want to tell her, so I just said I'd walked around. And she . . . she got angry at me. She said there was no point lying to her, that she knew I'd gone to see my family and asked me what I wanted with those Reds anyway. She asked me if I didn't think I was better off with her than with the Reds." Luisa closed her eyes. "She kept asking me and asking me. 'Can't you *see?*' she kept saying. She told me she'd known for years. That the people at the orphanage had known. And they'd never told me. For my own good. And then"—Luisa's chest heaved with dry sobs—"she made *me* say it. She made me *say* it was for my own good. I wanted to kill her right then and there."

"But you didn't," Tejada said encouragingly, patting her on the back. "There's no way you could have. You didn't, did you?"

Luisa pulled away from him and shrugged. "Not then. But a week later she told me I was a lazy slut, and she'd see to it Sergeant Rivas had Currito taken for a stroll if I didn't mend my ways."

Tejada opened his mouth to caution her and Luisa interrupted him. "I know the sergeant wouldn't have paid her any mind. He never did. But I was sick of it. Red slut this and jailbird's daughter that. She'd lied to me for five years." She stopped speaking, and Tejada found himself with nothing to say. Somewhere in the back of his mind he heard Amparo's voice saying lightly, "She was worried about one of the maids slacking off, I think." He wondered exactly what Doña Rosalia had said to Luisa. "I was just sick of it all," the girl said, in an almost contemplative tone. "And then I remembered. In Almuñécar my teacher was a botanist, and he showed us all kinds of plants, and I remembered him saying you should never crack cooked peach pits, because they were poison. So the next time I bought peaches I saved the pits and baked them, and then powdered them and put them in Doña Rosalia's wine." She smiled a little. "I wasn't even sure if it would work. But I figured at the least it would make her sick to her stomach. That would almost have been better. To have been able to make her suffer."

For the first time, Luisa seemed to notice the expression on the lieutenant's face. "The sergeant told me she was your aunt."

He nodded, speechless.

"Did you love her?"

Tejada thought about all of his interactions with Doña Rosalia and all that he had heard of her from her friends and family. He thought about Luisa, a bright, curious child who had gone through nine years of hell because of a war not of her making. He thought about what the newspaper reports would say: "One of Granada's most respected matrons, foully murdered by an orphaned girl whom she had taken into her home and to whom she had given her protection."

"I hated her guts."

Luisa blinked and then smiled at him, a little timidly. "Don't feel bad," she said perceptively. "I'm glad it's over, really. I'm sorry about Alberto, though."

For a moment, Tejada was confused. Then light dawned. "The pamphlet we found was yours?"

She nodded. "A friend of Mama's told me where to get it and asked me to bring it to her the next time I came. I was going to wrap a cake in it. No one ever looks at wrappings. And then when Doña Rosalia died . . . I needed a place to hide it, so I slipped it into the back of the cabinet when I tidied up the room. I figured no one would look there." She realized Tejada was staring at her again and added generously, "You can torture me if you like. But I won't tell you where I got it."

She met the lieutenant's gaze squarely, her eyes huge and luminous with tears. There was no bravado in her voice and no fear. Merely a kind of quiet weariness. "We have other evidence against Cordero," Tejada said quietly. "If we need more information, we'll interrogate him."

He had expected thanks, but she did not thank him. It did not occur to him that he had just told her that Alberto Cordero would be tortured in her stead. Still, she smiled a little, emboldened enough to make a request. "Do you think they'll let me see Mama again before the sentencing?"

He hesitated, unwilling to make a promise he might be unable to keep, and her smile faltered and disappeared. "Do you think . . . ?" she began, and her voice wobbled. "Do you think I could write her a letter? Just to explain. So she doesn't worry about me anymore."

"Of course." Tejada had a sudden vision of how a woman in prison would react to the news of her daughter's death. He shuddered. He had done guard duty often enough to dread the low howls of the bereaved that kept both prisoners and guards awake at three in the morning. Sometimes the prisoners were more brutal in suppressing those howls than the guards, and he had never blamed them. They were not a healthy thing to listen to at night.

"And maybe to Aurelia, too?" Luisa asked, her voice reminding him almost unbearably of Toño's. "I never got to say good-bye to her before. I never thanked her. And she was like another mother to me."

He nodded, and Luisa retreated to the pantry, returning a moment later with a tablet and pencil. "It'll just take a minute."

"Take as much time as you like."

She wrote standing up, leaning over the table, and forming the words carefully, sometimes scratching out a phrase and rewriting it. He watched her and felt words welling up inside him: *No one knows we've spoken, and no one can guess what you've said. Suppose we forget the whole thing. You're young, you have your whole life ahead of you. You dreamed the whole thing. Dreamed this conversation. I'll interview Fulgencio when he comes in and then go back to the post, none the wiser.* He was never sure later whether he kept silent out of the honest belief that Doña Rosalia's murderer could not be allowed to get away, or out of caution. The guardias and María José were aware that he had talked to Luisa. It was only a matter of time before someone else figured out the trick with the wine, and when they did, all the evidence pointed to her. He never knew whether he kept silent because he believed there was no point in postponing the inevitable or because he feared that if someone else tumbled to her guilt they would also deduce his complicity. She wrote for nearly forty minutes and finally folded the two notes in half. As she looked up, the words of pardon rose once more in the lieutenant's mouth, but before he could speak, she said quietly, "Aurelia's address is up in my room. Can I go and get it?"

He nodded, dizzy with relief. "I'll wait here for you." Then, in case she had not understood, he added gently, "Take as long as you need to find it."

She smiled slightly and went without a word of farewell, leaving the letters she had written on the table behind her. For a moment he willed her to pick the door to the alley behind the house, hoping she would understand that he would follow only slowly and clumsily. But she moved with firm footsteps toward the door that led to the interior of the house. He frowned, nervous, hoping she would remember that there were guards posted outside the front of the house. *But not at the back,* he thought. *And even if she leaves calmly through the front, like nothing's happening, there's a chance they won't stop her.*

To give her time, he picked up the letters and unfolded them. As he had expected, the recipient's address was neatly written in the upper corner of each. The first one was simple, barely more than a few lines:

Dear Mama Aurelia,

I'm sorry I couldn't write before, but they wouldn't let us at the orphanage, and then the lady I worked for wouldn't allow it. I'm afraid I won't be able to write again, but I wanted to tell you that I miss you and remember you, and that I love you. Thank you for everything. Tell Diana I love her and missed her a lot and that I hope she grows up to be a scientist just like she planned. Much, much love,

Luisa

The second one was even shorter:

Dear Mama,

I'm sorry. I know you told me to be brave, but I couldn't stand it anymore. I'm really sorry I can't come next Sunday like I promised, but last time you told me that anything was better than thinking of me in prison. So just remember that I won't ever be in prison anymore. Please don't be disappointed in me. I love you.

Luisa

The lieutenant smiled to himself. She was a gallant child to write so optimistically of never being in prison, but if she could make it to the mountains, the maquis would take her in. She was unlikely to live to old age with them, but at least she would die fighting. He wondered, with some concern, if she would make it to the mountains.

He put both letters in his pocket and then stepped out into the courtyard and walked toward the gate. It was already dark outside, and the wind blew cold as he opened the door to the street. Pinpoints of light shone in windows of the house opposite, and the guardias on duty were black shadows, with their cloaks whirling around them. One of the shadowy figures moved toward him, and he was about to salute and tell the man that all was well when a scream ripped across the courtyard. He froze. "*Luisa!*" The second scream had words in it.

Tejada's arm, already raised in friendly salute, frantically waved the oncoming guardia toward him. The man broke into a run. The lieutenant turned and sprinted back into the courtyard, bursting into the kitchen and through the door Luisa had taken earlier, the guardia he had signaled pounding at his heels. Tejada blindly followed the sounds of hysteria along the corridor, cursing himself for an idiot. How could he have been so stupid as to misread the notes? The girl's obvious intention? The cries were coming from the top of the house, and panic and anger at himself propelled the lieutenant up several flights of stairs at a run.

"Luisa! Luisa! Holy Mother of God, Luisita!" María José was cradling the girl, sobbing, when they finally reached the maids' room.

"Should I get a doctor, sir?" The guardia asked, breathless.

Tejada looked at the angle of Luisa's neck. Perhaps María José had unintentionally jarred it when she had tried to cut the girl down from the attic rafter. Perhaps not. He doubted it would have made a difference. "No," he said, his mouth dry. "Get a priest."

Chapter 23

The entire Tejada family went to the station to see the lieutenant and his wife off. All of them were in very good humor. Juan Andrés was pleased to take a morning off work and go strolling with his wife. His children, equally pleased by the idea of missing school for the morning, were exceptionally gracious to their little cousin. The children's mothers were both so relieved by their imminent parting that they managed to be quite cordial to each other. Doña Consuela enjoyed looking at the traveling dresses of the women setting off on journeys. Don Andrés Tejada León was perhaps happiest of all. He had spent the preceding evening at the casino, regaling his acquaintances with the story of his son's solution to the Ordoñez murder. The newspapers had printed an abbreviated version, saying that a deranged servant had confessed to murdering her benefactress and then committed suicide. But, as Don Andrés proudly pointed out whenever he was given the opportunity, the girl would never have confessed without the expert questioning of his son. "He's clever, my Carlito," Andrés had boasted. "Hardheaded, mind you, and damn irritating sometimes, but a smart boy. A good head on his shoulders. It's why I sent for him when I first suspected Aunt Rosalia had been murdered. I knew he wouldn't take any nonsense from anyone."

The only unsmiling member of the group was the lieutenant. He anxiously superintended the stowing of the luggage and then shifted from foot to foot, muttering that they needed to get on board as his family gave their final embraces and good wishes. He was inclined to snap at Toño, who was retrieved from a large luggage locker by an obliging porter. When he finally shepherded Elena and Toño onto the train, his entire family followed, except for his mother, who declined to risk crushing her clothing in the narrow passages. Juan Andrés good-naturedly shared the children's delight in the compartment and helped them to swarm over the tiny space. His wife urged Elena to write. The lieutenant found himself pushed up against the door of the compartment next to his father, who was wringing his hand and congratulating him again. To his disgust, the train was delayed, so his father's approbation went on for a long time. The din and his feeling of claustrophobia were nearly unbearable, and he began to wonder if the whistle would ever blow.

Finally, the porters shooed all nonpassengers off the train. Tejada submitted to a last handshake and embrace and pat on the back, and then he was alone in the compartment with Elena and Toño and the whistle sounded and the train crawled northward. He sank into a window seat and stared at the dry golden landscape without seeing it. The train chugged past fields where only the stalks remained after harvesting and dirty stone villages, their church spires dark against the azure sky, and then climbed into barren, bandit-infested hills. Forty minutes north of Granada the train jerked to a halt at a railroad crossing. They were near a small town, and the tracks ran beside a cemetery. The graveyard was filled with peasants, taking flowers and candles to the graves, under the supervision of a black-robed priest. Tejada blinked at the sight, wondering for a moment if it was a funeral. Then he remembered: it was All Saints' Day, the day of the dead. He watched the mourners. None of them looked up at the train's windows. They were probably used to trains stopping there.

He remembered Sergeant Rivas's anguished face two nights

earlier, when he had returned to the post to make his report. "She was distraught, right?" the sergeant had said. "A priest will certify that?"

"Clearly insane," Tejada had answered vehemently, clutching at a straw of comfort. "I can explain to the Father."

"You think he'll approve Christian burial?"

"He'd better!"

Rivas had said nothing but had looked at the lieutenant with cold, reproachful eyes. The priest had not challenged him either. But behind their respectful, "Just as you say, Lieutenant," he had heard the unspoken criticism: You drove her to the edge. Why did you leave her alone then? He wondered if anyone would bring flowers to Luisa's grave in a year's time.

"Grr-owl!" A stuffed lion butted Tejada in the chest, interrupting his reverie.

"For goodness' sake, Toño, can't you be a little careful with that thing!"

Toño snatched back the stuffed animal and looked up at his father with wounded eyes. "Drigo just wanted to play," he said, subdued.

"Well, have him play somewhere else!" Tejada snapped, hating himself as he saw the child shrink away.

Elena picked up Toño and Rodrigo. "Why's Papa mad?" Toño asked, his voice choked with unshed tears.

Elena sighed. "Papa's not really mad, sweetheart. He's just sad right now."

"Why's he sad then?"

"Because . . ." Elena cast a pleading look at her husband. He avoided her eyes. "Because his job in Granada didn't end the way he thought it would."

Toño said, "Don't be sad, Papa. I heard Grandpa say you did an amazing job."

The lieutenant snorted. "Yes. Thanks to me, he's a much richer man. And Tío Felipe won't get a penny of his mother's money." He saw that Toño looked puzzled as well as unhappy and he ruffled the boy's hair. "Never mind, Toño. I'm glad to be here, just the three of us again."

He made a conscientious effort to amuse Toño, but it was a relief when Elena took charge of the boy again, and he could go back to brooding. He looked forward to returning to Potes. He wanted to go on patrol, to ride through the mountains, breathless and sweating in the cold. He wanted to hear the Cantabrian accent, thick as a goose-down quilt; he wanted to go out with Guardia Mojica and get drunk on homemade *orujo*. And he *never* wanted to go back to Granada.

He thought that it was only his own impatience to reach their home that made the train seem to go slower and slower, and he pointedly did not look at his watch during the frequent stops. But when night fell they were still far from Madrid, and an hour after the train was scheduled to arrive in Atocha he was forced to face the fact that they were significantly delayed. Tejada glanced at his watch and optimistically hoped that the Santander train with which they had to connect would be equally delayed in starting out.

Elena had brought along lunch but at nine-thirty they still had not reached Madrid, and Toño began to complain again that he was hungry. At ten o'clock the Tejadas investigated the dining car and found that all the tables were full. At eleven they finally had a rapid and overpriced snack, but by this time Toño was unfortunately too tired to fully appreciate it.

By the time they reached Madrid, well after one o'clock in the morning, Tejada was in no mood to trek across the city to the Northern Station to see if there were still trains to Santander. He found a railroad employee, told the man he needed to send an urgent cable on official business, and rousted a sleepy telegraph operator out of bed to send a wire to the Potes post: TRAIN DELAYED. STOP. SPENDING NIGHT IN MADRID. STOP. LEAVING MADRID TOMORROW AFTERNOON.

They found a hotel across the plaza from the train station. Elena sat with Toño long enough to see that he was asleep and then changed into a nightgown. In spite, or perhaps because, of her exhaustion, she did not want to lie down immediately. Instead, she went to the window and stared out at the darkened city. The street lamps made cold puddles of light along the Paseo del Prado, but beyond them the botanical gardens sat in total blackness. She leaned her forehead sideways against the icy glass and was able to catch a glimpse of a few lights twinkling in buildings along the street. *Tomorrow,* she thought, *we'll take an afternoon train, and Toño will get to ride the hotel elevator again. We should take him to the park, too, so he gets some exercise. And he'd like a ride on the Metro. Just a short ride. We can take him to the Puerta del Sol.* She sighed and her breath condensed into a moist ellipse on the windowpane. It would be good to be back in Potes. But returning to Madrid was like returning to an old friend.

She blew on the window again, watching the lights outside blur on the fogged glass. She was not aware of her husband until he put his arms around her. "You're not cold?"

"A little." She leaned back against him and clasped her hands over his arms, glad to be embraced and grateful for his warmth. "But it's good to be here."

"And a little cold is preferable to going to bed with me."

Elena swung around, stunned by his tone. "What?"

He avoided her eyes and stared out at the darkened city. When he spoke, his voice was no longer bitter but rather contemplative. "I do good, don't I?"

"Do good?" Elena echoed, puzzled.

"I mean," Tejada hesitated, his voice pleading. "I work hard. I try to keep order. I've never taken bribes or abused my position. Right?"

"Of course." Elena's voice was soothing.

"So why isn't that enough?" Tejada whispered. "Why am I still such a goddamned stupid son of a bitch?"

"You aren't!" Elena hugged him ferociously. "You didn't know that poor girl would kill herself! You thought you'd arranged her escape."

"I should have *told* her."

"You didn't know."

"I didn't want to take responsibility." Tejada's voice shook. "So I pushed the responsibility onto her, and she died a worse death than the one I could have given her. She died like that because I was a coward."

"You gave her a choice," Elena comforted.

"I shouldn't have!" Tejada cried. "I should have made the choice for her. One way or the other."

"The same way you made a choice for Alejandra, when you sent her to Granada, six years ago?" Elena demanded. "Or the way you've made a choice now, to keep her there?"

Tejada breathed deeply. "Look, I didn't stand in the way of the Encinas kid going to France to study. But Aleja's my responsibility. It's for her own good." He remembered his last conversation with Elena and Carmen before leaving Granada. He had not seriously believed that Cristina Encinas would be willing to take Alejandra or that Carmen would willingly part from her daughter. But he had bowed to Elena's insistence that he at least discuss the possibility with Carmen. The woman's pathetic eagerness when she heard the word "France" had shaken him.

"She should grow up a *Spaniard*," he added a little desperately, knowing that Elena was about to argue the point again.

"Even if it means holding her prisoner against her mother's wishes?"

"It's what's *best* for her."

"How do you know what's best for a girl like Aleja?" Elena spoke so gently that the words sounded more like comfort than accusation. "Or like that poor Luisa?"

Tejada knew that somehow Elena's argument was flawed, but the answer to her question had always seemed so obvious to him that it was difficult to put into words. He looked for something to say. The best thing he could come up with was: "That's my job."

"You're not God," Elena pointed out, acid.

"I'm not much of a man either," he retorted.

"Don't be arrogant." His wife was serious but firm. "A man can't make decisions for other people. You have to leave them some freedom of choice."

Tejada stared out the window and watched clouds speed across the sky, as rapid and insubstantial as the certainties he had built his life on. "If I just . . . let everyone be free," he said, considering, "then what's the point of my job? If everyone could get along better without me, what's the point of my being here?"

"Your job is to enforce the law," Elena said. "But the law shouldn't make every decision in a citizen's life. It can't. That's the problem with a dictatorship."

"What about being a good husband?" Tejada demanded, in too much pain to debate abstractions. "A good father? If I'm *not* responsible for making decisions, how can I take care of you and Toño and do some tiny amount of good to make up for all the bad things I've done?"

Elena kissed him on the cheek. "Toño and I depend on you," she said. "We would be lost without you. But that doesn't mean we need you to be infallible."

Tejada knew that she was serious. He loved her, but he had never understood how she could love him—as he believed she did—without sharing his instinctive feeling that a man's role in a marriage was to protect his wife. A yawning pit of powerlessness far darker than the night threatened to engulf him.

"Then what am I supposed to do?" he asked.

"The best you can."

Tejada gave a laugh that was close to a sob. Elena's cheek was cold against his but she turned in his arms to stare out at the darkened city once again, impelled by a longing that he only half understood. He held her a little more tightly, wishing hopelessly that he could restore the prewar capital she had loved—in all its dangerous, chaotic fascination—or give her a longer vacation in Madrid or at least keep her warm against the November chill. *But if the war had never happened, she would love someone else,* he thought. *Even if I could turn back the clock, give her what she wants, I would lose her. The way we'll lose Alejandra if we give her what she wants. I'll send Alejandra to France, if that will make Elena happy. I would even support some kind of political "freedom" if it would make her happy . . . but I can't, because it would mean losing her.* He peered out the window, wondering what her gaze was searching for in the winter's night, and saw a few white-gray flakes drift past the glass. When he looked down at the street lamps he saw glittering motes dancing toward the pavement, their motion too slow and irregular to be raindrops. "Look, my love," he whispered. "I have brought you the snow."

Afterword

The events and people in this novel are fictitious, but the story of the children's colonies of Almuñécar is true in all of its tragic details. José Luis Entrala, currently an editor at Granada's daily newspaper *Ideal*, collected excerpts from his paper's archives to give a panorama of life in Granada during the Civil War in his book *Granada sitiada 1936-1939; lo que dijo el diario Ideal sobre la guerra civil.* The book tells the story of the children sent to Almuñécar, with extensive quotes and facsimiles of articles from *Ideal*. I have based the physical and political geography of the city of Granada on Juan Manuel Barrios Rozúa's *Granada; historia urbana* and Ian Gibson's guide *En Granada, Su Granada; guía de la Granada de Federico García Lorca.* (The latter is available in English as *Lorca's Granada*, and I highly recommend it as a guide for anyone fortunate enough to visit the city.)

The legend of the attempt to bring a "blizzard" of flowers to Sevilla is told in Richard Fletcher's book *Moorish Spain*. Fletcher adds that the story is "sheer literary convention, of course: similar stories are told of other princesses in other times and places." Tejada's use of the story is perhaps ill-advised, but the good lieutenant is incorrigibly literary, dating back to his first conversation with Elena about the *Iliad* in *Death of a Nationalist*.